THE PRANCESTOR PROJECT

THE PRANCESTOR PROJECT

CHRISTINE MORSE

STINGRAY PUBLISHING AND MEDIA

ISBN: 978-0-578-33155-3
Published by Stingray Publishing and Media
Cover design by Jessica Bell
Interior design and publishing assistance by
The Happy Self-Publisher
Published by Stingray Publishing and Media

*For the one who taught
me that I should play
my own game.*

PROLOGUE

As the truck bumped and splashed down the narrow road, Christopher was reminded that the last translator to be headed down a route like this, in the same passenger's seat, had disappeared. He stole another glance at his new boss, sitting quietly behind the wheel, and wondered how someone could care so little about a missing employee, especially after this morning's report: *Clyde Martin now presumed dead.*

The tangle of mossy vines and trees that had shaded the road for hours finally gave way to a clearing—a smear of oatmeal dirt leading to eight small dwellings, each topped with thatch and clinging to a riverbank. The scene of this tiny, hand-built village encircled by rain forest brought Christopher back, as if he had left the Congo just yesterday, not two decades ago. He could still remember staring up at the web of branches and fronds, inhaling the energy the jungle had exhaled, and feeling invincible.

But now what Christopher felt was sick—not to his stomach, but to his soul. What exactly was this business with no name, no headquarters? He knew that his boss was overseeing an archaeological dig somewhere else on the African continent, but that seemed more like an expensive hobby, not a moneymaking endeavor. Was Patrick Veeder simply a rich guy, following his eccentric whims—and needing a translator to do that? It had never been explained to Christopher, and somehow, he knew not to ask.

Once in the clearing, Patrick flattened the gas pedal, accelerating toward a sleeping dog. Christopher dug his fingernails into his seat until the skinny mutt opened his eyes and jumped out of the way.

"Would've done it a favor," Patrick said, braking hard and killing the engine. The clicks and chirps of a thousand bugs seemed to get a lot louder.

In the blink of an eye, a man holding a fish snare emerged from the wilderness, and two women carrying infants stepped out of a hut. Another blink and more men—curious, hopeful—appeared at the edge of the dense jungle. The women sported headscarves bursting with orange and red, and dresses to match, but the men wore hand-me-down T-shirts and tattered, off-brand shorts. Their unguarded smiles were just like Christopher remembered.

"Stop daydreaming!" Patrick snapped. "Let's get in and out. Stick to the script."

Patrick lowered his window to the man who approached it, the only villager dressed in a button-down shirt, who asked, "Mr. Veeder?"

The community leader tapped his finger to his chest. "Zo." His sun-wrinkled face waited for a greeting Patrick never gave.

Christopher heaved open his door and let his short legs drop to the mushy ground. He directed his words over the truck's hood, speaking in the African language of Sango. *"Nice to meet you, Zo. I'm Christopher, and I'll do my best to translate."*

Christopher knew his nausea came from the bullshit he was about to peddle and not from the foul odor of the nearby compost pile. *"Mr. Veeder was very happy to fund the pastor's mission here. He hopes your community is enjoying the supplies."*

Zo smiled and bowed, acknowledging Patrick as one would a king. He spoke in his native tongue and paused. Christopher translated: "He said, 'We have much appreciation for the pastor's kindness. We are making full use of the clothing and tools.'"

Christopher listened again to Zo, and then turned to Patrick. "He's asking us to follow him. He has the gift."

Patrick looked down, examining his designer boots—ankle high and made of leather—and lamented. Word of this offering had come after he was out for the day, having breakfast with yet another dignitary who wanted to schmooze with a wealthy American. Delaying the trip out here even thirty minutes—to go back and change or to buy new shoes—would have made it impossible to return before nightfall.

Of course, he could have set out the next morning, but that would have violated his motto: *Never put off until tomorrow what could make you rich today.*

Groaning, Patrick stepped into the sludge and resolved to replace his boots on his upcoming visit to California. He pressed his key fob and the truck beeped, prompting wide eyes from the shirtless boys who had come outside to play in a canoe.

Zo led the way into the shadows of the forest canopy. They weaved around tall trunks, dipped under branches of feathery emerald leaves, and passed by thick vines serving as ant highways. As a child, Christopher had stayed in a village like this, farther up the river, with his missionary parents. He smiled, recalling the caring women showing him which bugs were the best to eat and how to prepare them.

They came upon a private space, closed off with plastic tarps hanging from ropes tied between trees. Zo invited them inside, where they found a two-foot-tall object covered by a faded towel and placed on a flat piece of wood to elevate it from the soggy leaves.

With one stern look, Patrick reminded Christopher of his rule: *Keep your eyes off the artifact.* Christopher turned away.

Zo spoke to Patrick and then waited while Christopher said, "Mr. Veeder, I understand that you would like to remember our village with a piece of our history."

Christopher tried to emulate the gravity in Zo's voice. "Therefore, I have selected one of our oldest treasures to give you."

Patrick had locked onto his hidden prize. "Give him the spiel. His village is special. The gift isn't necessary. Play it up."

Christopher swallowed his guilt. *"Mr. Veeder says your village is special to him and will always be in his memory. A gift is generous and not necessary."*

These fishermen and their families, struggling for survival along this wide stretch of the Moulegi River, didn't understand the financial side of artifact collection. Zo had lived here his entire life, without occasion to acquire knowledge on the valuation of relics. He politely grinned. *"It doesn't have any gold or jewels, but it holds our hearts."*

Keeping his head turned away, Christopher translated. But Patrick wasn't listening; he had squatted down and now wiggled his fingers, awaiting the unveiling.

Zo tugged off the towel, exposing a stone carving of an ancient deity with a chip in its nose.

Patrick fancied the scar to be nearly perfect; the right kind of damage brought more attention to the age of a relic and could increase its worth. He stroked the artifact's gritty edges and narrowed his eyes as he estimated its time period, surmising that it would fetch nearly a million dollars at auction—or a million dollars' worth of influence with the right politician or CEO. He smiled at his own cleverness; it had only cost about $5,000 to send a pastor offering basic goods and, most importantly, making these villagers feel indebted.

Zo posed a question and Christopher, still averting his gaze, said, "He wants to know if you'll provide the resources for the pastor to come back."

Glaring into the deity's almond-shaped eyes, as if in a staring contest, Patrick spoke under his breath. "You're no magical lord. You're just a really valuable rock, and now you're mine."

Zo's eyebrows wrinkled in confusion.

Christopher winced from another wave of nausea. "Sir?"

Patrick intentionally mumbled, in case Zo had learned more English than he had let on. "Fine. I'll pay for that oddball to visit one more time with a few suitcases of secondhand shit and his stupid Bible talk. Don't promise these people anything else. Make it sound nice."

Christopher sighed, wiping away the beads of moisture that had percolated out of his forehead. *"Mr. Veeder says, 'Yes, you are like family. The pastor will be sent back for a visit.'"*

Zo bowed.

Patrick covered the statue and stood up, once again towering over Zo and Christopher. It was difficult not to notice the right angles in Patrick's body, from his square hips to his shelflike shoulders to the flat top of his head.

He whispered to Christopher, "Let's go. Time for the sedative."

Christopher did not agree with erasing the short-term memory of the gift givers in each of the villages where Patrick collected artifacts. But he kept his opinion to himself, especially since Patrick had more than once remarked that Clyde Martin's bad habit had been to disagree.

Patrick hoisted the sculpture into the center of his front truck seat, buckled it in, and switched out the towel for a blanket. He started the engine and, for no apparent reason, revved the gas. Christopher's hand trembled as he passed the towel back to the village leader along with a cold bottle of spiked water.

Perspiration dripped from Zo's earlobes as he eagerly drank.

Christopher leaned out his window. *"You may not remember that you met me, Zo, but I will never forget about you and your community."*

Patrick switched into drive, racing them away as he slammed his finger onto the button that rolled up the passenger-side window. He wasn't going to take a chance that another translator would realize the "sedative" was actually poison. Usually, the fatal liquid was slow acting, causing its victims to deteriorate over the course of a few weeks and eventually to expire from what seemed like an infection. But people sometimes reacted when they first drank it, convulsing or going into cardiac arrest.

Patrick shared a tight-lipped smile with himself in the rearview mirror as the reflection of Zo and the other villagers—joyfully waving—shrank away. A dead man could not change his mind or accuse someone of tricking him out of a valuable possession.

He would plant the stout deity at his own excavation site three hundred miles away for his workers there to discover. The civilized world would not question the man who held a master's degree in archaeology from Harvard and had funded the projects of renowned scientists. Last year, Patrick had put up the initial investment for a new museum in Washington, DC, and his long record of donating large sums of money to politicians from both major parties had endeared him to liberals and conservatives alike. He had become an internationally respected figure, and some were even suggesting that he should run for president.

He gestured for Christopher to retrieve a Nicaraguan cigar and a cutter from the glove compartment. "Careful," Patrick said, concerned not for the welfare of Christopher's fingers, but about him making the proper cut.

Patrick puckered his lips around the cocoa-brown stogie, puffing several times over the butane lighter in Christopher's hand.

Pungent fumes replaced the oxygen in the cab. Christopher longed to open his window, even just a crack, but he knew Patrick would yell at him for letting the air-conditioning escape. He rubbed his eyes and mustered the nerve to ask, "Will it harm Zo, wiping out his memory with that sedative?"

Patrick delighted in Christopher's gullibility—it was much easier to fool him than that sleuth, Clyde Martin.

Christopher cleared his burning throat. "Will it, sir?"

Patrick reasoned that being poisoned to death would be quicker and less painful than whatever disease or natural disaster would have eventually ended Zo's life.

"Nah," Patrick said, sucking in the cigar's peppery flavor and musing about what new boots awaited his purchase in California.

Chapter 1

"You've found something, Professor, haven't you?" The program director pushed his face close to mine, as if our relationship had spanned a lot longer than ten minutes. Was he inspecting my beard?

I stepped backward, but he closed the gap. "Your trek was short-lived." His words delivered the odor of stale coffee. "Because you made a discovery. Am I right?"

The backstage was cluttered with set-design pieces—a desk on wheels, a rocking chair, a tiger in a reared-up pose, staring at me. I retreated behind the sequined dresses hanging from a clothes rack.

Another text vibrated my phone, the fourth in an hour. Was it Mom? She was probably worried; I hadn't called in a while.

No, it was Peter Wendell, still text-yelling at me.

—*You must not say a word!*

"Two minutes and you're on," the giddy director said.

The Future of Humanity was an annual seminar, set this year in London, featuring speakers who offered ideas on how to achieve a better tomorrow. But this time the attendees—now starting to hoot and cheer as if they were at a concert—were curious about the deep past.

"Eight hundred people are out there, begging to hear what you've found." The director swiped open a space in the garments and scowled at me. "You can't disappoint them."

He checked himself in a mirror and then entered the stage, smiling and nodding toward the crowd like a rock star.

My body withered down the wall—bunching up my baggy suit jacket behind me—until my tailbone landed on the scuffed wood floor.

The director's assistant, a frail sociology student with bulky glasses, peeked around the clothes rack. Her voice shook as if the sight of me on the floor made her nervous. "Professor, sir, would you like some water?"

"Do you have any wine?"

"Um, it's nine a.m."

"Pretend it's nine p.m."

"Um, well, no sir, we don't have any."

Whistles and clapping interrupted the director's introduction. He spoke louder. "Yes, Professor and Cultural Anthropologist David Denlon is here, all the way from the United States. And although his lecture for our seminar addresses isolated tribes, most of you know, I'm sure, that he has been on the hunt for something very interesting."

"Zircon!" a man shouted from the second row.

"That's right," the director said. "Two years ago, Professor Denlon heard about a startling find. A billion-year-old zircon crystal. A superancient mineral that had preserved something special. What evidence had that crystal delivered to us from yesteryear? Evidence of life! The biogenic carbon in that tiny crystal inspired Dr. Denlon to create a hypothesis. And to prove it, he set out to find more of those crystals."

The director paused and then said, "Maybe today the professor will tell us what he's discovered."

I cringed. Applause and shouts stabbed my eardrums.

"I'll take that water," I said.

The assistant hurried over with a miniature plastic bottle, seeming to consider if I needed medical attention. She rolled the rack away with an apologetic smile.

The director continued, "What kind of life has Dr. Denlon been looking for in zircon crystals that were on Earth before dinosaurs?"

I sighed. Why hadn't I canceled? Why hadn't I conditioned my appearance on none of this being mentioned?

"What the professor has been on a quest to find, ladies and gentlemen, is an entirely separate humankind. A form of people, like us, who evolved into being an eon ago but then went completely extinct."

The crowd quieted.

The director shook his head. "Some people have written this notion off as crazy. But many of us are asking, 'What if this sister race not only existed, but evolved to the point that our own race has, or even further? What could we find, preserved in billion-year-old crystals, about how these other humans lived?'"

The red light of the backstage exit sign seemed to get brighter. I stood and marched toward it. The assistant rushed to me and set her hand on my arm, then pulled it away as if she'd committed a faux pas. "Sorry, Professor, but he's about to call you onstage."

We looked out past the tall curtains to see the potbellied director lean toward the audience, adding a whisper to his words: "Was there intelligent life on Earth that came and went before our human race was even born? Only the man who is about to walk onto this stage can answer that!"

A thousand feet drummed the floor. My stomach turned over.

"Please welcome our keynote speaker, Professor David Denlon."

The assistant took my bottle of water, though I wasn't done drinking it. I peered toward the exit sign again.

"You're on, Doctor," she insisted.

I stepped under the hot lights to a crescendo of screams. At the lectern, I slowly opened my binder of notes, ruing the day I had agreed to meet with a television producer.

Peter Wendell sat in the blue high-back chair that I had found in an antique store. He looked disapprovingly at my windowless office, acting as if I had been the one to request this meeting, instead of the other way around.

"I know you need money," he said. "And I'm inclined to give it to you, because this research is important. But you must keep your discovery a secret."

He pulled a contract out of his folder and clicked a pen. "I'm only interested in funding your project if it means I pull off this show. It's exactly what viewers are into now—treasure hunts, historical searches. We'll reveal what you find, each episode a new tidbit. But the network won't pick up something that everyone knows about. You must not say anything to anyone about your findings until the show airs. In fact, even hinting at what you've found will get you sued for violating the nondisclosure clause."

When I looked away, he reminded, "Full funding, Dr. Denlon."

Audience members shifted in their seats and cleared their throats.

I swallowed. "Humans have many oxymoronic callings." This usually led to a joke, but I didn't feel like making it. Instead, I stumbled through my slide pictures: Madonna the singer, from her early years, wearing ripped fishnet stockings and little else, then Madonna the mother of Jesus, with a yellow halo around her face like a bonnet. God the Father pointing across the sky to Adam, then God handing Adam a .44 Magnum pistol.

"Sex and chastity. God and guns. So many opposing notions. And yet another is the—"

"Where have you searched?" a woman yelled from the second tier.

"Bless you," I said, eliciting chuckles.

"Another conundrum we have"—my voice disappeared; I swigged water from the bottle the director had left on a stool for me—"is the question of bringing isolated tribes into the network of what we call 'civilization.'"

I turned the page to find black lines across the next paragraph. Droplets trickled from my hairline. I rambled through the approved parts of my speech over irritated coughs and sighs.

"What we've learned about these peoples—living in what we callously refer to as 'the bush,' completely unaware of freeways and selfies and processed food—is that they're doing just fine. They produce nothing that harms the planet. They have their traditions, their social structures, and"—I touched the white-zircon pendant hanging from my neck—"their treasures. They don't want or need what we are calling 'help.'"

The attendees looked around, silently asking each other if I were really going to be this big of a letdown.

The collar of my shirt pressed into my windpipe. Was my neck swelling? Before my discovery, audiences were riveted to learn that certain tribes had not yet been in contact with the rest of the world. The pictures taken from planes and drones—good enough quality to show the very wide feet of these humans, an evolutionary trend in the absence of shoes—had never failed to fascinate. Until now.

Twenty minutes into what I had promised would be an hour, I decided to end the crowd's misery. And mine. "I'll conclude with this: maybe instead of thinking about helping these secluded societies, we should try to learn from them."

There was a long stretch of silence before the attendees realized I was finished. A smattering of weak applause was drowned out by huffs and moans. I yanked at my tie and ignored a hundred hands shooting into the air.

"Thank you." I scooped up my binder and hurried down the stairs on the side of the stage.

Another woman shouted, "Professor! Tell us what you've found!"

A shrill ring answered her as I punched open the emergency exit leading to the street.

The director flew out of the front door of the auditorium and nearly crashed into me. "What kind of a presentation was *that?*"

"I can't tell them anything."

"Why not?"

I mumbled, "Because I sold out."

"You what?"

Above, tufts of white clouds hovered beneath the swimming-pool blue of the universe. Nothing about the calm sky was the least bit affected by the disgust on this conference organizer's face, disgust that stretched back his eyes and cheeks, making him appear as though he was sticking his head out the window of a speeding car.

I waltzed away. As I descended into the coolness of a subway station, I checked my neck pouch for the essentials—passport, credit card, cash.

"There you go again—grab your passport and run," my ex-wife, Melly, used to snipe. "That will solve the problem."

It absolutely solved the problem of me being caught up in something I neither created nor could fix. When I opted to tour historical sites and study cultures in faraway lands in lieu of enduring my colleagues' long-winded meetings, or my wife's dissatisfaction with her career, or any situation manifested by what people referred to as "the system," the ridiculousness would evaporate. And when I returned, the drama about which professors should serve on the dean search committee, or the critique of me being too much this or not enough that, or whatever nonsensical first-world crisis was flaming, would be embers. Every time.

I boarded the subway but could not shake the feeling that someone was watching me.

Two stops later, as the overcrowded train accelerated out of the Oxford Circus station, there was a scuffle and a squeaky scream.

I looked toward the noises, half expecting to see a puppy, but then an elderly man said, "Oh . . . God!"

"I'll give you anything!" I heard a woman beg. "Please don't hurt her!"

Passengers backed away, clearing my line of vision to the man causing the commotion. His marble eyes found their target.

"You!" he commanded me, as he gripped a little girl by her blonde hair. "You get off at the next stop with me or this child and everyone on this train dies."

I became a mute spectator trapped inside a statue of myself, staring intently. Nothing but my beating heart moved.

I hadn't suffered this paralysis in almost thirty years, but now the humiliation returned as if no time had passed. For most of my childhood, my brain had responded to sudden stress by locking me into an unflinching stare, and it often required a long, inelegant minute for me to break free. While I had never grown out of being what people called 'weird,' I had assumed since the tenth grade that this staring condition was behind me.

My frozen glare took in the fit man in a black knit hat. One of his fists clenched the whimpering five-year-old girl; the other propped open his jacket, revealing a clump of clay with two wires sticking out, strapped to his chest.

Could someone be *this* serious about getting me to reveal what I'd found?

CHAPTER 2

My father's voice finally whispered inside my head. *Breathe, Son, just breathe.* I inhaled through my nose and regained the ability to blink.

The train slowed into the next tube station. As the terrorist grabbed hold of a hanging strap, he peered out the window and spotted two constables on the platform.

I squinted at him. "Let her go."

The girl's face pinkened as if she had instantly become sunburned. "Mommy, help me!"

"It's gonna be okay, baby," her mother cried. "I love you!"

The terrorist took another look at the enforcement officials and snarled in frustration. He announced, in an accent I recognized as Eastern European, "No one moves or makes a sound, or I blow up the station!"

He pushed the girl toward her mother and sprang out the parting doors.

New passengers hurried in, twitching their eyebrows at our collective unease.

The man charged up the steps toward the station's exit; bits of paper trash whirled behind him. A businesswoman in high heels nearly tripped as she dashed from our train to the constables, pointing out where the man had gone.

I relieved my shaking knees by taking a seat facing the girl, who wailed uncontrollably. Her mother embraced her. "Carrie, I've got you, *ssshhhh.*"

As the train rolled forward, Carrie focused on the zircon pendant hanging from my neck. Her crying quieted to hyperventilation and then slowed to an occasional hiccup.

I had discovered this white zircon along with two other pieces, one blue and one brown, on the side of the massive Cayateña volcano. The white and blue crystals were an inch long and shaped like solid infinity signs. The brown crystal, a marquise, had been the jackpot—containing humanoid DNA, along with some kind of synthetic particles—while the other two had preserved nothing.

Given their unique shape and coloring, I had turned the white and blue specimens into pendants. Peter Wendell, the producer, had insisted on keeping custody of the blue pendant and the brown zircon containing the evidence. He had originally wanted all three pieces, of course, but after I started to retreat from the deal, he let me hold on to the white pendant.

The hint of a smile brightened Carrie's face as she fixated on the crystal. Her innocent curiosity reminded me of my ex-wife's second-grade class.

"Mr. David!" Joey ran to me after I'd said good-bye. "Can I do *ant-apology* when I grow up, like you?"

"Of course you can," I said.

Melly came outside, her skirt long and loose-fitting on her petite frame. "Get back in the classroom, Joey. Mr. David will visit again soon."

Joey hugged me, triggering an annoyed sigh from Melly.

"What?" I asked, as Joey trotted back inside on tennis shoes with lights that blinked red and blue with every step.

"I know, David. You want kids." Her tone was judgmental, as if I were being greedy.

"Stop telling me what I want," I replied, unable to hide my anger that she was making me attend weekly counseling sessions and then not listening to the advice. "I thought you were supposed to start, 'I feel . . .'"

"Well, at least you were listening as you stared out her window." She took a breath. "Okay. I feel . . . like I'm not ready to have children."

The tetherball chains clanged against their poles. The sound seemed sad, abandoned.

"Tell Joey and the others that I can't come back anymore," I said, "and that I'll miss them."

Instead of going to our next counseling session I had sent her papers to finalize the divorce. Melly wasn't ready to have kids *with me*. I didn't know if she thought I would make a bad father or she didn't want my weird genes passed on to her children, but if she wasn't ready to start a family with me after a decade of marriage, she never would be.

Carrie sniffled, her blue eyes still on me. I pulled the leather string holding the zircon over my head and handed it to her, prompting her ear-to-ear smile.

"You can keep it," I said, "for being so brave."

Her mother's hands were still trembling. "Thank you." She kissed her daughter and asked her, "What do you think of that?"

Carrie leaned into her mom's chest, rubbing her tiny fingers over the white zircon's hourglass symmetry. Her eyes dried and filled with light. "It looks like the clouds."

"Exactly," I said. "That's why I made it a pendant."

Transit security officers and more constables met our train at the next stop. I hurried to the front of the line to be searched.

One of them asked, "Can you step aside, please, and tell us what you saw?"

"Nothing," I said, knowing there would be nothing that I would provide that was different than what others would say—the system would catch this guy, or not, without anything to do with me.

I left the station and found the tour-bus stop but couldn't keep Melly out of my head. If she had been here, she would have accused me of running from the question I should have been answering.

Why did that man on the subway want me to go with him?

But that was another problem I had not created nor could fix.

My phone beeped. It was Pestering Pete.

—*Where are you?*

I quickly typed:

—*I don't understand why preproduction is taking so long, and why I can't go back to Cayateña.*

But then I deleted my text. Because Pestering Pete would come up with some Hollywood explanation, like he always had. Last time it was: *You have no idea about the unions and the red tape, or what it takes to get a network to pay for a crew on location when the location is a volcano.*

I found a seat on the coach and rested my head on the tinted window. As we pulled away, the sound of the engine reverberating through the glass, into my ear, brought Arthur's purr to mind. My long-gone cat—my childhood best friend—had always comforted me when I was a kid, but it had mattered most the day Mom's voice floated up through the heater vent to my room.

"I know, but I can't say it that way to my little Davey." She was on the phone downstairs in the laundry room. I slurped my chicken noodle soup straight from the bowl, and then I glided my hand, again and again, over Arthur's silky black hair.

Mom laughed. "He would get upset at that. Or ignore it. I have to ask him about those things one at a time. The book says to talk to him in a linear way."

I blew my nose. I didn't understand what she was talking about.

"Well, what else am I going to do?" Mom chuckled and sighed. "He's my Spectrum Boy."

My sore throat worsened, as if my soup were suddenly spiced with hot sauce. I lost my appetite and fell back into my fluffy pillows.

Spectrum Boy. That phrase rolled off her tongue as if she said it often. But she had never said it to me.

Arthur climbed onto my legs and gazed at me, kneading my blanket with his front paws. My mind moved completely into his purring, until he flopped beside me and we both fell asleep.

The next morning, with a handful of tissues, I waved good-bye to Mom from the school bus, wondering what my defect was.

I opened my eyes with a quick breath and almost expected to see Mom outside the bus, waving back at me. Instead, I saw oncoming traffic to the right of us, not the left, and remembered that I was in the United Kingdom.

Spectrum Boy. Mom's voice had emanated so much love when she said it. But there was a small monster inside that nickname. Something that worried or scared her.

Pestering Pete. Why had I so often given people nicknames? Even *Melly* was a nickname for my ex-wife, whose actual name was Melissa. Had I done that for more reason than to entertain myself? Like Mom, was I dealing with discomfort or fear?

The coach stopped and lowered with an air-release noise. I clunked down the steep steps and took in the rectangular wood trim on the building in front of me—the structure seemed fake old, like on a movie set.

I hurried through ticketing to avoid the slow-moving mass of people, and eventually arrived at the unexceptional bed that the prerecorded voice in my earbuds identified as the place William Shakespeare had come into the world. My heartbeat finally calmed.

But I soon found myself a few blocks away, ordering alcohol.

The snarling man from the subway yelled *You!* inside my head until I finished my second glass of Cabernet Sauvignon.

The barkeep rubbed his rag inside a mug, sizing me up. "It's your first time, across the pond?"

"No," I answered. "I get over this way two or three times a year."

"Oh. So you're one of those traveler guys, with a ton of stampings in your passport?"

I pulled my passport out of my pouch and held it out to him. "A few interesting ones."

He set the mug down, took the booklet, and shuffled through its pages. "Wow . . . frequent flier."

A newspaper on the bar taunted me with its headline: *American Executives Found Guilty of Bank Fraud; Punished Only with Fines.* I flipped it over and swallowed more wine.

Another text pulsated my pocket. Maybe it was Melly.
—*Where are you? Call me. Right now.*

I ignored Pestering Pete, shoved the phone back in my pocket, and swirled my third glass of wine. Its blackberry scent carried me away from Peter's relentless texting and to my discovery. Evidence of humans from an eon ago. Not from our kind. Had they come into being the way we had? Or arrived here from another planet? How far along had they evolved before going extinct?

I longed to get back to Cayateña, to search for more evidence. It had been five months since I'd come off that volcano, and three and a half since I'd signed Peter Wendell's contract.

The bartender interrupted my thought. "So, what is it? The job that takes you around the world?"

"I'm a cultural anthropologist."

"A what?"

"I research peoples, their traditions and customs . . . I teach, write, give presentations."

He pondered me as if I were an expensive piece of ugly modern art.

I got that look a lot. Like from my marriage counselor, before she would say *David, show a feeling.*

I leaned over the bar. "I feel it's important that I stay out of the system." My last gulp of wine numbed my chin. "That I'm in control of my life, and free."

The bartender's eyebrows shot up to where his hair used to be. "You're free from the system, huh?"

A man sitting three barstools to my right lifted his glass of Guinness in my direction. "To freedom!"

The man to my left, wearing a grease-streaked jumpsuit, pointed at the TV. "Take a look at this!"

A reporter appeared on the silent television as words ran across the screen beneath her.

On the tube in London this morning, a man with a bomb took a young girl hostage and demanded that another passenger go with him.

People stopped eating their battered fish to gawk at the television. I fumbled with my cash, and too much money fell onto the bar. I left it and hurried toward the door.

The bartender hollered, "Cheers!"

Three steps from the pub, I stopped near a parked Audi, pressing my hand against my pouch. It held only my credit card and cash. Had the bartender set down my passport after looking at it, instead of giving it back to me? Had I forgotten to pick it up when I scrambled to pay?

Just as I reopened the tavern door, a fiery roar erupted behind me. A scorching force pushed my body through the doorway, nearly into flight, and smashed me—sternum first—into the bar. My spine stung and I was suddenly panting.

Was I dreaming? Had I died?

CHAPTER 3

I turned around to something I couldn't make sense of. Was that a slice of sizzling metal lodged into a high-top table? Beyond the broken glass and through the window frames, screaming pedestrians darted down the street, away from a rolling tire engulfed in flames.

A reek so heavy I could taste it—burning plastic?— scratched inside my nostrils and down my throat. An orange blaze swirled into the entryway, making the pub feel like an oven.

"It's the car, out front, it blew up!" a woman said. She had curled into a ball in a booth.

The frantic howl of a dog next door penetrated the walls.

A terrorist points me out on the subway, and now a car bomb goes off right next to me?

The barkeep reemerged after ducking. "Holy God . . . Is anyone hurt?"

Seven or eight people were scattered on the floor, inspecting their debris-covered arms and legs for injuries.

The bartender tugged the fire extinguisher off its hook; I let him go by before I stepped over the man in the jumpsuit—who lay facedown, still covering his head—and stumbled to the bathroom.

The mirror startled me. Was that what I looked like? Wrinkled clothing? Where had I even gotten this baggy, caramel-colored suit, at a thrift store? When was the last time I had cut my hair? The single gray strand in my beard was longer, thicker, and whiter than I'd ever noticed.

I wet my hands and wiped my face, as if I could wash away my grizzly look. But the water seemed to magnify my vagabond appearance, making me look like a guy who had wandered inside, out of the rain, asking for drugs.

What was wrong with me? Sure, I was on edge after this explosion, on top of what had happened on the subway, not to mention the disaster that was my presentation, but the tired eyes that stared back at me had been suffering for much longer than today.

I missed my dad, but it had been more than a year since he'd passed. My divorce had hit me hard, but lots of people got divorces. The producer was a nuisance, but soon I'd have a television show that would share my astonishing find with the world, and because I'd agreed to that, I'd also receive a healthy budget to continue my research.

Did I have some problem, like a tumor, that had been growing for the last several years, and was about to kill me?

In a daze, I returned to the bar.

No one seemed to have suffered more than cuts and shock. Outside the unhinged pub door, the ashy skeleton of the Audi bled smoke.

"Drinks coming," the bartender said, rushing back inside. The extinguisher clanged a hollow tune when he set it down. He took the phone from the waiter and squeezed it between his cheek and shoulder, saying, "Yes, yes, Guild Street. Stratford-upon-Avon. Thank you." He popped off caps, then loaded the beer bottles and dimpled glasses onto a tray in the waiter's white-knuckled hands.

Despite the calamity, the barkeep diligently dried his foamy fingers on his apron before placing my passport next to a full glass of red. "You're okay, mate. Take a seat."

I sought comfort in evaluating my wine. I smelled its toasty aroma. Observed its deep purple color. Sipped.

Bordeaux.

Over the next forty minutes, a fire crew doused the charred car and law enforcement secured the area.

But that dog, why wouldn't it stop howling?

I approached the man who had flashed his badge (and then done nothing but stand around) and asked, "Can I leave?"

"Not yet. But you can go out front. The detective is there."

I stepped outside under the establishment's sign that dangled from S hooks in the smoky breeze. I hadn't considered why that image of a proud toad sitting next to a fluorescent-green shrub had enticed me into the Frog & Leaf. But now I realized it reminded me of something I hadn't thought about in a long time—the storybook *Alfredo Frog Leaves the Forest*. I had read that book so many times as a child that some of the pages had fallen out. But by then I'd memorized Alfredo's journey, which taught him that other places, like the ocean, were very different from his tree-filled home. That tale had introduced me to the sensation of hope, hope that I, like Alfredo Frog, could someday visit faraway places. Because seeing different people and places, my young mind had reasoned, might finally make me feel comfortable, since I was different no matter where I went.

"Excuse me, Mr. Anthropologist?" The detective waved his hand in front of my eyes. I shifted my sight away from the clouds to find his haggard face, his jowls sagging from the weight of acceptance that he and his comrades were unlikely to find the perpetrator of today's near-deadly event.

"It's just David."

"David, don't look so glum. We have some questions, and then we'll let you go."

I had been listening to the questions he was half-heartedly asking the others. "Did you see who parked the car? Did you see anyone suspicious before or after the explosion?"

He wasn't asking the one question that would matter. *Is someone stalking you?*

I practiced talking to him in my head.

You know that guy on the subway in London this morning with the bomb? I was the person he wanted. Maybe he followed me here.

Or maybe someone is trying to attack me before I reveal my secret. Because they disagree that we could be the second iteration of humans on Earth.

Nothing worked. Anything I said would sound crazy, break my contract, and probably result in me being detained by a system that was unlikely to protect me or my discovery.

"Now, David." The detective flipped over a page in his notebook. "How 'bout you, see anything suspicious?"

My entire body cramped. Motionless, I stared straight ahead.

The detective dodged the awkwardness of my silence by repeating himself. "Anything, David?"

Like all the times this had happened to me as a prepubescent child, I couldn't move. I remembered the day my pediatrician explained that having this affliction sometimes co-occurred with what I was—*a different kind of thinker,* she had said, which put me on something called *the spectrum.* Mom's secret nickname for me had finally made sense, but the phrase was still foreign.

For weeks after that doctor's appointment, I wrestled with the concept of a spectrum, and eventually pictured it as a rainbow with *David* written on the indigo stripe. Although indigo was one of the seven primary colors, it was often left out of depictions of rainbows—just as I had so often been excluded from social groups. That color and I shared exclusion, I had decided, because the shade in between blue and violet was, like me, difficult to figure out.

My father's words came to me. *Just breathe.*

I finally exhaled. "No, I saw nothing."

The return coach ride to London seemed never-ending. I used both hands to pull at my beard, repeatedly counting to seven. My left hand tugged at my left cheek, then my right hand at my right cheek, left, right, left. And then I repeated, pinching my beard between my fingers and pulling. My face warmed up and throbbed, distracting me from my nerves.

The woman next to me relocated herself and her expensive handbag to the front of the bus—rocketing out of her seat and jogging up the aisle as if she had to get away before I grabbed her.

Melly smiled at me from her contact picture on my phone. She had the eyes of a fawn—big for her face, vulnerable. One of our counseling sessions barged into my mind.

"Ah . . . David?" The counselor, an older woman with scraggily hair who always appeared as though she had just gotten out of bed, moved her head in front of mine, blocking my view out the window to the thin clouds scribbled across the powdery blue. "A tragic thing has happened. Let's not be so cerebral. Show a feeling."

I shoved the psychobabble knickknacks off the coffee table. The rock with the painted letters F-A-I-T-H banged into the wall.

"A tragic thing *has happened*?" I shouted. "She humped her boss! Cheating doesn't just *happen*, like a fucking tornado!"

The person in front of me reclined his seatback into my knees. I sighed, longing to get home.

Several hours later, I tripped into my rolling suitcase, trying to check behind me as I approached a subway platform.

The train screeched to a stop and its doors slid open. A wide-shouldered man with an eye patch studied me before turning toward the stairs.

"Hey!" a male voice screamed.

I jerked away from the noise, then realized it was a teenager calling out to a friend.

The doors closed and I bolted to them, but it was too late. My ride to the airport clattered away, leaving me alone, a hundred feet underground.

The bartender's words whispered from the dark tunnel: *You're free from the system, huh?*

Footsteps approached, slow at first, then more deliberate. From where? I backed up against the wall, praying another train was on its way.

CHAPTER 4

I scooped my hair out of the airport-bathroom sink and threw it, the razor, and the scissors in the garbage. I rubbed my smooth jawbone and then pushed a dollop of gel through my new, uneven hairdo.

Pestering Pete lit up my phone.

—*Our contract requires you to stay in contact with me! Where are you?*

I angrily pecked.

—*It doesn't say I have to be in contact with you every hour!*

Then I remembered that his funding would cover the expenses for a research team that I would be solely in charge of selecting. Food and supplies, equipment, laboratory fees, travel costs—all included. I had discovered DNA from a species within the realm of humanity, yet distinct from our own human race. This would rewrite evolutionary history, but only if I could thoroughly study and test it, and search for more of it. Without the financial support from Peter

Wendell, the project would be out of my control and potentially mishandled or not fully realized.

Once again, I tapped Delete.

A husky man with no luggage entered the restroom and glanced from person to person. He considered me for a quick second.

After pretending to dry my hands, I tossed the paper towels onto my hair clippings in the trash, and then did my best impression of walking nonchalantly as I left the bathroom.

I stood in the waiting area of my previously scheduled flight, second-guessing myself. Did I really think someone was stalking me, and that changing my flight plans would throw them off? Couldn't the subway and pub incidents have been random crimes, unconnected to me? What had I done to make someone want to kill me?

Melly had no reason for me to be dead. Indeed, she stood to lose money from my passing. As my ex-wife in the community-property state of California, she would receive plentiful payments from my television earnings.

My phone blinked again; now the producer was calling instead of texting. I hit Ignore and typed a message to him.

—*About to board a flight to Shanghai. Attending a conference there.*

A month ago, I had scoffed at the e-invitation for "Connecting the Cultures of the World," grumbling to my fruity glass of Pinot Noir, *Connecting cultures . . . yeah, right*

46

. . . so more people will be introduced to fast food and be tricked into thinking they need four-hundred-dollar tennis shoes. But now I was ready for any excuse to be among colleagues, and a last-minute destination change would hopefully outsmart a stalker.

Three quick snorts sounded off behind me. I lurched into a charging station, then rescued the phones I'd knocked into a mess of dangling cords. Two women cackled with delight, pointing at the small pig in a cat carrier, and then at me, apparently tickled by how it had scared me.

Within moments it seemed like everyone, even concession workers, were looking in my direction, enamored with the swine version of emotional support and wondering why I was reacting as though it were a rattlesnake.

My idea to surreptitiously observe the people getting on my old flight no longer seemed clever. Who was I looking for, anyway? How would I recognize an undercover assassin?

Was my stalker a bounty hunter, mistaking me for someone else? After finding asylum in a candy store, I scrutinized the latest picture on my phone, taken by the helpful staff member at Shakespeare's birth site. When— and more importantly, why—had I become frumpy, wearing baggy, rumpled clothing and having such a bewildered look on my face?

I ventured to Generation Vogue, a store overpriced even for an airport, to continue to become, hopefully, unrecognizable to whomever was after me. I reappeared in gripping jeans and a shirt that stayed untucked. The salesman had seen my grimace in the mirror and replied, "That's the style now, believe it or not."

When I returned to the two-story wall of glass next to the gate, a thirtysomething woman checked me out with flirtatious eyes. It had been several years since a look like that had come my way, but it had also been that long since I'd exposed my clean face to the world or worn something other than loose-fitting clothing.

The plane, and my old life—peaceful, not on the radar—disappeared down the runway. I would have made a connection at JFK and flown to Northern California, then driven to my home in the wine region of Shenandoah Valley. I could taste the bottle of new-world Barbera I would have enjoyed on my patio, overlooking rows of purple clusters that would someday refill my glass.

I had never cared about money. Why had this discovery made me so desperate for it that I would make a deal with the likes of an egotistical television producer? I wished I could call my dad. I looked up his old number in my phone, then stuck my phone in my bag.

A shuttle zipped me to another terminal, where I boarded my new flight. Soon after takeoff, a boundless layer of clouds blocked the planet's surface, and the hum of the aircraft pushed worry out of my mind. I faded into half sleep.

Two kinds of beeping kept me on edge. There was the steady, low-pitched sound of my dad's heart monitor and the less often, high-pitched *twee!*—a noise I could never figure out.

My dad winced as he swallowed his medication and struggled to adjust himself in the hospital bed. He had a large head, maybe too large for his medium frame, but my dad's big head had made him seem dashing. Now, however, it exposed more of his pain.

"No, I won't tell anyone," he wheezed. "You know you can trust me."

I described my upcoming secret trip to search for evidence of a human race that had gone extinct over a billion years ago. Then I filled the silence: "Dad, how cool is this?"

He closed his eyes and opened them again, choosing his words carefully, since speaking wore him out. "Let's talk about the business. I want to make sure you have the information. Just do it for me."

"Dad, I gotta go." I could not start another round of arguing about the American banking industry.

"Wait, Son, promise me . . . you won't leave on that trip until . . . I want you to be here for your mother when—"

He stopped talking when Mom came into the room.

Mom had always appeared strong to me, more muscular than other women. She was easygoing, with eyes that paid close attention and a mouth on the verge of a smile, if not already in one. But today she seemed weak, like her skin had dried up and she'd shrunk a few inches. She used the back of her hand to caress my dad's face, and then set down on his tray a fresh juice box with a picture of an apple on it.

My own arm hurt as I studied the IV biting into my dad's bruised skin.

In the early hours of the next morning, he opened his eyes. "Oh, David . . . you taught me . . ."

My dad struggled to talk. We held him until he went limp.

A week later I stood at his polished wood coffin, wondering, *What did I teach you?*

The left side of my head bumped into the plastic window. I looked down at the smelly apple juice that had arrived while I slept and wondered with intense hope if the last day had been a nightmare. Maybe I had gotten on my original flight and was on my way home.

I asked the man in the seat next to me where the plane was going and waited for the *are-you-mentally-impaired?* expression to clear from his face. He finally pointed to the navigation screen in front of me. Had it turned on while I slept? A cartoon airplane flew above an arrow that aimed toward China.

My shoulders slumped.

After a minute-long stare at my fists, my dad's voice came to me. *Just breathe.*

I held my tender chest—realizing how hard I must have slammed into that bar—as I maneuvered myself between elbows to arrive at the rear of the plane.

A woman in mid-thigh shorts walked toward me down the aisle. Despite only dim floor lights in the dark cabin, I caught glimpses of her smooth legs, legs that carried her with confidence, as if she were a runway model.

She arrived and considered me for a long moment. "Are you okay?" Her eyes rendered me speechless. They were like flawless emerald jewels.

I finally found my voice. "Yeah, I just needed to stretch."

"Economy keeps getting smaller." She scrunched her nose at the skinny seats. "What brings you to Shanghai?"

"A conference," I said, before I thought that I should be keeping my destination to myself.

She waited for me to say more.

I lied, "I'm going to some place called 'The Pearl.'"

She glanced down, as if disappointed. "What's your name?"

A man with only socks on his feet walked sideways through the small space between me and this curious woman, giving my groggy mind a chance to think. *Could she be working for my stalker?*

The man mumbled, "Thanks."

"No problem," I said to him, and then responded to this beautiful, inquisitive woman, "Roger. I'm from Ohio. And you?"

A bout of turbulence struck; we each grabbed an edge of the lavatory partition. The airplane *ding* sounded, and the pilot instructed everyone to return to their seats. We complied.

As I deplaned, I waved a *thank you* to the pilot. With a glint in her eyes, she said, "Happy to serve you."

I shuffled up the jet bridge from the plane to the terminal, scratching my jaw and remembering that I was clean-shaven now and wearing stylish clothing. I recalled what Melly had remarked two months into our relationship: *It's like you don't know that you're good-looking.*

I had left my response—*I'm glad your cultural programming finds my appearance pleasing*—unspoken. By that time in my life, I had learned that saying less around girlfriends decreased the chances of them breaking up with me.

I followed the airport signs toward the passport check and mentally scolded myself. Had I really been so paranoid as to assume that the woman with green eyes was an evildoer and not politely trying to get to know me? I searched for her as I went through customs and then as I waited outside in the taxi line. I didn't know what I would do if I saw her. Apologize for lying and ask for her number? Give her mine?

I reached the front of the line and tumbled into a cab. The driver, encased in a hard-plastic enclosure that captured the air-conditioning only for him, drove me through the steam room that was Shanghai in July.

After nearly an hour, I peeled my sweaty back from the seat and walked toward the Central Urban Building. I needed to get into that conference and tell someone who might believe me that I was being followed. Then if I went missing, someone would know to look for me. Or they would know, at least, that Weird David didn't off himself.

Maybe I would talk to Janice or William. They didn't get antsy when I sat next to them during faculty meetings, like some of the other professors. Janice usually snacked on cashews and would offer me some, especially when the meetings went long and I started knocking on the desk, seven beats at a time.

I walked through the underground pedestrian tunnel, planning my explanation. *I made a discovery; I can't disclose anything, but I think it has put me in danger.*

When I entered the building—through skinny doors that were nearly two stories tall—the stillness stopped me. Had there been a conference, there would have been registration tables. And there would have been more than a lone security guard in the lobby.

Like a sudden gust of wind, two men scooped me up from behind, one under each of my arms. They were quiet and careful as they moved me forward. Were they saving me from something?

CHAPTER 5

The men racewalked, still carrying me, as my marionette feet quickly tapped in between theirs.

A mirror reflected a third person behind me, reading my luggage tag. He yelled, "It says 'David Denlon'!"

The security guard wore black pants and a pressed light-blue shirt with an emblem on the left breast and black embroidered patches on the shoulders. He marched toward us as if that uniform would be message enough. I squirmed and wondered what the word for "help" was in Mandarin Chinese. He gave an order in his language, and when he was ignored, he switched to English. "Stop!"

A hefty pistol came at his nose from the man on my left. "Piss off!"

The guard yelped and dove behind a glass cabinet displaying delicate models of Shanghai landmarks.

The two men muscled me outside to a secluded courtyard behind the building. A beat-up sedan was there with its trunk open—a large trunk, large enough for a body.

I shoved my foot sideways in front of the man to my left, and as he faltered, I pulled my arm from him and tried to get my hand on his pistol. But the man to my right stepped behind me and squeezed me intensely, restraining my arms and resurrecting the pain in my chest.

With a desperate surge of energy, I kicked the man with the gun, planting my foot in his gut. He hinged over, labored to inhale, and snarled at me.

I had seen that curled, chapped lip before. Those bloodshot eyes. This was the thug who had singled me out on the subway. His shout echoed inside my mind: *You!*

He pointed his revolver at my forehead. "Count to five, Professor. You'll be dead before you finish."

The man behind me snapped a phrase in a Slavic dialect. Snarl Guy shook his head in disagreement and begrudgingly shifted the gun away from my face.

They stuffed me into the passenger's seat of the car. Squeezer sat in the rear seat, aiming his pistol at me. His swollen chest and arms made him seem more fat than strong; this was definitely the guy from the airport restroom. How had these men followed me here? Snarl Guy jumped into the driver's seat, shut the door, and hollered out the window in a language I didn't understand.

Three heavy seconds ticked by as we waited for the third man to load my bags in the trunk.

"Please," I begged, "just tell me what you want."

"We want you to be quiet," Squeezer said.

Snarl Guy again shouted to the back of the car. No response. No slamming of the trunk. No sign of the other man.

We slowly swiveled our heads toward the rear window.

My third kidnapper, even more plump than Squeezer, lowered the trunk lid and raised his hands above his head, staring at us in defeat.

A police officer stood behind him with a large gun.

Snarl Guy sneered, "Shitty hell!" He and Squeezer huffed out of the car.

The officer pushed the third guy to his knees and drilled the gun barrel into the back of his head.

Squeezer threw his hands up, dropping his weapon. Snarl Guy tossed his gun like a Frisbee into a planter box. "Don't shoot him!"

The officer pointed toward the driveway exit—a solid, wooden fence on wheels, blocking the twelve-foot gap in the courtyard wall—leading, presumably, to the street.

Snarl Guy and Squeezer exchanged dumbfounded looks before running toward the gate and sliding it open. The officer patted down the third man and released him. The three of them raced out of the courtyard, through the pedestrian traffic, and disappeared into the honks of crisscrossing cars.

I flung open my door. "Sir, do you speak English? Someone is trying to kidnap me!"

He removed his sunglasses, and there were those bright-green eyes.

The woman from the plane?

"Stay in the car," she said. "Get down and hide."

She ran to a plant with trumpeting red flowers, pulled a backpack from behind it, and returned to the driver's seat.

I wedged my bottom half between the glove compartment and the seat, and kept my head low. The car accelerated through long honks and shouts. She steered right, braked, and mumbled, "C'mon, let me in."

A sweltering three minutes later she said, "You can sit up now."

I climbed up from my fetal position and buckled myself into the passenger's seat, sucking in the air-conditioning and imploring my heart to stop pounding.

As the woman drove, she pulled off her wig and mustache and unbuttoned her police shirt enough to reach in and unstick Velcro accessories that had simulated muscles. Her eyes flew upward every half minute to check her rearview mirror and downward at the cell phone between her legs.

Her velvety, shoulder-length hair curled at its ends. I watched her right thigh flex as her foot pivoted from the gas to the brake and back again.

"I don't know what's happening," I said. "But there must be some mistake."

"Nope," she replied, matter-of-factly. "The mistake is what I made—you don't look like the picture my boss gave me. Didn't you have a beard? And you said you were going to the Pearl Tower. And you apparently thought I was coming on to you and didn't like that, so you gave me a fake name." She sneered at me. "So I didn't know until you showed up to the Central Urban Building that you were Dr. David Denlon, the archaeologist."

"It's just David . . . And I'm not an archaeologist. I'm an anthropologist."

"What's the difference?"

"Does it matter?"

She thought. "Depends on the answer."

I glanced out the rear window, relieved that no one seemed to be chasing us. "Well, archaeologists focus on who lived where, and we anthropologists look at *how* people live or used to live."

"Hm. Interesting." She switched lanes, barely scooting us between two compact cars. "But no, doesn't matter."

Her skin shined. She was the sexy kind of fit that I had only seen in magazines.

"I lied because I thought you might be helping someone catch me," I said. "Who are you?"

"Elaine."

I waited for her to say more.

"I've been hired to get you to safety."

"Who hired you? And how did you find me?"

"Don't worry about that."

"Why can't you tell me?"

She wrapped both hands around the steering wheel and said nothing.

"Can you tell me why there wasn't a conference? My colleagues emailed me about it."

"Your email was probably hacked. There's a way that messages can be sent to you from names and addresses you recognize."

"So I thought I was being smart, sneaking away to this conference, but really I was taking the bait?"

"Pretty much."

Elaine drove us into a park, stopped, and hurried out. She checked under the hood, then dropped to the pavement. I opened my door and almost fell headfirst to the ground as I peered under the car. She was trying to unscrew a device attached to the underside of the engine.

"Damn it," she said, straining. "I don't have my tools." Using a rock, she whacked at the small silver box, and a battery fell out. "That'll do."

She squirmed out of her uniform shirt and pitched it into a garbage can, leaving her in a black tank top and cargo pants.

Back in the driver's seat, she surveyed the area—an expanse of manicured lawn lined with sculptured plants, where locals walked, jogged, or pushed strollers.

She asked, "Has Dr. Imani been in touch with you?"

"Musa?"

Thirty years my senior and with the same PhD, Musa Imani had been my mentor since we had met in Cuzco, Peru. We had coauthored the textbook *World Societies*. His tranquility had always soothed me, particularly when I would withdraw into a frustrated simmer and he would say, "Is David stuck in his head? Come join me out here, my friend, everything is fine."

"Yeah, Musa Imani," she said, as she navigated our car out of the pristine park. "Have you been texting with him?"

"Not lately, no."

My phone vibrated. Mom was calling.

"No, don't," Elaine said. "I'm not supposed to let you talk to anyone. And your phone might be compromised. Give it to me."

I didn't move.

"David, c'mon, give me your phone." Elaine reached over, swerving the car and correcting before we crashed into a trailer truck.

I leaned away, bonking my head into the passenger-door window. I tapped my phone and put it to my ear. "Hi, Mom."

Elaine sighed, then whispered, "Okay. But don't say what's happening."

"Davey? Are you there?"

"Yeah, Mom. How's it going?"

"It's two a.m. here. I couldn't sleep. What's going on? It's been weeks since you called."

"Just one week, Mom." I obeyed Elaine's stern look. "Everything's fine. My plans changed. I'm at a conference in China."

My seventy-five-year-old mother nearly shouted, "China? *Chi*-na?"

"Yes, Mom, Shanghai."

After a pause, she started thinking out loud about what she wanted me to bring her.

"Silk pajamas? Mom, did you say—Mom? Or jade if it isn't too, what? Junky?"

A slight smile cracked through Elaine's impatience.

"Okay, Mom . . . listen, I have to go. I love you."

Elaine snatched my phone away and dunked it into the pocket of her door.

My body flew back into the seat as she accelerated and then jerked forward when we hit traffic.

"What's happening, Elaine? Who's after me? Why did you ask about my friend Musa? Is he in trouble?"

One of her hands left the wheel to rub her neck. "Just trust me."

"I don't. And if you weren't supposed to let me talk to anyone, why did you let me talk to my mom?"

Elaine's face turned sour.

I couldn't bring myself to ask my next question. *Because you think I might not live to speak to her again?*

Chapter 6

When Elaine stopped the car to pay a toll, I took off.

"David!" Elaine was sandwiched in the middle lane. "David, please! They'll kill you!"

All the taxis in the toll lines were full, so I skipped between car bumpers and ran through the brush dividing the highway, halting at the edge of the speeding traffic on the other side.

"Wait!" Elaine had merged her way to the side and parked, and now sprinted toward me, hurdling the scratchy shrubs.

As each vehicle zoomed by, wind smacked me into a wobble. The stream of cars was constant; if I made a run for it, would the drivers see me in time to brake?

Elaine rushed up and draped her hands on my shoulders. A face that close would usually bother me, but somehow, it was comforting.

"Whether or not you trust me, this is real," she said. "Someone is trying to kill you."

I scrutinized her bare lips; one of my lectures came to mind.

She wiped her mouth. "What?"

"Nothing. I was just thinking."

"Thinking about what?"

Elaine seemed more enlightened than the average person, and the combination of the rushing-river noise of traffic, the tangy smell of flowering weeds, and the embrace of humidity encouraged me.

"You really want to know what I'm thinking?"

"We're in China about to be arrested for standing on the side of a highway." Elaine nervously looked around. "But yes, what is it?"

I relaxed into my forte. "Lips are like fingertips. No two prints are the same. Navajo Indians point with their lips, because they believe using their finger to point is offensive."

A crow skimmed the atmosphere fifty feet above us, squawking like a car alarm.

I said, "If a Navajo were directing your attention toward that bird, he would pucker his lips as if he were kissing the air between him and its place in the sky."

I demonstrated.

Elaine's head slowly tilted to the side.

I continued. "I study things like this. I share stories about humans with other humans. Because it endears us to each other and, hopefully, makes us a little more accepting of our differences. That's all I do, Elaine. I'm not anyone worth killing or kidnapping."

Elaine's eyes eased away from *you're crazy* and warmed into something so nice that I thought about kissing her, and then blushed.

A toll guard blew a whistle and angrily waved for us to get back in our car. We obeyed.

Elaine latched her seatbelt. "We have to go to the other airport—Hongqiao."

"Where are you taking me?"

"La Paz."

"Bolivia? Why are we going there?"

"David, I'm sorry. I can't explain things to you yet."

"Why not?"

"In case we get caught. If we get . . . pressured."

"What are you saying?"

She hesitated, checking her speedometer and her side mirror. "I'm saying that what you don't know can't get beaten out of you."

I spread my hand like a starfish and grabbed the top of my head. My fingers pressed into the ripples of my cranium; I clenched my teeth.

"Hey . . ." Elaine's tone softened. "Please don't stress."

I wondered what people's reactions would be to my death. Would Mom ever stop crying? Would Melly miss me?

Elaine patted my arm. "I need you to tell me about the television producer."

"What about him?"

"How do you know him?"

I sighed. "I started a research project and ran out of money. He was the only one to offer funding. He said he'd pay for my continued work if he could do a show that followed my discoveries. *The Race Before Time* he said they'd call it."

"The race before time?"

"Meaning a different human race, before our own time on Earth."

"A different race, like different than black or white or—"

"No, when we say 'human race,' we mean 'humankind.' Just, you know, *humans*."

She shook off her confusion. "What directives has the producer given you?"

"To keep quiet about my findings while he's in preproduction. But my contract includes a cancellation fee. If he doesn't get the television network to green-light the project, my searching and analysis will still be funded for a year."

"Sounds a little too good to be true, doesn't it?"

Rays of sun lasered into the endless landscape of buildings off the highway to our left, blurring the metal and the windows into each other.

"You're saying I was tricked? Why would someone do that?"

"We think it all started with the presentation you gave a year and a half ago, in Dublin. That's all I can say."

"This is insane!"

Elaine stared out her side window so long I thought we would crash into the car in front of us. She finally looked forward. "Insane. That's been my whole career."

"This is really what you do? You run around with a gun, in disguises, risking your life? How do you even get a job like this?"

"My training was in the service. Intelligence, special operations." She nodded. "Yes, this is really what I do. But I didn't want this assignment."

"Then why did you take it?"

Elaine slowly, audibly inhaled. "I was motivated by money, too."

"How so?"

She squinted into the rearview mirror and changed lanes to exit the highway. "I've saved up for many years. This job will significantly increase my little nest egg. I won't be buying anything extravagant, but it'll be big enough that I can invest it, and live off it. Then I can finally be free."

A cozy sensation settled into me. "Free from the system?"

"Yep. Able to get up in the morning, have a cup of coffee, and turn the smallest thing, like watching a butterfly, into the agenda for the day."

I smiled for the first time since I'd left my London hotel for the Future of Humanity conference.

Elaine pulled our car into a space next to a stack of pallets in the parking lot of a small restaurant. She asked, "What's your phone's password?"

I thought about not giving it to her.

"David, please, I'm helping you." She pulled my phone from the car door, and her thumbs paused as she eyed me.

"Nine four seven, two six six."

Her face asked, *Huh?*

"It spells 'zircon.'"

She shook her head again as she opened my texts. "This first one is the producer, 'Pestering Pete'?"

I nodded.

She spoke as her thumbs assaulted the phone. "I was almost kidnapped after landing in Shanghai. Police helped me and I'm safe now. They explained that it must have been an attempt to rob me. I'm shook up and going to head home."

Elaine questioned me as if my life depended on giving the right answer: "Is that how you would say it?"

"That's not what happened."

"Listen. We think someone posed as a producer to steal your evidence. We don't want him to know that you're being saved by people who are onto him. Or that you're going to La Paz. So tell me, is that how you talk?"

"You're saying there's no TV show? That was a total lie?"

"That's what we think. Now help me, okay?"

I craned over to read what she had typed. Her hair smelled like coconut.

"I wouldn't say 'shook up.' Erase that part. Press the voice command."

Elaine held my phone toward me. I said, "I'm looking for a flight back to the States. Phone doesn't work the same here, goes in and out of Wi-Fi. Maybe it's my plan."

A hint of surprise landed on Elaine's face. "That's good."

She reread the message to herself and pressed Send.

"C'mon, we're going inside. We have a lot of time before our flight." She stepped out of the car.

"Can I bring my laptop?"

"Okay, but no internet."

She retrieved my computer bag from the trunk, and I followed her into the teahouse. Golden metal saucers decorated the walls of the entrance. Soft footsteps grew louder until a woman appeared with ruby-colored wands in her hair bun. She glided her open palm away from her as if she were introducing curtain number three. We seated ourselves at the table beyond her hand.

I waited for the woman to leave and asked, "Are we safe here?"

"I hope so."

"You hope? That's it?"

"Yeah, everyone thinks this kind of work is so calculated, but actually, we do a lot of hoping." She handed me a menu with pictures of food next to Chinese characters.

Fifteen minutes later, she ate vegetables and rice, nibbled on biscuits, and sipped tea as I watched, wishing my stomach were cooperating.

"Don't you want some dinner?" she asked.

I had not eaten in nearly two days, since the bland continental breakfast before my presentation debacle. But my gut was in a nervous mood.

"I'll stick with the tea."

Elaine kept an eye on the windows.

"So," I whispered, "what do you think of my hypothesis?"

"What hypothesis?"

"What I presented in my Dublin lecture."

"I didn't see it."

"What? I thought you said that lecture is where this started. Isn't it important to you?"

"No."

I pushed my nose into my cup and rested my forehead on the rim.

"David? Um, I mean . . . I'm sure it's really meaningful. A big deal, looking for a sign of early human life from a million years ago."

"A billion," I mumbled without lifting my head. "And not early forms of our own humanity. A completely different mankind that came and went before us."

"Wow. Cool. But I still don't really get it. Anyway, look, I'm just doing my job of apprehending you."

I raised my head. "Kidnapping. You're kidnapping me, Elaine."

She sighed and looked at her phone.

My fingers danced on the table. "I've got my Dublin presentation on a flash drive. Wanna see it?"

"A whole presentation?"

"You said we have time. And it's very informative."

Elaine crunched her biscuits and said nothing.

My marriage counselor pleaded in my head. *Show a feeling.*

I took a long breath. "Elaine, I feel small—like you're this smart, superhero woman, and I'm some quirky researcher. I'd feel better if you saw me doing the one thing I'm sort of good at."

Elaine's face blossomed with energy. "All right. Let's see it. But I'm no superhero, and quirky is okay. Quirky is . . . interesting."

My pangs of hunger disappeared.

I hit Play and positioned my laptop on the table in front of Elaine. She saw a lecture hall with three movie screens, all showing a graphic of the Earth sitting in space. She watched me at the lectern, where I confidently said, "Everything that has existed on Earth is still here, as the planet's gravitational pull does not allow matter to escape."

Elaine smiled. "There's the beard and longer hair."

"Oh God. I look like hell."

When Elaine chuckled, her lips unveiled glistening straight teeth.

Geysers spouted and volcanoes erupted on the screens, pulling her attention into the computer. The grungy me narrated: "Substances that were here long ago are sometimes transported to the surface of the Earth via geysers and volcanoes, or they are discovered when people drill down into the planet's crust."

Giant rocks appeared on the screens, surrounded by ocean, as my presentation continued: "This is Canada's Baffin Island. Old, hardened lava here was found to hold geochemical materials that existed on Earth four billion years ago."

In my lecture, I posed this question: "Instead of only looking for humankind elsewhere in the universe, why not search our own planet, but look for that life in a time period that we have not yet thoroughly considered?"

A vacant, blistering desert appeared on the screens, and then the scene morphed into an ocean covered with sheets of ice.

"Scientists have determined that young Earth was too hot or too cold or had an otherwise inhospitable environment for biological activity, declaring extensive segments of the past as almost entirely lifeless. In fact, the period between eight hundred million and 1.8 billion years ago has been labeled 'the Boring Billion' because that entire billion-year period has been written off as barren."

Elaine saw a timeline appear, highlighting an era lasting about eighty million years.

"However, evidence has recently come to light that suggests there might be a shorter span of time within this billion-year period that was anything but boring."

The timeline faded into sunrays beaming onto a meadow of orange poppies at the foot of a tree-covered mountain.

"Evidence that Earth offered hospitality to a humanlike species in the distant past has come to us through a sliver of something called zircon." Sky-blue, translucent crystals came on the lecture-hall screens. "Zircon is nearly indestructible. It's the oldest known mineral of terrestrial origin—some specimens are over four billion years old."

The screens zoomed into the center of one of the crystals.

"And when zircon traps other material, it preserves it. Recently, a billion-year-old zircon crystal was found to be harboring graphite, and that graphite had the isotopic structure of organic matter. The existence of organic matter—from plants, insects, animals, or even humans—a billion years ago is something that most scientists previously agreed was impossible. But the discovery of this organic material, preserved in a crystal, points to an environment on Earth an eon ago that hosted biological beings."

Elaine's eyes twinkled with intrigue.

"Could zircon have trapped DNA evidence from a preancient humanoid species and preserved it? Yes, it certainly could have."

Elaine reached across the table without taking her eyes away from my laptop; I nudged her cup to her hand.

Footage of brown rocks, in the shape of small logs and sitting in shallow, clear water, emerged on the screens.

"Stromatolites were in what is now Australia at least 2.7 billion years ago, and possibly as early as three and a half billion years ago. They are evidence of the kind of complex biological activity that could have led to the evolution of a human race similar to our own."

Next, pictures of rust-colored stones filled the screens.

"Klerksdorp spheres are alleged by scientists to have been created by intelligent life, and they were made more than a billion years ago."

Video played of archaeologists in the field brushing dirt away from bones.

"Perhaps we will someday find billion-year-old human fossils. We continue to exhume fossils of prehistoric life-forms we never knew existed. A species of dinosaur recently found, *Yueosaurus tiantaiensis*, inhabited this planet one hundred million years ago.

"Or maybe"—I had paused at the lectern, allowing three beats of silence to build anticipation—"maybe *fossils* of our sister race are not what we should be looking for."

Elaine's fascination dissolved my concern that she was kidnapping me. I reached for her hand, which felt too delicate to shoot guns and pound off car trackers.

"This is it," I said. "This part explains it."

There was her smile again, like the one that snuck out when I was on the phone with Mom.

My presentation continued. "Perhaps it isn't fossils, but zircon crystals preserving superancient DNA, that will show us who walked the Earth in the distant past. But where do we look for crystals from so long ago? Maybe in eroding granite, or in areas where material has been launched up from beneath the planet's crust."

Orange molten rock bubbled and smoked on the monitors in the lecture hall.

"The Earth's mantle. Where matter from yesteryear melts and hardens and melts again. A process that zircon crystals survive. And some of them are shot up through geysers, ocean vents, and volcanoes."

In slow motion and set to classical music, streams of yellow and neon-red lava rocketed from stratovolcanoes.

My lecture concluded: "There has been plenty of time and opportunity for Earth's intricate ecosystem to have introduced a species, including beings of humanity, more than once."

Dozens of smiling faces, of various ages and ethnicities, emerged on the screens. "It's not impossible that a human race came and went before our own—in fact, it's likely. Let's get to searching for preancient zircon, to see who these people were, and what we can learn from them."

The audience's applause cut off when Elaine closed the laptop.

"This is a bigger deal than I thought." She seemed more alarmed than enchanted.

Three vehicles had pulled into parking spaces outside the restaurant windows. Elaine's hand moved toward the gun that now sat between her legs on her chair, under her cloth napkin. People exited each car—parents with their child, a single woman, and a man with an elderly lady.

Elaine relaxed but observed the newcomers. "So how does Darwin's theory fit in with this?"

"It fits in just fine. He said species evolve over time and share a common ancestor. Leading up to our own existence, plants came into being, then bugs, then fish, then mammals. And then we humans evolved from the order of primates. Right?"

"Yeah, okay."

"Well, why can't a Darwinian progression like that have already happened once, an eon ago? From single-cell organisms to animals and then to a human species. And after that race of humans existed for a while—maybe even longer than we have—they, and most everything else, went extinct. And then a Darwinian evolution started all over again, leading to the existence of our own human race."

"Wow." Elaine gazed at me. "What happened after you gave this presentation? Did you go searching for the crystals?"

"Not at first. No one would fund the research. Not even my own university would give me the minimal grant funding to travel and test zircon samples."

"Why not?"

"They called the premise 'improbable.' But that wasn't why. The donors are into the future. They want to invent rocket ships that go farther and faster. They want to put a mobile-home park on Mars."

"So what did you do?"

"I funded my own search. Sold my travel trailer, withdrew my savings, went on sabbatical, and spent several months exploring volcanoes and geysers until I found . . ."

Elaine's eyes asked why I was no longer talking.

I wondered the same thing.

CHAPTER 7

A tickle had crawled into my throat. I coughed, talking to myself in my head. *You were nearly blown up yesterday, and today you were almost abducted. You could still die. You might as well share your secret with the woman who saved you—the woman who may be the most incredible person you've ever met in your life.*

"What did you find?"

I cleared my throat. "I was on a stratovolcano in Guatemala. It had this energy—I don't know how to describe it."

My memory transported me back to the black pebbles that carpeted the side of the broken mountain, where only a handful of plants had struggled their way to life among steaming holes. My electron microscope rested on a board next to my generator, and under the lens was the evidence of a soul from a humanoid species, who had called this planet home over a billion years ago.

"David?"

The thrill of the discovery washed over me again. "The crystal was brown. Marquise-shaped. And more than a billion years old. I took it back to a NanoSIMS laboratory and confirmed the evidence it had preserved—humanoid DNA, unrelated to us."

"Unrelated?"

"Not in our line of evolution. We're not even born out of any organisms that were here when they were."

"My God."

Sharing my secret reminded me that it was real. This discovery would change everything. I struggled to quiet my voice. "There were synthetic particles in the crystal with the DNA. I know it sounds crazy, but I think this evidence— the DNA and these particles—was put there. Like, 'Here's a sample of us and our materials.' Anyway, I ran out of money to keep testing, but my original analysis showed that the particles are from materials we have yet to invent."

"What does that mean?"

"It means these humans who came before us probably got further along in their evolution than we have."

Elaine's eyes shut and reopened bigger.

I raised my cup for a drink but couldn't stop talking. "If we can confirm that these humans existed, the next step is to learn about how they lived, especially if they evolved beyond us. What did they do well, and what mistakes did they make?"

As if the force of her thought had shoved her, Elaine's back hit her chair. "Yeah, this is why he wants to kill you."

"Who? What's going on?"

Elaine sipped her tea.

"C'mon," I said. "Why can't you tell me what's going on?"

"I told you why. If you know information and we get captured, they'll torture it out of you. Now, tell me. How did this discovery lead you to that producer?"

I pulled at my cheeks since my beard was no longer there. "Tortured?"

"Let's hope not. The producer?"

"Um, well, even though I had kept my search and my discovery to myself, it was no secret that I had been looking for financial support. And the Dublin presentation you just saw had gone viral. The producer, Peter Wendell, saw it and contacted me. He signed an agreement not to disclose what I told him about finding the DNA. He explained about the TV show and offered me the funding."

"Did he give you the money?"

"No. He wasn't going to hand over cash. He was going to pay the expenses directly."

Nausea crept onto Elaine's face. "And you turned over your findings? The zircon crystal with the DNA and the foreign material?"

"Not everything. There were two larger crystals that had not captured any material. I put them on leather straps, to wear as pendants. I did give one—the blue one—to Peter, but I kept one for myself."

"At least you have something."

"Well, no. I gave my pendant to a little girl in London."

Elaine pressed her fingers into her temples. "I can't believe you gave everything away, and that you trusted someone who said he was a television producer."

I leapt to my feet. The lady with the hair bun eyed me suspiciously from across the room. I returned to my seat and held my hand over my mouth until I was sure that I would not shout. "He said he needed it to develop the show. The contract said he couldn't disclose any of it."

"I'm not blaming you."

"But you're looking at me like you think I'm dumb."

"You're not dumb. You seem kind of brilliant, actually. Just naïve."

"Naïve? Because I didn't suspect that someone was blatantly lying to me? Because I didn't think, 'Hey, maybe these references answering their phones and vouching for this producer are orchestrating fraud?' Because I didn't worry that someone might try to steal a scientific discovery of no monetary value?"

She pushed her empty cup aside. "Calm down. And everything has monetary value."

"No." I looked around at potted plants and marble statues, finding only my napkin to throw. I chucked it on the table. "Not the stories of people. The site of Machu

Picchu gave us a story about the peaceful, intelligent Incas, but that story wasn't for sale. The Great Wall of China is a story of peasants, convicts, and soldiers who were forced to heave stones every day, across generations—you can't put a price tag on that information. I'm not a pirate searching for treasure. I study people, their beliefs, their community structures . . . stories that can't be patented or trademarked. They're shared with everyone and owned by no one. This show was supposed to be about determining who these people were, how they lived, and what we might learn from them."

I gulped down my water.

The host nearly ran to our table with a pitcher. She refilled my hard-plastic cup, nodding and smiling at me until I returned the head bobs.

Elaine asked, "Is that why you do what you do? Because people's stories aren't merchandise?"

"What?"

"On the side of the highway a few hours ago, you said you learn about people and share what you learn. Is that your thing? Because it's so far from a capitalistic job where something is for sale?"

Elaine stabbed my gut and healed it at the same time. I felt scathed and relieved in one sensation.

She checked her phone. "You can let that be rhetorical. Don't move. Seriously, you won't leave?"

"Where am I gonna go?"

Elaine hurried away through a slender door with a picture of a stick figure wearing a skirt.

A Caucasian man in a T-shirt and jeans entered the teahouse and did not wait for the host before heading into a private dining room. He moved too quickly for me to get a good look at him. Was it Snarl Guy? Or was I being paranoid?

A waitress in a red silk robe with dragons outlined in black poured more tea into my cup. The babbling-brook sound of the trickling liquid sent my mind to my sixth year of marriage.

> Melly poured lemonade into her tumbler, leaving a green paint smear on the thermos. She dove back into her canvas, stroking with her brush and smudging with her fingers, until there was a scene of white water cascading down a steep, minty-green mountain, just as in real life two hundred yards above her easel.

> I kissed the back of her neck. She relaxed into my arms, and soon we were naked in the untrimmed flora, making love.

My semester as a visiting professor in Bergen, Norway, had given us the opportunity to visit the fjords. This was long before our irreconcilable differences, when Melly and I had regarded our marriage as a portal through which we had found wealth without needing the actual money. I was paid to speak and teach around the world—enough money to bring her with me—and this delivered her to unique places to paint. By day, I would lecture while she painted exotic scenes; by night, we would sip wine, eat out or order in, and have sex.

I had always known this way of life could not be sustained when children came along. In fact, I had looked forward to missing the trips—to warming a bottle in the middle of the night and rocking my baby to sleep, reminiscing about how Melly and I used to travel.

But Melly had a different idea about her future. After our Norway trip, she accepted a job teaching art in an elementary school. Soon she was obsessively studying to earn her credentials, and then she was Miss Melissa the second-grade teacher, at a school whose mascot was a swordfish.

However, by the end of her first year—during which she paid for her classroom's safety scissors, glue sticks, and allergen-free granola bars because the school was short on supplies, and, more seriously, visited one student's home every weekend because protective services said his bruises were not severe enough to warrant an investigation—our dinner-table discussions often ended abruptly with her snapping, "You're the prestigious professor; I'm the glorified babysitter."

I experimented with several responses, such as "Your students love you; ignore the crooked system that doesn't appreciate you." But no matter what I said, it seemed to have the same result—her losing interest in sleeping with me.

Two and a half years into Melly's teaching career, her boss, Principal Owens, screwed her in the photocopy room. From the details Melly reluctantly shared after our counselor had pointed to the round rock on her coffee table that read *Honesty*, they had been going at it when I was touring a castle in Hollókő, Hungary.

There was a year of marriage counseling and Melly's move to a different school district to follow, but really, those efforts were emotional preparation for divorce.

"David?" Elaine's gentle fingertips brushed my arm.

I came back to the now with a blend of physical and emotional pain. I was divorced. I had no children. I was being stalked. And I had traded my greatest discovery for a false promise of research money.

Elaine moved her hand to mine. "You okay?"

I told her about the man in the T-shirt and pointed toward the private room.

Elaine picked up the padded bag holding my laptop. "Go in the bathroom and climb out the window."

"What if there isn't a window?"

"It's my job to know there is."

She set a colorful bill featuring a lotus flower on the table and did not follow me.

I toppled through the screenless window and fell into a seated position on the ground, next to a plant with purple leaves. I rested there, studying the sky. The clouds had clustered into bigger, whiter puffs. They floated by in slow motion, reshaping themselves as they moved.

Elaine's question about my career repeated in my head. *Is that why you do what you do, because it's so far from a capitalistic job?* Had I pursued teaching and nonfiction storytelling because I loved it or because it was the opposite of my father's business of mortgage pushing?

Elaine whistled. She had gone out through the kitchen and now stood at the rear of the car. "C'mon." She deposited my computer in the trunk.

I examined Elaine's toned legs, her flat tummy, and her bosom, stuffed into her shirt against its will. She was smart in a way that inspired me. Strong in a way that made me realize that I was strong, too. I could follow her anywhere.

But I didn't move.

Elaine shut the trunk and came to me. "David, let's go."

"Elaine, I need to know what's going on. Is my friend Musa okay? Who's chasing me? What's happening with my discovery?"

"Get in the car."

"Not until I get more information."

"David, I can't."

My face and body stiffened. I couldn't move, but I didn't want Elaine to see me like this.

"What's wrong?"

I ordered my tongue to answer, but nothing happened. I begged my brain for release, to no avail.

"David?"

Just breathe.

Air slowly filled my lungs. My face relaxed and my muscles worked again. I pushed my way out of the foliage and bounded for the street. I was a failure at marriage, a fool in my career, and now I was freezing up like an old, glitchy computer.

Elaine tailed me. "Please don't make me force you to come with me."

I spotted an approaching vehicle. Before I could flag it down, Elaine grabbed and twisted my thumb and wrist. Stabbing pain sprinted up my arm to my jaw.

"Damn! Okay, okay!"

As soon as we pulled away, my mind climbed into the croon of the car's engine.

Elaine's eyes bounced from side mirror to windshield to rearview mirror. She adjusted the vents to ensure that cold air landed on me. "I'm sorry. I don't know how to do that move gently."

I tuned in to the transmission's automatic shifting from second gear to third and back to second. Then, away from the packed urban area, the engine settled into high gear.

The pavement glided beneath our car at an even pace, fading away in my side mirror.

Elaine's voice was light and sweet. "How's your hand?"

It was sore, like I'd fallen on it.

Elaine reached over and stroked the thumb she had nearly torn off. "I need you to get on this plane with me without a scene. We're being watched. It could mean our lives."

Magnolia trees had been planted along the road in a wavy line. If I stared long enough, they seemed to be ebbing and flowing, like waves on a beach.

"Listen," Elaine said. "If I promise to break my orders and explain things to you once we're safely on this flight, will you cooperate?"

Chapter 8

I draped on the sports jacket, and Elaine squirmed into the beige muumuu. I dunked my head into her backpack. "Nothing in here that goes a little better with humidity than a tweed jacket?"

"Sorry. Elderly-people disguises are the only ones I've got. To add age you hide youth, like with that big jacket. Because older men don't usually have"—Elaine drew circles in the air at my torso as if she were casting a spell—*"that."*

My cheeks warmed as I buttoned the extralarge jacket that covered my muscular arms and chest. I stopped resenting my doctor, who had prescribed a weight-lifting routine after droning on some years ago about me turning forty and needing to avoid weak bones.

She unrolled a pair of baggy pants with an elastic waistband and tossed them to me. "Over your jeans," she said. "It'll make you seem heavier."

Our compact car sat under a carefully clipped tree, surrounded by the clean concrete of the business-center parking lot. In the back seat we applied stage makeup to each other to simulate wrinkles and rubbed streaks of white into our hair.

"You need more here." She smeared foundation around my mouth. "Don't eat it."

"It tastes like crap." I laughed into her hand.

A cane—in her backpack as two pieces and now screwed together—completed my old-man disguise. She pushed a gold band onto her ring finger and handed me one. When it slid off, she said, "I went big, because I can't fix small. I'll bring out some tape to wrap around it, to make it tighter."

Elaine clicked pictures of us on her phone and uploaded them to a computer inside the store. She printed them on special pages that affixed into passport books, items she had brought in what I now regarded as her Backpack of Tricks.

I watched over her shoulder as she fiddled with her phone.

"Who are you sending our pictures to?" I asked.

"My boss. He's got to get them into the system, so they come up when our IDs are scanned."

In the airport, my face tensed up at the stoic security official checking our documents. He glared at me, as if to ask, *What's your problem?* I thudded my fist under my throat, trying to feign indigestion, but quickly realized that I had no idea what indigestion felt like or why it would cause my hand to pound the upper region of my chest. What the hell was I doing? Indicating I was choking?

Elaine remained calm. Her grandma voice said, "Take your glycerin, dear."

The official waved us on.

As we approached the gate, a slight-framed man holding a broom and long-handled dustpan swept in our direction.

Elaine handed me my phone, whispering, "Only use it in an emergency. I mean it."

She returned to her role. "Sit here, dear, I'm going to have a look out the window. Let me use your cane."

The man swept a path over to the window, beside Elaine. She tapped his shoulder and pointed to the cane, motioning to its torn rubber bottom. He took hold of it and disappeared behind a closet door near the men's room. When he returned, the cane had a new rubber tip.

I struggled to keep my questions to myself through the forty-minute flight delay, the boarding process—where I kept forgetting to shuffle like an old man—and takeoff.

Thirty-nine thousand feet in the air, Old Lady Elaine finally relaxed into her aisle seat. I sat in the window seat next to hers, thankful that this plane offered the two-chair configuration on either side of its cabin, with a wider row in the middle, giving us relative privacy.

"Start talkin', sugar." I spoke as much like the Elderly Weird David that I might someday become. "And don't leave out what happened there with Mr. Sweeper."

Elaine's cute nose crinkled up as she again revealed her snow-white teeth.

"What's so funny?" I asked.

"I'm the only one who can hear you," she whispered, "and you don't have to fool me into thinking you're an old man."

We laughed, our foreheads nearly touching.

"Okay." She sat up straight. "Here's what I know."

I drank my orange juice.

"If you're captured, hold out as long as you can before divulging any of this. 'Cuz they'll kill you anyway, once you've told them."

I quickly pulled the cup back under my chin as I coughed, spitting out the liquid. "Why do you keep talking about me getting beaten or killed?"

Elaine handed me her napkin. "Sorry. So, where to start. I work for an agency run by my boss, Paul. At least that's what I've called him for fourteen years. I don't have a last name."

Frustration hissed between my tongue and the roof of my mouth. "Is Paul his spy code name or something?"

"It's not like in the movies. Anyway, he does international covert operations."

"Huh? Like what?" I looked away from her only to unwrap my chicken in mushroom sauce, which the flight attendant had delivered after setting a gentle hand on Elaine's shoulder.

"Like secretly helping the US fight terrorists. But governments aren't willing to go after bad guys when there's no political support. And that's Paul's specialty. Bringing evil to justice when no one else will."

Elaine stabbed a piece of chicken onto her plastic knife, but before devouring it, she said, "You seem confused, or pissed off?"

"Both." Wilted mushrooms stared up at me from their mini container, emitting a school-cafeteria aroma and threatening to produce havoc in my stomach. "I don't understand what's going on, and I want my project back. Tell me about Musa. Is he okay?"

"All right, I'll start there."

As Elaine talked, Musa's face appeared in my mind. Creases framed his weathered eyes like parentheses.

According to Elaine, it was a week ago that Musa's digging crew, at my discovery site, uncovered the corner of something silver and glossy.

"He described it as 'strange material protruding out of the dirt,'" Elaine said.

Invisible nettles attacked my feet—a thousand itches too far under my skin to scratch. I stopped chewing my rubbery chicken. "Something was discovered at my site? Why is Musa at my site? How can this be? When did you talk to him? Why were *you* talking to Musa?"

"*Ssshhhh!*"

The attendant appeared and asked about dessert. Elaine answered, "Can I have the fruit, and my husband, the carrot cake?"

A white plastic box landed on my tray.

The attendant moved on, and I nearly screamed at Elaine, "You've known all this time that something more was found at my site? Why didn't you tell me?"

"Whisper! I thought it was some ruin or something. I didn't know it was from a whole different human race. From a bazillion years ago. I didn't know anything about it until you showed me your Dublin presentation."

"I can't believe this. Is it related to the evidence I found? Have they dated it? Is it made of natural material, or synthetic?"

"David, I don't know any of that. Please, just listen."

I grunted and tore into my little box.

She continued. "Musa said he talked to the other researchers there, and they agreed something must be wrong, because you wouldn't only text them, you would travel to the site."

"What other researchers?"

"Jeremy and Meredith."

"Jeremy Johnson? Meredith Fry?"

"I don't know."

Jeremy had always skateboarded into class, usually late, but he had proven to be an excellent analyst and had scored at the top of my research-methods class. Meredith's writing skills had earned her a position as my teaching assistant two summers ago.

"And what do you mean, I 'wouldn't only text them'? I haven't been texting Musa, Jeremy, *or* Meredith."

Elaine held her hand up. "Stop, David. You need to listen."

I used my finger to scrape the gelatinous icing off my tiny cake. "Can you at least tell me why Musa and my former students are excavating at my site? How'd they even hear about it? Peter told me that we'd start work in the field later, after preproduction, and he didn't tell me he'd be hiring anyone to—"

"Listen to me, David." Elaine unpackaged her wet wipe and handed it to me. "We think this guy, posing as a producer, found Musa Imani because of your professional association with him. Didn't you coauthor a book?"

Musa was more than my coauthor on a textbook. He was my mentor, and now that I thought about it, my only friend. "Yes."

Elaine explained that Peter Wendell had shown Musa the contract he and I had signed, and it indicated that Peter should hire Musa to bring on a research team to test more sediments at the site where I had found the zircon containing billion-year-old humanoid DNA. Soon after, Musa had received text messages from me, confirming this arrangement.

"No, that's not what I signed . . . and I told you, I haven't texted Musa."

"You signed a signature page, yes?"

"Yeah."

"So he typed up other stuff and added that page. And he tapped into Musa's phone and pretended to be you."

"Why are you saying this as if it's no big deal?"

"It's a huge deal. But it happens more than you think. Can I finish?"

"I don't know. How much worse does this get?"

"Peter told Musa, like he told you, that this search had to remain a secret until the show aired. Musa and your former students agreed to the terms and therefore to use telephones and computers that were monitored by Peter and his assistant, Darin, to ensure that they were not leaking any information."

I squeezed my cake into the foil wrapper that had covered my mushroom chicken, pumping it like a stress ball. "No. No! This is not at all what we agreed on. It's all a lie!"

"*Ssshhhh!*" Elaine scooped a grape out of her fruit cup and put it in her mouth. "I get it. You've been scammed. But I'm here to help you. Now listen."

The old woman across the aisle observed me, as if she were trying to figure me out. Every wrinkle on her face led into her nose in a look of angry suspicion, like she had spent so much of her life being annoyed that one day her face had frozen into that expression. I coughed like my grandfather used to, until she looked away.

Elaine continued, "Musa told me the texts from you never rang true. He said that one time you texted, 'Long faculty meeting. Phone will be off.' But Musa said you dread faculty meetings and, in fact, that you often send complaining texts to him while you're in them." She smirked. "Really? You do that?"

I shrugged. "They meet for hours, arguing over committee assignments, and they use superfluous words like 'pedagogy.'"

Elaine laughed and offered me the last square of tasteless cantaloupe from her fruit cup.

"Well," she continued, "since Musa was suspicious about why you weren't there, when he found the top of that mysterious object, he decided to rebury it and not say a word to Peter's assistant Darin, who checked in at the site every other week."

"My mentor is a smart man."

"And resourceful. When he and Jeremy went to Antigua on their normal run for supplies, Musa left Jeremy at the street market and borrowed a phone from a tourist to call me."

"How does he know you? He never told me that he knows spy people."

"We're covert operatives."

"What's the difference?"

"Does it matter?"

I thought. "Depends on the answer."

"Well," Elaine said, "spying is secretly gathering information. Covert operations are behind-the-scenes, undercover efforts, such as overthrowing a government or exposing someone."

"Okay, fine," I said. "That does matter. You're operatives. But Musa didn't tell me he knew covert operatives."

"He couldn't tell you or anyone he knows us. Suffice it to say he gave us some information about tunnels in Turkey that helped us nab some really bad people three years ago."

Elaine gathered up the garbage from our trays. "And when he called me and relayed all of this, I said, 'Keep reporting to Peter and Darin that nothing's been found.' And I called my boss, Paul."

I pushed up my tray. "Paul No-last-name?"

"His last name is Smith. But I know that's not his real last name and I don't know what is."

"And he assigned you to kidnap me?"

"Intercept you."

"Well, is someone *intercepting* Musa, Jeremy, and Meredith from the site?"

"I don't know. I only know my assignment."

The mushroom sauce slithered up my esophagus. "My project has been totally hijacked. Why would this Peter guy do this to me?"

"Talk quietly, David." Elaine handed our trash to an attendant passing by with a bag. When he had collected his way ten rows ahead, she whispered, "We don't think Peter is a producer or that his name is even Peter. And it looks like his plan is to off you and then claim everything for himself."

"That's ridiculous."

"It's pretty solid, actually."

"You're complimenting his plan to kill me?"

"I said 'solid.' Meaning 'able to pull off.' I didn't say 'moral.' We have to think about this objectively if we're gonna figure it out. If his plan is to take over your project, he can make your death look like an accident, then reveal his version of the contract to the world and commit to going forward anyway, saying it's in your honor. It all fits, because it looks like you hired your own people."

"What the hell?"

"Think about it. You get killed in a car wreck or while being robbed. This guy comes forward and says how tragic it is, and that he was in contract with you, planning to produce a show where you would have continued searching. He explains that he used the 'Peter Wendell' name to keep the project a secret. And he announces that he will go forward with everything—more searching, trying to get a green light for the show—because it's what you would have wanted. Then everyone thinks he's a good guy for doing you a posthumous favor. But moving forward, most people associate this discovery with him."

I shivered from a chill that sought out only me and began clicking my tray lock right and left, counting to seven. I thought about the seven continents and the seven days of the week. And seven was me, according to someone who lived in a beachfront studio apartment so laden with the smell of marijuana that it had made me forget about the Pacific Ocean, crashing its sea-salty scent to shore behind me.

Venice Beach, California, was cloudy, as Melly and I often found it on our weekend stays, and I questioned why so many people liked it.

"Let's have some fun," Melly said, swatting through a curtain of beads and leading me to an obese woman with long toenails. I was still mulling over the meaning of the sign we had passed on the way in. *Numerology Psychic.*

Madame Jewel spoke to me without hesitation: "You correspond with the number seven. You have your own mind. You believe yourself over others even when everyone else believes one thing and you believe another."

She slurped from a cup of tea with green foam on the top. "You seem withdrawn because you are in your head so much. People think you're strange, but really, you're just living your own version of life."

Why had I agreed to pay someone to tell me that I was a quiet misfit, and why was that insult supposed to be more palatable because it was associated with the number seven? Who had given seven such a bad rap, and why did everyone agree with its meaning?

I switched the tray lock right and left seven more times.

Elaine's voice seemed loud, as if she were repeating herself. "Put your tray back down, dear. More coffee is coming."

The flight attendant asked Elaine, "Cream? How many sugars?"

Before she could restate the same questions to me, I interrupted, "No, and just one."

Words crowded on my tongue, as I waited for the attendant to ask every single person if they wanted cream, and how many sugars, cream, sugars . . . Had flight attendants not come up with a more efficient way to question so many passengers in such a small space?

The attendant finally moved out of earshot and my pent-up sentiment rushed out of my mouth.

"I don't know who you deal with in your covert world. But in my world, things don't go down like this."

Unaffected by my outrage, Elaine simply stated, "They do now."

CHAPTER 9

"Listen," Elaine said, after nearly twenty minutes of silence. "We think we know who's pretending to be Peter Wendell, the producer. He's a really bad guy."

My voice had gone into hiding and I had to clear it twice to speak. "What's his name? Or is there some reason why you don't know *his* name either?"

"His name is Patrick Veeder."

I felt weak, as if my soul were sucked down a drain before I could catch it.

"He fools poverty-stricken communities out of their art and relics," she said, "and then sells them to high bidders. Dead people are left in his wake."

My mind ran from Elaine, into the whistle-hum of the plane. In all my flights, I had never come to understand this sound. Was it how the human brain processed the scream of the jet engines? Was it the atmosphere whirling by the windows?

My right arm moved. I blinked and saw Elaine's hand shaking it. "David?"

My limp hand came alive and gripped her wrist. "No one, Elaine. No one is a match for Patrick Veeder."

Her pulse quickened under my fingertips. "You know him?"

I released her and dipped my knuckle into my hot coffee. It stung, but I kept my finger submerged, welcoming the burn.

I had already mounted a stool when Patrick Veeder strolled into the candlelit bar in Cartagena. His black hair nearly skimmed the top of the entryway as he passed through it.

The bartender recognized him and nervously scrambled to have his cognac poured and sitting on a napkin.

Veeder covered the ground from the door to me in four big steps. He stopped and stood behind the stool to my right, with no intention of sitting down. His pale hand grabbed the glass of cognac. "A refill for my colleague," he said to the bartender. "I see he's started without me."

I tried to make small talk. "Another power outage, I guess."

His contempt was palpable. Was this the same polite person I'd met that morning? "You said you're a professor, David? Then you're surely bright enough to understand this. It's not that you do the right thing and I do the wrong thing. It's that you do your thing and I do mine. The world is big enough for both of our passions. As long as you stay out of my way."

"These people are starving, Patrick. The gemstones were found on their land."

"Where these gems were found is none of your fucking business."

His manicured eyebrows enhanced his look of admonishment. I realized his earlier invitation for a drink, after complimenting me on my research, had been a ploy to get me alone.

"You keep pushing this issue," Veeder said, "and you're gonna get someone killed. Someone like you."

He finished his drink and clunked the heavy glass on the bar top. "What do you think happened to Timothy?"

Timothy was the young journalist who had been writing a story on corruption in the Colombian government. He had been given an anonymous tip to investigate the relationship between the Colombian president and Patrick Veeder.

I concentrated on steadying my voice. "No one knows where he went. His parents are still looking for him. The gossip is he killed himself, but that doesn't make sense."

Veeder grinned, giving me just enough time to connect the dots. He tossed back his drink, threw ten US dollars next to a sign that read *Colombian Currency Only*, and charged out.

I took my finger out of my coffee and wiped it on my shirt. My dry mouth formed one word: "Water?"

Elaine passed me her cup of ice water and I finished it.

"Can you confirm that it's Veeder?" she asked.

"I don't know."

"When you met with him, to do the contract, he would have been in disguise, but think about his features. How tall was he? How big were his feet? Think of things that probably weren't in disguise and compare them to when you saw him before."

He awaited me, outside my office, standing as tall as the highest door hinge. His coarse hair and mustache bore a matching hue of yellow blonde, so fake I assumed he had dyed them.

Hollywood, I nicknamed him in my head.

"Sorry I'm late." I neglected to tell him that I had come all the way from my home in Shenandoah Valley and not from my apartment near the campus.

"No problem at all, Dr. Denlon."

"Call me David, please, and nice to meet you." My hand reached for his thin, pale fingers.

"Peter Wendell. Only a four-year degree in cinema, so, no title."

We laughed and entered my office. The sharp angles of his firm, slender body lowered into my blue chair.

I nodded. "It's him."
"How do you know?"

"His skin, his height, his creepiness. I'm going to the police."

"You can't."

"Yes I can, Elaine. This is my life, and *my* project."

"It doesn't work that way. The police won't believe you over what powerful, well-connected Patrick Veeder will tell them. And there's not enough evidence to link him to anything significant. People like Veeder talk their way out of things, and then hide and wait. And years later you eat some pie in a coffee shop and die from poison."

I handed her my coffee, slammed up my tray, and twisted to face the window. My mind dove into the bed of cumulus clouds. After half a minute, my fingernails stopped pinching into my palms. Tension seeped out of my body, and my feet quit their bouncing, finally becoming still and resting on the floor.

Peter Wendell is Patrick Veeder.

Like cancer or Satan, Patrick Veeder was too evil for a nickname.

My gaze lifted from the clouds to the limitless blue atmosphere, and I thought again about my habit of nicknaming.

Snarl Guy.

Squeezer.

Melly.

My ex-wife Melissa had become *Melly* to me because, when she got angry, she reminded me of Nellie Oleson, the spoiled girl from *Little House on the Prairie*—a TV show I watched when I was young. Melissa wasn't nearly as evil as that rich brat of a character, but when she threw a fit, she seemed to take joy in seeing me suffer, with that *you're beneath me* look that the actress playing Nellie had perfected. Melly rhymed with Nellie, which I found entertaining, and since it used part of her real name, Melissa never suspected that it was anything other than my pet name for her.

Melly's tantrums followed a yell–throw–silent-treatment pattern, and their frequency had increased when she became a teacher. The final time I had tried to connect with her—planning to take her on a picnic, as recommended by our poorly groomed therapist—one of her tantrums shut me down. She had *yelled* at me first: *I have to teach AND manage thirty children; you tell a story about a tribe in Venezuela and get paid twice as much!* Then she had *thrown* the Venezuelan quilt off the recliner. Finally, she gave me the *silent treatment* when she locked herself in the den with chocolate and chips, ignoring my pleading outside the door. I had then taken the picnic basket to the porch, where I drank the wine and threw my sandwich, bit by bit, to a twitchy squirrel.

I now realized that calling Melissa *Melly* had given me a loving way to strike at a part of my ex-wife I didn't like. And referring, in my head, to my hunters as *Snarl Guy* and *Squeezer* had dulled my fear of them.

It must have helped Mom accept my weirdness, coming up with that nickname.

I turned back to see Elaine cuddling a gray sweatshirt in her lap as if it were a curled-up Chihuahua. She asked, "Do you want to know anything else?"

The question I had was the same one that had pounded on the inside of my forehead decades ago, when I was riding away on the school bus, under my newly discovered moniker, *Spectrum Boy*.

"What am I supposed to do now?"

"What do you mean?"

"Patrick Veeder stole my discovery. You say law enforcement won't help. So what am I supposed to do?"

Elaine smiled. "Steal it back."

CHAPTER 10

Elaine used my cane to stand up and pretend to stretch. Her eyes darted around the cabin. When she sat back down, I whispered, "Who else is on the plane?"

"Don't worry about it."

"Elaine, you weren't looking for someone, you were looking *at* someone." I popped up and surveyed a hundred bleary-eyed people around us. I attempted another old-man cough, but it came out like a garbled sneeze.

Elaine pulled me down. "Stop! Jesus, don't do that!"

"Who is it? You said you'd tell me everything."

"Fine. Yes. We're onto someone who thinks he's onto us. Be quiet and let me do my job."

The cream-and-sugar lady presented a tray of rolled-up washcloths. "Warm towel?"

Elaine collected herself. "Yes, dear, that's so thoughtful." She turned to me. "Honey, would you like one?"

I clicked my tray lock back and forth.

"Honey, did your hearing aid fall out?" She touched my bicep. "Dear?"

I winked at the attendant. She had one of those hairdos that was so perfect it seemed like a wig—black hair dropping straight to her jawline, puffy bangs sitting just above her eyebrows, not a strand out of place. "No, darling, all I need right now is a kiss from my bride."

Elaine gasped and smacked my knee. "You've always been trouble."

The flight attendant smiled. "This is so nice to see. How long have you been married?"

"Forty-seven wonderful years." I puckered my lips toward Elaine.

The flight attendant cooed and waited.

Elaine evil-eyed me as she brought her lips to mine. They were soft, like rose petals.

"So sweet," the attendant said, and resumed offering her cloths to the next row.

Elaine blushed, whispering, "I don't know where this mood has come from, but I guess it's better than the pouting you've done for the last hour."

"I wasn't pouting, I was thinking. And I'm happy now because I know what I'm going to do."

"What are you talking about?"

"As soon as we land, I'm announcing my discovery to the world."

"No, you're not."

"Hear me out. I'm going to say that Patrick Veeder is funding the continued search, and in exchange for his funding, I gave him the rights to whatever is found."

"David, no . . ."

"Veeder will be checkmated. He won't say, 'No, actually I tricked Denlon.' He'll have no reason to kill me. He gets the notoriety, which he can have. He won't get to walk away with anything, because the whole world will be watching. And I can uncover the story of our extinct sister race, which is what *I* want. Because that's the most important thing here, Elaine, determining how these people lived and how that can inform us. Good God, I can't stop thinking about it. What could that strange thing be that Musa found? A building? A machine?"

Elaine's head had fallen toward her chest. She slammed her eyes shut. "Announcing that you're working with Patrick Veeder will only solidify his reputation as a do-gooder. He's a thief and a murderer."

"But we'll never be able to steal the site back from him. We're going to end up dead and the discovery will be pilfered!"

Elaine grabbed the same thumb that I thought she had broken before. "Talk quietly."

I turned toward the window again and consulted the shaggy clouds. My free hand reached for my pendant and found only the skin of my neck.

Would Carrie remember how she had gotten her zircon crystal, and share that story throughout her life? Is that how I would live on?

Elaine changed from holding my thumb to caressing my hand. "David, it may not seem like it, but everything is okay." I snapped my head around, silently accusing her of being ridiculous. But she continued. "You've discovered something amazing. After this plane lands, we'll go to the safe house and work on getting your project back. Okay?"

I didn't believe her, but I liked her hand on mine. My jaw unclenched.

Elaine patted my hand as if to say good-bye to it, and went to work. She concealed my cane under her blanket. I peeked underneath to see her extract a gun from it.

"Man," I mumbled. "I can't even sneak on four ounces of shampoo."

She smiled. "Mr. Sweeper."

It took me a minute to figure it out. The new rubber tip had been a cover for what the janitor had really done— place a gun inside the cane's specially designed handle.

Elaine attached a silencer that had been packed in her carry-on in pieces and then said, "Unhook my necklace."

As I searched for the clasp in the warm space between her hair and neck, I noticed that her necklace consisted of bullets alternating with pearls.

Elaine loaded her gun. "He hasn't peed. This whole flight."

"Who?"

"He's one of the guys who tried to kidnap you. Look, I could use your help. If he goes to the bathroom, follow me.

When he opens the door to come out, I'm going to shove him back in and get information about Veeder. While I'm in there, do not let anyone come near the bathroom, no matter who it is, even an attendant. Stall them. Ask a question. Pretend to be sick. Whatever. Okay?"

I could not formulate a response.

"David, you can do this."

My prayers were denied forty-five minutes later when Snarl Guy, emotionless and wearing a baseball cap, stood from his aisle seat eight rows ahead of us, stepped into the attendant workspace, and went, presumably, into the bathroom.

Elaine shuffled toward where he had gone, past the slim food carts parked in their spaces, and disappeared from the view of the other passengers. I scurried behind her.

When the lavatory door unlatched and bent inward like an accordion, Elaine stuffed the tip of her gun into Snarl Guy's mouth before he could get out. She squished herself into the closet-sized restroom with him and shut the door.

I wondered if I would see her alive again.

A boy who seemed about twelve years old arrived, and his eyes flickered at the banging around the corner.

"Hello, young man," I said. "I suggest you use the bathroom in the rear. The one up here is going to be occupied for a while."

He backed up in confusion, spun around, and skip-walked down the aisle.

The flight attendant who had taken a liking to us gently tapped the boy's head as he passed her. Then she marched her neat, square hairdo toward me.

A furnace ignited inside my rib cage. Not one word came to mind to deter her from entering her workstation.

A *peh-thud!* rang out from the bathroom. People sitting nearby looked left and right before returning to their magazines and seat-back TV screens.

The flight attendant picked up speed. Had she heard the banging?

The lavatory door clattered and shook.

Just five rows away now, the attendant asked me, "Is everything okay?"

I couldn't find an answer in my head.

A heavyset man with dark circles under his eyes stood up and blocked the attendant's path, describing his flight connection and asking her which terminal he would need.

Elaine's hand slugged into me; she had flown out of the bathroom and now pushed me past the man and the attendant.

"So sorry," she said as we bumped into them.

We sat and fastened our belts, stealing glimpses at Snarl Guy as he sulked into his seat with flushed cheeks.

My body locked up. I could not budge even my eyeballs, no matter how desperately I commanded them.

I imagined my dad kneeling next to me when I was a child. But before my memory replayed his soothing voice, Elaine rubbed my shoulder and said, "Just breathe."

I thawed. "Why did you say that?"

Elaine kept her hand on my shoulder. "You looked like you needed to breathe."

"Yeah, sorry, I . . . have this staring thing."

"No worries."

I knew that was just a phrase, like *no problem*, or *have a nice day*, but I really did have fewer worries around Elaine.

She lowered her voice. "That guy yapped on about some pastor. Liam is the name I got out of him. Sound familiar?"

"Liam? A pastor? No idea. So now what?"

"We land in La Paz. The hideout is there."

"Musa and my students will be at the hideout?" I asked, worried. Musa was in his seventies now. Jeremy was bright but unsophisticated. And Meredith, although independent, had more Southern charm than survival skills. "They've been rescued from the site?"

"I told you I don't know. Someone else is on that."

Stomach acid squirted up to the back of my throat. I swallowed the stinging. Sweat formed all at once, all over my body.

My fingers madly searched the seat pocket and yanked out the airsick bag. The second time I encountered the mushroom chicken was no worse than the first, save the pain of my stomach trampolining into my throat and landing back in my gut.

Elaine handed me a napkin. I cleaned my quivering lips and looked up to find the adoring attendant.

"We're almost there, hon. I'll get you some crackers." Her gloved hands took my bag.

Since my two-month stay with the remote Venezuelan tribe known as the Yanomami—a friendly community whose digestive systems were, of course, more accustomed than mine to charred caterpillars—I had made it routine on my trips to pack salt, baking powder, and powdered orange juice, as recommended by the World Health Organization. These simple ingredients, mixed with bottled or otherwise purified water, did a decent job of treating an ailing stomach.

I nursed this concoction and ate salty crackers until my mind refilled with curious thoughts, like wondering who chose the fabric for airline seats and if there were specific factors considered. Did certain colors or patterns instill patience and tranquility in the human brain?

And then my stress evaporated as I fell into laughter. I silently shook, a wide grin across my face, enjoying the release of endorphins.

Elaine contemplated me. The sensation of her attention felt like sunshine on a winter day.

She finally asked, "What could possibly be funny?"

"I shouldn't say."

Elaine raised her eyebrows into question marks.

"Okay, if you want to know. I was thinking that what we just pulled off with the bathroom is not the mile-high club I would have preferred to join with you."

Her attempt to keep a straight face didn't last long. "Yeah, okay." She smiled. "That's funny."

The pilot announced our descent into La Paz.

Chapter 11

I staggered off the plane, dizzy and weak, but thankfully, no longer nauseous. I headed for the first restroom I saw.

"Don't use a urinal," Elaine whispered. "He knows our disguises now, and he got off ahead of us. His tennis shoes are blue. Check under the stalls before going in one."

I left my bags with her and walked through the doorless round entrance to find tired men with disheveled hair relieving themselves in a line. Feet and shins were visible beneath the doors of half the stalls—but none were Snarl Guy's.

I checked twice that I locked the door of my stall and glanced up at the top edges of the walls as I peed. Someone jumped to the ground next door, but I had thought that stall was empty. I zipped up my pants as the door unlatched behind me.

Snarl Guy was inside when I turned around, nearly on top of me, pointing his knife. Had he used the blade to pry open that flimsy lock? His foot pushed the door shut behind him.

He kept his voice quiet. "Yell and it will be the last sound you ever make. Give me your phone."

I considered dropping to the floor and rolling out of the stall, but between the toilet and Snarl Guy, there wasn't enough space.

"Your phone!" he hissed.

I handed it to him.

"Turn around," he commanded.

I faced the wall. Why was I complying?

His breath hit my neck. "Where's the other site?"

I stared, but this time, as I involuntarily froze into stillness, I felt more relief than embarrassment. It was as if my brain had retreated to some place of safety, and not being able to move let me off the hook for having to deal with my fear.

He whirled me around and touched the knife to my throat. "You live if you tell me where that other damned site is."

I stared.

He shook me. "The other site, where is it?"

I recalled Elaine's words. *You can't have beaten out of you what you don't know.*

But I knew. In my digging and analysis of sediments on the sides of volcanoes and around geysers, a second site had revealed zircon crystals similar to the first. But I had run out of money, leaving me unable to test them. I hadn't collected anything, assuming I would return to the area when I'd secured more resources.

I had told Peter Wendell—ergo, I had told Patrick Veeder—that a second site existed, but that I would not make it part of our contract. My reasoning had been to have a bargaining chip for when I negotiated future seasons of the show.

But now, I inferred, Veeder wanted to know about that second site, given that Musa and my former students were reporting that nothing had been found at the first one.

"Professor, snap out of it. Answer me."

It made sense. On the subway, Snarl Guy wanted me to go with him. At the Central Urban Building, they put me in a car. They had been trying to take me to Veeder, who would torture me until I told him the location of the other zircon, and then kill me.

Urinals flushed and faucets turned on and off.

If I yell and he stabs me, will someone get help before I bleed to death?

Snarl Guy's fist came at me like a bolt of lightning. I blinked as if waking up, taking account of my position—bent, squatting, and leaning against the wall. My cheekbone tingled. My stare was gone.

Everyone quickly pattered toward the exit, leaving the tiled room in silence.

Snarl Guy locked the stall door. "Still refusing to answer, Professor?"

Yes, you bastard.

His knee slammed into my chest, rebruising my sternum. And then I remembered eleven-year-old Wayne Durkson.

Granules of sand filled my nostrils, and for some reason, after years of being picked on, this nose-plugging sensation was the last straw. I squirmed out of Wayne's hold, and as he yelled, "Freak," I grabbed his ears. I pulled his head down fast, intending to throw his face into the sand as he had done to mine, but our tussling had shifted us to a different spot on the playground. Instead of sand, his mouth pounded into the metal seesaw, knocking out his freshly grown front tooth.

That night Mom fretfully chopped celery, murmuring about umbrella insurance. But my dad snuck me a glass of new-world Cabernet and joyously squeezed my kneecaps.

I shot up and powered my fist into Snarl Guy's nose, crumbling cartilage and busting open a fountain of blood. His eyeballs floated in different directions. One of his knees buckled and he fell into the wall.

I reached toward the latch, but Snarl Guy wrestled me back. His warm blood splashed on my face as he thrust his knife toward my neck. My hands wrapped around his and we both pushed—I tried to keep the knife away; he pressed it toward me.

My hands trembled as he outmuscled me and the knife sliced into my throat. My peripheral vision caught Elaine peeking over the top of the stall. I focused harder on Snarl Guy's mutilated nose, to make sure my eyes didn't alert him to Elaine's presence. It took all my might to keep the knife from sinking deeper, toward my trachea.

Elaine reached down, and before I could process what she was doing, she had fired a bullet into Snarl Guy, near where his neck met his shoulder. The gun's silencer did little to muffle the ringing explosion. Snarl Guy gasped and released the knife; surprise hit his face, as if someone had poured cold water down his back.

Was that necessary? Couldn't we have fought him off? Will he be okay?

I opened the door and stepped out to find Elaine hopping down from the toilet next door. She leaned her head back to draw in oxygen but couldn't seem to get enough.

Snarl Guy stumbled toward the mirror and studied the man in front of him, as if it were not his own reflection. His right hand caressed his cheek, and his concern became terror. His legs collapsed; he smacked onto the floor, exhaling a high-pitched whimper. A scarlet puddle formed beside him.

"David," Elaine panted, checking me over and then pointing to the towel dispenser, "dab your face, to get the blood off. Don't mess up your makeup. Pull your shirt up over the cut on your neck."

"But, is he . . . ?"

"Hurry!"

I did as she asked and then bent down and extracted my phone from Snarl Guy's pocket. I expected him to wake up and take hold of my arm.

"C'mon," Elaine said. "Act old."

"The cane." I ran to the stall and back to Elaine.

"Move slower. You're old," she said.

We scampered through the circular exit and collected our bags. Two men had been stopping people from entering the bathroom, and the shorter one lurched back at the sight of us.

We all stared at one another until Elaine said, "There's a bad man in there! My poor husband had to hide."

The men didn't seem convinced.

I said, "I think he attacked someone in a stall."

"Help is coming," the taller man said, tipping his head toward the security officers sprinting our way.

The stream of arriving passengers continued moving by. One person had stopped and now asked no one in particular, "Was that a gunshot?" Most travelers veered around the onlookers, unaware of the incident and fumbling to retrieve their passports from purses and pockets. Elaine and I weaved into the flow and trudged forward.

But Elaine couldn't keep up. Sweat carried her fake wrinkles down her cheeks. "I think something is really wrong."

I tried to forget about Snarl Guy's shocked eyes and the crack of his skull striking the floor.

"My heart." Elaine put her hand to her chest.

I followed her to a bench and helped her sit down.

"Is it racing?" I asked. "Like you just ran a marathon?"

"Yes. Am I having a heart attack?"

"No, Elle. It's the altitude."

"Elle?" She gave me a quizzical look.

"We haven't been through enough yet? How much more has to happen before I can shorten your name?"

Elaine barely smiled, eyeing the spinning lights on the police golf carts.

"Listen," I said. "This is one of the highest cities in the world, twelve thousand feet." I set my hand on her shoulder. "What's happening to you is normal. Your body will adjust."

"I know about the effects of altitude. But I don't usually get them."

"Have you been *this* high before? And you know, just because you weren't affected by altitude some other time doesn't mean you couldn't be now. That's how it works."

Elaine peered back at the bathroom. Security personnel shooed people away and nervously spoke into their radios.

"I can't believe I feel this weak," she said, "just because I'm at altitude."

"Believe me," I said. "This is my third time here. Once I didn't notice it at all. Today, it's getting to me. Feel." I lifted her soft hand to my chest. My heart pounded into her palm.

Elle examined her hand as it sat on *that*—my pectoral muscle. Her princess eyes sparkled.

I kissed her forehead, then sat next to her.

"There's no need to pretend to be intimate," she said.

"I'm not pretending."

We held each other's gaze; our breathing synced.

But worry yanked her away. "We've got to get out of here."

I helped her up and we scuttled to the long customs line beneath a dusty television monitor on a wall mount. The title of the evening news segment on *Noticias Internacionales* was in Spanish: *Strange Incident in Shanghai*.

Police officers leapt down an escalator.

Elaine stood up on her toes. "This line isn't moving."

I investigated the luggage tag on my carry-on, trying to get my mind off the news report and the second bunch of hurrying police officers. Was the bulky black stitching around my undercover name and address plastic or leather?

Elaine bent over—acting as though her backpack was much heavier than it was—and approached an airport worker. "Dear, I'm really having a hard time. My ankles are swollen. Is there a different line for older people?"

After mumbling something into her radio, the woman escorted us to the front.

The man in the bulletproof booth handed back our falsified passports through a square opening, saying, "Welcome to Bolivia."

All at once, every phone in every customs booth rang. We hurried away from the checkpoint, elongating our strides but resisting the urge to run. I glanced over my shoulder to see the agents reaching for their phones.

Elaine tugged my arm. "Don't look back like that. We're on camera."

We zigzagged through hallways, down a stairwell, and past baggage carousels. I didn't know how to act old while rushing, so I limped, then jogged, then limped again. Outside, buses and hotel shuttles jammed up the street. Police officers seemed to be multiplying themselves before our eyes.

One official questioned a woman and her teenaged daughter in Spanish. *"There was an older couple on your flight, have you seen them? The man used a cane."*

We quickly put our backs to them and walked away; I picked up my cane and tried to hide it in front of me.

"That's them!" the woman said.

We darted behind a group of people in matching shirts, handing their luggage to a bus driver.

Elle used my arm to keep her balance. "I can't run. You need to go."

"I'm not leaving you."

"David, you have to get out of here!"

I snuck a peek from behind the tourists. Law enforcement officials wearing bulletproof vests had drawn their handguns and were quickly approaching.

I whispered to Elaine, "We'll talk to them. We can explain what's happening."

The woman yelled, *"He's in the brown jacket!"*

"David," Elaine insisted. "We can't explain murder."

CHAPTER 12

A taxi skidded to a stop. Elaine squinted for a better view of the female driver and said, "This way!"

She used the last of her energy to crawl into the back seat of the yellow car. I tossed my briefcase and bag in the passenger's seat and slammed the door before they toppled out. Landing on the seat next to Elaine, I pulled the door shut as the car tore away.

Behind us, six police officers charged into the street. Up ahead and to the right, officers in pickup trucks with blinking overhead lights stuck their arms out and pressed their palms at us.

"Ann." Elaine gasped for air. "I'm so glad to see you."

Ann smiled and waved at the police as if she didn't understand their *stop* gestures. She yelled out the passenger window, with a tinge of airheadedness, "Gracias!" before steering our car away from the terminal.

"You too, sweetie," she answered Elaine. "Did you have a nice flight?"

Elaine took off her backpack. "You know I don't like to fly."

Ann smiled. "Oh good, no bugs."

I must have looked puzzled because Elaine said to me, "'Did you have a nice flight?' means 'Do you think you're being recorded?'" She inhaled. "And 'I don't like to fly' means . . . 'no.'"

"Ah." I set my hand on Elaine's head as she planted her face on the back of Ann's seat, too winded to hold herself up. "Well, what if someone *were* listening in?"

Elle's arms fell limp beside her. "Then I would have said, 'The pilot pulled off a great landing.'"

Ann zoomed onto the freeway and then her brown eyes found me in the rearview mirror. "There's lots of things she could have said, actually. Anything in the negative, like 'I don't like to fly,' means 'no,' and anything in the positive, like 'the views were spectacular,' means 'yes.'"

I held my hand up to Ann's reflection. "I'm David. And that just means 'I'm David.'"

Ann's sweet laughter—almost childlike—lowered my anxiety. She was an in-shape, flirty woman in her early forties, wearing a blue running shirt and yoga pants that grabbed her legs until her calves, where they flared out and ended, leaving the rest of her legs exposed. As if she were turning her athletic look into high fashion, she also wore a long dark-blue sweater, open in the front.

"Hi there, David. I'm Ann. It's nice to formally meet the star of this show."

I laughed. "I certainly don't feel like a star."

We drove into southern La Paz and Ann throttled our rickety taxi up a steep cobblestone avenue. Near the top, she turned into a square opening in the face of the wall-to-wall dwellings.

The garage door whined as it closed. We hobbled out of the car; Elaine moved gingerly, trying to keep her heartrate low.

Ann unlocked the two medieval-looking deadbolts and slowly swung open the weighty door, evoking a sense in me that we were entering a crypt. "There's a bathroom to the right," she said.

I knew immediately that the house had been staged, with a jacket carefully strewn over a new couch and some dishes without food stains neatly piled in the kitchen sink. The walls bore impersonal decorations, like in a hotel room. A painting of a river. Tapestry woven into the shape of an alpaca.

In the bathroom, I rinsed the makeup off my face and out of my hair, took off my baggy pants—leaving me in the jeans I'd worn underneath—and changed back into my untuckable shirt. The bright-pink slit on my neck had finally stopped trickling blood.

Elaine had taken her wedding band off in the car, but mine was still on my finger. It was a cheap ring, undoubtedly fake, more yellow than gold. Nothing like my real wedding ring, which was thick and heavy, with a brushed finish, and sitting now on the floor somewhere at home in my kitchen. I hadn't noticed where it landed, after I'd thrown it at the refrigerator, aiming for the picture of Melly and me in the Mirabell Palace rose garden in Salzburg, Austria. I had determined that rings were useless symbols, excuses for jewelry stores to make money. But now I found myself reluctantly pulling this toy of a ring from my finger, smiling at the tape wrapped around it, and wanting not to lose it. I put it in my pocket.

Elaine had changed and washed up in the kitchen.

"We're down there." Ann pointed toward a dark stairway that led to what I anticipated, given the modest size of the house, was a small basement. She toggled an intercom, moving close enough to kiss it. "On his way."

A cheer erupted out of the speaker and then was silenced by Ann releasing the button.

Who was down there?

My skittish stomach cramped as I descended toward the warped door. The rusted lever stuck until I jiggled it, and then I slowly entered.

Light bulbs inside glass globes bordered the large rectangular room, giving the whole space an ultra-white, heavenly glow. Although the room could fit ten, there were only two desks; one held a laptop, the other a desktop and a printer. A microscope stood on a tall table next to petri dishes and containers with tags. Dry-erase whiteboards—covered with writing, symbols, and graphs—stretched the entire length of one long wall; the opposite wall held shelves stuffed with files and was interrupted only once, in the middle, by an opening that led to a hallway.

Two men I didn't recognize stood next to Sunny Brown, one of my former students. *Doctor* Sunny Brown, I had to remind myself. They all stayed quiet, seeming to give me a chance to take everything in.

In the center of the room, a kitchen island with a two-burner stove, a mini refrigerator, and a sink added a homey flair to an otherwise command-center ambiance. The counter held a microwave, a coffee maker, and an electric teapot.

Near the island was a folding table, and on it were napkins, salt and pepper shakers, and open files. A magnifying glass had been set down on a mess of what looked like printouts of pictographs. Mismatched chairs surrounded the table.

By my estimation, this bunker occupied the space beneath several homes. Despite having no windows, the air was fresh—a pleasant mix of garden vegetables and lavender-scented cleanser.

Sunny's cheerfulness boiled over; he had no choice but to release his scream: "Professor Denlon!"

As he bounced toward me, I recalled the first time he had loudly participated in class, and I wondered, like I had then, if he was unable to control the volume of his voice. Bushy black hair and a gentle, boyish face—the face of a nerdy high school student, not a twenty-nine-year-old with a PhD—topped his tall, skinny body.

I seldom remembered students' assignments, but Sunny's research paper on hieroglyphic translation had earned a solid A from me, a rare feat.

"Professor, I want to hug you." We embraced—more him slamming into me while I tensed up to avoid falling over—and then he spanked his hand on the tall table in jubilee, causing the petri dishes to shift. "You're gonna love this!"

I remembered my secret nickname for him when he had been my student—Pipsqueak. The label was partly accurate, describing how frail and naïve he seemed, and partly sarcastic, a mousy name for such a loud-talking person. A surge of remorse hit my gut, as calling him Pipsqueak, even in my head, now seemed cruel.

Behind him, the two other men were stoic. "We'll get the bags," one of them said. They hiked up the stairs.

Sunny held out both of his hands in front of the long span of dry-erase boards as if to say, *Ta da!* The panels sparkled under the lights, displaying red, blue, and green drawings of amoebas, dinosaurs, rats, apes, and other creatures. A timeline depicted human evolutionary milestones, identified by notations such as *Control of fire*, *Understanding the solar system*, and *Inventing the wheel*.

The information overwhelmed me. I swayed backward.

"It's a lot." Sunny ran to the lip of the board and picked up a photograph of a drawing carved into a rock. It was a round, black circle with a brown rod through the center, like a wheel with an axle. "I think these are painted petroglyphs," Sunny said, "because they are etched into the stone, but also in color. Your site is a gold mine!"

"That's a picture of a carving you found at the site?" I asked.

"Yes!" He carefully balanced the picture back in its place and slapped a desk with both hands. "You were right. They existed!"

I looked back toward the stairwell. Was I being fooled? Was this a trap?

"This can't be," I said. There were so many photographs— set up along the board, scattered on the desks. "You've found all these etchings at the site? You've dated the paint? And the rocks?"

"Yes, and it's not paint! The colors are from granules of zircon, as old as your specimens. And we used radiometric dating for the stones. There's unknown material mixed in with the granite that seems to have preserved it. Professor, these engravings are over a billion years old!"

"My God." The throbbing pains in my jaw and chest— from Snarl Guy's beating—shrunk to small itches.

Elle and Ann smiled at me and then at each other, as if they were my parents, elated to see my reaction on Christmas morning.

I peered into the microscope, adjusting the focus. "Zircon."

"Yes," Sunny said. "That piece preserved graphene."

I took a moment to think. "To use as a semiconductor?"

"Computers!"

My legs lost strength.

The men returned with my carry-on and briefcase, and Elaine's backpack, and finally greeted me, albeit with reserved smiles.

"Okay, then," Sunny said. "We're safe, and finally together. It's time for dinner. And then my update!"

"But what about Musa?" I asked. "Jeremy, Meredith?"

"Not here." The blonde-haired man sounded like he wanted to head off my questions. "We'll speak with them soon, remotely."

Sunny opened the refrigerator and pulled out more than I thought it could hold—carrots, celery, hummus, and a glass dish of cooked pasta with meat sauce. His second dive inside produced bottles of water and juice.

Ann dealt paper plates around the table like cards, making the rounds again with cups, and then with plastic cutlery, while the microwave heated up the pasta.

I couldn't let go of my concern. "Musa and the others are safe?"

"David, we need to stay healthy," Ann said. "Come get your food."

As we each found a seat, Sunny said, "All right, now for introductions. I'm Sunny. I'm a researcher. The other researchers are Jeremy, Meredith, Musa, and of course, Professor Denlon."

"Thank you, Sunny," Ann said, looking toward the blonde, muscular man in his thirties as if it were his turn.

"I'm Casey." He spooned hummus onto his plate and dipped a carrot into it. "Security."

Elaine caught her breath. "I'm Elaine, security." She turned to Sunny, the only person in the room she apparently didn't know, and snuck a smile my way before saying, "You can call me Elle." We watched her consider the pictures and the multicolored markings on the shiny boards. "I've worked for Paul a really long time. But I've never been on an assignment like this."

"Neither have I," Ann said. "I'm security. My husband works for the CIA. I used to work there, but I like this kind of work better. And I'm mad at my husband, so when Paul called me about this gig, I took it, to get out of the house."

"Poor Mark." Casey twirled spaghetti around his fork. "Whatever it is, tell him I'm on his side."

Ann smirked at Casey, and then motioned to the other man who'd carried our bags. I tried not to stare at his scarred cheeks.

"This is Miguel," Ann said. "He doesn't talk much."

Miguel flashed me the peace sign. I returned the gesture.

Sunny asked, "Professor, can I introduce you?"

"Sure. But it's just David."

"Ooohh no. This is Dr. Denlon, the professor and cultural anthropologist!"

"Thank you," I said.

I took another look at the people I'd just met, memorizing their names. *Confident, toned Ann; quiet, rough-faced Miguel; cocky, poster-model Casey.*

After repeating their names twice to myself, I asked, "Elaine tells me that we can get the site back?"

"Whadayamean, Professor?" Sunny diverted a forkful of pasta back to his plate. "We've already done that."

"Not quite yet," Casey said, agitated by my question. He scrubbed spaghetti sauce and hummus from his hands with a wet wipe and turned to his keyboard. "We're still working on getting a bigger security team to the site before we confront the person who took it."

"And who is that?" Sunny asked.

I covered my full mouth, anticipating that food might fly out. "You didn't tell him?"

Elaine's hand landed hard on my arm. "Let's not get into that with Sunny."

"Bullshit." I pulled away from her grip. "If we move forward from here, together, we start with the truth."

Casey stopped typing and turned his chiseled body toward me. "You're safe now, David, no need to worry."

"Don't patronize me. You have to tell Sunny who we're dealing with."

A troubled look took over Miguel's banged-up face.

"What's going on?" Sunny glanced around. "Who are we dealing with?"

I stabbed my fork into the air. "A murderer, that's who."

"Okay, hold on," Elaine said. "Paul's got this under control."

"Does he?" Ann poured more juice into Sunny's cup. "I think David's right. We're in this together, so everyone gets full information."

"We're not in this together like that, Ann," Casey snapped. "We're in an operation. We take orders from Paul, and we keep the researchers safe—we're not supposed to have a friggin' roundtable discussion."

Sunny asked Casey, "What are you keeping us safe from?"

I stood, my legs infused with adrenaline. "I don't believe this. You have to tell him how much danger he's in! What about Musa, Jeremy, and Meredith? Do they know?"

"Sit down." Elaine's tone disclosed her mental fatigue. "This isn't the time to talk about this."

"*When* to talk about *what* is up to *me*! Musa and my students are working on this project because they're loyal to *me*! They're going to learn right now what's happening, and if they want out, we're going to help them get out, immediately."

Miguel shook his head and stared down at his plate.

"I trust and respect Paul," Ann said. "But David is right. It's time to tell Sunny what's happening."

"No," Casey said. "It won't do anything but worry him."

"Listen." I reluctantly sat down. "Only with full information can Sunny make a decision to be involved in this." I addressed Sunny. "His name is Patrick Veeder. And if he finds out that you're part of this effort, he'll kill you."

"David!" Elaine spilled her juice. Ann and Miguel threw their napkins on the cranberry liquid.

Sunny's face crumpled into a blend of shock and confusion. He grabbed a fistful of his hair and tugged his head back.

Casey's hard legs pushed his chair away from the table. "I appreciate that this is your project, David, but this isn't your operation."

Elaine picked up the soggy napkins and plopped them onto her half-eaten pile of pasta. "Stop with the 'operation' shit, Casey."

"Well, what the hell else is it?"

Miguel threw his hands in the air and walked toward the cellar door.

Ann flung her words like knives across the table toward Casey: "We're dealing with the fate of these innocent people and with a project that could change the course of humanity."

Casey singled out Elaine. "The orders were clear; you weren't supposed to tell him."

"Things have changed," Elaine countered.

"That's not your call," Casey fired back.

Elle cast her eyes up to the ceiling beams. "I'm too exhausted for this."

Ann spoke but Casey spoke over her, and then Elle lit into both of them. A screeching argument ensued.

Sunny meandered to one of the lists on the dry-erase board: *Animal etchings—deerlike, wolflike, seal/platypus.* He stared at the scribbles as if they were windows through which he could see into the vibrant world of yesteryear's human race.

Miguel kept his back to us and parked his hands on his hips.

Ann, Casey, and Elle's squabble became an inarticulate racket. The fresh air that had welcomed me fell stale.

In a sudden move, Sunny faced me, mouthing the words, *They . . . sent . . . us . . . a . . . message.*

Hoping to get the others to shut up, I asked, "What did you say, Sunny?"

Sunny cleared his throat. "They sent us a message. That's what I was going to explain, in my update."

Arguing became silence.

"What? Who sent us a message?" Elaine asked.

Miguel came back to the table with a furrowed brow.

"Our cousins from a billion years ago." Sunny smiled. "They weren't just documenting things or making art with these etchings." He glared at me. "They're talking to us."

CHAPTER 13

Sunny, his giddiness restored, pushed a plug into Casey's computer. A grainy video feed appeared on the flat screen mounted above the dry-erase boards—bringing us the slim, older black man that was my good friend and mentor, Dr. Musa Imani.

Musa's cheekbones had become more pronounced over the years. His skin had gotten thinner, but the light in his eyes had never been brighter. He adjusted his computer, slightly tilting our view of him.

"Musa." I held Casey's screen with both hands, looking into the camera. "I'm so sorry."

"David! It's good to see you. Why are you sorry? My friend, you've given me the highlight of my life."

My former students—happy-go-lucky Jeremy and kind-hearted Meredith—entered the scene behind Musa.

Meredith sang out in her Southern drawl, "Hey, Professor! It's so very nice to finally have you with us!"

Only one of Jeremy's eyes was visible behind his grown-out hair. He fist-bumped the screen. "Dr. D, you're here! Now we're really in business."

The ridges of rocky terrain behind them—more defined in the setting sun—sparked my memory. Twenty yards beyond their campsite, two men and a woman, in khaki pants and with holstered guns, stood guard.

"Hold on," I said. "Is that . . . ? Are you guys still at the site?"

Casey grew irritated. "David, don't worry about—"

"No, Casey, don't! Musa, your lives are in danger. You have to get out of there!"

Meredith wrapped one of her braids around her finger as the three of them looked at each other, bewildered.

"And wait, Elaine, aren't their devices being monitored?" I asked. "How can we be talking to them?"

Casey's tone was displeased, having to explain to a rookie. "Paul had an operative meet Musa in Antigua, on his supply run. Snuck him laptops and a separate internet connection." He paused, forcing himself to be polite. "We know what we're doing, David."

"Hi, Musa, good to see you." Elaine peered into the screen, clearly attempting to change the mood. "Jeremy, Meredith, I'm Elle. Now that we're all here, we'll explain everything."

Jeremy and Meredith opened canvas chairs and squatted onto them. Musa reached for a mug.

Elaine assumed her business mode as she found her breath. "Musa, as you know, the person who hired you—the guy who called himself Peter Wendell—lied to you, saying he was working with David. He did this to trick you, to convince you to join the project, and then for you to hire the researchers. It looks like his ultimate goal was to claim for himself whatever you and the researchers discovered."

Nods came from the screen. Sunny agreed.

"The reason David has not been with you is that this guy lied to him as well. He told David that he wasn't needed at the site because work on the"—Elaine used air quotes—"'television show' would begin later."

Jeremy cut in. "Yeah, we know. Casey told us. This dude pretended to be a Hollywood producer. Acted like he was gonna do a show, and we were part of the crew and had to keep everything quiet. But he was really trying to be the first one to see what we found." Jeremy smiled. "But the joke's on that jackass because now we're lettin' him spend his big bucks so we can keep doing our work, but we're hiding everything from him and giving it to Dr. D. Right?"

"Yeah," Sunny said. "Right?"

My eyes visited each member of the security team—Elaine, Casey, Miguel, and Ann—pleading to speak the truth.

Casey turned away, but Miguel bowed his head, and Elaine shifted the computer toward me.

"Go ahead," Ann said.

"That's almost right, Jeremy," I said. "But there's more to the story. The person posing as the producer is Patrick Veeder."

Jeremy pulled his hair aside, revealing both of his perplexed eyes. "Who's that?"

"Veeder?" Musa stiffened.

"That bigwig, egomaniac art-collector guy who hangs out with politicians?" Meredith asked.

"Yes," I said. "Please believe me, your lives are in danger. I want you to leave that site right away. Musa, you know what I mean."

Musa was the only person I'd told about my Cartagena encounter with Veeder. His advice had been to immediately abandon all my research in that country and get out.

Musa sipped from his mug, regaining his composure. "Thank you for the truth, my friend. But nothing will get me to leave here. Jeremy and Meredith will sleep on it and give us their decisions in—"

"I'm staying," Jeremy interrupted.

"Me, too," Meredith said.

Musa studied each of them until he was satisfied. "Well, that's that."

I grasped the screen again. "But if Veeder finds out that you're fooling him, he'll kill you!"

"David," Musa said. "Calm down, come out of your head."

"No, this isn't like that! Listen to me!"

Musa set down his mug. "All of humanity is in danger, and from forces greater than Patrick Veeder. But what we're pulling out of the side of this volcano might just save the human race."

Casey turned back, intrigued.

Musa examined the purple evening sky. "I think it's dark enough to give you a peek."

Jeremy and Meredith jogged off screen. Musa fiddled with the computer until it faced away from him and toward an unremarkable expanse of ground, with the tip of the mountain barely visible in the distance.

In the bunker, we gathered shoulder to shoulder around the flat screen.

"What is it?" Elaine asked. "I don't see anything."

"Just watch," Sunny said.

Jeremy and Meredith arrived at different sides of the rocky dirt patch. Each switched on a floodlight that illuminated the ground.

Elaine and I exchanged blank looks.

After crouching down, Jeremy and Meredith started tugging at something. What had appeared as dirt and gravel was actually brown and gray camouflage netting, spread out across the terrain. As they rolled up the netting, the tops of large headstone-like slabs came into view, each with a deep hole in front of it.

Musa's even-paced voice could have been narrating a documentary. "Our sister race has left us a series of stones that deliver a detailed message. The stones bear pictures and symbols arranged in a manner that seems to present a full story."

The ground now uncovered, several rows of rectangular rocks were exposed, sprouting just above the pebbly soil in a perfectly aligned garden. About ten feet from one another, they formed a massive grid, five hundred yards beneath Cayateña's jagged cone. Only their top edges were visible to us because we could not see, from this angle and in the near darkness, into the holes in front of them.

"We've removed enough sediment to step into the holes," Jeremy explained, "to photograph the carvings on each monolith. But we've left the rest of the dirt in place, so nothing protrudes too far above ground."

"And we keep everything hidden with the camouflage," Meredith said, "in case someone visits the site or spies on us overhead."

It looked like a graveyard, or maybe a monument, honoring their dead or their heroes.

"Musa," I asked, "are you sure it's a message?"

"There's too much on each stone for them to be simply marking a person or an event. And the rocks seem to relate to one another."

"You think it's a message for *us*?" I asked. "Intended for a *future race*?"

"It seems purposeful that they situated these slabs the way they did," he said, "and that they knew this volcano would form and lift everything up to what would be the new surface of the Earth, making all this accessible to whomever would be here an eon later."

"Professor," Sunny said, "the answers to our questions are right there, in the symbols on those stones."

Musa directed the computer back at his own face, lit up on one side by the flame of a lantern. "David, we need you and Sunny to translate the symbols."

Impossible. Translations took months, sometimes years. And the urgency in Musa's voice indicated that we likely had only a few weeks, or less, before Patrick Veeder discovered what we were up to.

I ran from his demand, switching the topic. "What about that big object—what you originally found and told Elaine about?"

His enthusiasm waned. "Yes, well, the top of that is nine hundred feet up the hill. It's made of material the likes of which our kind has never seen. But I don't know how we're going to excavate it."

"Musa," Casey said, now invested. "Paul has more security coming, along with earthmoving machines. David is safe. We're gonna get Veeder off your backs so you can do your work."

"Don't make it sound so easy," I said. "Getting rid of Veeder is probably impossible."

Ann set a plate of brownies on the table. "Oh, David, we're only called in when the job is 'probably impossible.'"

"How are you keeping this from Veeder?" Elaine asked into the laptop.

Meredith responded, "We tell his assistant, Darin, when he checks on us, that we put netting down to mark where we've already searched and found nothing. He doesn't inspect."

Jeremy chuckled. "He's kind of a nimrod."

"That's only gonna work for so long," Ann said, before announcing, "Okay, everyone, I'm calling it. As amazing and exciting as this is, we can't function without sleep. Let's regroup in the morning."

"All right," Musa said. "But one last question for David, if I may."

"Anything, Musa," I said.

"Have you given this pursuit a nickname?" He winked.

"I haven't," I said, smiling. "So let's see. This is the discovery of a human race that came and went before us. Our prehistoric ancestors . . . What does everyone think?"

Sunny mumbled, "Our *prehistoric ancestors* . . ." Then he slapped his hands together. "They're our *PRAN-cestors*!"

"Oh wow." Meredith's accent distorted her words. "Prancestors. You've done made up a great word, Sunny."

Miguel gave a thumbs-up.

Everyone eyed me, asking if I approved.

"PRAN-cestors." I found the term accurate and unique. "Yes, Sunny, that's who they are. Our prancestors."

"So it's Operation Prancestor?" Casey asked.

Elaine and Ann got lost in thought.

Then I heard Quiet Miguel's deep, confident voice for the first time: "This is the Prancestor Project."

CHAPTER 14

The digital clock displayed *2:03 a.m.* My legs slid off the mattress and pulled me out of bed.

I had no robe, but I was too anxious to take time to dress.

In my underwear, and clutching the flashlight Miguel had left me, I crept down the hallway and into the lab. The dry-erase boards were waiting, begging me to absorb their information.

The grooved lip beneath them held an eight-by-ten-inch photograph every five feet, from one end to the other. I tiptoed to the left side, near the door to the stairway, shining my light at the first photo, labeled *Full view of stones, taken by drone.* A black arrow had been drawn onto the picture, pointing out the stone in the center.

The next photograph was labeled *Evolution Timeline* and was taken facing that center stone, which differed in size from the rest; it was much skinnier, about a third the width of the others. It offered a vertical display of engravings that seemed like significant evolutionary events. The top one depicted a half-standing gorilla-like creature.

A few sketches down, a fully upright humanoid held its hands over a fire.

The research team had taken pictures of each scene—each major evolutionary step of our prancestors—from top to bottom on this narrow monolith. Sunny had laid the photographs out, down the boards from left to right, and had written notes above each one.

My gut seized up. Our prancestors were telling us the order of their evolution, so we could compare it to our own. But this was a foundation. What were they really trying to convey to us?

I directed the flashlight down the wall, pushing the darkness away from the rest of the photographs—each one a thin square leaning backward onto the boards.

What was our prancestors' ultimate milestone, portrayed at the bottom of that center rock? What was the final knowledge or ability they had acquired before they fell into extinction? Was it there, at the end of the board, in that last photograph?

I charged toward the other side of the room; my elbow crashed into a desk lamp. I caught its metal arm and froze, listening for anyone I had awoken.

No sound was detectable except the *whirrrr* of the desktop's internal fan.

I arrived at the last picture. Nothing but question marks occupied the board above it. I lifted the photo to bring it closer, and saw dark scratches over human figures, as if a grizzly bear had clawed into the rock. A blood-red river snaked beneath the illustration.

Sadness nearly choked me. This was their demise. But how?

My heartbeat thumped into my awareness. I whispered, "We're gonna figure out what you're trying to tell us."

The lights flipped on and the cellar door banged open; I landed on all fours.

"Oh man, it's you." Casey holstered his gun.

"Oh . . . God," I panted.

"Sorry, dude. But we told you we each take a watch." Casey opened the refrigerator and took out a bag of something green. "And we have alarms set up. You can't sneak around here at night. Or ever. Security has to know your movements."

"Okay." I got up and returned the picture to the board.

He crunched on a stalk of celery. "It's the middle of the night."

"Yeah." I pressed my shaking hands onto my legs.

"Why don't you get some sleep?"

"Okay. See ya, Casey."

"See ya. And by the way, I totally would have guessed *briefs*."

"Nope." I clicked off my flashlight and walked, in my boxers, back to my room.

As I snuggled my legs under the puffy softness of the comforter, a whiff of peaches breezed over me. A pair of silky legs rubbed up against mine. My eyes hadn't adjusted to the dark. "Elle?"

"You have to ask? Were you hoping for Ann?"

When I didn't answer, Elaine muffled her laughter.

I finally laughed, too, and then said to the ceiling fan, which slowly materialized in the faint light of the digital clock, "This is so crazy."

Elaine's tired tongue slurred her words. "I know. I can't sleep either. Tell me more. How did you come up with the idea to look so far in the past for human life?"

"Okay . . . a bedtime story."

Elaine scooted closer to me.

"Hm. How did I come up with the idea? Frankly, I was trying not to throw up. I was on a ferry from England to France. Seasick as hell."

"Oh no," Elle mumbled. "You get that?"

"Not usually. But the waves were like hills." I remembered the salt sticking to the windows after the ocean splashed the glass. Sitting in a plastic chair that was bolted to the floor, I was piercing my elbows into my knees, distracting myself from the impulse to gag, and cursing the fire that had shut down the Chunnel.

"I don't know if I fell asleep, or passed out, or what," I said. "But I was thinking about the news report of the ancient zircon crystal that had just been found, with the organic matter, and I started seeing the double helix of DNA. And I could see the planet, like from space; it was blue and white, and so beautiful."

A rush of embarrassment heated my face, and I paused.

"Dave?" Elaine asked. "Is something wrong?"

"This is just, it's kind of strange, when I say it out loud."

"Why? It's your truth."

My eyes warmed and stung. I had never heard that phrase, but it gave me a kind of peace I'd not felt before. I suddenly understood that it didn't matter if I was weird, or if anyone thought so. My truth was all mine, and it was valid simply for being truth.

Elle touched my shoulder; my fingers grazed her thigh.

"And so, in my head," I continued, "I started exploring the concept of evolution. I thought about how the same insects have evolved into existence in different parts of the world, in different places that have the same conditions but are isolated from each other. If the same things can evolve into existence in different places, then why couldn't they evolve into existence in different time periods? And why wouldn't things that *e*-volve also *re*-volve? Can't biological beings that have gone extinct evolve into being again? Is every life-form here today something that's never been here before? That seems unlikely."

"Mmmm," Elaine said. "You're brilliant."

"I'm not brilliant," I laughed. "I'm quirky. But you said quirky is interesting, right?"

"It is to me."

I kissed the tip of her nose. "Get some rest."

"Yeah, you, too."

I stroked her arm for several minutes, until she fell asleep. I felt like I should have been more excited. Elle was in my bed! But mostly, I felt safe. The faint whistle of air moving in and out of her mouth slowed down my thoughts.

My eyelids finally drooped, and my body released its tension. But it was always here, in this state of almost sleeping, that my agonizing memory returned.

The beeping persisted above my dad as he slept. I knew those machines were there to help him, but I resented them for constantly reminding me how sick he was.

Mom whispered, "If he wakes up, don't fight with him. Just let him say whatever he wants."

She shut the wide bathroom door behind her.

My dad's eyes opened; he exhaled with a groan. I put the small drink box near his mouth.

He sipped from the straw and then pushed the box back. "I'm sucking kiddie juice, for crying out loud. Where's your mother?"

"Bathroom."

"David, please take over my business."

"Mom said not to fight with you."

"Then don't. Just take it."

"I don't want it."

"I worked my whole life. You could have it easy—you could be free. Do your research stuff as a hobby. Please, just do it for me."

"Dad, your business is part of the problem."

"Here we go. Capitalism is evil."

"It's not that simple."

"Capitalism is the reason the business thrives, and that business paid for the ten years of college it took you to get your fancy PhD."

"You act like there's no other way to make money than to trick people."

"Oh, now helping people become homeowners is a trick?"

Mom came out of the bathroom, her hands still wet. "David, what did I say?"

"What am I supposed to do? Lie to him because he's dying? I don't want to take over a mortgage-loan business."

I hurried out of the room and down the hall to the vending machines. I squinted through the glass at the brightly colored wrappers of candy and chips. Hospitals provided junk food to those who were not healthy. Banks provided unfair loans to those who were not financially savvy. And my dad's mortgage business helped the banks harm those people. I banged the machine seven times.

A nurse with red-rimmed glasses and no smile appeared next to me.

I returned to the room. "Dad, you really want me to be free?"

Mom grabbed my arm. "No, please, he's so sick."

"That's why I need to tell him this. Dad, the only way I'm going to be free is to go as far away as possible from a business that tells some hardworking couple that a jumbo loan is where their money should go."

As my dad pointed at me, the monitor over his bed sounded an alarm. "You think you're finding freedom by flying to some other part of the world and learning what those people eat? Studying how they cut their hair and what holidays they celebrate? Give me a break."

He struggled to breathe. Two nurses rushed in. One squirted a syringe into his IV tube; the other adjusted a knob on the machine, saying, "Mr. Denlon, relax."

"David, for heaven's sake," Mom said. "Why can't you just appease him?"

The sedative invaded my dad's bloodstream. His head slowly rolled toward his left shoulder.

Two hours later he forced open one of his eyes. "You guys should go home. Come visit me in the morning."

"It is the morning, Dad. It's four a.m."

Mom spanked my knee. "Davey, be nice."

Then my dad did something I'd never seen him do. He smacked his lips together over and over, almost as if he were using them to bite at the air.

"Are you hungry?" Mom asked. "Do you want some juice?"

His mouth relaxed. "No, thank you, love." He smiled, and I realized I hadn't seen him smile in weeks. "David," he laughed. "Oh, David. You taught me . . ."

He studied something at the foot of his bed, looking it up and down. We saw nothing.

The gloom that had set into his eyes months ago cleared away. He became mesmerized by the air above his swollen ankles.

"Dad?"

But then he was nauseous. He struggled to say, "Son, I can do this, because you taught me . . ."

A green hue intensified on his waxy cheeks. Mom pressed the call button. My dad mumbled gibberish.

A nurse appeared as my dad seemed to be reacting to a rancid taste in his mouth, squeezing his eyes shut and sticking his tongue out and down toward his chin.

"Hold on to him," she said. "Talk to him."

Mom asked, "Is he choking on something?"

The nurse stared at Mom, not wanting to explain.

Mom held his left hand and I held his right.

"We love you," Mom said.

"We're right here, Dad."

He stopped holding our hands.

I sat up and searched my brain for clues. Was I in the hospital? Mom's house? My house? The digital clock was only vaguely familiar to me. It read *5:16 a.m.*

A warm hand came to my lower back. "You're okay. It was a dream."

Each puzzle piece fell into place. *The discovery. Elle. Patrick Veeder. The laboratory-hideout.*

I rested my fevery neck on the pillow and Elle embraced me for several minutes without saying a word.

Then she slowly asked, "I think you said 'dad' . . . Is your dad okay?"

"He passed away."

"Oh God, I'm sorry. How?"

"He was born with a heart defect. Wasn't supposed to live beyond his twenties. Made it to sixty-two."

"Wow."

Playing with the curly parts of Elle's hair calmed me. "What about *your* parents? Your mom?"

Elle nestled her head onto my shoulder. "I don't want to talk about it."

"Okay, your dad?"

"Never knew him."

"Why not?"

"He was married. Had an affair with my mom, and my mom got pregnant with me."

"Damn. Who was he? Wait, another spy person? Or, covert-operative guy?"

She laughed. "It's really not that cool. Yes, another operative."

"An enemy?"

"No, no. Also working for Paul. When I was really young my mom told me that 'Daddy was far away.' But when I was fifteen and demanding a real answer, she said when I turned eighteen she'd let me know who it was. But by then I didn't want to know."

"Do you want to know now?"

"I'm not sure. It's hard to think about."

"Any brothers or sisters?"

"No, just me."

"Me, too," I said, and thought for the first time that maybe, after having *Spectrum Boy*, my parents had decided against more children.

Elaine ran her fingers up and down my arm and then asked, as though she would be disappointed with the answer, "Are you in a relationship?"

"No."

She came closer, settling her head on my chest. I asked her the same question.

"With this job?" She laughed. "No."

"I get it," I said, petting her cheek. "Your work has so much to do with people, but it leaves you alone."

Elaine squeezed me. "Yes, exactly."

Her warm breath tickled my face. She brushed her mouth over mine, tenderly, igniting an electrical current, an intensity that drew me into it. I came alive with exhilaration, but, for several seconds, I was too nervous to do anything other than gently return the kiss.

My eyes closed as I accepted that I couldn't see—thankful for the lack of light, actually, so that I could focus on looking through my fingers. I rubbed her breasts, pinching into her flesh, but then I internally scolded myself for grabbing at her like a horny high school boy.

I lightened my touch, as if skimming over braille, and carefully read her chest. Hard tips alive with desire, not desperate or begging, but elated, celebratory. Raw womanhood vibrating into my hands, welcoming me.

A sensation then struck me, almost painfully, shooting from my groin, quaking my stomach and hitting my heart. It was both hot and cold, and frightening at first. I realized she was fondling me, indulging in personal communication with a part of me that had not received affection from a woman in a long time. I hardened and she squeezed more; I stretched up and she stroked faster.

When her hands left me, a rush of abandonment pushed a whimper from my throat.

She squirmed out of her T-shirt and panties and relief overcame me, as if I would have died had she stopped our encounter. Happy anticipation flooded my nervous system, engorging me to the limits of my skin.

I had almost forgotten how to get out of my boxers, finally kicking them off as she turned away, onto her side, and tucked into me, trusting me. She was nearly pulsating, inviting me to please her.

Her breathing, now short and fast, reminded me of her concern.

"Elle," I whispered. "Are you sure you feel okay, with the altitude?"

She choked through a swallow and almost giggled. "Yes, though I may not be able to move much."

"I'll take care of that."

Chapter 15

My hips had a mind of their own, thrusting faster and harder, although I had become light-headed.

I was so damned attracted to the completeness of Elaine. She wasn't looking for me, or for anyone, to make up for a part of her that she felt was lacking. I could only add to her happiness, to her life experience, and only if I brought my own completeness. My own truth.

Elaine yelped into her pillow, jerking almost into crunches as orgasmic waves pulsed through her. I exploded inside her, forgetting entirely about Patrick Veeder and my stolen discovery.

We gasped for air, our hearts pounding. She rested her head on my chest again.

I whispered, "Elaine the Magnificent."

"What?"

"That's why I had to shorten your name to 'Elle.' Because 'Elaine the Magnificent' is too long to use all the time."

She shook her head and quietly laughed, rolling out of bed. Her breathing increased again as she put on her long T-shirt and pulled up her thong underwear. "See you at breakfast."

"Wait."

Her sleek, messy hair flopped over half her face as she posed with her hand on the doorknob.

I tried to form a question. "Why did you . . . was this . . . ?"

She came back and kissed me. "You are so you." She quietly opened the door and walked down the hallway.

Satisfaction filled my heart while my head remained confused. What had just transpired?

An hour later I bit into buttery toast, which accompanied the sweet bacon and fluffy scrambled eggs that Ann, in another snazzy yoga outfit, had lovingly served me from the basement kitchenette.

Was the universe giving me a great send-off, since I was about to be murdered? Incredible sex. Beautiful women who looked at me as if I were normal. Delicious food. And my discovery revealing itself to be bigger and better than I had ever dreamed.

Ann's sexy arms flexed as she scrambled more eggs. Her formfitting top and tights accentuated her thin, muscular figure. "Sunny has a presentation planned for us," she said. "We're a small team and this is a big deal, so he wants everyone, even us on security, to know what's up. He's very excited."

"He's always excited," I muttered, prompting laughter from Miguel and Casey, who'd just finished some morning exercise routine of push-ups and jumping jacks.

Miguel gave a thumbs-up to Ann as she toppled eggs onto his plate.

Casey took a seat on top of one of the desks, constructing two bacon-and-egg sandwiches with four pieces of toast. The baby-smooth skin of his face barely wrinkled as he took large bites out of his first sandwich.

Elaine came into the room and found my eyes before anyone else's.

"Good morning, sweetie," Ann said to her. "Come get breakfast."

"Professor!" Sunny jogged in, squeezing his hands into fists as if that helped to keep him from shouting. "I hope you like the presentation!"

"I'm sure he'll love it," Ann said, handing him a glass of orange juice. "Before Musa and the others call in, can I brief David about security?"

"Good idea," Sunny said.

Ann explained, "As we said, Casey, Miguel, Elaine, and I are your security team. We'll be here, with you and Sunny, as you guys translate the markings on the stones. When Paul gets a larger security presence to the site, Musa,

Jeremy, and Meredith will start digging up that artifact. And when it's safe, we'll escort you there."

"Sounds great," I said, sipping my coffee.

Sunny's computer beeped, and he pressed a key that produced a live shot of Musa.

"Good day to all of you." Musa's white, matted hair glistened with water; his pajama-like sweats hung from a body that was bony and muscular at the same time.

"Whatcha doin', Moose?" Sunny asked.

"Just finished my meditation. David, you slept well?"

"I had a good night." I peeked over at Elle, who firmed up her face to avoid a smile.

"I found him wandering around the lab in his underpants," Casey said.

Quiet Miguel made an *oh-my* face.

I smiled. "I thought you said that would stay between us, Casey." A quick, collective burst of laughter broke out.

Meredith's hair again hung in two braids that sat on her collarbones, but today she wore a knit cap with pink and yellow flowers. "Namaste, y'all." She put her hands in the yoga prayer position and bowed forward.

Jeremy's lanky body always seemed relaxed. His shirt displayed the words *I'm with her* next to a picture of planet Earth. "So honored to be doing this work with you, Dr. D."

"Thank you all for your dedication," I said. "I can't wait to be there with you."

Musa took a drink from his steaming mug. "Fire it up, Sunny."

Behind Sunny on the large flat-screen TV was the Guatemalan volcano that had gifted me the evidence of our prancestors. "Our site is on Cayateña—where Professor Denlon found the DNA in the marquise crystal—and this presentation is a summary of what we've learned so far."

A picture of the rock garden appeared.

"The site has revealed a square plot with tall, rectangular stones, and the fact that this stone configuration has stayed intact suggests that our prancestors were aware of how the tectonic plates, particularly the Cocos and Caribbean Plates, were going to form and migrate over time."

The monitor took us under the sea to plants that looked like brownish-green noodles, swaying with the tide. Those plants faded into the scene of a blue whale breaching, sending a wall of white water into the air. The ocean scene then dissolved into people walking, jogging, and biking in New York City's Central Park.

"Approximately five hundred million years ago, there was something known as the 'Cambrian explosion'—when life began to rapidly evolve, resulting in the creatures that are on Earth today. And we used to believe—until Dr. Denlon's discovery—that the planet, pre-Cambrian, hosted nothing more than scarce, single-celled organisms."

Sunny couldn't keep his voice down. "But that simplistic explanation of Earth's history is wrong! It's like when people thought the world was flat. Or when scientists believed the universe was static, but Edwin Hubble came along and proved it was expanding!"

A timeline stretched across the screen, starting at 2.2 billion years ago and running to a point five hundred million years ago, labeled *Cambrian*. Highlighted in the middle of the timeline was the period from eight hundred million years ago to 1.8 billion years ago.

"Shown here, before the Cambrian explosion of life, is the billion-year period known as 'the Barren Billion,'" Sunny said. "It's often called 'the Boring Billion,' because it's believed that no significant life developed within that time."

A circle appeared on the timeline, around the mark indicating 1.1 billion years ago.

"However, zircon has brought us evidence of a short span of rapid evolution, hidden within this supposedly barren eon. More aggressive than the Cambrian, this life-abundant period lasted about eighty million years."

A cartoon explosion appeared on the left side of the timeline.

"About 2.2 billion years ago, a meteor crashed into Earth. The impact heated up our planet and ended an ice age. The crater it left, called Yarrabubba—in what is now Western Australia—is the oldest crater on Earth."

A bright-yellow meteor smeared across the monitor, soaring toward Earth with a fiery tail.

"Meteors deliver cosmic material, including the building blocks of life-forms, from other places in the universe. The genesis of our prancestors likely came from meteors like the one that created the Yarrabubba crater."

I realized I had stopped breathing. This was no longer a crazy idea in my head. We really were the second iteration of humankind on this planet.

"These microscopic seeds of life mutated," Sunny said, "launching eighty million years of development that eventually produced an advanced human race. A race that came and went long before our own."

No one moved, not even to chew.

"But this period of life remained a needle in the Boring Billion haystack until zircon led Dr. Denlon to it. And now, what our prancestors are telling us"—Sunny gestured toward the whiteboards and the pictures from the Evolution Timeline—"is that they inhabited Earth for the last five hundred thousand years of that eighty-million-year period." He sighed. "And then they, and all life-forms from that era, went extinct."

On the screen, a grassy knoll degenerated to brown weeds, the weeds became dirt under a smoky sky, and the dirt faded into ice in the shadows of navy-blue clouds.

"The planet, again, became inhospitable. But after hundreds of millions of years, the atmosphere changed and the Cambrian explosion of life occurred, restarting evolution all over again, with single-celled organisms leading to the development of plants, and so on, until another advanced human race—our own—came into existence."

Soda cans lying in a creek, with factory smokestacks in the distance, appeared on the screen.

"Had our prancestors solved any of the issues we currently face? Did they find out how to eradicate disease or reverse harm to the planet? We are certainly hoping that the detailed message our prancestors put so much effort into sending us will answer these questions."

Sunny took a deep breath, focusing on me. "Professor, I know you want us safe from that Patrick guy. But this is the most important discovery ever made. Ever." His voice cracked. "We have to pursue it, no matter what."

Misty-eyed, he continued. "Our prancestors had evolved to a level that made it possible for them to predict we were coming. Their dying wish was for us to know the message they lasered into those stones."

He turned away.

Meredith shouted from the computer screen, "Sunny, darling, we love you!"

Miguel went to Sunny, setting a hand on his back.

"You're right," I said. "It doesn't matter how we got here or who's trying to stop us. Our mission now is to translate the message from our prancestors."

"You've done excellent work, Sunny," Musa said.

Sunny wiped his nose with a napkin and turned back around. "It's not gonna be easy to decode what's on those stones."

"You and Dr. D can do it!" Jeremy shouted.

"Yeah," Casey said. "You got this."

A swell of excitement lifted me out of my seat. "I couldn't imagine why you would stay involved in such a dangerous project, but now I know." I stared at the notes and figures on the panels, then pondered, again, the picture of the gigantic mountain of Cayateña that had returned to the monitor. The base of the volcano was wider than most and crowded with evergreen plants and trees. Toward the center it became gray, and farther up, dark-brown, and rocky. The top had been blown out, leaving behind uneven pinnacles. "We're being called by our brothers and sisters from yesteryear, and what they have to say could save us."

Elaine's nose became pink.

"Yes!" Ann said.

Meredith yelled, "That's right!"

"Before this project I'd lost hope," I continued. "Because governments around the world give so little attention to our precious past." Words came easily; I'd never spoken with this tone—as if I were leading a protest—but couldn't stop myself. "Tiwanaku, for example—we still haven't fully studied and explored that site. It's right outside this city." I pointed to what I thought was west. "People who lived there two thousand years ago invented tools with precision we have yet to re-create. They knew how to store the sun's heat, how to insulate their crops. Why is this not the talk of the media, the focus of our politicians?"

I now understood Sunny's struggle to keep his voice down. "I never see the discoveries of Tiwanaku on the news, but I do see pictures taken from the luxury camera sent to Mars. For our fellow humans, moving outward, into the future, has been a lot more tantalizing than pondering the past. But the past is where wisdom comes from! No one ever uses tomorrow to learn how to approach today. Indeed, if we don't use what we know from yesterday to get there, we may not ever *see* tomorrow. But now, thanks to each of you, we can look into the past and see beyond our present. Because our prancestors have already lived our future, and they want to tell us about it."

Elaine's eyes twinkled as she clapped; Casey and Ann nodded and smiled.

A loud rumble and *Boom!* from upstairs rocked the basement. The desks and tables vibrated; files and petri dishes scattered onto the floor. Two of the dry-erase panels unhinged from the wall.

"Watch out!" Casey screamed.

Musa looked closer at his screen. "David! What's happening?"

The video feed cut out.

We dropped to the floor.

Elaine asked, "Earthquake?"

"I don't think so," Casey said. "It's like a bomb hit upstairs."

Ann stepped over a mess of photographs and papers, strapping on a gun holster and checking that her Hi-Power pistol was loaded.

Sunny stayed hunkered beneath a desk. "What's going on?"

Miguel retrieved more semiautomatic handguns from a rack.

"Gather everything you would if we had to leave here forever," I said to Sunny, as I climbed over a broken lamp.

"What?"

"Remember what we talked about, Sunny," Casey said. "The essentials."

Sunny and I packed the laptop computer that was on the nearby desk, along with flash drives, folders with pictures, and small containers of specimens.

Ann nodded to Casey, then opened the cellar door. She snuck up the stairs and out of our view.

Machine-gun fire pierced our ears. Ann charged back down and locked the door.

Miguel's deep voice commanded: "Tunnel!"

Sunny rummaged through desk drawers. "I can't find the backup flash! It has everything on it! We can't leave it!"

"Yes we can!" Ann said as feet stomped down the stairs.

Miguel waved Sunny and me into the hallway. He pushed part of the wall; it slid sideways—revealing itself as a secret door.

I shouted, "Elaine!"

Miguel shoved me and Sunny into the tunnel. "Go to the split."

He shut the door and small yellow lights ignited on the brick ceiling. Water dripped down the chipped-concrete walls. The floor dipped in the middle, to accommodate the leaking water.

"Where are we?" Sunny asked.

"It looks like this connects to the storm drain system."

We traveled down the musty tunnel, hopping back and forth over the small ditch, until we found the junction. One passage continued right, the other, left.

More shots rang out inside the hideout.

"Sunny, if the others don't make it into the tunnel, I think I'm supposed to go one way and you go another."

Sunny's lip quivered. "Why can't I stay with you?"

"Patrick Veeder wants me dead. He may not even know who you are. You're safer if you're not with me."

Sunny peered down the black shaft to his left and hugged his duffel bag.

The secret door flew open. Casey and Ann sprinted toward us; Elaine labored to jog after them. Miguel shut the door behind him and helped Elaine.

When they reached us, Elle leaned her rag-doll body against the wall.

Miguel pointed to Ann and Casey. "Take Sunny."

Ann grabbed Sunny's arm. "With us, okay?"

Sunny stared at me.

I tried to sound confident. "You'll be fine."

Casey bent down to Elaine. "You can do this. I texted Paul. He's gonna find a place to meet up."

The tunnel door shook.

"Go," Elle whispered to Casey. "See you there."

Ann and Casey charged down their passage with Sunny. I put Elaine's arm around my shoulder, and we limped after Miguel.

The door busted open behind us. I could hear feet striking the ground, faster than ours.

CHAPTER 16

We scurried out of a street drain and ducked into the doorway of a store selling goods made from alpaca fur. The man at a nearby bus stop, holding a rolled-up rug under his arm, glanced from us to the drain and back again.

We left the doorway and found an alley, where Elle gave in and slumped to the cobblestones. She squirmed out of the straps of her backpack and stared at the empty pouch on the side of it. "I didn't have time to grab my water bottle."

I had no water to offer, and not being able to help Elaine, together with wondering if we were about to die, brought back the constricted sensation that had attacked my chest at the first sight of Snarl Guy on the subway in London.

Pushing his gun into the back of his pants, Miguel walked to the mouth of the alley, standing at the cross street. He looked back and forth, up and around, before turning to us and nodding *we're okay for now.*

Elaine took hold of her phone and swiped across it several times, groaning.

I knelt beside her. "What's going on?"

The zoom of a speeding car climaxed and faded away, as it passed on a nearby street. Miguel walked to the opposite corner.

A gust of wind raced between the walls of the narrow alleyway, sending shivers through Elaine. She tugged her sweatshirt out of her backpack and angrily punched her arms into the sleeves.

"Elle, please," I said. "Take it easy."

"We're in a lot of danger," she responded. "I'm sorry, David. I'm holding us back."

"No, Elle."

"I wonder," she said in a way that didn't seem to include me, "is this what my mom felt?"

She twisted her hair into an elastic ponytail holder and stood up. "Is this it? My mom was cornered like this, or incapacitated like this, and mad as hell? And then that was it? Goddamn it!"

"Elaine? What are you talking about?"

"She's dead. My mom is dead. She was murdered."

I held her shoulders, urging her to sit back down. "I'm so sorry. What happened?"

"My mom tried to retire. But she took one last job—one final mission because she wanted to earn enough money to pay off my college, so I wouldn't owe student loans."

I knelt in front of her, rubbing the infant-soft skin just above her ankles.

"She was killed in North Korea, near the border. I posed as a journalist to visit the area. I found part of her blouse."

Elaine pushed her face into her hands; her belly tightened as she sniffled. I searched her backpack for tissues but found only toilet paper. I handed her a clump of it.

Miguel was out of earshot, but he watched Elaine with concern.

She dried her cheeks and nose. "My mom's blouse." She smiled. "It was this print, funny polka dots. I used to tease her about it." Sadness consumed her smile. "It was stuck in barbed wire. I can't imagine what happened; did it rip off when she maybe tried to climb the fence?"

Elaine unzipped the sweatshirt she had just put on, and as she did, I remembered that it was the garment she had cuddled on the plane. She exposed the inside of it—the front left side, over her heart—and I saw a patch of white rayon with blue and pink polka dots. She had sewn the only remains of her mother into her clothing.

I hugged her. But I couldn't think of anything to say.

Again, the zoom of a car. Closer this time. Elaine re-zipped her sweatshirt.

Miguel jogged past us again, to the other end of the alley.

"Look," Elle said, "when we get split up like this, Paul suspects we might be captured or that someone else might have access to our phones. So he switches to texting in code."

"Code?"

She pointed to her phone. "Paul gives me a clue to decipher, one that no one else will know. Directing me to a meeting spot."

The screech of car brakes sent Miguel ducking behind a dumpster; he furiously waved at us. We scrambled to a parked moped and crouched behind it. The car accelerated, whooshing by the alleyway too quickly for us to perceive anything but a red blur.

Elle whispered, "Shit. They're not gonna give up."

"Paul gives you clues?" I asked.

"Right. He interviewed me about my life, things that only I know. He did it for each of us. He sends me clues based on my answers. That way, if someone else sees a clue, it won't mean anything to them. And if I'm captured and asked to translate a coded message, I can make up any meaning."

Miguel darted back to us, picked up Elaine's backpack, and motioned for us to follow him.

Up the road, we retreated into an entryway where colorful flags hung on poles next to a sign that read *Hostel*. A teenaged boy and his much shorter mother greeted us with smiles and we-don't-speak-English shrugs.

The boy said in Spanish, *"The receptionist speaks English. She comes in soon. The rooms are available in three hours."*

A request I had made more than once in my travels seemed worth a try: *"We just got off a long flight. We are willing to pay for both last night's stay and tonight's, to get in and sleep."*

The boy translated, in the dialect of Aymara, for his mother. She nodded approval.

Our sparse room offered three single beds, two end tables, and a wooden chair with baseball-bat legs. Miguel ventured down the hall, to the shared bathroom.

Elaine sat down on the middle bed, removing her sweatshirt and resting it in her lap. She slouched, pressing her palm on the material from her mother's blouse.

The bed creaked when I sat next to her.

"I had a close call a year ago," she said. "An ISIS member shot at me—I had no vest." Elle's laughter revved up as if she were suddenly crazy. "The gun jammed. The fucking loaded gun a foot away from my chest didn't shoot."

"Jesus."

She recovered her breath. "I quit the field. Limited my work for Paul to research only. But here I am doing one last field job because I want to secure my retirement like my mom wanted to pay off my loans."

A surge of mixed emotions overloaded me. I stepped to the window and saw into the past.

> At the park with the tall, circular slide,
> I searched my brain for a response to the
> two boys who had asked me to pick a
> superhero.

My dad took a knee and whispered, "Hey, Son, what are you thinking?"

I couldn't get my mouth to work.

"Look at that sky," my dad said.

Luckily, I had been facing the side of the park without trees when I went into my stare.

"The clouds are so fluffy," he said, "like big pillows, look at that."

The white-and-blue dome above me was endless. It had always been there, and always would be. It dwarfed the boys and their game.

"Just breathe, Son. In through your nose, out through your mouth."

I had never thought about my breathing before.

"That's it. Now, what are you thinking?"

The wind chilled me all over my body, except for the warm space on my shoulder under my dad's strong hand. "I don't know what they mean. I don't know what to do."

One of the kids overheard me and lisped through his dental retainer, "You pick a superhero, and then you pretend to be him. And we play that this is our fort and we're being attacked."

The other kid said, "I'm Batman, so you can't be Batman."

I asked, "You play a superhero by pretending?"

"Yeah," Batman said. "C'mon, it's fun."

"See," my dad whispered. "Just breathe, and you'll come right out of those stares."

He returned to the bench with the real estate section of the newspaper.

I took a deep breath and said to the boys, "I don't know which superhero to be."

"I picked mine because of his skills," the lisping kid said. "You gotta climb on this fort. That's why I'm Spiderman."

It occurred to me that defending a fortress would take strength. "Can I be Superman?"

"Oh yeah!" Batman said. "We need Superman!"

I smiled to myself. Those kids and I warded off attacks from make-believe villains every Saturday for the summer I was six. Long before I could imagine that real villains existed.

"What are you looking at?" Elle asked.

"The sky." Clouds spread across my view like puffs of steam from a train engine. I unstuck my forehead from the window. "Elle, you're in danger because of me."

"This isn't your fault."

Miguel stepped inside and locked the door. He pointed at Elle's phone.

"I can't decipher the clue," she sighed. "So no. I don't know the meeting spot."

"Can't you call or text this Paul guy?" I asked.

"How will he know that I'm not being forced to contact him? How do we know that someone isn't listening in?"

I turned to Miguel. "What about *your* phone?"

He moaned his way into the unstable chair. "Had to leave it."

"What's the clue, Elaine?"

Miguel's eyes asked, *Yeah, what is it?*

A knock on the door brought us all to our feet. Miguel walked through the silence and, after peeking out, fully opened it.

The young boy smiled; his adult speech and polite gestures were endearing, but they revealed a childhood lost to running a business. *"Thank you again very much for being our guests. My mom says thank you, too."*

Behind him, his leathery-skinned mother wore a round brown hat and a blanket-style poncho. She smiled as the boy continued, *"If you're not needing anything, we will be going to the market. The receptionist should be here soon."*

"We have everything we need," I said. *"Thank you."*

Miguel and I walked them out the front and watched as they hiked down the curved street. I looked up at the sagging mess of electrical wires hanging overhead, then peered across the valley, where every inch of the neighboring hillside was packed with reddish-orange rooftops.

After we returned to the room, Elaine tossed her phone on the bed. "It has the same description as my dream wedding."

"What does?" I asked.

Miguel slapped my arm.

"Oh," I said. "That's Paul's clue to the meet-up point?"

The same car engine—it rattled and growled, as if it were powerful but with a loose part—accelerated up the steep road and skidded to a stop outside the entrance to the hostel.

Miguel closed the drapes after frightened pedestrians trotted by the window.

Elaine asked him, "No back door?"

His eyes fell shut as he shook his head no.

The shout of my last name boomed out: "Denlon!"

A twinge hit the middle of my back. I warded off shakiness by securing my thoughts to the business of decoding. "What's in your dream wedding?"

Elaine's eyes remained bugged out in the direction of the wail. She whispered slowly, as if in hypnosis, "A lot of details, none more important than the other."

A gunshot burst into the sky.

I stole a glance from behind the curtain. "It's the other two men, of the three from Shanghai," I reported. "How the hell did they find us? And if they've found us, why don't they seem to know exactly where we are?"

Elaine inspected her phone. "They knew we were in the bunker, and now they've followed us here. They must have slipped a tracking device on one of us. Seems like they're using triangulation."

"Oh my God." I pulled out my phone. A tiny black button, nearly as thin as a sticker, had been stuck onto the back of it.

Miguel took my phone and scrutinized the device. He nodded and handed it back.

"I'm sorry," I said. "The guy in the bathroom. He took my phone and told me to turn around. He must have . . ."

"My fault," Elle said. "I should have checked it when you took it back."

Elaine put her sweatshirt back on and rubbed it, as if she were preparing to die in it.

We gathered at the door and I whispered, "Let's work on the clue. What were some of those wedding details?"

When Elaine didn't answer, Miguel nudged her.

She sighed. "I wanted tulips to line the entrance to the ceremony."

"Denlon! It's over, come out!"

I recognized that voice. *Squeezer.*

Elaine touched my arm. "Breathe. C'mon, you're gonna be okay."

After a long minute, my throat allowed air to escape. "What else about your wedding?"

Elle answered as if it were pointless. "Luggage tags as the favors, 'cuz everyone I know travels so much."

"Made out of leather or alpaca fur?"

"I hadn't thought about it."

We moved to the hotel entrance. Elaine pulled the door open two inches and squinted into the gap. "Their car, let's take it. The door's open. I can see they left the keys."

Miguel's thumb shot upward.

I nervously asked, "We're getting in their car?"

"We gotta get away." Elle heaved in a breath. "And thanks to this altitude, running or fighting aren't options for me."

"We have to decode the meeting spot," I said. "What else?"

"About my wedding? I don't know. I wanted to have it at night, under moonlight."

We drew our heads back when another shot rang out. They seemed to be in a courtyard, in the apartment across the street. We snuck a look out the door and saw a family—two children, a mom, and a grandmother—dart out from a nearby dwelling and flee down the road.

One of our hunters screamed, "Denlon, you're pissing me off!"

The men rushed into the street; we hid behind the door. They booted the door next to ours until it broke open.

I whispered, "Did you say moonlight?"

There was a location outside La Paz that Neil Armstrong, the late astronaut, had visited. It was an expanse of naturally formed sandstone spires, and his remark that it "looked like the moon" had given the valley its name.

"The meeting place is Valle de la Luna," I said.

Elaine tilted her head. "What?"

"Elle, you're not dying for me. Musa and the others are a great team. They'll take care of the project."

"David, what are you—"

"Valley of the Moon, okay? Miguel, got that?"

I pushed myself in between Elle and the door. "Miguel, take care, man. Elaine, get out of here and out of this line of work."

"Wait!" Elaine pleaded, but I kept going.

I marched into the street and called out, "Hey, guys, are you blind? I'm right here."

Squeezer and the man who had put my luggage in the trunk in Shanghai rushed outside, aiming their guns at my chest.

I didn't know how to make someone shoot me, but the more shots they fired, the less time I would suffer. "You're gonna catch a lot of flies with those open mouths."

Squeezer gripped his gun. "What's the trick, Denlon? Where are the others?"

"There is no trick, you idiot. It's only me. Kill me or take me to the asshole who sent you after me."

The nose of the other man was long and slender until the tip, where it turned into a round ball. He moved his gun up in front of his face to secure his aim. "We asked you a question."

"You asked me two questions. Jeez, maybe this is why you can never catch me. You're too damn stupid. Is this your car?"

They argued with each other in their Slavic tongue; I climbed into the back seat of their rusted Nissan.

"Stop!" Squeezer commanded. He ripped me out and hard-patted me all over.

"In the front," he said, shoving me.

I stumbled to one knee and stayed there, pulling my head back to glare into that dome of infinity.

"Get up, Denlon!"

"Oh, now you're tough, when I've surrendered."

They both cocked their guns. Long Nose said, "You should shut your mouth. We could kill you."

I stood, taunting, "You could kill me? Then do it!"

Squeezer handed Long Nose his gun. He rammed me into the front passenger's seat. "You're not gonna get off that easy, Denlon. And I can't wait to see what a smart-ass you are when your fingernails are being ripped off."

CHAPTER 17

His eye color was dark, almost black, and his irises were unusually large.

This wasn't Patrick Veeder. Who was it?

He served me tea and left me unbound.

"Dr. David Denlon, my assistants have made several attempts to bring you to me. But I understand why you were afraid. Vladmir and Gustav do not seem to understand how to be gentlemen."

He looked over to Squeezer and Long Nose, who bowed their heads and dug deeper into the task of cleaning up our tattered laboratory bunker, to which they had returned me.

Were they taking it over? Rummaging through it for evidence?

"Let us start with a prayer to calm your fears."

A prayer . . .

I recalled Elaine's whispers on the plane, after she had confronted Snarl Guy in the bathroom. *He yapped on about some creepy pastor. Liam is the name I got.*

The volume of his voice lowered, pulling in my attention although I didn't want to give it. "He will not fail thee, neither forsake thee: fear not . . ."

Vladmir and Gustav pitched menacing looks in my direction as they pushed aside pictures, picked up lamps, and repositioned the desks against a wall.

While my captor uttered biblical phrases with closed eyes, I studied the men I had called Squeezer and Long Nose. One marveled at how the ink on the board could be erased while the other squinted into an empty petri dish. New nicknames came to my mind—Tweedle Dee and Tweedle Dum—and I smiled, triggering a much-needed release of stress.

Dee caught my happy face as he picked up the side of a desk. He clenched his fist in my direction; the *da-bam* of the desk falling from his hand to the concrete floor startled the pastor out of his mumbling.

"Amen! Dr. Denlon, how are you feeling?"

"I'd feel better if I knew who you were."

"Forgive me, so much is going on."

He sat his pudgy hips into a chair and brought the sugar bowl closer to us, readjusting it twice before pulling his hand away.

"My name is Liam Ericson."

This *was* the pastor. But how was he related to Patrick Veeder?

I surveyed the whiteboards that remained on the wall, most of them crooked. Only one panel had been erased by the lazy efforts of Tweedle Dee. The majority of the graphs, notations, and evolutionary milestones were still there, comforting me.

Could I fool Liam and escape?

"This tea is good," I lied. I had not been drinking it because Elaine's comment had grown roots in my brain. *And years later you eat some pie in a coffee shop and die from poison.*

"It's special tea," Liam said. "It helps with altitude sickness."

Dee and Dum steamed.

"You'll be happy to know," Liam said, sipping his tea, "I'm helping you."

I smiled at Liam, as much to lead him on as to tease the Tweedles. "Helping me? Well then, I suppose I should be saying 'thank you.'"

Dum slammed a file box onto a table behind Liam and flashed me his middle finger.

Liam turned around, just missing his gesture. "You can't clean up the place without making a racket? You're bulls in a china shop!"

I smirked like a smug older brother. When Liam turned back around, I asked, "How is it that I might help you?"

"I shall explain." Liam beamed with pride. "I'm a traveling pastor. I bring God's Word to people who are far from churches but who need Him the most. To do this, I move into a village, bring supplies, and preach there for three or four months." He scooted the salt and pepper shakers to be exactly in line with the sugar bowl. "My sponsor provides the resources for me to conduct these missions, and he has asked me to do him a favor. In fact, he is unable to fund any more of my missions until this favor is done. Therefore, you can imagine, Denlon, I'm anxious to get this favor over with."

I pretended to swallow my tea, trying to put everything together. *My sponsor* . . . Veeder? But why was Patrick Veeder funding a pastor?

"I'm assuming I can help you with this favor?"

"If you choose to tell me the truth. And once the information you provide is confirmed, you will be free to go."

The doorbell rang.

Liam smiled. "The supplies. Vladmir, get the door. Gustav, the dolly."

Dee ascended the cellar stairs; Dum lugged the dolly up behind him.

"What information do you need?" I asked.

"Truthful information." Liam carefully plucked a wet wipe from its case and used it to rub circles on the metal table, cleaning up invisible traces of food or dirt. "This world is full of lies, because Satan has a hold on it. The devil standeth not in truth . . . for he is a liar and the father of all lies!"

My throat tried to swallow my tongue.

Dee and Dum carried the loaded dolly down the stairs, arguing and cussing in their language.

Liam ambled over to inspect the delivered boxes. "Good. The scanner. Our food. Set out the cans. Labels straight."

The Tweedles began lining up cans of soup, beans, vegetables, and chili on the desk they had cleared off.

Liam observed and corrected, adjusting the cans so an equal amount of space separated them from each other. He contemplated the display, then slightly rotated a can to the left, ensuring it joined the others in facing one direction. Had he forgotten about the conversation we were having? What favor could he want from me?

When his phone chimed out the tune "Amazing Grace," he hustled down the hallway, toward the room where I had made love to Elaine.

I imagined running out the cellar door, but the Tweedles were closer to it, and they were armed. I considered charging to the tunnel, but that's where Liam had gone. I swiveled in my office-style chair to see what other options I might have, and saw a man—a hostage?—seated in the far back corner of the room with his arms and legs tied. He bit down on his gag, scowling at me as if his predicament were my fault. I had not noticed this bald, tattooed man fifteen minutes ago, when Dee and Dum had thrown me into the laboratory like they were kicking me out of a bar.

My mind pulled away, from the Tweedles unloading cans, from the seething hostage, and from my worry that Veeder would show up and tear off my fingernails.

I pictured Elle's caring green eyes. Would I ever see her again? Could someone like Elle ever fall in love with someone like me? If she could, would I screw it up?

I recalled my marriage counselor asking me to think of a time—long before *the incident*, as she had insisted on calling my ex-wife's infidelity—that I had let Melly down. I had ignored her question before, shrugging at her misbuttoned blouse and keeping my thoughts to myself. *Why are we focusing on everything but the fact that she fucked someone?*

But, for some reason, it was now easy to remember a time when I'd not been the best husband to Melly.

Napoleon Bonaparte's hat sat in a glass box. A dark-brown helmet, round on top, extending out on either bottom side, as if to protect his ears. As the story went, he had left it behind in this Parisian restaurant, after dining there two hundred years ago.

Melly and I sat at a table with three of my colleagues, watching them bungle their attempts to greet the long-suffering waiter in French.

All of them were far less brilliant and talented than Melly, but Dr. Tom Gray was a particular dimwit. It was only with the strenuous pulling of extensive strings by his father, who had preceded Dr. Gray as a professor, that he had made it—with one vote to spare—into the haven of tenure.

After struggling to order his food, Dr. Gray asked Melly, "Being the wife of a professor on the international speaking circuit is a wonderful gift, now, isn't it?"

I rolled my eyes and returned to studying Napoleon's hat.

Upon returning to our hotel room, Melly said, "Can you believe that Tom asked me that . . . being a wife is a gift?"

"The students call Tom 'Dr. Gray Area,'" I reminded her. "No one ever knows what the hell he's talking about. He's a stupid ass trying to sound smarter than he is."

"Those silly, old white men, they don't get why sexism is wrong. They are the real victims!"

As usual, I had realized too late that she was not simply making small talk. Why did people—particularly women—calmly ask me open-ended questions when they were actually fired up and wanting me to say something specific?

Before I could make sense of the moment and offer a better answer, Melly *yelled*, "Thank you for ruining Paris!" She *threw* her palmier cookie in the trash and retreated to the bathroom in *silence*.

As the steam from her long shower billowed into the main room, I stood at the glass door of our Juliet balcony, ogling the Latin Quarter's historic buildings. Clusters of short chimneys—round and ceramic— poked out of the rooftops. Corbels in the shape of spades supported ledges; beneath them, ribbony lines and snail-shell swirls protruded out of the walls. Underneath each generous window, all the way down the block, bushels of pink flowers had outgrown their containers.

I imagined how sad and confused I must have appeared to anyone peering over at me from their apartment. I could nearly feel myself being painted into an oil on canvas, *Love Lost in Paris*, that would hang in a back hallway or spare room, attracting more dust than attention.

Being married to me was a gift? Why hadn't I told Melly that I was the one receiving the gift? A beautiful wife who could capture the essence of a scene with a paintbrush, who gracefully endured sexist, socially inept professors because she loved being with me. Why hadn't I ever thanked her for what she tolerated, or even acknowledged it?

Liam charged into the room, trying to stuff his phone back into a pants pocket that was too tight to receive it.

"Denlon. We are aligned, you and I. We both want to return to our careers—preaching for me, teaching for you. Do we not?"

"Amen," I said.

"I don't know why the funder of my missions is so preoccupied with this blasphemous idea of yours."

I forced my face into stillness, hiding my reaction. *Because it's the greatest discovery ever, and Patrick Veeder wants the world to think he was the one who found it!*

"Surely you aren't serious that there were people put on Earth by someone other than God?"

An answer jumped out of my mouth, in a more agitated tone than I wanted: "I'm not trying to disprove any religion. God might be the one who created evolution."

Liam considered my response and then seemed to consider how to change the topic. "Well, anyway, the sooner my sponsor has his information, the sooner he sends me back to my ministry."

I knew what he was going to ask. Of course. How had I not figured this out before?

"It's simple, my friend. Relax," Liam said, observing the frustration on my face. "When you give me the exact location of the second research site, we both win. Just tell me, where is it?"

Patrick Veeder had defrauded me out of my greatest accomplishment. And now he was using Pastor Liam to steal from me again. He would never learn of the second location, even if it meant my life, and it probably did.

I searched Liam's cloudy eyes. He trusted me.

"It's the Mount St. Helens volcano in Washington. I can draw you a map, no problem."

Liam grinned. "I knew we'd be friends." Then he looked over to Vladmir and Gustav. "Witness allegiance to God. Witness how Denlon earns peace."

Smoke nearly came out of the Tweedles' ears. The hostage shook his head.

Could I find where Liam had hidden my phone? Would my call be tracked? I needed to alert the others that

I would be sending Veeder on a wild goose chase, giving Musa time to dig up that mysterious object, and Sunny time to translate the message.

"How long will it take to confirm the information I provide?" My voice shook. Dum trained his gaze on me.

"Not long," Liam said. "And I will enjoy your company while we wait. Not to worry, we have plenty of food and supplies."

I peeked at the perfectly aligned cans of food, wondering which ones contained Veeder's poison.

CHAPTER 18

Liam arranged several candles on the table in the shape of a cross and lit them with a long-reach lighter. My guess was that he was attempting to set a peaceful mood, but flames assembled into the most prominent symbol of Christianity made me feel like we were in a funeral home.

We followed his lead, bowing our heads over chili, olives, and artichoke hearts, until the conclusion of his prayer.

The bald hostage—allowed one free hand and a break from his gag to eat—angrily stabbed bits of food onto his fork, protesting the meal and his company. Who was he?

Tweedle Dee and Tweedle Dum had configured the seating so that I was between them; every time Liam looked away, they snuck elbow jabs into my sides.

For about the tenth time, I brought a forkload of food to my mouth, pretended to eat, and then scattered the food around my plate. When enough time seemed to have elapsed, I said, "Thank you for dinner." I rubbed my forehead. "I think I should lie down."

Dum's mouth came at me as if to bite off my nose. "Yeah, right. What about the map, Professor?"

"Gustav, clear the table," Liam said. "My friend Denlon will make a better map after some prayer and some rest."

Pastor Liam, as a nurse would accompany a patient, led me out of the laboratory and into the room where I'd slept with Elaine. He knelt and murmured next to me as I covered myself with bedding that still smelled like peaches.

He stepped out and closed the door.

I hopped out of bed and searched the room. Could my computer be where I had stored it when I was here before? My hand found nothing in the dark space of the nightstand. I checked under the bed, finding only dust balls.

Where had Liam put the possessions we'd left behind?

I flopped onto the bed, pondering the ceiling fan. The last time I had examined it, my body had been tingling. I reimagined every second of my encounter with Elaine, from her arching back to her pulsating orgasm. I devoured the peachy scent of the sheets and wondered if she was all right. Had they made it to the Valley of the Moon?

The "Amazing Grace" ringtone sliced into my daydream. The clock switched from *9:36* to *9:37 p.m.*

The church tune grew louder as Liam came into the hallway, just outside my room. I tiptoed to the door and pressed my ear to it, hearing Liam's defensive tone. "But, Mr. Veeder . . ."

After a pause, Liam said, "But Denlon will be informing us of exactly where that second site is."

My anger and swelling urge to scream collected in my shuddering fists. *Actually, Denlon will be tricking you like you did him!*

Liam finished his call and I leapt for the bed. The door swung open.

"Denlon!" His shark eyes were suddenly three inches above mine. "The map."

"Coming right up," I said.

"Good man." He charged out to the main room and I followed.

"It's time to go," he said to the hostage. "God's will."

As I sat down in front of a desk, Tweedle Dee pleaded, "That's not necessary, Mr. Ericson. He doesn't need to be killed. He's learned his lesson."

Liam tied the hostage's hands behind his back and lengthened the chain holding his feet together.

"What was that, Vladmir?" Liam said. "Not necessary? This man had my clear orders to avoid using deadly force. And he blew up a car in Stratford-upon-Avon anyway."

I squeezed my pencil so tightly it split in half. *This guy nearly killed me and the others at the pub.*

Liam unfastened the bandana around the hostage's mouth. "Would you like to confess your sins?"

The hostage squealed, "Denlon's lying, you dumb preacher! Your funder wants him dead, can't you see that? I was doing you a favor."

Liam pointed a gun at the hostage's back and pushed him toward the cellar door. "The soul that sinneth shall die . . . the wickedness of the wicked shall be upon him!"

He shoved the hostage up the stairs and Dum followed until Liam yelled, "No, stay back!"

We heard the complaints of the hostage and Liam's repeated command—"Keep walking!"—until the back door on the main floor slammed shut.

Vladmir fell to a seated position on the floor. Gustav put his hand on Vladmir's head and shouted at me: "What the fuck are you looking at, you lying piece of shit!"

Vladmir looked up. "Better get to that fake map."

I called to mind the most difficult part of Mount St. Helens to reach. That volcano, given its relatively recent eruption, had been the first place I'd searched, but it had produced no positive findings. With travel, excavating, and testing, Veeder would be distracted, at least for a while, before he came up empty-handed.

As I drew a vertical line to indicate north and south, a short burst of what sounded like machine-gun fire rang out from upstairs, startling my hand across the page.

My head throbbed to the beat of my pulse. I spent the next twenty minutes forcing my shaky hand to draw the map and label it. My instructions would clearly lead Veeder to an exact spot, but there would be no zircon nor prancestor DNA.

Dee and Dum became preoccupied with a small safe, mumbling to each other. Vladmir turned the combination lock one way, and then the other, then back again. When the safe didn't open, Gustav pushed him away and tried turning the lock himself.

Liam's patent-leather briefcase was open and standing next to a pad of paper on the other desk. I leaned over to it from my chair, keeping an eye on the bickering Tweedles. Peeking inside, I saw a folder that read *Village Gifts to P. Veeder*.

As Dee and Dum fiddled with the lock, I slowly reached into the folder. My fingers slid across something thin and slick.

Liam banged down the cellar steps; Dee and Dum scrambled away from the safe. I pulled my hand out of the file and saw that I'd fished out three-by-five photographs.

When Liam flung open the door I hopped up and pushed the photos into my jeans. I couldn't think of an excuse for having my hand down the front of my pants as he approached me.

But his focus was on his filthy hands and arms. He showed no remorse for whatever he'd committed—murder?—but was frenzied with concern over how quickly he could wet-wipe himself, from his forearms to his fingernails, to remove the chestnut-colored dirt.

Finally clean and his conniption abated, he arrived at the side of my desk, squinting as if he had made a mistake in trusting me.

"I finished the map," I said. "It shows two different perspectives. It will be easy to follow."

He inspected my notations. "Very good. Soon we will be out of this underground room and into the light of day."

Liam's scanner buzzed my map through cyberspace to Patrick Veeder. Angst twirled around in my shrinking stomach. Were Musa, Meredith, and Jeremy safe at the site, and had they discovered anything more? Did Elle and Miguel find Ann, Casey, and Sunny in the Valley of the Moon, and had Sunny been able to spend any time translating the prancestors' message?

Our extinct sister race spoke to me through the notes on the board. I pondered the evolutionary milestone written in blue: *Industry*. I remembered the photograph of the corresponding etching—a square structure with two smokestacks, producing six identical gadgets.

"Time for bed," Liam announced.

I happily left the main room, tossing a phrase over my shoulder: "See you in the morning." One of the Tweedles grunted but I didn't turn around.

Relieved to be in the bedroom alone, I kicked off my shoes and wondered if I'd be able to fall asleep. In what seemed like a second after my head hit the pillow, I awoke in a coffin. I sat up, shoving open the heavy casket lid and then realized I was dreaming. Perspiration had pasted my hair to my forehead. The clock read *6:52 a.m.*

I checked the tunnel door. A latch had been screwed onto it and secured with a padlock. Someone stirred in their sleep. I didn't move until the snoring resumed.

I crept through the laboratory and up the cellar stairs, wincing at the creaky step. Up on the ground floor, plastic garbage bags had been taped to the side wall, presumably to hide the hole blown through it yesterday. I dismissed my idea of escaping that way; there was too much tape to quickly—or quietly—rip off.

The front door and the door leading from the kitchen to the garage were also padlocked. I considered how much noise it would make to open one of the windows, and moved on.

Thankfully, the back door opened without a sound. I gently stepped onto the red-and-gray tile in the courtyard.

The morning air delivered the perfume of flowers. The sunrise was too young to provide warmth, but its yellow light spilled into the blue atmosphere like the drippy yolk of a fried egg.

Beyond the courtyard, amid a small patch of rocks and plants, dirt had been piled into a mound. Over the dead body of the hostage?

I cursed myself for not grabbing my shoes. Could I climb the back fence, or one of the fences on either side of the small yard?

"Going somewhere, Denlon?" Behind me, Liam's breathy question ended with the click of a cocking gun.

Chapter 19

My paralyzed stare found a chattering bird. His twiggy legs supported a red-feathered body on the back of a metal chair as he urgently chirped his case.

"Turn around," Liam commanded.

I couldn't move. The little bird tweeted at me as if he were explaining something very important.

After about twenty seconds, I drew a breath in through my nose and released it. My body thawed and I faced Liam.

He sat beneath a vine of heart-shaped leaves, in one of four chairs around an outdoor table, aiming his pistol at my head.

"Liam." I smiled. "I'm not running away in my socks. I came out to get some fresh air. We're friends, right?"

A flash of moisture flooded his eyes and then evaporated. He kept hold of his gun, but rested it in his lap.

Could I distract him? Wrestle away his gun?

"Killing that hostage," I said, taking a seat next to him, "must have been difficult for you."

The bird stopped chirping as if to listen to Liam's response.

"Mischa was his name," Liam said. "It means 'who is like the Lord.'"

"Do you regret it?"

He shifted in his chair. "Do you regret *your* killing?"

"What?"

"In the airport bathroom—surely you haven't forgotten?"

"Liam, he attacked me."

"I was on the line, on the microphone in his shirt pocket. He asked you a question. Had you answered it, you would not have been harmed."

"He had a knife to my throat."

Liam examined me from head to toe. "C'mon, Denlon. Let's have some breakfast tea."

Back in the bunker, Liam handed me a warm cup with a teabag string hanging out, and then walked toward the hallway, hollering, "Rise and shine! You haven't finished picking up this place!"

I dumped the tea in the sink and crouched down behind the counter. The mini refrigerator still housed the leftover pasta that Sunny and Ann had served. I stuffed a handful in my mouth, hoping to settle my growling stomach.

The Tweedles staggered into the room looking like they'd had a rough night. Swollen eyes. Hair sticking out in every direction. One filled the coffeepot with water, the other slapped a filter into the basket and poured dark-brown grounds into it from a paper bag. As Dum rinsed out a mug, I caught the slight shake of his head, as in, *I can't do this anymore.*

Liam took a seat at a desk, adjusting his five pencils—sharpened to the exact same length. He sipped his tea. "Gentlemen, less chatting and more cleaning today."

Dum snapped, "I've had enough of your orders. You haven't paid us a dime." He dried his hands as if he were readying them to fight. "When do we get paid?"

Pastor Liam pounded the desk, launching his carefully arranged pencils into disarray.

I jumped backward.

He shouted at Dum: "He that is greedy of gain troubleth his house! He that loveth silver shall not be satisfied with silver!"

Dum puffed his chest. "You and your Bible quotes. You're such a freak!"

"Hey," I involuntarily reacted, regretting the words as they were coming out of my mouth. "He's not a freak. He's living his truth."

Vladmir and Gustav looked at each other. After giving up on figuring out what I meant, they took large steps over to me, curling their fingers into claws. I leaned away from the stench of their unbathed bodies.

"You're such a liar," Dum barked. "Mr. Ericson, Denlon is playing you. He's not your friend."

Liam stood. "It is not in the purview of your job assignment to provide your input on who is or is not my friend."

Dum pulled out his Glock, and I wondered how he had stored it in his sweatpants. He pointed it at Liam. "You owe us money. Pay up!"

Liam reseated himself. He carefully straightened the stapler to be in line with the side of the desk, and next to it the calculator, and then the automatic pencil sharpener. He did not look up when he spoke. "You understood the arrangement when you accepted this position. Your payment comes at the end. The end is when my sponsor learns about a location revealed by Professor David Denlon. He has learned of that site and is confirming it as we speak. But don't listen to me. Listen to the Lord." Veins bulged out of Liam's temples. "In due season we shall reap!" His spittle landed in tiny effervescent balls on the desk.

Liam's head slowly tilted upward, bringing Dum into his view. "But your overeager friend did things his way. Would you like to visit him? He's under a pile of soil in the yard."

Dee took the gun from Dum. "We just haven't had our coffee yet. We'll have the rest of this place cleaned up in an hour."

I exhaled, resolving to find a way out of this basement. Preferably after I recovered the flash drive Sunny had not wanted to leave behind. I glanced at the scanner, wondering how long Veeder would test sediment at Mount St. Helens before he realized I had lied.

The "Amazing Grace" jingle startled all of us. That song had always been soothing to me, but now it reminded me of an air-raid siren.

Liam answered the call in a subservient tone: "Good morning, sir," and disappeared up the cellar steps.

Veeder. I'd come to know when Veeder was on the other end of Liam's phone line, because only for Veeder did Liam assume the disposition of a slave.

Dum packed files and photographs into a garbage bag as Dee erased the graphs, pictures, and notations from the boards. Although Sunny had photographed the information, I still cringed.

"Oh, Professor," Dum mocked. "Are we messing with your little experiment? Your stupid research?"

When I didn't respond, Tweedle Dum marched to me. "You're a dead man, Denlon. It's a matter of time."

My hands barreled into his doughy chest, pushing him backward. He regained his footing and put up his fists.

Dee yelled in their language and Dum reluctantly brought his hands down to his side, saying, "You're just as fucking weird as Liam."

I retreated to the hallway and waited to see if they'd follow me. When they didn't, I snuck by the locked tunnel door and frantically searched each room for the flash drive Sunny had screamed about.

Reaching the last room, I darted in and checked the armoire—nothing. I pulled open the drawer of the bedside table—empty. Dropping into a push-up, I peered under the bed.

There was my computer bag.

I inspected its contents. My computer. My phone, which they'd taken from me after I'd surrendered. A wallet with identification I didn't recognize. Another phone—Miguel's? And a thumb drive, hopefully Sunny's backup.

Dee called out, "Where the hell is Denlon? He's not in his room."

I peeled the tracking device from my phone and forced the phone into my left pocket. I grabbed the flash drive and shoved it into my other pocket.

Dum yelled, "Did you find him?"

Dee paced down the hallway toward me. I pulled a pen out of my computer bag and pushed the bag back under the bed.

Dee's stocky figure blocked the doorway.

I clambered to my feet, holding up the pen. "There aren't pens in this place and I needed one."

"Bullshit." Dee's voice was calm. "I knew you'd screw up. When I tell Ericson about this, he's gonna bury you in the backyard, too."

I could think of nothing to say or do.

Dee yelled down the hall, "He was snooping through Liam's things."

"He's a dead man!" Dum exclaimed from the main room.

Dee and I heard Liam clomp down the stairs, fling open the door, and question Dum: "Why aren't you cleaning? You're like children! Can't be left alone!"

I followed Dee out to Liam.

Dum bounced onto his toes. "Go ahead, Vladmir. Tell Mr. Ericson what the professor has been up to."

"You'll have your turn to talk," Liam said. "I've just received news that can't wait."

"But, Mr. Ericson," Dee pleaded. "You have to hear what Denlon did."

"I'll tell you what Denlon did!" Liam held up his phone. "He provided the correct location."

The Tweedles shot surprised looks at me: *How did you pull that off?*

Liam smiled. "My sponsor didn't want me to share the good news, but I cannot resist. He said the map was spot on. His crew at Mount St. Helens discovered zircon. Lord only knows why that's so special." He turned to Vladmir and Gustav. "Pack your things, you are about to receive those generous paychecks you've been clamoring for. And I'm about to ship off to my next mission."

Vladmir and Gustav were stuck between hatred for me and their desire to collect their money and go home. Gustav sneered at me and then asked Liam, "Right now? You're gonna pay us?"

"My sponsor wants his arrival to be a surprise, so let's just say it's a matter of hours. He's bringing you bags of cash."

Gustav smiled at Vladmir and they discarded their concern over me, hustling off to their rooms.

My body filled with icy alarm. Even if there were zircon to be found on Mount St. Helens, it couldn't be discovered in half a day. Veeder had never intended to follow a map.

He would soon arrive, put on a show of congeniality, and then send Liam off to preach.

It was the perfect cover. When Liam got word that I had died, he would never suspect that Patrick Veeder had murdered me.

Chapter 20

"Praise God," Liam said, as we felt the vibration of a helicopter descending onto the house.

Too big to swallow. How could I get rid of the backup flash drive before Veeder killed me?

Liam set down his gun on an unopened supply box, freeing up his anxious hands to correct the display of food cans and the arrangement of his pencils.

Footsteps clattered down toward the open basement door. I warded off a frozen stare by breathing in, *one two three four five six seven*, and out, *one two three—*

A blue-eyed man in tailored slacks and a shirt with a pointed collar entered the room, holding a small duffel bag.

The color in Liam's face drained away as the man gave him a judgmental look and said, "You screw everything up."

"I don't answer to you, Darin," Liam retorted. "Where's Christopher?"

"That wimp is not far behind me," Darin said. "Don't know why he asked to come; there's enough English spoken in this shithole for us to get by."

Liam hung out near the stairs in hopeful anticipation.

"Where are your manners, Preacher?" Darin complained. "Aren't you going to introduce me to the professor?"

"Dr. Denlon, this is Darin." Liam's voice had taken on a gloomy pitch. "My sponsor's assistant."

Darin was sarcastic. "The wonderful Professor. How do you do?"

There was a padlock on the tunnel door down the hallway behind me. In front of me were Darin, Liam, and, soon enough, Patrick Veeder.

I adopted Darin's tone. "Never better."

More feet bounced down the stairs. A short man with a thoughtful look on his face arrived, carrying a duffel bag larger than Darin's.

Liam's face lit up. "Christopher, how are you?"

"I'm good, Liam, and you?"

"Great. Happy to be getting my missions back on track. Let me introduce you. This is Dr. David Denlon. Professor, this is Christopher Kiser, my sponsor's translator."

Christopher bowed his head. "A pleasure."

Studying me and the room as if he were worried, Christopher gently placed his bag on a desk and spoke to himself in another language. He peeked up at me. When he saw my blank look, he unzipped his bag and mumbled in yet another tongue. Again, he glanced up at me and realized I could not understand him.

The Tweedles pranced out from the hallway with their bags. While Darin snapped at Liam to introduce him, I studied Liam's pencils and spoke softly in French, *"I speak French, Spanish, and Portuguese."*

"I understand," Christopher responded in French, pretending to busy himself with the contents of his bag.

Another set of feet walked heavily down the stairs. I looked over at Liam's gun again, still sitting on a cardboard box, out of my reach.

Patrick Veeder strutted into the room, smiling. His hair seemed darker and he stood even taller than I remembered.

We all looked at him and waited, silently acknowledging him, the alpha dog.

He slowly brought his hands together. "We all know each other now, I presume?"

We nodded as if we would be in trouble if we didn't.

Patrick Veeder was in his element. In charge and relaxed, as if he knew everything would work out precisely as he had planned.

"Darin, please take care of the payment to Pastor Ericson's assistants."

"Will do." Darin set his duffel bag on a desk, opened it, and produced two zippered cloth bags.

"Please count it," Veeder said. "I will not be offended."

"No need. We trust you." Gustav started for the door.

"We are grateful," Vladmir said, following Gustav. "But we must be going."

Veeder had given Gustav and Vladmir the willies, and not even the chance of seeing me suffer could tempt them to stay.

"I understand," Veeder said. "But I have a gift for you." He nodded to Christopher, who pulled a bottle of vodka out of his bag.

Gustav read the label and stuttered in disbelief. "This . . . this is too generous."

"Nonsense." Veeder smiled. "Enjoy it and your hard-earned money."

After Gustav and Vladmir ascended the stairs, Veeder carefully shut the door. The click of the lever seemed louder than I'd noticed before.

Veeder turned to me with eyes that knew I was onto him. He continued his performance for Liam.

"Dr. Denlon, I have a gift for you as well. Because I'm so appreciative of that detailed map."

Christopher produced a bottle of Cabernet Sauvignon. He faced the emblem toward me—an eagle in a square.

"Wow," I said. "Top shelf."

"Or as they say in French,"—Christopher looked straight into my eyes and switched languages—*"poison."*

I held back my gasp and managed to smile. "Nice." I tried not to glance at Liam's gun.

Veeder pinched the leather strap hanging from his neck, pulling out from behind his cardigan the pendant I had handed over to him when I thought he was a television producer. He quickly twitched his eyebrows up and down, rubbing in how he had fooled me.

Finding that powdery-blue crystal together with the white one—the one I'd given to Carrie—had brought me back to that day in the park when my dad urged me to breathe, and to focus on the blue-and-white sky. In that moment, there had been something about really noticing the uncatchable clouds and the uncontainable universe, something that had convinced me that I, too, deserved to be free.

Veeder directed Christopher to open the wine. "Let's toast a new arrangement. Pastor, glasses for the professor and me?"

Darin snapped at Liam to find wineglasses. As Liam rummaged through the storage cabinet in the corner of the room, I told myself to do something. *Anything.*

"I saw some wineglasses in a box over here," I said, walking toward Liam's gun.

Liam started to disagree, but by his third word I had seized the pistol. Aiming the barrel at Veeder, I hurried backward until no one was behind me.

Darin elevated his hands. Liam's mouth fell open.

But Veeder smiled. He held his hands out in a welcoming gesture, as if I had just entered his home for cocktails. His wavy hair stayed in place as he nodded. His gold pinky ring sparkled, as did a bulky watch on his left wrist.

"You see, Liam, I told you Denlon was not going to cooperate."

Liam's face bloated in shock. "Mr. Veeder, I'm sorry I doubted you."

"Shut up," Veeder quipped, before he returned to the role of gracious host and said to me, "You fooled my little preacher. We have that in common."

He ignored my gun and walked toward me.

My urge was to step backward but I forced myself to stand my ground. "Liam, Veeder is using you to steal this project from me."

Darin's worried eyes shot back and forth between me and Veeder.

Christopher's look was much different. His eyes implored me to shoot. He had moved out from behind Veeder, clearing a path for any stray bullets.

But I had never discharged a gun, and this one was larger than I'd seen on TV. Did I have to load it? Unlatch something?

"Clearly, David," Veeder said, "I'm in a position to allow some bargaining." He took another step toward me. "I'm open to sharing the reward. Let's talk, Professor."

Liam's cheeks broke out in pink blotches. "You are servants of Satan!"

Veeder ignored Liam and smiled at me. "Let's write up a new contract and include that second site. Then you can do your thing and I can do mine. Easy. Peaceful. No one gets hurt."

"You don't care about artifacts or history." My gun-holding hand shook. I used my other hand to steady it. "This is about you gaining more power."

Veeder came closer to me. "Put your gun down. We don't need weapons to solve this."

I walked backward, tripped, and regained my balance.

"David." Veeder sounded like he was talking me out of suicide. He was five or six feet from me now. "We're intelligent men. Let's work together."

Christopher's face tightened as Veeder stepped toward me, reaching out.

I discharged a gun for the first time in my life, pulling the trigger five times. Only one bullet hole appeared on Veeder, near his right shoulder, and for a moment, I stood in disbelief at how I could be so close to a target and miss four of five shots.

Blood dribbled down his expensive sweater as he fell to the floor.

Liam whispered, "Mr. Veeder?"

Darin screamed, "Why did you do that?"

Christopher mumbled in French: *Shoot him again. Make sure he's dead.*

A buzzing noise started up at the tunnel door. Was someone sawing through it?

Veeder pressed his left hand to the front of his shoulder and then inspected it, seemingly confused at how quickly it had become drenched in blood. He struggled up to his knees, with his right arm dangling like a fake attachment, and attempted—awkwardly, as he clearly was not left-handed—to retrieve the gun from the back of his pants. "Darin, shoot him!"

"S'il vous plait," Christopher begged me.

Behind me and down the hall, the sawing stopped. Part of the door tumbled onto the floor.

I pulled the trigger again, aiming toward Veeder's chest. Nothing happened.

Veeder yelled, "Darin, he's out of bullets! Shoot!"

Darin whipped out his gun and unloaded it in my direction.

Chapter 21

I peered down at my toes, trying to remember the last time I had seen my bare feet. The heat of the water penetrated my shoulder blades and my body finally relaxed. The massage of the shower begged me to forget about everything, just for a few seconds. But my mind refused to clear, replaying my escape as if I was convincing myself that it had really happened.

As I charged away from Darin's blasting gun, Ann poked her head through the hole she had cut in the tunnel door.

"Hurry!" she said.

I crawled through the opening, and we sprinted down and into the left passageway. After scaling a wall ladder up through a storm drain, we emerged to the relentless shriek of a helicopter landing in a plaza.

The chopper pointed down at us like a hungry, horror-movie insect. Its two huge windows were tinted, making it impossible to see inside it.

"Oh my God!" I shouted.

"Run to it!" I could hardly hear Ann over the thundering blades. "It's Veeder's—we took it!"

I hoisted myself inside. The pilot didn't need to turn around for me to recognize him. That build and thick blonde hair. *Casey.*

He checked that we were secured in our seatbelts before flying us into the safety of the sky.

We had now taken refuge in a high-rise hotel, one of many that spoiled the traditional look of this sacred South American city.

The heat held on to my skin as I dried off. I started to wrap the towel around me, but it was refreshing to be naked and clean after days of wearing the same clothes. I pitched the towel to the floor and strolled into the bedroom.

Elaine was seated on my bed.

I stammered, "I . . . I didn't know you had a key . . ."

Elle nearly leapt to me. Her hands held my face and then rubbed downward, over my stiff nipples.

Her eyes pooled. "I thought I'd never see you again."

Our lips came together like magnets, our tongues seeking shelter inside each other. The connection between us had become its own force, declaring itself our master, ordering us to let go of boundaries and follow the sensation of pleasure wherever it took us.

I lifted her out of her sandals and brought her to the bed; she tore at her clothes to get them off, ripping her underwear. I kissed my way down her belly and dove in, determined. She was the cure to my every illness, the key to any potential I had to ever really be satisfied. I didn't relent until her legs trembled and a noise came from her that was part squeal and part something I'd never heard before.

I climbed up and she hooked her heels onto my back like a sexy Cirque de Soleil performer. My skin was slick with sweat, radiating life and strength as I slipped through the gates of heaven.

We moaned in harmony, each thrust another attempt to reach deeper. I lost myself and my sense of time.

Elaine yelled and gasped, and then shook. My body released, wave after wave. Our grips on each other slowly unclenched. My body fell limp beside her, into the coolness of the sheets.

A fast beat rattled the door. We ignored it, lying still, willing the noise to be something that didn't involve us.

Another knock, a harsh reality we couldn't deny. We scurried into our clothing, threw the bed back together, and patted down our crazy hair.

Someone banged again. I glanced through the peephole before turning the knob.

"Professor!" Sunny stepped inside and hugged me with his free arm.

"Hey, Sunny, how ya doing?"

"You're not gonna believe this!" He used his laptop to call Musa.

Ann, Miguel, and Casey filed in and shut the door.

"Dave, dude," Casey said. "Don't do that anymore."

"Do what?"

"Any and all of what you did with the *I'm surrendering* and the *I'm gonna take on Veeder* shit. Just . . . no."

Miguel patted my back.

"We gotta debrief," Ann said. "While it's fresh in his head."

Miguel held a phone under my nose, and I assumed it was recording.

Ann asked, "Who is Liam?"

"A pastor, well, self-proclaimed I think—"

"How does he know Veeder?" Casey asked.

"Veeder funds his missions to villages."

"What villages?" Ann asked.

"I don't know . . . he said he reaches people far from churches."

Musa, Meredith, and Jeremy appeared on Sunny's screen.

I sprang to the computer. "Hey, it's good to see you guys."

Musa grinned. "David, stay with us."

"I don't want anyone dying for me."

"I know, my friend."

Sunny started to yell, but Ann held his arm. He gritted his teeth as if keeping himself from shouting was painful. "Moose! Tell him!"

Musa gestured toward Jeremy and Meredith.

Jeremy pushed his long bangs out of his eyes, and they immediately fell back into his face. "We got more generators here. We were able to do GPR."

My head jerked forward. "To look at the object? The one above the stones, made from the foreign material?"

"What's GPR?" Elle asked.

I smiled. "Ground penetrating radar. To see things underground or in concrete."

"It's not an object," Meredith said. "It's more than a half mile long. It presents like a cruise ship or a really tall strip mall."

"Dear God," I said. "Is it part of a city?"

"It certainly could be," Musa said.

"Okay, Musa, but please," I said, "I don't know if Veeder is dead or alive. We have to get you out of there. We have to do this another way."

Musa stared. "You don't know?"

Everyone in the room smiled as if they'd just yelled *Surprise!* on my birthday.

Elaine said, "Musa, we thought you should be the one to tell him."

"Tell him?" Musa said. "I'll show him."

He turned his computer around.

An army of a hundred men and women wearing blue-and-green fatigues, with black rifles strapped over their shoulders, guarded the site. A helicopter painted in camouflage colors sat on a plateau. Four armored trucks were parked in a row alongside the rock garden.

"You see that, Dr. D?" Jeremy stuck his nose and one eye into the camera. "You got your site back!"

My fingers gripped the top of my head.

"Yes!" Sunny smacked the hotel desk.

Elle's soft hand rested on my shoulder. "Even if Veeder survives your bullet, he won't be taking this site back anytime soon."

I searched the room for a chair to sit in before my knees gave out.

Ann kissed my cheek and then explained, "Kind of a good thing that your site is in Guatemala because Paul's got a pretty good relationship with the Guatemalan government. He made a deal. They need money and we need secrecy and protection."

I asked, "How much money does this Paul guy have?"

"Kind of a lot," Casey said. "But we still gotta hurry."

I exhaled for several seconds. "Okay, excellent work with the GPR! Sunny—"

"I know," he said. "We gotta translate the message on those stones!"

Musa panned his computer, allowing us to see the large bulldozers chomping into the pebbly brown earth. "Our diggers had to widen the trail leading up here, to bring in bigger equipment. We're working around the clock to uncover this thing."

"Okay, Moose," Sunny said, "over and out!"

We ordered everything on the room-service menu. And I let the others choose the wine.

Two hours later, stuffed and wobbly on our feet, we played the third round of our made-up drinking game: David the Sommelier. The game had one rule—every time I correctly identified the origin and type of the wine, we had to finish the bottle.

I relaxed on the recliner as the others glared at me.

Ann handed me a half-filled stemmed glass.

I swirled. Smelled. Noted the color. Tasted. "Old-world Cab."

Casey asked, "Sunny?"

Sunny stared into his computer. "He's right. French. Old-world. Cab. That's my professor!"

Elaine handed me another glass.

I swirled and sniffed. Tasted. I smiled at her. "How did you know?"

She winked at me. "I do my homework."

"Thank you," I said.

Miguel's hands and face asked, *What's going on?*

"Barbera," I said. "From where I live. Shenandoah Valley."

"Man," Casey said. "You went six for six. Is this like an autistic thing?"

The room fell silent. The others eyed Casey as if he had said something wrong.

"I don't know what you people call it," I responded. "I call it 'me.'"

Laughter started up and then grew louder, like the beginning of a good song, and infected everyone, including me.

"Well, you're awesome," Casey said, as he poured more wine into our glasses, spilling it in between them.

Ann thumbed her phone, and a familiar 1980s pop song blared out. She and Elaine gyrated to the beat, sing-yelling the words and sounds: "Oh! Hoo!"

Miguel and Casey wiggled their hips in their chairs. Sunny hurtled onto the bed and flailed around—was he dancing or swatting away mosquitoes?

I excused myself to the toilet. As I washed my hands, I saw my phone charging on the bathroom counter and remembered that I had borrowed a converter and charger from the front desk.

My dead phone had finally turned back on, and it was showing that Melly had called while I was in the bunker with Liam. But she hadn't left a message.

I relived, for what might have been the hundredth time, the memory of glancing out my front window, after arriving home from Hollókő a day early. Melly was being dropped off by some man, and it looked like she had leaned over to kiss him before getting out of the white Volkswagen Jetta.

I coiled back my arm, preparing to throw my phone into the wall, but then I remembered that I needed to check in with Mom.

Drunken wooziness consumed me.

I recalled Elaine's warning that my phone could be compromised, but ignored it. Listening from inside the bathroom door, I determined that they were now playing a rap song. I pressed Call.

Casey knocked. "Hey, man, all this wine makes me need to pee."

He came in as I walked out and hid in the closet alcove.

"David?" Mom was tentative.

"Hi, Mom. Sorry I haven't called in a—"

"Oh, Davey," Mom cried.

In the background, Melly yelled, "David!"

I stared at the clothes hangers in confusion. *Why are my ex-wife and my mother in the same location? And where are they?*

"Mom, what's going on?"

"I love you," she said.

An unfamiliar man's voice penetrated my ear. "If you want them to live, you'd better get to Amsterdam."

"What? Who are you?"

"Instructions will be texted." The phone beeped. *Call ended.*

I mumbled, "Jesus Christ."

"Ssshhhh," Elaine said. "David? Are you saying something?"

I tried to speak but knew I would weep instead.

Miguel came to me; Ann shut off the music.

"What'd I miss?" Casey asked, walking out of the bathroom.

All I could give were half-sentence explanations.

Elaine took the phone. "How long were you on? Less than a minute?"

"Uh, yeah."

Casey poured himself more wine. "Shit. Patrick Veeder had your mom and ex-wife kidnapped. This guy *is* evil."

Sunny's hand covered his mouth.

"This means Veeder's alive?" Ann asked the others.

Elle shook her head. "Not necessarily. He had to have arranged the kidnapping before he came to La Paz. He couldn't have been shot and then orchestrate this, all in twenty-four hours."

Casey drank his wine as if it were a shot of whiskey. "Right. Only time will tell if Veeder is alive."

"Look." I collected myself. "Enough. My mom and Melly can't die because we're making some cool discovery. We have to go to the police."

"With what?" Casey asked. "Don't you think we'd love to call 911 and be done? We have nothing to tie Veeder to this, and we can't tell our story without admitting some shit we've done that is kind of illegal."

"It's one hundred percent illegal," Ann said. "We do illegal stuff."

Casey argued, "We have reasons."

I stared. Sweat seeped out of my scalp. Elle rubbed my shoulder.

I finally exhaled. "Goddamn it!" I swept my arm across the desk, clearing the phone, lamp, and papers to the floor. "What, so now my mom and Melly just die? I can't do this anymore. I can't! We're going to the US embassy!"

I lifted a bottle of wine straight to my mouth and swallowed.

"David, it doesn't work that way," Elle said.

I banged the bottle down onto the empty desktop. "What are you referring to with the 'it'? Life? Speak for your own. International spy games? I'm not playing them anymore."

Ann waved Miguel, Sunny, and Casey over to her and out of the room. She said to Elaine, "Get him to bed."

Nausea begged me to lie down. Elaine covered me.

I shut one of my eyes so the other could peek inside my empty wine bottle. I pictured myself shrinking and crawling inside it.

"Elle," I cried. "Can we save them?"

Chapter 22

I was back in the La Paz airport, no longer an old man—this time as Miguel. I had memorized his birthdate, place of birth, city of residence, and other information I might have to produce rapidly. We were almost the same height and weight, and Ann had fattened up my nose and scarred my cheeks with makeup.

Miguel now resembled me, which had been harder to achieve, since his nose had to be made to look skinnier. The solution was to simulate a bruise, so that the bigger nose would be explained by swelling. His scarred cheeks went along with the injury disguise.

An officer walked by, his eyes more in a daydream than on patrol. Had he been among the police officials that had chased me and Elaine the last time we were here?

I readjusted myself in my chair, but there was no getting comfortable. Were they torturing Mom and Melly? Starving them?

The sign at the New York gate read *Delayed*. On top of that, counting the hours, New York wasn't even halfway there, because I would endure a layover before the second flight to Amsterdam. I pressed the pads of my fingers into my scalp until both my head and my fingers hurt.

An entire structure, maybe even a city, from an extinct race of advanced human beings was about to be excavated, and I was numb to it. My mind wouldn't release me from images of Mom and Melly—crying, resisting advances, attempting to squirm out of chains—for even a moment, not one tick of time for me to sit in awe of the magnitude of this discovery.

The only reason I had so far resisted rolling on the floor and screaming, which I knew wouldn't help but somehow seemed like it would feel better than sitting quietly, was the calm—almost boredom—that Miguel, seated next to me, exhibited.

As he studied my driver's license, I said, "Being me puts you in danger."

He shrugged.

"It does, doesn't it?" I asked. "I mean, you could be killed."

Miguel pushed a gust of air out of his nose. "Unlikely."

His attention went to a suitcase that a woman wheeled over near us and quickly abandoned. When she returned to it, he stood and raised the strap of his carry-on over his shoulder. "See you in Amsterdam."

We hadn't been able to find seats on the same plane on such short notice.

When he walked away, I followed. "Wait."

He turned back and gave me a good-bye salute.

"Wait, please," I insisted.

Miguel looked around to see if anyone was noticing the scene I was making. "Don't worry. Just follow the plan."

"No, what I want to know is . . . why are you involved in this?"

A woman's voice began to announce his flight over the speakers.

He contemplated me. "Knowing my story helps you?"

"Yeah."

The woman completed the announcement, in Spanish and then in English. "Please proceed to the gate."

We walked to the wall, away from the foot traffic.

Miguel whispered, "My wife was killed. Antiabortion people bombed a clinic. She was a nurse there. The main guy got off on some technicality. I hunted him. Shot him in the legs. Crippled him. Becky would not be proud."

He made sure no one was watching us. "I'm on the run. Got a new name, cut up my cheeks. I knew Ann. She got me on with Paul, 'cuz I gotta eat."

He smiled. "Does that answer it, Professor?"

I realized I was shaking my head no. "I mean, yes, I just can't believe it. Miguel, I'm sorry."

"Yeah. Now let's go get your ladies." He pushed a white earbud into one of his ears and sauntered away.

I turned around just as Ann strolled by in a short-haired red wig. She had pasted a simulated diamond to her nostril as a nose ring, and stuck a decal mermaid tattoo on her bicep.

I approached her. "Hey."

"Can I help you, sir?" she said, annoyed.

I whispered, "Really? We have to pretend like this? Miguel didn't."

She whispered back, "Well, he should have."

I spoke a little louder. "If your flight isn't leaving right away, I'd like to buy you a drink."

"That's a pretty good cover," she said softly. "A desperate guy, trying to pick up a woman in an airport."

She turned into a nearby bar and I trailed her. "Desperate?"

We sat in a booth.

"How old *are* you?" I asked.

"Forty-two," she said, and smirked. "But playing younger."

We ordered drinks.

I lowered my voice. "Um, can I ask you, why are you doing this?"

"Doing what?"

"This job. Is it really to spite your husband?"

"It's a long story. And a personal one."

Her drink arrived—a slushy kind of juice blend with a splash of gin. She dumped it into her travel mug and hid the mug in her backpack. "Fast and clean on this. Follow the plan."

The waiter returned with my Irish coffee. I sipped it and kept my thoughts to myself. *Your plan is crazy.*

"David?" Ann asked. "You've got the plan down, yes?"

I wondered if Mom had her medication.

"Listen," Ann explained. "You and I will be standing outside. The place is right in town, so we'll act like tourists. A couple on vacation. And remember, you look like Miguel."

"Yeah, okay."

"Focus. We can't pull this off without you. Miguel, disguised as you, will approach the door and ask to lay eyes on his mother and ex-wife. When you see your mom and Melly, if it's really them, you'll open the app Elaine downloaded to your phone and press the button—pretend to take a picture or something when you do it—and Miguel's phone will vibrate in his pocket. If his phone vibrates, he knows it's your mom and Melly. If it doesn't, he bails."

"What if no women are there?"

"Don't press the button."

"What if I'm not sure?"

"Don't press the button."

"What if it isn't them?"

She shook her head no.

"But, Ann, if it's other women, or no one, then what have they done with my mom and Melly?"

"One step at a time, David. I gotta go." She stood up. "Thanks for the drink, stranger."

I paid the bill and headed for the pet relief room.

Elaine was already waiting, smiling into a small dog carrier with a zipper around one of its ends, allowing it to open like a mailbox. We entered and shut the door.

The pungent odor of urine competed with the smell of sanitizer. Plastic grass took up half the floor. Elaine tossed the empty carrier on the small counter next to the porcelain sink. "We gotta make that call. You ready?"

"I guess I have to be."

"You can do this. We're just confirming that . . ." Elaine looked for something to do with her hands. She pushed the carrier farther onto the counter.

My throat stung. "That they're still alive?"

"Yeah. And don't give up any information."

I called Mom's phone as I had before. No answer.

"They'll call back," Elle said.

I plucked at the carrier's zipper for five minutes.

Elle listened to the garbled noise from overhead. "Your flight is boarding."

My phone buzzed. I answered, "Yes?"

Melly asked, "David?"

Where was Mom?

I tapped my phone into speaker mode. "Melissa, I'm on my way. I couldn't find a flight at first, but I'll get there."

Melly spoke like a robot, as if she were reading. "You must come alone or they will hurt us."

Elaine screamed at me with her eyes: *Do not screw this up*.

"It's just me," I said. "I'll be there alone. I promise."

"We're not far from the museum for Anne Frank," Melly said. "You know, where I painted that scene with the birds, remember?"

I didn't remember. Melly didn't usually paint animals.

"Is my mom okay?"

There was a pause.

"She's fine, David. How are you?" The voice was synthesized. But the cadence and the fake small talk gave me the shakes.

I mouthed to Elaine: *Veeder?*

She cupped her hands and whispered into my ear, "He's hiding his voice in case you've got detectives listening."

I pleaded, "They're innocent. Don't hurt them."

"You've made an enormous error, Denlon. Never shoot if you aren't going to kill. These women are innocent, indeed. But they're dead if you don't get to Amsterdam soon enough, and alone."

"Listen to me," I said. "My mom takes medication—"

"No. *You* listen. If you don't do everything exactly as you've been told, here's how it will go down. I will kill Melly first. By chopping her into pieces while she is still alive. In front of your mother. Because I want your mom to witness horror before I slit her throat and watch her slowly bleed to death. Oh, Dr. Denlon, you are no longer in your benign world of academia."

The call ended.

"Ignore it," Elaine said.

I couldn't breathe.

Elle squeezed my arms. "Bunny rabbits. Ice cream. Have you ever seen a snowball in the desert?"

"What the hell?"

"Take your mind somewhere else. What color is a clown's nose?"

"What?"

"What color?"

"Red? Elle, that was Patrick Veeder for sure. He's alive and he has my mom and Melly."

"Yeah, you knew that. And you already knew he could kill them. He's using threatening words because that's all he's got. He's scared."

"He didn't sound scared. He's angry!"

"Anger is fear. He's lost control of the site, he's losing his whole secret life, and don't forget, he's having to hide out. Because he can't risk being recognized by someone when he has an injury he can't explain. He's in some house or hotel with a gunshot wound, and some doctor friend is treating him without the benefit of a hospital."

Elle peered out the skinny window in the door. The man announcing my flight for the second time ended with "Immediately proceed to the gate."

"What's up with the birds?" she asked.

"Huh?"

"Melly. She painted birds?"

I thought.

Elle asked, "You guys went to Amsterdam?"

"Yeah."

"Did she paint a scene somewhere she's trying to tell you about? Did you go to a restaurant with the name 'bird' in it?"

"Amsterdam, um, she painted bicycles . . . bicycles lined up by a canal."

Elle spoke to herself. "He had people kidnap your mom and Melly and take them to Amsterdam?" She set out to pace, but nearly bumped into the wall. "And now he has joined them there?"

She turned and walked back to the counter. "No. He wouldn't tell us where he is, or where his assets are being kept. But if he's not in Amsterdam, where is he?"

I switched the sink on and off seven times, running away from the thought of Mom and Melly as assets.

"Go with the plan," Elle said. "You'll be fine. See you in a few days, okay?"

She kissed me for several seconds, but I was too worried to enjoy it.

We heard the final boarding call for my flight.

"You gotta go. Here"—Elle handed me a phone—"this is a burner."

"A what?"

"Safe to use, but for a limited period of time. And it's got the application. Practice it with Miguel when you get to Amsterdam. Call me at your connection."

I stayed put, holding her hand until she pushed me out of the room and nearly into the man I'd met an hour ago, outside the airport. He sat in the driver's seat of an electric shuttle and acted like he'd never seen me before. "You called for assistance, sir?"

"Could you take me to the New York gate?" I limped into the seat.

"Of course."

He leaned toward me. "You know, I'm grateful for Paul every day. Got me away from some bad shit. Gave me a new life."

A raised scar stretched from his earlobe, down his neck, onto his shoulder.

"That's good to hear."

He glided to a stop at my gate. "Make sure you have everything, sir."

I picked up the briefcase I'd given him outside the airport.

Shortly after the Boeing 747 carrying me and two hundred other people leveled off above the clouds, a flight attendant said, "Mr. Miguel Sanchez? There's a gentleman waiting for you in the upstairs lounge."

"Thank you," I said, and added, under my breath, "that's just great."

Was it Veeder? Was he expecting Miguel or me? I shot two mini bottles of vodka.

While most people were taking out their cell phones and electronic notebooks, I shifted the pistol in my briefcase to where I could retrieve it in a hurry.

The flight attendant pointed me to the stairs. At the top, I met a handsome man in his late sixties. He smiled warmly and spoke with a British accent. "David, my good fellow, won't you come in."

I pulled out my Glock and inspected the room.

He ignored me, relaxing onto a vinyl stool next to a bar offering normal-sized glasses and bottles of alcohol. He wore stubble like a criminal; his aquamarine eyes twinkled beneath white hair.

"Where do you fit into this mess?" I asked.

"Put the gun down. Let's chat."

"I can chat and aim a gun at the same time. Start talking."

He took a drink from his glass. "Well done. You've become a good operative. Not bad for an academic chap."

The vodka I'd slammed hit my bloodstream, calming me. I asked, "Where does Elaine want to get married?"

He smiled. "She wants a lunar event."

I tucked my Glock back into my briefcase. "I think this is where you offer me a drink, Paul not-your-real-name Smith."

He laughed and poured tonic water and vodka into a glass at the same time, then handed the glass to me. "To Zircon."

"Cheers."

We gulped toward insobriety.

"But since that discovery," I said, "all I've done is almost gotten killed and put the lives of too many people on the line."

"We'll recover your mother and ex." He used his glass to point at me. "And you've done a lot, David. You've brought us critical information about Veeder."

I tossed back my drink. "Then we finally have evidence to take to the cops?"

"Not by a long shot," he said. "Dave, I have a confession. You might not like it."

"Then don't tell me until I've had more to drink." I set my glass back on the bar. "Hold the soda."

CHAPTER 23

I called Elle as I hustled from the arrival gate to the flight bound for Amsterdam.

She answered. "You good?"

"I met Paul."

"On the plane?"

"The lounge."

"Ah, yes, that's Paul. Is he with you?"

"No, he had some job to check on in Manhattan."

"Right. Listen, did you give any more thought to Melly painting the birds?"

"There's nothing about Amsterdam and birds."

"Forget Amsterdam. Just anything. Anything at all. Did you have something you used to say to each other about birds? Did you have a pet bird?"

A woman with long, curly fingernails lost the grip on her suitcase; it toppled to the floor in front of me.

I hopped over it. "Forget Amsterdam?"

"Yeah, just think."

I flipped through Melly's paintings in my mind. The fog cleared from my memory of one of her canvasses where birds flew over slate rooftops. I closed my eyes to see more of it.

My shoulder banged into a man's backpack. He lurched sideways.

"Sorry," I said.

The rooftops in the painting were part of a large castle. I stopped walking.

A young woman slammed into me. "Hey!"

"David?" Elle asked.

I searched for a list of departures, spotted the screen, and darted to it, cutting off a ten-year-old boy.

His dad reprimanded me: "Watch it!"

"David? Are you there?"

A flight to Paris flashed *Boarding*.

"Elle, I'm going to Paris."

"What?"

"Thank God for you, thank you so much. Elaine, I, I . . . I really have to go."

"Tell me what you're doing!"

I rushed down a wide hallway. "Melly painted birds flying over Mont-Saint-Michel in Normandy. Those were the only birds she ever painted. They're in France, not Holland!"

In a full sprint, I cut around people and their rolling luggage as I headed toward the gate.

"I found a website," she said, and began reading to me. "'Mont-Saint-Michel, surrounded by water at high tide, was built in honor of the archangel Michael.'" She muttered to herself, "Yes, right, whatever . . ." She continued, "'There are several floors, rooms, and passageways—'" She interrupted herself and then said, "Okay, here, listen to this: 'It is completely deserted at night, as it now functions as a tourist attraction. It has recently been shut down to the public for renovations that are to begin next month' . . . You cannot go there alone, David."

"I'm not going there. Miguel is." I hung up the phone before she could talk me out of it.

I fell into the counter at the gate. "Are there seats left?"

The clerk squinted into her computer. "I have seats. But you'll have to go to ticketing and back through security." She glanced at her wrist gadget that kept track of her steps. "You have fourteen minutes."

I raced away with my briefcase, contemplating where to hide a gun. I ducked into a bathroom and waited for a lull. I pulled a food bag out of the trash, stuffed my gun into it, and threw it back in the bin.

After purchasing the ticket, I convinced security to let me go through ahead of others, given that my flight was about to leave, and then I charged back to the restroom. A janitor finished tying off the garbage bag in which I'd placed my gun and put the bag on his cart.

I gave up on the gun and ran to the gate.

The same woman was watching for me. "It's been twenty-five minutes."

"Please," I panted. "My mom is in France. She's sick."

"We have rules and it's past the—"

"Oh, Gladys!" another woman in uniform said. "He's not a terrorist. We haven't closed it yet. Let him on the damn plane."

Gladys pushed my ticket under the scanner.

"Thank you both." I pulled a tissue from a box on the counter and swabbed my sticky forehead, careful not to touch the makeup on my nose and cheeks. "Thank you so much."

Immediately after boarding, I pressed Mom on my phone and bent over to hide from the flight attendant who had requested that all cellular devices be turned off.

Liam's voice slithered into my ear. "Dr. Denlon. Your shenanigans are keeping me from my missions."

"Liam! Has my mom gotten her medication?"

"David, if you'd let the Lord into your heart, your stress would be relieved."

I felt the confused stare of my seatmate searing into my left shoulder. I twisted my head toward him and smiled at his rusty mustache.

His look transformed into a nod. "Hello."

I nodded in return and then used my hand to cover my mouth and the phone. "Answer me, you son of a bitch, if my mother has already died, I'm not coming. I'm about to board a plane to Amsterdam, and I'm not setting foot on it if I don't hear my mother's voice!"

"Calm down, Denlon."

Dead silence made me worry that the call had dropped.

The flight attendant headed toward me, motioning to my phone.

I sat up and took my hand from my mouth to put one finger in the air.

"Davey, sweetie . . ."

"Mom, you're okay? You're taking your meds?"

"Yes, dear."

The attendant set her hand on my shoulder. "Phone, honey?"

"Mom, you're in that storybook, my favorite when I was a kid, right?"

Mom was quiet.

I smiled at the attendant, keeping my finger in the air.

"Oh. Yes," Mom said. "That's right. It's just like in the book, exactly, your *very* favorite."

"Satisfied, Denlon?" Liam asked.

I hung up.

"Thank you, honey." The flight attendant pushed her face too close. "And I have to ask, what was your favorite storybook?"

I looked past the two people to my left, out the oval window, beyond luggage carts parked on the asphalt, and to a small patch of blue-and-white sky. My fluttery stomach settled.

I turned back to the fiftysomething woman. She wore orange lipstick to match her airline-issued orange silk scarf, and eagerly awaited my answer.

"It was about a frog who leaves the forest and discovers a big castle overlooking the ocean."

"How nice." She lingered with that look, the one I'd seen so many times. *Something must be wrong with him. What is it?* I stared at my knees until she left.

The next eight hours did not go to waste. I ordered extra food and drank several bottles of water. After upgrading my Wi-Fi pass, I memorized the driving directions from the Charles de Gaulle Airport to Mont-Saint-Michel, studied the floor plan of the monument, and reserved a rental car.

Soon after landing, I was speeding by furry green fields on the A13 toward Normandy. The angler's shop I had researched wasn't far off my route; I acquired a folding knife and returned to the road.

The knife sat, closed, on the passenger's seat, and I imagined it talking. *What the hell are you doing with me? You can't even cut vegetables without making a mess. How do you expect to use me to defend yourself?*

My mind ran away from the knife and into reviewing my discussion with Paul, on my flight from La Paz to New York.

"Okay, that should do it." My empty glass hit the bar. "What's your confession?"

"Saving you and this project is not my sole objective," Paul said.

"What else are you doing?"

"I've been after Veeder a long time."

"You're using me and my project to get Veeder?"

"It's more like I'm taking this opportunity to—"

He found my hand in front of his face. "Using me to bring down Veeder. Yes or no?"

Paul sighed, finished his drink, and poured another.

I pushed my glass toward him. "Yes or no?"

He gushed more vodka into my glass. "Yes."

An urge blasted up from my gut and down my arm, and although I refrained from throwing the glass, my hand still jerked, splashing my precious vodka.

"David, I appreciate the import of this project. So much so that my agency is now funding it. I may be after Veeder, but I'm also going full throttle to protect you and the researchers, so that you're free from concern and can focus on your work."

I fell into my head. *Free from concern.* I picked up my glass. *Free.* I lightly banged its green-tinted bottom edge on the bar. *Tap-tap tap-tap tap-tap tap.* I hadn't been free in a long time. I closed my eyes and saw my untied Snoopy shoes, as I skipped down a seemingly endless row of grapevines in our neighbor's vineyard, *free from all concern.* Back then life was storybooks, petting Arthur, daydreaming, and grilled cheese sandwiches. Until a cold virus stuck me in bed and I learned that I was *Spectrum Boy.* Then the deluge of stress over navigating school, college, and my PhD program. Melly's depression, her infidelity, our divorce. My dad's defective heart slowly failing. *Tap-tap tap-tap tap-tap tap.*

"Let's talk about something else," Paul said. "Do you know how difficult it was to find this airline that still uses 747s to fly from La Paz, so we could have this lounge to talk?"

"Lounge," I slurred.

Paul's eyes stayed on me.

"You don't see *first-class lounges* in tribes, among members of communities that depend on each other and live off the land."

Paul seemed to feel a draft. He adjusted his watchband.

I continued, "People in tribes and small villages have special community spaces, of course. Places where leaders meet, sacred areas of worship. But they haven't designed their society with places of *leisure* for those who are stronger, better hunters, or have gathered more food while those with less are excluded."

He took in the orange-and-gray décor as if for the first time. "We're a disgusting lot, humans. We tend to leave ethics behind as we advance." His half smile was shaded with worry that he hadn't gotten the answer right.

"That's what I don't understand," I said. "Your reaction. Just now."

Paul looked down at himself and then back up.

"I tell you something I've noted in my exploration—most tribes don't exclude based on a class system. And you become distressed. Like instead of stating a fact, I said something untrue or scary."

I swallowed my vodka as if it were water. "Everybody loves my insight when I'm giving a presentation. Up on stage. Entertaining. But say the same stuff one-on-one? In a serious conversation, to make a real impact? Then I'm crazy."

"Not at all." Paul rested his knuckles on my arm. "It's just unexpected, such profound information in a chitchat. When you said that bit about lounges and exclusion, it grounded me, and I hadn't known I was up in the wind."

I sighed.

"How's Joseph?" he asked, changing the subject again. "Does he seem happy, working for the airport?"

"He says he's grateful for you every day."

I entered a roundabout and exited toward the city of Avranches. My mental playback continued.

Paul took a deep breath. "It was nuts what you did, surrendering yourself to Gustav and Vladmir. But it was productive. You brought us valuable intelligence and my agents have used it to find more. Veeder, I'm afraid, is using Liam as a front. And it's flawless."

I slumped. "What do you mean?"

"It seems, from what we've learned, that Veeder pays for Liam's travel to places of scarcity and hardship, in historically significant locales. Specifically, in communities with relics that Veeder wants to get his hands on."

"Wait." My inebriated brain struggled to understand. "So Liam thinks his missions are funded by some rich guy who cares about helping people. But really, Veeder sends Liam to preach in remote areas where there are artifacts he wants to claim?"

"You got it."

"That's fraud. He's swindling people out of their valuable heirlooms."

"You know Patrick Veeder is smarter than that. He's careful not to label anything an 'exchange.' He asks only for Liam to suggest to the community leaders that they provide a token by which Veeder can remember the place where 'the Lord's work has been done.'"

I slowed for the next roundabout. White cows with brown spots rotated their lower jaws, almost in sync, on the hillside to my right.

My phone rang for the fifth time. I shut off the ringer and checked my rearview mirror—nothing suspicious.

"Tokens?" I asked. "Like gifts?"

Paul tried to pour himself another drink, but nothing came out. He inspected the bottle as if it had malfunctioned.

"Here's how it works," he said. "Liam brings his version of biblical teachings, along with tools, medical supplies, and other things that, at least temporarily, make life easier to endure in remote places with scant resources and unhelpful governments. He asks the people to express gratitude, not in money, but by donating a symbol of their culture. Some run him out of their villages. But from the information we have now gathered, most of these struggling people appreciate his kindness and offer one of their relics."

I tipped the last of my drink into my mouth, savoring it.

"Of course," Paul continued, "these people have no concept of a global market wherein these items could fetch large sums of money."

I drove around a traffic circle twice to ensure that I was choosing the right exit. My phone flashed again but I ignored the call.

"Sadly," Paul said, deflated, "Veeder's scheme is clean."

"How could it be?"

"It's clean because people *gift* these artifacts. They arguably have received inspiration to make the donation, as Liam's preaching is provided in earnest. Liam doesn't directly profit and seems genuinely unaware of the piles of money the relics are realizing."

We searched our empty glasses before returning them to the bar.

Paul shrugged. "Patrick Veeder merely makes religious donations, which Liam legally uses for traveling and subsistence while he's preaching. No law enforcement agency or system of justice could make any charges stick to Veeder, in terms of theft. Murder, on the other hand . . . But he hides that far too well."

"Okay," I said. "This is a lot of heartache that I can't do anything about."

"Oh, David, you've done the most wonderful thing of all. You've impaired the mighty Patrick Veeder. You've set him back. This changes everything. This gives us the upper hand."

"It doesn't feel like it."

Paul rubbed his chin and smiled. "Poetic, really. Your first go-round with a gun, I'm assuming? And now he's compromised. We must not let up. If we are to find a way for Veeder to be held accountable, it will be now, when he is weak and knocked off his game."

I didn't smile.

Paul collected himself. "I know you're nervous about your mom and ex-wife."

"I am, but that's not it. I don't think Veeder is the big catch."

"Do explain."

"Patrick Veeder is a caricature. He's one-sided. Easy to hate. You don't labor over destroying him any more than you deliberate about getting rid of lice. But the system that rewards and insulates him? The societal construct that encourages people to revere him? To consider him for public office? That's the problem. And what about Liam? He is a victim and a perpetrator at the same time. We can't just arrest all of the Liam Ericsons. Indeed, we've abandoned the Liam Ericsons. And it is through them that the Patrick Veeders of the world gain power."

Paul slowly blinked. "Well, even pissed on vodka, you are ever the professor, eh?"

I decided that I liked Paul.

"Ah, there's a smile," he said. "Thank you. Warms my heart. Listen, you may be right, philosophically and all, but let me tell you something.

"Call him one-dimensional, but Patrick Veeder is a narcissistic, power-hungry man who kills for access to rare, historical objects that are often the only items of value for sorely underprivileged people. The few who have attempted to bring his crimes to light have disappeared. Veeder doesn't just kill people who question or challenge his esteemed global status and monumental wealth; he erases them, leaving their loved ones with no understanding of the assumed death, and no remains to bury or burn."

"Yes, Paul, I know. And he's gonna kill me, too."

I pushed Paul out of my mind and focused on the road. There were many miles between me and that castle, and I had to get there before Veeder realized that I hadn't gone to Amsterdam.

CHAPTER 24

Windswept clouds hovered above rolling hills for a perfect picture I had no time to take. Paul lit up my phone again.

I answered.

"David." His voice—heavy, on edge—came through the car's speaker. "Elaine updated me. You must not go there alone. I've redirected everyone to France; Casey should be there first. We can strike tomorrow morning."

Mont-Saint-Michel appeared on the evening horizon. A majestic, dominating edifice seated on a giant rock in the English Channel.

"That will be too late."

"Listen to me, David. There's something that happens when you get shot at but not hit, and have close calls, like explosions, that don't harm you. Are you listening? Your mind starts to discount the danger. The activity becomes familiar. And Liam, too. He seems less of a threat because of your time with him."

A flock of birds flew over the road on which trams would soon deliver visitors to the renovated Mont-Saint-Michel. Just as in Melly's painting, their outstretched wings carried them over the slate rooftops that snuggled up to the base of the fortress.

"David?"

The mountain-castle, with an abbey at its peak and a medieval village in its foothills, stood precariously on a tidal island. Were Mom and Melly in its dungeon? I pictured them in shackles until a memory took over my mind.

My dad and I sipped Sangiovese as we restacked storage containers in the garage.

Mom came out to pick up our dirty rag pile. "Sweetie, he's sixteen."

"Exactly." My dad smiled. "In Europe he'd be drinking wine at home without anyone thinking twice about it."

Our garage always had a wet-dog smell even though we didn't own a dog. I found relief by sniffing the earthy aroma in my fat wineglass.

Psychology textbooks caught my eye through the clear plastic cover of a storage bin. I opened the lid.

"Oh, leave those." Mom snapped the bin shut.

"I thought you got your degree in English, Mom."

"I did. Go on, put the box up."

"Why are you saving psychology books?"

My dad chimed in: "She was shooting for her PhD in that subject."

I drank more wine, until Mom pulled away my glass and handed me a bottle of water.

Twelve years later, when Mom cried as she read my dissertation, I had considered that raising *Spectrum Boy* had kept her from finishing her own PhD.

"David, are you there?" Paul's tone had become desperate.

The sharp spire at the top of the monument took on a shiny appearance in the afterglow of the recently departed sun.

"David?"

"It's my mom in there. I have to get her."

"No. You'll call and tell Veeder the plane was delayed. It's one day!"

"Paul, I know you've done this sneak-around spy shit for a long time. But has your mother ever been the person you were trying to save?"

"No. And that's precisely why you cannot go. You're making an emotional decision. You don't have the training for this. Veeder's deal to release your mother and Melly in exchange for you was a ruse—you know that, right? We only get them back covertly, or by force."

I parked. "You're just afraid I'm messing up your chance to land Veeder."

"No, David. Veeder has only kept your mother and ex-wife alive to bait you. As soon as he has you on the hook, you all die. What more can I say to convince you?"

Mont-Saint-Michel became gray in the twilight.

"I don't know much about Veeder," I said, "but I know this. He operates with very few people in his inner circle. That's good for keeping secrets, but it's bad for surprise attacks. He's recovering from being shot, waiting to hear that I've arrived in Amsterdam. His guard is down for two more hours at best. The chance to save my mom and Melissa is right now."

Paul's sigh was more of a moan—long and filled with sadness.

I picked up the folding knife and practiced opening and closing it, nearly slicing off my finger.

CHAPTER 25

The tide would soon consume the shore, cutting off Mont-Saint-Michel from the mainland. I had no idea how I was going to get Mom and Melly out of this monument, but it would be a lot harder if we had to swim.

At the base of the front wall, it took two tries for my nervous fingers to type a text message to Miguel and Ann.

—*Ready to call?*

Miguel sent a thumbs-up.

With him and Ann secretly on the line, I called the number in the directions I had been texted.

Liam answered. "You've arrived."

My gut contracted. Could he see me? I read the notes I'd written on a torn piece of paper. "I'm where the directions said. On the street called Prinsengracht? There are lots of bikes. The canal is on my left. Where do I go?"

"You'll see a streetlight with a green ribbon around the pole," he said. "Go to the entrance of the nearest building."

"You'll be at the door?"

"No. Gregorio will verify that you are alone and unarmed."

Liam hung up, terminating the conference call.

Inside the front gate, a watchman in a kiosk read a book under a construction light. A nearby sign read *No Entry. Closed for Renovations.*

Was he just a security guard? Or did he work for Veeder?

I lobbed a rock over the steep-pitched roof to his right. It banged down the walkway, drawing him, more curious than concerned, from his post.

I climbed over the gate's slick metal pickets and sprinted up the Grand Rue, away from the watchman. The narrow street ascended into the belly of the fortress and was crowded with signs in various shapes—an ice cream cone outside a dessert shop, a black sheep in front of a sweater store. For years, this cobblestone avenue had delivered the medieval-village experience to thousands of tourists, but now the feel was ghostly, with every establishment's wooden door closed and locked, and the overhead lamps, strung on chains, turned off.

I charged up the steep staircase to the abbey. A stone floor led me into the nave of the church, and from there I could see a large, arched opening. It was the entrance to a vacant courtyard—an open, outdoor space with another construction light perched in the middle, on a sturdy tripod. The light illuminated the center of the yard but relinquished the walls to the blue haze of near night.

A cell phone rang. From the other side of the courtyard? Wasn't there a balcony on that side, according to the layout I'd studied?

I walked sideways across the yard, scraping my back along the stone wall, to discover that my memory was correct. With a peek into the balcony, I saw shadowy figures and a battery-fueled lantern on a marble-top bistro table. A second look revealed Patrick Veeder stretched out on a beach lounger, facing away from me, with a cashmere blanket tucked neatly over his legs. His assistant, Darin, stood beyond him at a portable table, battling the wind as he organized pill bottles and a container of ointment. Two other men huddled in conversation in the far corner.

Mom and Melly were not there. *Could there actually be a dungeon in this castle?*

One of the two men said in French, *"But I don't care about the money, I need to get out of here."*

The other man responded, *"Do you know any other doctors who could take over for you?"* I knew that voice. *"If you leave, I'll be punished."* It was Christopher. The man who had alerted me to the poison wine, and who had begged me to shoot Veeder until he was dead.

The doctor sounded both infuriated and terrified. *"Tell him I said he's healing and doesn't need any more care. The bullet's out, just watch for infection. And get him inside, out of this wind."*

Veeder, oblivious to their exchange, lay in his chair with a phone to his ear, surveying the approaching sea over the low parapet wall.

He said into his phone, "Denlon's arrived? Invite him in, make small talk. Point him down the stairs, then throw the acid."

I pulled my head back and pressed myself into the wall, texting Miguel too quickly to be accurate.

—*They goin throw acid n you!*

With satisfaction, as if Veeder knew I could hear him, he uttered, "Burning skin should get you to talk, David."

I worked up the nerve to peek in again. Veeder's free hand rotated slowly at the wrist, in a twirling motion. His spiny fingers fiddled with something blue attached to a leather cord.

My zircon pendant. But not only that. The small white box containing the marquise crystal—the brown zircon that had preserved the sister-race DNA and the foreign material—sat beside him on the bistro table, with a rock on top of it to keep the ocean wind from blowing it away.

It was all right there. My original finds, except the pendant I had given to Carrie.

I watched Veeder's pale thumb rub up and down my helpless blue crystal and remembered how I had made that discovery. My digging had led me to a football-sized rock, and I had drilled into it, out of curiosity, given its shape. The rock broke apart, almost too easily, exposing the zircon pieces—the blue and the white, contoured like solid figure eights, and the brown marquise.

"Time for your pills," Darin said.

Christopher added, "When you finish with your call, I'll tell you the good news from the doctor."

Darin stepped toward Veeder and looked my way. I pushed my back into the wall and stayed still. Had he seen me?

"What was that?" Darin said. "Christopher, did you see that, like a shadow, in the courtyard?"

Should I run?

Veeder said into his phone, "What? How did he get away? Go after him!"

Miguel had escaped.

"What shadow?" Christopher said. "You better give him his meds."

Silence. What was happening?

"I'm sorry to interrupt, sir," Darin finally said. "But you need to take your medication."

I quietly scampered out of the courtyard and set about finding Mom and Melly. Recalling the floor plan, I was reassured when I came upon the rectangular patch of grass surrounded by arches—my reference point. From there, I ran through the doorway that, according to my understanding of the layout, would lead me up to the bell tower. But instead of locating an inside set of stairs, I landed outside on another terrace.

How had I gotten disoriented?

I backtracked, feeling my way down a dark stairwell, and found myself in a vast, empty room. Candles formed a cross on the floor. *Liam.*

There were two mammoth fireplaces—big enough to store cars—but the candlelight was too faint to disclose more than their openings.

Whimpers echoed about the room.

"Mom, Melissa?"

The sounds multiplied from gagged mouths I couldn't see. I turned on the light on my burner phone and there they were—Mom and Melly, in one of the giant hearths.

I rushed to them, less careful about being quiet than I should have been. Melly's stringy hair hung in her ashen face; puffy skin circled Mom's eyes. Handkerchiefs had been pulled between their lips and tied behind their heads.

Liam's voice reverberated down the stairwell. "Do not take that tone with me, Darin. Tell Mr. Veeder I'm getting them now."

As Liam continued down the stairs, Mom and Melly panted faster. I shut off the phone's light and unfolded my knife, trying to figure out how to stab someone.

Darin called out from beyond the top of the stairwell.

Liam responded, "I can't hear you! Hold on." We listened until we were sure he was stomping back up the steps.

I cut the thin rope, unstrapping their hands from the iron ringlets on the wall, then bent down to the twine around their feet. Was it reinforced with plastic? I sawed and swiped at it until I cut through. They removed their gags.

Mom held the back of my sweatshirt and Melly squeezed my hand as we jogged through a small exterior walkway and into a room with rotund columns.

I whispered, "Are you guys okay?"

Melly stared at me. *What did you do to get me kidnapped?*

"Davey," Mom asked with wide eyes, "what happened to your face?"

I felt my cheeks, bumpy from the fake scars.

"Oh, no. Mom. I'm fine. It's just a disguise."

Liam's shoes hammered the floor behind us as he called out in a tone that was almost affectionate: "Where are you gals? Don't do this!"

I got my bearings and led Mom and Melly up to the bell tower, down spiral steps, and across a room with walls made of large stone blocks. "You okay, Mom?"

"Keep going!" She hopped down the next set of stairs before I could help her, and we dashed by the drape-covered tables in the gift shop, arriving outside, back on the Grand Rue.

Melly's scalding eyes continued her silent demand. *What did you do?*

"I went on that trek I told you about," I whispered. "Looking for evidence of a previous human race. I found it, Melly, I found it. But this creep, Patrick Veeder, wants to steal it. He kidnapped you to bait me. I'm sorry. I had no idea this would happen. Jesus, Melissa, really . . . I had no idea."

Her face softened. She nodded. "Let's get out of here."

They followed me down the road and into an alley. "I'll get the guy at the entrance to leave his post," I said. "And then you help each other over the gate. Stay in this alley until it's safe to go." I pressed my keys into Melly's palm. "The car isn't too far away. If I don't make it out behind you, get help."

Mom and Melly held on to each other.

I raced down until I found the watchman, outside his kiosk and staring upward, straining to hear the garbled shouts between Darin and Liam.

He searched in the direction of my footsteps, the overhead light in his eyes. He drew his gun.

I stopped and put my hands up, noticing his scrappy build and crooked teeth.

I asked, "You speak English? You're working for Patrick Veeder?"

He didn't answer and kept his gun pointed at me.

"He's trouble, believe me," I said. "You should get out of here."

"Shut up. Go back up there," he ordered. "Move!"

I walked backward up the street as he came at me, his gun aimed at my face. After we passed the alley in which Mom and Melly were hiding, I stopped. "Where are you taking me?"

Melly peeked out at the guard's back.

"You don't get to question, keep going!"

Out of the corner of my eye, I saw Mom and Melly tiptoe downward and dissolve into the darkness.

I purposely tripped and fell backward.

"Get up!"

Darin burst out of the gift shop and nearly stepped on me, gasping, "Who is that? Wait, Denlon? Shit!"

He laid into the watchman. "Where'd those women go?"

"What women?"

Darin spotted Liam waddling after him through the gift shop. "Liam, go back! Tell Mr. Veeder that Denlon's here!"

"That's Denlon?"

Darin screamed, "He's in disguise, you moron!"

I stood up. Liam looked at me, speechless, before jogging away.

I craned my neck to see downward, over the shops and into the circle of light at the front gate. Mom was balancing her knee on Melly's shoulder, searching for a handhold on the spiky fence.

Darin observed me, the gears of his mind turning. He scolded the guard. "You left the front gate! They're getting away!" He charged down the Grand Rue.

Enticing the guard to give chase, I blasted up the stairway. After several steps, I stopped and turned around.

The guard was quickly climbing up toward me, leaning forward, watching his feet.

I launched myself onto his shoulders; we tumbled down to the landing. His gun bounced out of sight. He drove his elbow into my nose, and my brain felt like it had been punched. I rolled on top of him and jammed my knee into his groin. After getting to my feet, I again found the view of the gate below.

Mom fell to the ground on the other side of the fence. Melly pitched the car keys to her as Darin arrived.

"Go!" Melly yelled. "Get us help!"

Darin sprang onto the fence, but Melly jumped on his back; they slammed to the ground. He pushed her away, and before she could jump on him again, he scrambled over the gate, and sprinted after Mom.

The watchman, below me on the landing and back on his feet, reached for something strapped to his leg. When he withdrew a knife, I pulled out mine. His was bigger.

He leapt up two steps and posed, ready—and seemingly very able—to slice the blade into me. My kickboxing aerobics class rushed to mind. I hopped into position on my left foot—diverting his attention—and used my right leg to roundhouse-kick him in the head, sending him to his knees. We both panicked at the realization that our knives had flown from our hands and disappeared behind a thorny hedge.

An engine revved. I looked down to the entrance but saw no one. I heard a car screech and speed away.

Was Darin driving away with my mother? Where was Melly?

I pinched my bleeding nose and tried to stop shaking. Had I just made everything worse? Paul was right. I didn't have the training for this.

Chapter 26

I took stock. Darin had gone after Mom, and the guard was here, on the steps, holding his head and staggering. Who was protecting Veeder?

I stormed up the stairs again, this time feeling the burn in my legs. As I passed the winged statue of Saint Michel, I double glanced at the doctor trying to hide behind it—his frightened eyes begging me not to harm him.

When I bolted into the courtyard, a gunshot exploded and something whizzed by my ear. The bullet? I dove to the ground and scooted to the wall, far enough from the construction light to notice the stars dotting the moonless sky.

"Denlon!" Veeder had relocated himself away from the balcony. But where was he?

"I've swindled away your greatest discovery." Was he on the west side, his voice echoing east? "I've kidnapped your mom and ex-wife. Now I'm hurt. Unable to fire a straight shot. Can't you take me out?"

Hate filled me, powered me. I would charge so quickly across the courtyard that his bullets would miss me. I would choke him slowly, staring into his eyes—his last moments of life would be spent begging me for air.

Paul's words came to me: *You're making an emotional decision.*

I scurried toward the balcony instead.

Veeder shot, and *crack!* A shard of stone nicked my forehead.

I crouched down and went still.

The tired-out guard entered the courtyard. "Mr. Veeder?"

"Find Denlon," Veeder responded. "He's by the wall. Use the light."

The guard trotted toward the construction light.

"Oh, Professor . . . " Veeder said. "I saw Darin running after your beloved mother. I'm sure he has caught her. He will not only kill her. He will have his way with her first."

I could tell his location now and was supercharged with strength. I would sprint toward him, an attack from the side, and he would not be able to aim quickly enough to shoot me. I would knock the gun out of his hand, drag him to the balcony, and launch him into the rising tide, a hundred-foot fall.

I raised my back end up like a track runner in a starting block.

Just breathe. It was the voice of my father.

I exhaled and didn't move.

The guard lifted the tripod and waved the light, erasing the shadows that concealed me. I hurried through the entrance to the balcony.

The lantern was turned off, but there was enough glow from the construction light for me to see the blue zircon and the box on the bistro table. I removed the rock and took hold of my plastic container, then put the leather strap over my head and tucked the blue zircon into my shirt, pressing it to my heart.

The watchman said, "I don't see him, Mr. Veeder."

"Check the balcony."

I dipped my head over the edge of the wall. Wind soared up the fortress and blew the water out of my eyes. No ledges to land on. I lay flat on my back on the cold ground, pushed up the lounger and slid under it, and let it fall back down, on my nose.

The guard arrived behind the chair and shined his flashlight into the corners of the balcony.

I squeezed the box of evidence and the crystal, as if I could carry these things into eternity.

After half a minute, the guard said, "Not here, sir."

"Take my gun," Veeder said. "Stand out here and watch. I've got to lie down."

"Yes, sir."

Veeder moaned as he drew near the entrance. I snuck out from under the chair and stepped to the darkest corner of the balcony, away from the edge, stuffing the evidence box into the waistband of my pants. Veeder used a small flashlight to find the lounger and then carefully sat on it, clutching his chest.

I crept into position, reaching my hands out to choke him.

But I reeled them back in, reasoning that his guard would shoot me dead before Veeder would asphyxiate.

After catching his breath, Veeder extended his hand toward the marble-top table. He patted in several spots, slowly at first, then furiously, whacking his pillbox and the rock to the ground. He trained his light on the empty table, then at the floor.

The guard hurried over. "What was that? Are you okay?"

"I'm missing my . . ."

The guard noticed me. Before he could speak, I plunged into him, pushing his gun sideways into his chest. I pinned him against the wall and turned to Veeder.

"You're missing *what*? *My* evidence? It was never yours. Nothing is ever yours! I'm taking it back, you son of a bitch!"

I sprinted across the courtyard, somehow eluding the guard's bullets that pinged and ricocheted around me. I sped through the church and to the stairway.

My feet quickly drummed down the steps until I banged into someone running upward; we both flopped onto the landing. We slowly stood and stared at each other through the starlight.

It was Christopher.

I reached under my shirt, catching the evidence box that was about to pop out of my pants. Christopher held up his hands.

Did he really think the box under my shirt was a gun?

"I just want to leave," I said. I glanced over his shoulder, looking for the watchman, before continuing down the steps.

"Wait, please!" he said. "You're kidnapping me."

I stopped. "What?"

"Please. Veeder will hunt me down and kill me if I run away on my own."

I checked again for the guard.

"Listen," Christopher said. "I know a way out of here that isn't the front gate. I'll show you."

The guard shined his flashlight at us.

Christopher yelled, "Hector, stay there!"

Hector halted. I held the box on the inside of my shirt, pointing it toward Christopher.

"Step aside, Christopher," Hector said. "This is an easy shot."

"No, don't, Hector," Christopher said. "He has a gun!"

I yelled, "Get back in the courtyard or I'm going to shoot Christopher, just like I shot Veeder!"

"I'm not going anywhere," Hector said.

"Hector!" Christopher screamed. "I'm the only translator for the only doctor who will treat Mr. Veeder. Don't get me killed!"

Hector begrudgingly backed off, into the archway.

Christopher trotted down, past me, and I followed.

"David!" Melly whispered. She was hiding in the entryway of a souvenir shop.

I waved her to me, and we tracked Christopher through a passageway to the back of the restaurants, where we stopped.

Melly tucked her hair behind her ears and tried not to cry. "What's happening?"

"Don't worry," Christopher told her. "I know you saw me working for Veeder. But I'm helping you escape, and I'm leaving with you."

"Okay then," I said. "How do we get out of here?"

"Over the wall," he said blankly.

I crawled to the wall and peered over. The murky sea had reclaimed most of its territory, thirty-five feet below.

I considered and then ignored the possibility that Christopher was a double agent.

"Melly," I said, crawling back. "We have to go over that wall."

"What?"

"They won't think we had the nerve to do it."

"I *don't*."

"The water isn't deep yet. The sand is soft. We can land without hurting ourselves, and if we hurry, we can make it to the road before the tide covers it."

"This is the lowest spot in the whole place," Christopher said. "Anywhere else is too high to jump from."

Another car started in the distance and peeled away.

"The doctor," Christopher said. "Good for him."

We saw Darin shining a light from a balcony at the top of the fortress. A touch of relief calmed my stomach. "Mom must have gotten away."

Melly smiled, but only for a moment.

"Look, I'll go first," Christopher said. "But I'm telling you, we gotta go. Now."

Christopher lay on his stomach on the ridge of the wall. He spun on his belly until he was facing us and let his legs hang down behind him. He shut his eyes and then dropped out of sight.

We ran to look over the wall. A splash torpedoed up into the wind and became mist. We saw nothing else.

Melly sank down to the ground. "David, you know . . ."

"Yes, I know."

Melly was afraid of heights.

I put my hands on her shoulders. "Remember when we jumped off the rocks into that river, that time we were hiking?"

"I only jumped to shut you up. And that was half this distance!"

It had been a fifth of this distance, at the most.

"Okay, I know. And again, I'm sorry. But you survived, right? It didn't hurt?"

Her eyes welled with tears of acceptance, acceptance that she would be free-falling three stories into cold black water.

Melly would change her mind again if I didn't act. I sat on the wall and ignored my own fear. The wind screeched like a tea kettle. I hung from both hands and then questioned what I was doing. How deep or shallow was it? Was I about to break both of my legs and drown? Was Christopher going to attack me?

Melly put her hands on mine. "David!"

"It will be . . . okay . . ." I strained and then my hands slipped and my stomach shot up to my neck.

The water was deeper and colder than I had predicted. I stung all over and nausea dizzied me. The salty bitterness surged into my mouth as I found the surface.

I grabbed at the zircon around my neck. The box of evidence was gone. I frantically felt around in the water. The floating white container shimmered in the glow of the Milky Way. I retrieved it with numb fingers.

I lied: "Easy! C'mon!"

Melly sat on the wall for too long. Two flashlights twinkled from above.

"Melissa! Now!"

She screamed when she fell.

I swam to her as she thrashed. "*Ssshhhh!* You did it. C'mon."

We doggie-paddled to where our feet could touch ground and then fought the suction of the sand.

"This way!" Christopher guided us out of the muck and onto the mainland.

The three of us racewalked down the road, away from Mont-Saint-Michel, trying unsuccessfully to control our shaking.

A car slowly approached us head-on, its lights off. Had Veeder called one of his henchmen from a nearby town? The land around us was level and open; there was no place to hide.

The car stopped and the rear window hummed down. "Davey?"

"Mom!"

Casey was at the wheel. He asked, "Who's the guy?"

Christopher put his hands up.

"Um," I said. Nothing else came to my lips.

Mom yelled, "He's with the men who took us!"

"I'm escaping, too," Christopher said. "I'm unarmed."

Casey tore out of the car and patted Christopher down, then handcuffed him.

"He's okay," I said. "He helped us out."

"He's riding in the trunk," Casey said.

"Seriously?"

I let Melly have the front seat for better access to the heater vents. I sat in the back seat, dripping, next to Mom.

Casey closed the trunk and relocated a piece of luggage to the floorboard in front of Mom.

"He's on our side," I said, as Casey got back into the car. "He's the one who told me about the poison."

"Don't worry about him," Casey said. "I switched his cuffs to the front and covered him with a jacket."

Casey turned the car around, scolding me as he peeled away. "David, you don't listen. I told you to stop doing this shit."

Mom held my cold, wet hand.

"How'd you know to come here?" I asked.

"Paul wasn't going to leave you hanging, even though you decided, again, to go rogue." He checked his side mirror. "I was with Sunny, not on the Amsterdam assignment, so Paul could quickly reroute us here."

"Where's Sunny?"

"I left him at a bar in the village up the road."

"How'd you find my mom?"

"Was driving to the monument and saw someone skid into a gas station. Your mom got out and she matched the description, so I intercepted her. Your rental car was bigger, so I took it."

"Tell me we are finally going to the police."

"Paul says no."

I shuddered. Mom rubbed my shoulders to warm me up, inspecting my face again.

"And the others?" I asked.

"Miguel and Ann got out of Amsterdam and are headed to the meeting point. Elaine's flight was delayed, but she'll get there."

Elaine. Just hearing her name soothed me.

We hadn't fully parked when Sunny ran out of the pub, hugging his computer bag.

Mom stepped out of the car.

"Professor's mom?" He embraced her, nearly dropping his bag.

"Yes, hi, sweetheart," Mom said. "We gotta go. Sit by David."

They got in and Casey took off again. Sunny examined my face. "Does that hurt?"

"What?"

"Your nose is swollen and your head is cut."

"I'm fine, Sunny. Look what I got."

I clicked on the ceiling light.

"No," Casey said with a frown. "Dude!"

"What?"

Mom said, "When you're sneaking away in the dark, dear, you don't use lights."

"Exactly," Casey said. "Even your mom knows."

"Okay, just a sec—"

I fished down my wet shirt to pull out my zircon, and I showed Sunny the white box.

"Professor! You got the evidence back!" Sunny used the back of the passenger's seat as a punching bag. Melly leaned forward.

Casey quietly said to Melly, "He gets excited, don't worry. I'm Casey, by the way."

"Melissa," she said, still with her chin to her knees. "Nice to meet you."

Sunny studied the zircon.

Casey peered at me in the rearview mirror. "You snuck that stuff away? As in, Veeder might not know you took it?"

"I told him I was taking it, and I called him a son of a bitch."

Casey sighed. "We have to go over the meaning of 'covert.' What about your new friend in the trunk?"

"Made it look like I kidnapped him."

"Holy Jesus," Casey said. "And really, can we turn off the light?"

"Wait!" Sunny said, his fingers rubbing along the edges of the crystal.

Mom smacked the light off and patted Casey's shoulder. "Thanks, Mrs. D."

Sunny mumbled, "I bet that's one of the keystones."

"Keystones?" I asked. "What are you talking about?"

"Musa showed me this morning on our video call," Sunny said. "They've uncovered these little spaces, where things need to fit. Things shaped like an hourglass, like this zircon."

"Spaces on what?"

"On the top of the city or whatever they're digging up."

"Hold on, Sunny." My frigid hand gripped his arm. "How many spaces are there—how many keystones are supposed to fit into them?"

"Two. Did you find another crystal like this at the site?"

I stared. My teeth chattered.

"Oh, Davey," Mom said. "You have to change out of those wet clothes."

Sunny asked again, "Professor? Do you have the other zircon crystal?"

CHAPTER 27

"David, you're sure of that?"

"Yes, Paul, American."

Casey stood next to me at the window as we enjoyed a far-reaching view—all the way up to the bell tower of the monolithic church. He slowly enunciated the town's name. "Saint Ee-MEEL-yon."

I corrected him: "Sahn ah-mil-lee-ohn."

"Mate," Paul said, handing me a glass of wine, "you said your knees were shaking. You had just seen a bomb and a frightened young girl. Are you sure—"

"I'm sure! Their accent was American."

Casey left the window and settled himself on the chaise longue. "Paul, that mom and her little girl were probably from the States, on vacation in London. Or visiting someone. I think the white crystal is long gone." He used his toes to push off his shoes. "On another note, this house you rented for us is amazing. Love the furniture."

Miguel pulled the thick drapes shut in front of my face. He returned to his laptop to monitor the feeds from the cameras he had mounted outside.

I spun around. "Paul, we could have died. Darin could have gotten to my mom. Melly could have drowned. Catching Veeder isn't worth our lives. Certainly he's done enough for us to go to the police?"

"Who is this magical group you keep referring to as 'the police'?" Paul seemed startled by his loud voice. He lowered it. "Local law enforcement agencies are just that—local. They'll turn this over to a federal or an international agency. Who do you think has more influence at that level—us or Veeder? I know this isn't your cup of tea. But you are a brilliant fellow. So please notice that Mr. Veeder has the kinds of connections which allow him to shack up at a fucking UNESCO World Heritage site."

I swallowed more wine.

"Well, Dave?" Casey said. "Show Christopher your talent."

Christopher meekly sat with one hand cuffed to a chair, while Elaine researched information about him on her laptop.

It calmed me, sniffing my glass. I sipped one more time. "Cab Franc, this region."

"Damn," Casey said. "You should go on, like, *Wine Jeopardy!*"

I watched Elaine's silky hands typing on her computer and wondered when I could hold them next.

Paul relaxed into a recliner. "This furniture *is* nice." He set down his drink, careful to use a coaster. "David, there is every reason to celebrate and no need to be upset. Your mom and Melly are rescued and unharmed. You recovered the blue-zircon pendant, and the crystal with the evidence. The discovery site in Guatemala is Patrick-proof. And the icing on the cake is that Christopher has joined us, and he has provided extensive intelligence on Patrick Veeder's secret operations. This, Professor, is what is called 'turning the tables.'"

My nervous stomach disagreed with him. I used one finger to slightly part the drapes and tried to lose myself in the afternoon sky.

It was our second day in the village of Saint-Émilion—one of France's many historic towns with ancient yet sturdy walls, and pedestrian-only flat-stone corridors lined with window sills holding flower pots. The first day had been spent shopping in the larger, neighboring town of Libourne, to stock up on clothing, food, and office supplies.

Sunny pinged around the open-concept house—the kitchen, dining area, living space, and front entry occupied the same room—setting up the printer, connecting the television monitor to his laptop, and spreading out pictures and notes.

Mom and Melly diced and stirred, creating a garlicky aroma.

Miguel spotted Ann in one of the live-feed windows on his screen, walking up the driveway. She entered the house with a small white bag, saying, "I love pharmacies in Europe."

Mom's blood pressure medication.

"Thank you, Ann," I said.

Casey added more wine to my glass. "David, you're sure you don't remember if they said what subway station they were headed to?"

"That's enough." Elaine shut her laptop. "You've gotten everything out of him that he knows."

Mom shook salt into a pan, nodding in agreement.

I reached my hand out to Elaine but she leaned away from it. I followed her to the bedroom. "Thanks for saving me from their grilling. I wasn't going to remember anything else, no matter how many different ways they asked."

Elaine's frustrated tone didn't match her words. "You seem like everything is okay with Melly."

"Ah, yeah, her and my mom are both okay. Shell-shocked. But better now."

"So . . . you and Melly are working things out?"

"Working what out?"

"Well, *she's* workin' it."

"Huh?"

"David, don't."

"Don't what?"

"Christ!" She stomped away.

Sunny called out, "Hey, they're probably awake now, at the site."

"Very good," Paul said.

I tried to get *confused* off my face as I returned to the living room.

Casey freed Christopher's hand. "Don't give us a reason to put the cuff back on. Or shoot you."

"Welcome to the team." Ann handed Christopher a glass of wine.

Musa was on the screen in a flash.

"What's your update, Moose?" Sunny asked.

"We've gotten a lot of digging done." His voice cut off. Meredith put her arm around him as he coughed and cleared his throat. "There aren't words."

Jeremy reached for the screen. "Let's just show them." He spun his computer around.

They had unearthed the upper part of the structure.

"What . . . in the world?" Paul said. "Where are you guys?"

"Down slope, but up on a ridge," Meredith said. "Easier to see the whole thing from here."

"It looks like a huge luxury hotel was built into the volcano," Ann remarked, flabbergasted.

Made of what looked like squares of black glass, it stretched into the distance, maybe covering the length of three aircraft carriers. It gleamed in the sun as if it were fresh off the factory floor, and not coming out of a billion-year-long hibernation.

"What kind of material is that?" Casey asked, not expecting an answer.

The shiny structure was tilted toward the volcano and the top edge, the only part we could see, reflected the clouds. Smooth granite appeared to have been whipped up as a cream and placed to harden at either end of this behemoth, holding it in place. In the sloping land beside it, the legion of seven-foot-tall tablets, now fully excavated, stood at attention, begging for their etchings and symbols to be interpreted.

"How are you exposing it so quickly?" Elaine asked.

"We remove soil from the bottom, and it triggers landslides, pulling the dirt away from it," Jeremy said.

The range top hissed and smoked; Melly and Mom darted back to the kitchen.

We heard Meredith's Southern drawl. "You lay your eyes right on it, but you still can't believe it."

Casey nodded. "Yeah. It's like a cross between a skyscraper on its side and a super-stretched-out yacht."

"Isn't it awesome, Dr. D?" Jeremy shouted.

"Good Lord!" Christopher said. "I thought you had found old artifacts from early humans. What is this? It looks like it comes from the future!"

Paul studied it. "We'll fill you in, Chris. Musa, how's the protection there?"

"Good, but how do you protect something like this?"

"It won't be long before someone flies by," Elle said.

"I know," Jeremy concurred. "No more hiding it."

Sunny wiped his eyes. "It's beautiful."

I put my arm around his skinny shoulders. "We've gotta figure out what our prancestors wanted us to do with this, before the site becomes a media zoo, or starts a war."

Musa sighed. "There's no way to finish excavating this without attracting attention. In the next phase, we'll remove several hundred feet of the mountain. We're setting up conveyor belts to relocate the rocks and soil. Cayateña will be a different shape when we're done with her."

"I'm sorry to tell you guys this," I said. "I . . . I gave away one of the crystals—one of the keystones that fit into those spaces."

"Can you get it back?" Jeremy asked, turning the computer back around to their concerned faces.

"I gave it to strangers."

"We're thinking about how to locate them," Casey said. "A mother and daughter."

Meredith asked, "Where are they from?"

"The United States, maybe," Paul said.

"Don't you have names?"

"The little girl is Carrie," I answered. "The mom, I don't know."

"One first name and only a guess at the country?" Jeremy said. "That's all kinds of impossible."

"The bigger issue," Musa said, "is the translation. Have you made any progress?"

CHAPTER 28

Sunny smacked his hands together. "We can do this! I think I've already deciphered some of the symbols. If these make sense to you, we can rely on them to translate other words, and then move on to sentences."

His fingers pecked on his computer, and the field of propped-up rocks appeared on the TV screen. "This is their message to us, and it's a long one."

Miguel and Casey moved closer to the monitor to study the rows of tablets, eleven across by eleven deep. "How do we know which way to read those lines of characters?" Casey asked. "And what order the message goes—does it move from rock to rock?"

Sunny zoomed in, focusing on a pair of lines on one of the stones. They started off thick and became fine, disappearing at their ends. "I think these are arrows. They seem to be pointing in the direction we're supposed to read each rock face, and then they direct us to the next tablet."

"Oh yeah," Ann said, investigating a photo in her hand. "It snakes. Those lines, or arrows, are saying we read from left to right along the front row until we finish the last rock, and then the message continues on the rock behind that, and goes back across, from right to left, until the end of the second row, and then behind, and back across, weaving until the end."

Elle was stuck in thought. "We have to learn an entire language without anyone to teach it to us?"

"They *are* teaching it to us," Sunny said. "We just have to interpret their method."

"Hey, Christopher," Ann said. "How many words do you need to know in another language to really understand it?"

He tipped his head left, then right. "I think a thousand gets you in the door. Two or three thousand is good. After that, you can start to learn other words by context."

Sunny zoomed in again, to another carving of symbols, this one with a curvy line beneath it. "Okay. Let's start here. I think this says 'river.' Do you see that?"

No one responded.

Sunny zoomed out. "Now?"

Ann scratched her head. "I think it says 'tree by the river.'"

"Do they mean 'bird over river'?" Elle said.

Miguel shrugged.

Sunny asked, "How do you see that it says 'tree' or 'bird'?"

Casey pointed to the screen. "That's a tree, isn't it?"

"No, the tree is over here." Ann trotted to the monitor. "And that's not a bird."

Casey asked, "Isn't it? The wings are there and there? Maybe it says, 'bird *in* the tree'? Christopher, you're the translator. What do you think?"

Christopher shook his head. "I'm still trying to see how it would say 'river.'"

The guessing continued, sometimes flaring up into an argument.

Paul poured himself a vodka tonic. "I thought a bunch of code-deciphering operatives would be better at this."

CHAPTER 29

As the others yapped into a frenzy over what they saw or didn't see in the etchings, Sunny's muscles seemed to fail, one at a time, until he was a pile of bones on the floor.

Paul and I took seats on the couch, on either side of Sunny's bushy head. "Hang in there," I said. "We'll figure this out."

"But I spent days on this," Sunny said. "We're all seeing different things. We're running out of time."

Paul offered Sunny a sip of his vodka. He swallowed without considering it, and every feature on his face seemed to melt. "Holy crap!"

"Yeah, I know," Paul said. "But you forgot about this shit for a second, eh?"

Mom brought Sunny a glass of water; he sipped from it but wilted again.

Casey abandoned the monitor to open another bottle of wine. "This is like reading tea leaves."

Melly rose from her chair. "I have an idea."

Sunny pulled his head out of its droop and looked up to Melly. Everyone quieted.

"I think we need to determine the perspective they wanted us to have," she said. "The layout of the rocks"— she held up a picture of the entire crop of monuments—"I think there's something else going on."

Melly and I exchanged smiles, sharing the memory of what she used to tell me: *Painting is all about perspective.*

Sunny swigged his water and came back to life, flipping through his catalog of etchings, thinking out loud. "These close-up pictures of the symbols and carvings were taken from inside those holes right in front of the stones."

"So that means," Ann finished his thought, "that we're considering only one part of one rock at a time."

Sunny dropped a picture of the entire rock garden to the floor and then hopped up on the couch and peered down at it. "But maybe we're supposed to be taking in the whole scene."

After a lengthy discussion, we video called the others and explained our idea.

Jeremy chewed on beef jerky, each bite pushing him deeper into thought. "Okay, I think I see what you mean."

He aimed his laptop camera at the outcrop of rocks, then slowly walked. "Tell me if you see anything."

We examined the grouping of rectangular gray stones, almost white in the sunlight. The angle of our viewpoint changed as Jeremy continued to walk.

"Nothing outstanding," Paul mumbled.

"Wait," Miguel said.

Jeremy stopped. "You see something?"

Miguel pointed out four stones on the screen, like he was silently counting them.

"Those have shifted," I said. "Is that what you mean? Two are slanting forward, and the others are cocked to the side?"

Miguel nodded.

I poured myself a glass of wine. "But after all this time, the geological metamorphoses, the tectonic plates subducting, I'm surprised they're not in pieces."

"Yes! That's it!" Sunny shouted.

"A little quieter, Sunny," Ann reminded.

He lowered his volume. "Miguel, good call. They didn't mean for us to see them leaning or twisted."

"We can fix that," Meredith said. "Give us a bit."

Meredith hiked down toward a small backhoe as the video call ended.

We used the time they took to restore the tablets to their upright, outward-facing positions to create a display similar to the bunker's dry-erase boards. The printer spit out pictures of the stones that Jeremy had emailed us, and we taped them to the walls. We re-created the Evolution Timeline—from top to bottom, in the exact order that each depiction appeared on the center stone—using a tall bookshelf.

After Christopher, Mom, and Melly watched my Dublin lecture, Sunny delivered the presentation he'd given to us in the La Paz hideout. As Sunny spoke, Christopher rubbed his head and repeatedly stood up only to sit right back down. Mom nodded as if something she'd wondered about her whole life now made sense. Melly barely moved, and with her half open mouth and one eye squinting, her face looked like a Halloween mask of a crazy woman in shock.

"They're calling," Elaine said.

The monitor came on to Jeremy's big eyes. "It's amazing!"

"Y'all ready?" Meredith asked. "Check it out."

She walked with the laptop as Jeremy had before, allowing us to see the batch of stones—all of them now standing straight.

"It's right here," she said, stopping.

We saw nothing but the rocks, appearing like oversized gravestones.

"Wait, almost . . ." Meredith adjusted her computer. "There. Do you see it?"

"Dear God." Christopher sprang to his feet.

Melly's hand flew to her chest.

"Look at that!" Mom said. "It makes one huge scene. It all blends together, like . . . Davey, is that 3D?"

I stepped toward the monitor, nearly falling over the coffee table. "I don't know. Sort of. But more information comes out."

"Hold it there, Meredith," Ann said. "We're taking pictures."

"How is it doing that?" Casey asked.

Viewed from the precise location at which Meredith stood, the rocks, their etchings, and the grainy terrain combined to form what looked like a hologram the size of a baseball field.

"It's like a picture dictionary," I said. "And it's in layers. I think it's showing us how symbols are grouped and how they make a sentence."

"There's your two thousand words," Christopher said to Ann.

In a split second, it disappeared.

"Where did it go?" Elaine asked.

We heard Musa, off screen. "The clouds. They've moved overhead. It must only work in direct light."

"Musa, you keep digging that structure out." Paul had grown anxious. "We'll study that picture thing, and be in touch."

Sunny, Christopher, and I dove into contemplation of the holographic grid, and I noticed that our research team had expanded. Without any fanfare, Ann and Elle had asked for a section of the grid to dissect, and Casey had begun organizing our guesses at translations. Even Paul, Melly, and Mom pitched in, sharing their hunches about how clusters of symbols related to each other. Miguel backed up our files when he wasn't monitoring the security-camera feeds.

A peaceful feeling tingled through me; I had never been part of a team.

But there was a hole in that sensation—a draft of cold worry leaking into my heart. What was wrong with Elaine? Had she stopped liking me?

Chapter 30

I woke up into the memory of coming home early from my trip to Hungary. I tried to fall back to sleep, to escape the insistence of my mind, but once this particular mental movie started, I could never stop it.

Melly leaned over to kiss someone before getting out of the white Jetta. I left the window and sat at the table, my gut on fire.

"Oh! David." She came in and fumbled with the knob, blanking on how to close a door. "I thought you were coming home tomorrow." She smeared her hand across her lips as if she could erase the kiss.

"I wanted to be at the board meeting this evening. To say something on your behalf."

She couldn't bring her voice out of falsetto. "Oh! Sweetheart, wow . . ."

At the meeting, Principal Owens—a gleam in his eyes—gushed, "Melissa has such heart, dedication, and drive. She really should be the person selected for this position."

Uninterested, the board chair picked at his wiry eyebrows and read from his notes. "Okay, thank you, Principal Owens. And the next speaker is, David Denlon?"

I was out the door before he completed my name. I followed Owens, and when he approached a white Volkswagen Jetta, I picked up my pace. As I caught up to him, I pinched his bicep.

"Ah! Oh, hi, uh, David, is it? I didn't see you."

"Where was it?"

"I'm sorry?"

"Where did you fuck my wife?"

"David, um . . . I don't know what you're . . ."

I stepped closer to him as Melly jogged across the parking lot, yelling, "David! Don't!"

I squeezed his arm again. "She's afraid I'm going to hurt you because she told me. She told me everything. She just didn't tell me where it happened." I pressed harder. "Where was it?"

Sweat beaded up next to the age spots on his forehead.

Melly arrived as he finally said, "It wasn't in your house."

"Van, no!" Melly said.

"Van?" I questioned. "Your first name is Van?"

I let go of his arm and turned to Melissa. "You fucked a guy who's older, uglier, and less accomplished than me, and whose name is Van?"

I had never seen someone's face display shame and offense at the same time. I studied Melly. Then I walked away.

No one else was up, although it was already eight a.m. Jet lag, mental exhaustion, and working until three a.m. had taken its toll. I checked the security cameras and saw nothing but a crow prancing down the narrow village road with a nut-like thing in its beak, as if it were showing off. After stuffing the bed back into the couch, I showered in painfully hot water, washing away the bitterness of Melly's betrayal. And then I got to work.

I scoured the pages of our potential translations— lining the floor, coffee table, and couch. Nothing was clear. I studied an arrangement of symbols, whispering, "Animal ocean? Not a sentence." Then I moved two symbols next to a third. "Person with stick?" I sighed. "Where are the verbs?"

By ten a.m., everyone had crawled out of bed and was watching over me as if I were doing a jigsaw puzzle.

"Those characters are under the same picture of fire from the Evolution Timeline," Christopher said, setting his finger by the symbols. "So do they mean 'there is a fire'?"

"Or 'we made fire'?" Ann asked.

No one had an answer.

Mom filled our mugs with coffee that sent a burnt-toast smell into the air. We sipped, each of us in quiet thought, except for Melly, who found an apron in a drawer and began clanking around in the kitchen.

An hour later she took a quiche out of the oven. "Be sure to eat," she said to me. "You know you get an upset stomach when you don't eat."

Elaine turned on her heels and I thought I caught her rolling her eyes.

"Our translation is off." Sunny rubbed his forehead and stared at his block-lettered notes. "Or the pictures don't go with the symbols."

He moved to his computer and put the image of the hologram on the television screen. "We're missing something."

"We have to resist the urge to assume." Paul held his cup out as Mom tipped the coffee pot over it, giving him the last of the black liquid. "If we accept that we're in a mountain forest, we might only look for pine trees."

"Huh?" Miguel's deep voice asked.

"What Paul means," Mom said, heading back to the sink, "is maybe we're in a forest of bamboo stalks or of bright-yellow aspens, but we're only looking for evergreens, so we don't think we see any trees."

Paul winked at Mom.

"Oh, right." Casey sliced into the quiche—an eggy pillow with bits of sausage, cheese, and asparagus baked into it—and dumped a piece onto his plate.

I remarked, "I'm just glad we haven't heard from Veeder."

"That should actually make you nervous," Casey countered.

The vibe in the room turned dire, the opposite of my intention.

"Silence is what you hear before a mountain lion leaps from a branch and devours you," Casey said, stuffing his mouth with a lump of quiche. "Nothing is what you detect before a sniper sends a bullet through your brain."

"Casey," Paul said. "Enough."

I moped to the kitchen and screwed a metal opener into the cork of a bottle of wine. Miguel scrunched his eyebrows at me and looked at his watch.

As we worked, hours sank away like gold nuggets dropping to the bottom of the ocean. Mom poured us fresh coffee and set out plates of crackers and sliced bell peppers.

"I give up. I can't do this," Casey said, pushing his papers and note cards aside.

Ann yawned as she spoke, making it difficult to understand her. "I feel like I'm assembling something and I'm missing the main part."

Christopher's face swelled with disappointment. "I translate for a living. I speak eight languages. But the more I stare at these symbols and pictures, the more confused I am."

Sunny picked up a slip of paper with a symbol on it and placed it next to another. "Look, Professor, what do you think this means?"

I inspected. "Maybe 'person drinking?'"

"I agree," Sunny said. "But what about this?" He moved the symbol away, combining it with a different one.

I studied the new phrase. "'The clothes drink'? That can't be right."

We looked around at each other, leaving our collective thought unspoken. *We're a long way from understanding this language.*

Chapter 31

Elle balled up a piece of paper and chucked it into the waste can. "Damn it! We think we've found a meaning, but then in the next phrase, it doesn't work." She tossed her note cards down and peered into the kitchen at Mom. "What are you making?"

"Dessert." Mom set a hot tray of cookies on the counter and closed the oven door. "And dinner is lasagna."

"Yum!" Casey said. "Can you come on all our missions?" Both of Miguel's thumbs flew into the air.

I found myself standing in front of Mom's cookies, enjoying the sugary wet-wood scent of cinnamon.

"Why don't you test a few?" Mom suggested. She wrapped two in a paper towel and handed them to me.

I asked Miguel, "Can I step outside?"

He checked the camera feeds. "For a minute."

My bare feet sank into the lawn. The buzz of a small plane came out of nowhere, grew into a roar overhead, and then drifted away, cleansing my mind.

I bit off a chunk of the warm, sweet dough and chewed slowly, remembering Mom's soothing voice from when I was thirteen and trapped behind acne.

"You both are working so hard. Have some cookies."

I ignored the plate Mom set down, choosing to stay angry.

"David," my dad said, "you're very smart."

"How can I be smart if I can't get this? Jimmy gets it, and he doesn't have to work with his dad for two hours."

"Jimmy gets it because, unlike you, Jimmy isn't thinking beyond it."

Mom scolded, "Leave Jimmy out of this."

My dad laughed. "Jimmy will someday be serving David food, or rotating his tires. Because David is going to take over my business."

"Enough." Mom swatted him with her dish towel.

"And it might be sooner than later." He rubbed his hand over his heart. "This ticker is on extended play."

"Don't talk like that," Mom said. "Finish up, it's late."

My dad continued, "David, you know the answer. You just don't know how to get it out of your head."

"Is this more spectrum bullshit? I hate math. That's the problem. Not the way my brain works."

My dad gestured toward the cookies. Their spicy fragrance had already started to calm me, but I didn't want to admit it.

He pointed back to my algebra book. "There's no way you can't do this."

I gave in and put an entire cookie in my mouth, seeing how long I could keep it on my tongue before it dissolved.

My dad smiled. "Remember the game we played when you were younger? Where you say the opposite?"

He tapped the page, next to the algebra problem: $5 \times (4 - 2) = ?$

I had written the answer incorrectly as eighteen.

He said, "When parentheses are added, you might think the order of operations stays the same, but . . ."

The cookie was gone. When had I swallowed it? The Opposite Game came back to me. "But actually . . . when parentheses are added, the order of operations *changes*."

He handed me the pencil. I erased *18* and subtracted, then multiplied and wrote *10* in its place.

"You see?" my dad said. "Perfect."

Laughter from an approaching group of tourists brought me back to Saint-Émilion.

I put the whole second cookie on my tongue. *It doesn't make sense when the symbol is moved and its meaning stays the same.* The dough crumbled against the roof of my mouth. *It makes sense when the symbol is moved and its meaning changes.*

I darted inside, nearly choking.

"Sunny!" I looked around. "Where's Sunny?"

"In the shower," Mom said.

I ran to the bathroom door. "Sunny? Can I come in?"

"Professor? Are you okay?"

I entered the steamy room and spoke to the curtain. "Those symbols, the ones we can't figure out, they mean something different when paired with different things. You know, like the letter *o* says 'oh' in the word 'tone' with the silent *e*, but it says 'uh' in 'ton' without it?"

Sunny shut off the water. He charged out of the bathroom with a towel around his waist, nearly pulling the shower curtain down. "Professor, yes!"

Christopher joined us in the living room. "What is it?"

As we flicked through printouts, Elle, Ann, and Casey came over, a little worried.

"What's going on?" Casey asked.

"Here," I said, pointing to a symbol.

Mom and Melly looked over as they set the table.

"Yes!" Sunny said, almost losing hold of his towel. "It means 'fire' there but over here, with these characters, it means 'fuel.'"

Elle returned to her notes. "Oh, that's it. The same with this, the symbol for 'run.' With this character it means 'go.'"

"And check out the water one," Christopher said. "Here it means 'drinking.'" He moved the symbol toward the other cluster. "And here . . ."

Together, Casey and Ann read, "Washing!"

Sunny landed on the floor, staring up to the ceiling with a smile on his face. "Please? I have to get it out!"

"Go ahead," Paul laughed. "Give us a yell."

"Thank you, God!"

"Be careful about your towel, Sunny." Christopher chuckled. "There are women here."

"It's nothin' we haven't seen before," Mom said, dumping lettuce into a salad bowl.

"We have to build a dictionary," I said. "Then we can translate faster."

Within minutes, Ann's phone produced piano notes that fluttered around the room. Sunny decoded symbols on handwritten pages, then passed them to me and Christopher. We further honed the meanings and verified any different ones when paired with other symbols.

Along with thick slabs of meaty lasagna, Mom served us fresh bread from the boulangerie two streets away. The pieces, torn from a baguette, were crunchy on the outside and fluffy within, and each bite left me wanting more.

We silently gulped down our food and got back to work.

Casey captured a picture of each symbol and typed in its meanings. He shared his entries by flash drive with Ann and Elle, who organized them into a dictionary and cross-referenced their translations. Miguel updated the backup drives as he kept watch on the security cameras.

When the cheap metal clock—a mismatch to the rest of the home's classy décor—read midnight, Ann said, "Four hundred. Sunny, we have four hundred dictionary entries for their language."

Sunny was in a trance, staring at his latest translation. "Sunny?"

He went to his computer and sent a picture of the discovery site to the TV monitor. "Look at that," he said. "What do you see, when you really look at it?"

The upper section of the glimmering structure—the only part so far visible—was covered in what looked like solar panels and seemed to be the top of something that could hold a small town.

Casey shrugged. "I see the top levels of an enormous apartment building from the future, which might also be a cruise ship."

"Yes," Sunny said. "That's exactly what it is."

"What?" Melly asked.

"Only it flies." Sunny handed me his notes.

I read them to myself. "Call Musa," I said, pouring a full glass of wine.

Musa's eyes were always a welcoming sight. Behind him, the gargantuan structure, more of it exposed now, cast a long shadow down the rocky volcano.

"David, everyone, good afternoon—or night, for you," Musa said.

Jeremy and Meredith dusted off their hands and waved at us.

I blurted, "It's a transporter."

"What?" Meredith asked.

"It's a huge transporter. Sunny decoded the word."

Musa, Meredith, and Jeremy slowly turned around, reconsidering the dominating structure.

Elle and Paul froze, mouths open, eyes toward the monitor.

"What does it transport?" Meredith asked. "And did it come from somewhere else, or is it going somewhere?"

"Don't know yet," Sunny responded. "Can you give us a better view of it?"

We congregated at the screen to witness the largest vehicle on Earth. The crown of this colossal, black-paneled spacecraft was a gentle arc of smooth gray material that sparkled as if tiny diamonds were set into it. The ends were still restrained by round towers made of granite and an unidentified substance that gave the granite a rubbery look. The dirt had been removed down a vertical strip at the transporter's center, as if Cayateña had been unzipped, revealing that the ship had forty—fifty?—levels, all covered in those glass-like squares. At the very bottom of the exposed part was a wide break in the paneling, filled in with the same gray material from above—was it a ramp to a loading bay? A trail along the outer ridge of this sunken part of the mountain led up to the top, providing access to the space cruiser's highest level.

Casey sat down on the coffee table. "That thing goes up in the air?"

"My God," Ann said, falling onto the chaise longue.

"Listen," Musa said, "I don't want to pressure you guys."

"What is it?" Paul asked, pouring more vodka into several glasses. Miguel took one for himself and handed another to Ann.

"We can't keep this a secret any longer." Musa's excitement had deteriorated into worry. "The guards at the outposts have seen incoming drones."

"We're making headway with the translations," Sunny said. "We'll keep going, as fast as we can."

"Being short on time is just the first thing . . ." Musa's voice trailed off.

Mom and Melly exchanged looks of concern.

"We've now cleared the soil from what we think is the main entrance." Musa glanced back at the transporter.

"Whoa," Sunny said. "Did you go inside?"

"We can't," Musa replied. "There's an etching on the door panel, like an instruction. It shows those zircon pieces, the ones shaped like figure eights, put in place up on the top. It's telling us, David, that we can't unlock the front door without those crystals. You're sure you can't get the white one back?"

Chapter 32

I heard a stranger say my name and opened my eyes to Mom shutting the television off.

"Mom, what are you doing?" I sat up from the couch bed, realizing—from how bright it was without any lights on—that it was already morning.

"Oh, it's bad, the news."

I cleared my croaky throat. "Huh?"

She shook her head. "I turned it off, it's awful."

"What did they say?"

"Terrible things about my Davey."

"Mom, don't worry. You're doing great; we're eating so well thanks to you."

"Are we going to die?"

The skin on Mom's face retained its youth, and made her hair seem prematurely gray. She had never bothered with dye, leaving her hair long and styling it, from curls to snazzy updos, just as she always had.

I hugged her. "We're okay. Go get your shower in, before everyone else wakes up."

After she closed the bathroom door, I clicked the TV remote.

A female reporter on the BBC channel spoke with consternation. "Denlon, a university professor, attracted a lot of social media attention after setting out to find evidence of another species of humans from the distant past. He gave a speech three weeks ago in London, but he refused to say what he'd found."

Paul stumbled out in a T-shirt and shorts. "What's this?"

"Several hours after that speech, a car blew up outside a pub that Denlon visited. Two days later, a security guard at the Central Urban Building in Shanghai was threatened at gunpoint after a taxi dropped Denlon off there."

Casey stepped into the room, patting down his floppy hair.

"They're making me sound like a criminal," I mumbled.

Ann stopped before she got to the kitchen. Christopher appeared with sleepy eyes and squinted toward the television.

"A dead man was found in an airport bathroom in La Paz after a flight from Shanghai had landed there. The passenger list did not include Denlon, but FBI officials suspect he had begun using a disguise. Two of the passengers from that flight have yet to be tracked down."

A picture of me—looking more like Unabomber Ted Kaczynski—filled the left half of the screen. "Anyone who has seen David Denlon is asked to—"

The television shut off.

Paul set down the remote. "David, you have translating to do. Let's get some coffee."

Elaine walked out of the other bathroom with wet hair and saw my scared eyes. "What happened?"

"Just a news report." Paul turned the coffee maker on. "What we'd expect."

Miguel came through the front door holding a pastry box. Our energy pushed him back a step.

"No worries, Miguel," Casey said. "Just the news. Dave, eat a croissant and forget about it. Did I say that right? Cruh-sahnt?"

Melly and Sunny were the last to emerge, busying themselves in the kitchen.

Elaine sat next to me. "It's okay."

I whispered, "Whatever I did to make you mad, I'm sorry."

She held my gaze and then walked away.

In half an hour, studious whispers and the patter of typing surrounded me, like white noise. Elle, with earbuds stuffed into each ear, searched news reports on her laptop. Casey was at the kitchen counter, on his computer, continuing to pick out of the pastry box.

"You looking for a date?" Christopher asked, watching Casey click through Facebook profiles.

"I wish, but no," he said. "Maybe Carrie's mom posted about her subway experience. If we could find her comments and then her account, we'd be able to find her, and hopefully, the white keystone."

Paul paced up and down the hallway with a phone to his ear, directing his operatives and securing another payment to the Guatemalan government. Cheery, familiar chopping noises floated out of the kitchen, where Mom and Melly stood at cutting boards.

"C'mon, Professor!" Sunny said. "We need you!"

I willed myself out of my funk, and we set up another translation relay, from one end of the couch to the other. Our English-Prancestor dictionary tripled in length.

Miguel backed up the flash drives every thirty minutes and surveyed the camera feeds.

The clock stared me down. "We don't have time to learn every word before we start," I said. "Ann, can you print out the dictionary? We've got to begin interpreting the message."

For dinner, we each remained where we were—on a piece of furniture or on the floor, note cards and papers carefully set out around us. Mom and Melly made do, handing us plates where we sat.

Mom picked up the last plate—holding a bowl, a spoon, and a piece of sourdough bread. "Where's Sunny?"

"He's working in the guys' bedroom." Ann could barely speak with her mouth full. "Mom, this stew is delicious."

"It's Melly's recipe," Mom said, carrying the plate to Sunny's room.

"David always loved it." Melly smiled at me.

Elaine delivered her full spoon back to her bowl.

Mom returned from the bedroom, disheartened. "He doesn't want it."

"What?" I set my dish on a notebook and tiptoed through the maze of cards in front of me.

Inside the room, Sunny sat on his single bed, holding a thin stack of note cards. His pads of paper, loose pages of notes, and a copy of the prancestor dictionary covered the space around him. The side of his face rested on his left knee, and a sock hung off the toes of his other foot. His fuzzy hair was determined to become dreadlocks.

"Sunny, you have to eat."

"You said to start translating the message." He didn't look at me. "So I did."

"Great, but please, eat."

"We have to go. It says we have to go."

"Go where?"

"A billion years to get to this moment, and we're gonna screw it up."

I coaxed Sunny out to the recliner. He brought his index cards.

"Sunny, my boy," Paul said. "What's that perplexed look doing on you?"

"He's translated some of the message," I said.

"What does it say?" Casey asked.

When Sunny didn't answer, Christopher rubbed his shoulder and Ann brought him water in a glass that seemed too nice for a rental unit—was it crystal?

"Sunny will share when he's ready," Mom said, sitting down to her stew.

After dinner, Musa and Jeremy joined us on the television monitor. Paul was at the sink now, barely rinsing off dishes, unfamiliar with a sponge. I took the spoons and bowls from him and fit them into the dishwasher, asking toward the screen, "Whatcha guys got? Isn't it the middle of the night for you?"

Meredith showed up. "Safer to work at night. We're fixing to remove that granite. They left pockets in the rock so we can insert rods and move it out in pieces."

Casey handed his empty bowl to Paul. "How 'bout now, Sunny, when everyone's here?"

"Are you saying," Elle asked, "that Sunny's about to read the first part of the message? This is what our prancestors are telling us, directly? Are you sure, Sunny?"

Sunny still refused to touch his stew. "Yeah. But it's a rough translation. I'm not sure of some words yet."

"Does it identify who's doing the communicating?" Paul asked. "Is it a leader or a representative?"

"I can't tell."

"Let's hear it," Musa said.

Sunny took a breath before reciting from his first card. "Future of your people is . . . *or wait,* 'relies' on you receiving and doing this . . ."

"The future of our people *what*?" Meredith asked.

Paul shut off the water. "Relies on us getting this message and following it."

We huddled around Sunny as he continued.

"There are many details to . . . talk to you, but . . . *emergency matter? . . . hurried matter?*" He threw his hands up.

I offered, "Urgent?"

Sunny scribbled on his card. "But urgent matter . . . is transporter. This is . . . second ship built."

He flipped to his next card. "We know too late . . . we *knew* too late . . . we needed to transport to another planet. Limited resources and a grow . . . growing population divided us, to . . . war."

An empty wineglass slipped out of my hand and bounced without breaking on the Persian rug.

He kept reading. "First ship built by our . . . *What does this say?*"

He handed the card to Christopher, who inspected it and consulted the dictionary. "I think that would translate into 'nation,' or 'country.'"

Sunny's pen ran out of ink; Ann handed him a pencil.

I picked up my glass and filled it with Cabernet.

"First ship built by our nation was . . ." Sunny set the card on the coffee table. "I couldn't get the end of this."

Christopher considered the symbols. "That's the weaponry phrase."

He turned the card toward Ann. "Oh my God," she said. "It was shot down."

"Holy shit," Casey said, pouring himself wine.

Sunny started again. "First ship built by our nation was shot down by . . . enemy." He scanned the next card. "Some of us build transporter in secret. We spend final years building second transporter. We . . ." He stopped and squinted, saying to himself, "I think it says 'placed it' or 'put it' . . . where Earth deliver to your . . . study people, from our study people."

"There it is," Paul said. "It's from an underground group."

"From our *what* people?" Musa asked.

Sunny shook his head. "I think it translates to 'study people' or 'the people who study'?"

After inspecting his note card, Christopher and I shrugged.

Sunny read the last of his translation. "By having fully built transporter before you . . . enter war, you can launch to the next world, starting new life, saving from . . . extinction."

Jeremy turned to view the transporter. "We have to launch to another place, or humankind dies off?"

Meredith sat down and covered her nose and mouth.

"They're giving us a head start," Mom said, "to save humanity, because they couldn't."

"No pressure," Miguel grunted.

I grabbed at Sunny's scattered cards. "Scientists."

"What?" Ann said.

"The study people—the scientists. Because who would think to use a volcano to hide a transporter, and who would most likely find it there? Geologists, archaeologists . . ."

"Anthropologists." Mom grinned.

Mostly talking to herself, Meredith said, "They couldn't stop fighting, even to avoid extinction."

Ann plucked out the blue zircon crystal from where we kept it—in a candleholder made of blown glass on an end table—and held it, like a baby bird, in her palm. "As they were dying off, a group of their scientists decided to reach across a billion years and give us the chance to get it right."

"How do we do that?" Christopher asked.

Sunny finally tasted his stew. "We have to get that transporter into space, before it's destroyed."

"And then what?" Melly asked.

"I guess we'll know when we translate the rest of the message," Ann said.

"How fast can you guys get here?" Musa asked.

Elle was on her laptop, one step ahead of his question. "I'm looking for a flight." Her eyes enlarged. "Uh oh."

Miguel examined her computer, then linked it to the television monitor.

"This report is trending," Elaine said. "It's from a national network in the States. Musa, I've shared the screen, can you guys see it?"

"We got it, yes," Musa said.

At the bottom of the screen, beneath a male reporter sitting at a news desk, was the question: *Is rogue professor planning to destroy the world?*

Chapter 33

The reporter's cakey makeup was uneven on his face, as if he had sweat through it on his forehead and above his lips. Had he stayed for an extra shift? Was there so much horrible news to tell about me that he couldn't fit in a makeup break?

He took big swallows of water and then set the plastic cup down on his news desk, unconcerned that it was still in the shot. "For those of you just joining us, the FBC is offering its services to the president in a public-private effort to reach out to Dr. Denlon and to confirm any evidence of a past human race."

Ann asked, "What's the FBC?"

"The Federate Banking Corporation," I said, retreating to the side of the room.

The FBC spokesperson, a white man in his forties with a roll of neck fat and cheeks so round they hid his ears from our view, appeared in his office, wearing a pinstripe suit. "We may be a private entity, but we care about humanity."

"No you don't." I pushed the top of my head into the wall.

"In fact, Dr. Denlon's late father ran a mortgage-loan business and held a contract with us. We reach out to Dr. Denlon with a friendly hand."

I pulled at my cheeks. "No you don't!"

The spokesperson continued. "Our mission is to obtain, if it exists, the evidence that has been found. And to contain anything that could be harmful."

The screen split, putting the news reporter on the left and the FBC spokesperson on the right. The reporter asked, "What is the concern—what could be harmful?"

Behind the spokesperson, on a credenza, stood a stone carving with a chipped nose.

I bolted to the kitchen and checked three wine bottles. All empty.

The spokesperson said, "We don't know what Dr. Denlon has found. But if there really did exist past people who evolved to a level beyond us, they could have left behind highly destructive weapons or deadly chemicals."

"What the hell?" I said. "Who's saying that weapons and chemicals were found?"

"Patrick Veeder," Elle said.

"What?"

Casey dished ice cream into mugs since we'd dirtied all the bowls. "Dave, dude, did you think Veeder was just gonna give up? You spoiled his plans, stole back the evidence, snuck your mom and ex-wife out from under him, and, if I recall correctly, called him a son of a bitch. And as far as he knows, you also kidnapped his translator. Oh, and, kind of the main thing, you shot him. He was always going to have a next move, and it was going to be big."

"But why this? Why tell the public that the discovery is dangerous?"

Musa's voice came out of Sunny's laptop. "He thinks it will bring you out of the woodwork."

I fell into a stare, but this group had gotten used to them. True to form, these operatives reacted without drama, and somehow that seemed to shorten my paralysis.

"Breathe," Ann said. "C'mon, that's it."

I coughed when I finally inhaled.

"Musa's right." Paul said. "He's hoping that you'll come forward to set the record straight."

The reporter continued, "Let's turn to our next guest, Patrick Veeder, an art dealer and philanthropist."

Christopher shook a fist and then turned away from the television.

Veeder glared into the camera lens, knowing I could see him. I moved baskets around on the kitchen counter and opened and shut cabinets. No alcohol.

"Now, um . . ." The reporter referred to his notes. "I understand that you're working with Denlon on this project?"

Veeder's confident voice explained, "My contractual relationship with Dr. Denlon is to search further in the area where he found the initial evidence and to bring what we find to the world."

"And where is it that he made these initial findings?"

"The contract does not permit me to disclose the location without Dr. Denlon's permission."

The reporter put his elbow on the desk and leaned into it. "Well, how long do you plan on waiting for him? His mother and ex-wife have gone missing as well. At what point will you consider him to be intentionally hiding from you and therefore breaching your contract?"

"Very soon indeed."

Christopher still faced away from the TV, but mumbled, "You evil bastard."

"I bet those drones at the site were Veeder's," Casey said. "He knows something's there."

"Thank you, Mr. Veeder." The reporter's look turned grave as he focused back on the camera. "Dr. Denlon, if you're watching, you must reach out to law enforcement or a news agency. It is extremely important that we get in contact with you."

I withstood the inclination to shatter an empty wine bottle on the TV. "Why is Veeder now acting like he's following the contract, like he has to keep the location under wraps?"

"He's making you an offer, David," Paul explained. "Veeder is saying, 'Seek me out, while I'm still keeping this a secret, and make me part of it, and for that, I will let you keep your reputation.'"

My eyes found Elle. "But years later I eat some pie in a coffee shop and die from poison."

"Bingo," Miguel said, inspecting the security-camera view across the alley behind our house—a wall of rectangular beige stones with white shutters flapped open from an inset window.

"Let's work this through," Ann said. "What's going to happen when David doesn't reach out?"

Paul found a seat, mug of ice cream in hand. "Veeder will get a lawyer to advise that David's disappearance is a breach of contract. The world will understand, because, look"—he pointed to the television—"Patrick is a nice guy who's giving David every chance to come forward."

Jeremy and Meredith cringed.

"But when he doesn't," Paul continued, "Veeder will announce the location of the site and act shocked that there's an army protecting it. He will then issue his statement, something like 'Denlon has secretly moved forward on more research, breaking our contract. He must have ill intentions; maybe he's found something dangerous.' And this will engender public support for the use of armed forces to take the site away from us."

Jeremy yelled, "No way! You gotta get here before Veeder tells the US government where this is."

"The US government, and many others, are going to find this on their own," Musa said. "Yesterday, in town, people were asking about what's going on up here."

Christopher came out of his contemplation. "What if we all explain the counternarrative to Patrick's story? I can describe how he drugs people that end up dead a few weeks later. Musa can explain how Patrick hired him with a false contract."

Casey passed out napkins. "That will be a he-said-she-said clusterfuck. It may tarnish Veeder a bit, but what he'll make up about you will be disparaging as well. And if he doesn't go to prison, you'll have to hide out from him for the rest of your lives."

Melly asked, "Where'd Sunny go?"

"Sunny," Mom called. "Sweetie, come back out here."

Sunny appeared in his doorway with more note cards.

Meredith requested, "Can y'all turn the computer? I can't see him." Elaine complied. "There you are, Sunny. Why did you leave?"

"I'm translating!" Sunny squealed. "I wanna know everything our prancestors were trying to tell us even if we end up failing them."

"We're not failing them, Son," Paul said. "We're getting to that site. Miguel, go to the store and get David a splash. Ann, let's work on transportation. Casey, pack up. Elaine, come up with disguises that match the identifications I've got left."

Paul turned to the hopeful eyes of Musa, Jeremy, and Meredith. "Get that transporter out of Cayateña's grip and ready to blast off. We're on our way."

CHAPTER 34

By midnight I would have kissed Patrick Veeder had he walked through the door.

I plunked another empty vodka bottle into the trash and set about uncorking a bottle of wine. "Did someone see if Mom took her meds?"

"Right before bed," Ann slurred.

I climbed onto the table and lay on my back, clutching my wineglass in one hand and the bottle in the other. I felt weightless, as if the table were a raft, sailing me away. "My mom is the only human being who doesn't suck."

"Hey," Melly said. "That's not fair. What about the rest of us?"

"Ooohh. The person who screwed Principal Prick is now proclaiming that I'm the one out of line."

"Don't call him that," Melly said.

"He fucked my wife. I get to call him whatever I want."

Miguel laughed and stumbled into the kitchen counter. He inspected the label on the beveled bottle of brandy—

as if to make sure it was alcohol and not cologne—and poured himself another glass.

Paul's expression of relaxation—eyes half closed, mouth resting in a gentle smile—went cold. He slid his feet off the ottoman and sat up, perturbed.

"There's no need to call up the past, David," Ann said, trying to line up a bottle of wine with her glass before the liquid came out.

I adjusted my head on the lumpy fruit bowl. "Ann, you want into this conversation? Okeydokey. You said you were on this crazy mission because you're mad at your husband . . . Yeah, he cheated on you."

"Fuck you, David."

"What else could it be—he didn't take out the trash? Christ. You people call yourselves covert operatives. But even from the spectrum, I can see you, plain as day."

I lifted my head enough to sip some wine and then let it bonk back down onto the apples. "Who's next? Come on in. Try your luck with Weird David."

Casey grabbed my wine bottle and I pulled it back, splashing Syrah on my face.

"Fine," he said, "I'll open my own."

"Oh, Casey. Portrait-ready Casey. Those legs, have they been taken from Apollo himself? You have personality. And smarts. And yet no lover? You do know that we are well into the twenty-first century. You can admit you're gay."

Casey's fist landed in my stomach; I struggled to hold my wine bottle as I kicked him and toppled to the floor. He palmed my head like a basketball and straightened his arm, keeping me down in a squatting position. I used my free hand to pinch his bicep, but his skin was taut and impossible to grab.

Paul rushed over and poked his fingers into Casey's chest, encouraging him to let go of me.

When I stood up, Christopher moved in front of me, so close he had to tilt his head back to look up to my face. His tone was timid. "Stop, okay?"

Elle sat up from the Persian rug, coming out of her stupor. For the first time, I noticed the rug's pattern—blue and gold flowery shapes, mirroring each other along the four edges, and in the center, forming a diamond inside another diamond. I had to blink to stop the shapes from dancing, and again to keep the diamond formations from cascading into themselves, like in a kaleidoscope.

"Maybe it's time to stop drinking, David," Christopher said.

"Who the hell are you to tell me that, Christopher?"

He backed away from me.

I pointed to the collection of short bottles near the kitchen sink. "How many beers have *you* had? Wait, let's stick to my first question . . . Who the hell *are* you? Why would you work for someone like Veeder?"

All eyes were suddenly on Christopher. He shrugged. "Um, well . . ."

We continued to stare at his rosy cheeks.

"Okay." He relented. "Like I told you before, I was born in the Republic of the Congo. My parents were missionaries there."

Miguel moved one of his hands in quick circles. *We know this. Get to the good stuff.*

Christopher continued. "I grew up being exposed to different languages, and I found them easy to learn."

He opened another beer bottle and played with the cap in his hand. "It worked out because I didn't much care for all the Bible study, but since I could help translate, I sort of got a pass from having to do the religious stuff."

He brought the bottle to his mouth, reconsidered, and set it down. "When I was twelve, we came back to the States, and I missed all the people from the villages. They had cared for me, taught me, and, well, practically raised me, since my parents were always so busy. I realized that by learning their vocabulary and their expressions, their jokes, their slang, I had gotten closer to them than even my parents had."

"Blah blah blah," I yelled. "Get to the point where you joined forces with a murderer."

"Jesus, dude," Casey said.

"I was interviewed by Liam, not Patrick," Christopher said. "It seemed like a dream come true. A translation job that would take me back to the kinds of villages where I grew up. I mean, yeah, Liam did seem a little weird, but only Bible weird, like my parents. I didn't really worry about it, because Liam brought assistance to people who needed it, and he treated them with respect."

He dumped the beer down the sink.

"Hey, Elaine!" I teetered and then found my footing. "Why don't I hear you calling Christopher 'naïve' for getting involved with Veeder, like you did me?"

She made a tsk noise and rolled her eyes.

I lost my balance and flopped into a chair. "Oh, right. David's the bad guy." I swigged from my bottle. "No. David is human. And it's humanity that's fucked up."

"Hey, we're all pissed," Paul said. "Let's call it a night."

I stood back up. "I'm drunk, but I'm not wrong. Humans—you, me, all of us—are total bastards. Useless to each other and dangerous to the Earth. Our prancestors were nuts! Why the hell did they want to save such a putrid species?"

The others seemed to sober up, except for Miguel. He had made himself comfortable in the chaise longue, facing me with a satisfied grin.

"I can hear your thoughts," I said to the group. *What's he talking about? He's so weird!* But you know what's weird? You! Strutting through life, pretending everything's okay when it isn't."

Casey and Christopher looked at each other, silently agreeing that I was being a jerk.

"Let me say it like a professor, then maybe you'll listen: human beings are a precarious mix of stupidity and selfishness."

Ann shook her head.

"No? How else do you come up with concepts like 'buyer beware'? Sound familiar? The notion that it's the buyer's fault for not assuming that the seller might be a trickster? That a seller who can pull a fast one is good at business?"

I drank my wine only for theatrics. In truth, a headache had engulfed my skull, and everything that hit my tongue was sour. "We seem to ignore the direct correlation between people gaining power and those people getting to break all the rules. Our pathetic attempt at justice is to try to hold administrations or policies accountable. But holding a system accountable is like handcuffing jelly."

"David, it's time for bed." Ann stepped to me, but I moved away.

"What else, but the combination of stupid and selfish, would assert that banks are too big to fail? CEOs who commit fraud—the nicer term for theft—are too politically connected to jail, but poor people have to plead to violent crimes they didn't commit because their public defenders have too many cases to put on a decent trial?"

My legs wobbled.

"And look at how well we fight against each other—millions of dollars spent on sporting matches, political campaigns, wars—but it's a chore to battle hunger, poverty, disease? Oh yes, we are magnificent warriors, just not against the real enemies."

Paul waved for everyone to move farther away from me. I couldn't tell if he was doing me a favor or giving them space for their own protection.

I nearly sung my words. "We *believe* having more than the next guy, more of something unnecessary and harmful to the environment, like expensive *cars,* is better than everyone having something necessary, like health care. How are we going to save the godforsaken human race from extinction if we can't even save poor people from the *flu?*"

I threw my empty wineglass onto the couch cushion next to Casey. He flinched, but then caught the glass by its stem before it fell to the tile floor.

"I've spent my adult life researching human behavior. All I see is a feeble, greedy, slow-learning species that brings nothing of value to Mother Earth."

I ranted on until Mom and Sunny walked out of their rooms.

"Pipsqueak!" I yelled at Sunny, using my old, secret name for him.

Sunny's shoulders slouched. "What did you call me?"

Mom grumbled, "He's drunk. Leave him be." She lasered a look of disgust at me and returned to her room.

But Sunny remained, asking with his eyes how I could be so mean.

CHAPTER 35

Soft morning light hit the closed drapes, causing their paisley design to glow. I picked my head up from the kitchen floor and quenched my parched throat by slurping water from the faucet.

One by one, like zombies coming back to life, the others raised themselves from the rug, couch, recliner, or, in Ann's case, the plastic leaves of the fake plant that had toppled to the ground.

Sunny, Mom, and Christopher puttered in the kitchen.

I swallowed the urge to vomit. "Sunny, I'm sorry about what I called you. I had too much to drink."

He kept his eyes away from me.

Mom handed me a glass of orange juice. "Drink this." Her loving tone had been replaced by irritation.

Elle picked up wet towels from the floor and dropped them in a bucket. "There's another mess by the door," she said to me. "Take care of it."

I mopped up the rancid fluid and went back to sipping my orange juice.

Ann returned the pillows to the couch, staring at me as if she were wishing something terrible.

"Man, there's a dark side to you, David," Casey said.

I pounded my glass down, sending the liquid shooting toward the ceiling. Everyone became still.

"Stop with your looks and your call-downs," I said. "Why the hell did you all drink last night? Were you having a little party? Having some fun, before you dye your hair and get another fake ID and escape to your normal lives? You all have that option. But not me. I didn't see that reporter talking to anyone else last night but *me*! I'm the one they know, not any of you. *I'm* the one they're insinuating is a murderer!"

Mom moaned and sat down, pushing her face into her hands.

"Do you know why *I* drank? Do you know why I turned from that news report to search the kitchen for something to numb my friggin' brain? It wasn't for fun. Elle, why don't you call up that report again. Look at what's sitting behind the FBC spokesperson. On his credenza. Do it!"

Elle sat next to Ann and opened her computer.

I tore at the zipper on Paul's duffel bag and dumped its contents on the table.

"Where are they?" I demanded, fishing through passports and tiny gadgets. "Where are the pictures I turned over to you, from the 'gifts to Veeder' file—the ones I stole from Liam's briefcase?"

"Over here." Paul took the ice pack away from his hungover head and opened his binder.

I fanned out the pictures. "Liam took these of the relics, before they were given to Veeder." I plucked one out. "Here!"

I tossed the photograph with a fast flick of my wrist. It twisted through the air and landed in Ann's lap.

"See any resemblance?" I asked.

Paul plopped the ice back on his head and stayed where he was. Melly, glossy-eyed and in the corner of the room, clutched her coffee mug with both hands, too nauseous to drink from it. Everyone else moved over to Elle's laptop.

I hustled into the bathroom just in time to puke. Stomach acid, orange juice, alcohol, and chunks of stew meat—had I even chewed it?—landed in and around the toilet.

In between my bouts of retching, I imagined Elle and the others rewatching the news report. Had they spotted the stone carving of an ancient god behind the spokesperson, and compared it to the picture I'd thrown of Veeder's stolen artifact—a two-foot-tall statue with a scarred nose—and realized they matched?

"Mother of God," I heard Ann say.

"That's about the size of something Patrick got from a village in the Congo," Christopher said. "I was with him."

"That's what you were talking about, Paul?" I heard Mom ask. "Patrick Veeder tricks poor people out of artifacts like that one? He auctions them off, or uses them to gain influence over people like the directors of the FBC?"

I didn't hear Paul's answer. It took all my focus to collect bunches of toilet paper and, with shaky hands, clean the seat and nearby walls.

I surrendered to the floor. The cool tile reduced the fever in my face.

Elle came in and shut the door. Without talking, she drew a bath and helped me undress. As I soaked in the hot water, she scoured the bathroom. The lemony scent of the cleanser relaxed me; her scrubbing motions—constant, overlapping circles—lowered my blood pressure.

"Elaine," I whispered.

She kept cleaning, not looking at me.

"Meeting you is not some bonus, added to this discovery."

She slammed down the squirt bottle and kept her face turned away from me.

I paused, fighting through the ringing in my ears to find the right words. "What I mean is, this discovery is just a bonus. The real find, for me, is you."

Her eyes finally connected with mine. "But you and Melly are getting back together."

"What do you mean? No we're not."

"Why didn't you tell me that?"

I took a moment to think. "Why would I tell you something that was *not* happening?"

Elaine's smile, slow at first, then wide and showing all her teeth, made the room feel brighter.

My weak legs almost didn't allow me to stand. As I closed a towel around my hips, Elaine gently rubbed and kissed my chest, igniting my whole body with energy. Everything felt right again.

"Elle." I pushed her satiny hair away from her face. "I don't understand some things that everyone thinks I should. I didn't know that I was supposed to tell you something I wasn't doing. I'm sorry."

Casey banged on the door. "Let's go. We've got our flights. We're going to Guatemala through Tucson."

I kissed Elle's forehead. "Always talk to me, even if you think I should know what's going on, okay?"

"I will." She gently pushed her lips onto mine.

"Hey!" Casey knocked again.

Elaine sighed and then opened the door, asking, "We're going to Arizona? Why?"

Casey waited for me to look into his eyes before he answered. "Because that's where Carrie and her mom live, and they still have the white crystal."

CHAPTER 36

I secretly nicknamed him Brutus. His beefy upper half seemed more than his skinny legs could hold. He was one of Paul's operatives, here to escort Mom and Melly to a different location.

"We're a wanted group," Paul said. "According to the news, law enforcement understands that David has a small posse helping him avoid detection. It's best not to be around us."

"What place in the world is safe for them?" Sunny asked.

"Anywhere not with David."

I bowed my head, mumbling, "Especially when David drinks."

Sunny leaned his shoulder into mine and smiled.

"I'm sorry, man," I said.

Paul gestured to Mom and Melly, opening the door.

"Don't forget your medication, Mom," Casey said. "It's in the kitchen. Want me to get it?"

"Nope," Mom said. "I'm not leaving."

Paul looked at me. "Dave?"

"Mom, this is really dangerous."

She folded her arms and didn't move.

"Paul, I've never told my mom what to do. I'm not starting now."

He smiled at Mom. "I'd love for you to stay. Just providing the option."

"But Melissa, dear," Mom said, "you should go where it's safe."

Melly tearfully hugged Ann and then Miguel.

I slipped out the door and consulted the gray clouds. Brutus smoked a cigarette by the car, looking up into the sprinkles. Melissa finally came out of the house, carrying a reusable plastic bag with the few personal items each of us had acquired in Libourne—a change of clothes, a toothbrush, deodorant.

"Paul said this guy has money for you, to get more clothes and stuff," I said.

She blinked away raindrops from her eyelashes. "I'm sorry," she said. "I'm really sorry for everything."

"So am I. It's behind us."

I wrapped my arms around her. "This is how we should have ended before."

"Yeah, I know."

The drops fell harder, stinging when they hit, helping us end our good-bye. The mud-brown Peugeot descended the hill, shrinking into the distant line of asphalt between two fields of grapevines. Brutus was delivering Melissa to Lucca, an Italian town that she had said was "perfect for painting." He would stay there as her guardian.

The summer shower drifted away to nourish the rest of the Dordogne Valley, but drips still tapped out a tune around me. *Pa-ting* on the gutter. *Puth . . . puth* on thick leaves extending from the tree in the next yard.

I returned inside to Ann and her hair clippers. "What's my character for Tucson?"

"Nothing crazy." She rubbed a towel on my wet head and then covered my shoulders with it. "Clean-cut guy. Round-rimmed glasses." She handed the glasses to me. "The lenses are nonprescription. Elle found them this morning at a charity shop."

Elaine pondered me like a casting director. "I couldn't find any pics of you online with a buzz cut or glasses. So I figured, make you look like nothing they can compare you to."

A three-ring binder hit my lap. "Your copy of the dictionary," Sunny said. "Lots of time in the airport and on the plane. I'm giving everyone a section of the message."

Ann ran the clipper from my forehead up over my head and down to my neck.

Miguel walked in and emptied his bag on the table. Twenty cell phones tumbled out.

"We use these phones from now on, and only once," Elle said, as she picked one up and started pressing buttons.

Casey placed his open computer on the binder in my lap. A video of a news reporter played: "I'm here with Lynette Frieson, a Tucson resident who alerted authorities when she saw the news about Dr. Denlon and realized she had shared a subway ride with him in London last month. When an unidentified terrorist grabbed Frieson's five-year-old daughter and threatened to blow himself up, Frieson says it was Denlon who told the terrorist to let her daughter go, and the terrorist complied."

The reporter asked Lynnette, "What can you tell us about Professor Denlon—do you think he knew that terrorist? Do you think he's dangerous?"

Lynette spoke into the microphone pointed at her chin. "I don't know Mr. Denlon. All I can tell you is that he was kind to my daughter and gave her his necklace to cheer her up."

"What kind of necklace?"

"It's a crystal of some sort."

Casey pulled the computer away as Paul said, "Here's what we're betting. That Lynette won't call the cops if you show up asking for the zircon back."

"Why is that your bet?" I asked.

"Because she was sympathetic to you in the interview," Ann said, folding down my ear to shave around it.

"And more importantly," Casey said, "we're assuming law enforcement doesn't know the pendant is a keystone and that you need it."

"However," Elle said, "there's a chance Veeder will pay Lynette a visit, in search of the zircon, since he's undoubtedly seen this report."

"What are we doing about that?" I asked, as Ann's clipper hummed up the back of my neck.

Paul mumbled, "Hoping."

"Hoping?"

"Hoping Veeder doesn't get to Lynette before we do."

The house became quiet as people left to load themselves into the minivan driven by Paul's local operative, Jenny.

Ann smack-dusted my head, sending hairs onto the towel. Then she just smacked.

"Ow!" I said.

"That's for saying my husband cheated on me."

I vaguely remembered that piece of my drunken tirade. "Oh yeah . . . I'm sorry."

She swept the floor as I shook the towel out over the trash, expecting her to swat me with the broom.

"Pesticides," she mumbled.

"What?"

"Why I'm mad at him. And an electric car."

I held the dustpan as she swept my brown hair into it. "What do you mean?"

"We got married twenty years ago. We didn't talk about these things. Turns out, they are kind of a big deal to me. He wants to live in the country and spray weed killer all over. He wants a truck when we have nothing to haul. I want to be in town so I can bring my mason jars back and forth to the food co-op. He makes fun of me and he's not budging, and I don't want to be married to someone who doesn't give a shit about this and worse, who doesn't care that I do."

I put the broom in the slender closet near the back door. "Yeah, that's a real issue, and you have every right to be upset."

Ann smiled. "I like you again. I'm sorry I hit you." She heaved her backpack onto her shoulder. "And while you were wrong about me, you were right about Casey."

"What did I say about Casey?"

And then I remembered.

"Oh man, I'm such an ass."

CHAPTER 37

The plane was filled mostly with Americans, and took us from Paris to Chicago, the first leg of our flight. We had divided the cabin into segments to monitor, and Miguel and I were nearly finished with our shift.

Bored and anxious, I eavesdropped to learn the red-shirted man was with his mistress and missing his kids; the woman with the rhinestone glasses had developed type 2 diabetes; and the fidgety grandmother was furious that her grandson had not wed a woman who shared her religion.

Our prancestors called me from the pages of symbols in my bag. But I focused on the person who had unclicked his seatbelt and moved into the aisle. He opened an overhead compartment, pulled out a sweater, and wedged himself back into his seat.

Casey pretended to wait in line at the lavatory. I met him there.

"My turn to watch," he said. "Any issues?"

"No. Hey, I'm sorry about what I said last night."

Casey gazed at the floor for several seconds before looking at me. "You essentially told me that I'm handsome and smart and shouldn't be ashamed of who I am. I mean, my sexual orientation is none of your damn business, but . . . yeah, I gotta work through some stuff."

The air around us seemed to grow thicker, as if we had more privacy than a carpeted wall panel near an airplane toilet could provide.

"You know, Casey, I used to think that, too," I confided. "That I had stuff to work through—that I had to put in some great effort to finally accept myself. But that wasn't it. I never had an issue with who I was. It was other people who had the issues. What I had to accept was that there would always be people who didn't like me. Who would judge me. Who wouldn't feel comfortable around me. And once I accepted that, there really wasn't any work to do. I just went about being me."

Casey's face became peaceful. "Thanks for sharing that, Davey."

Back in my seat, I looked in the beverage menu for alcoholic drinks. I could taste the Merlot pictured next to the word *Complimentary*. I could feel the relief of the vodka in the bottle next to its price, *US$15*.

I slipped the menu into the seat pocket and poured my mind into translating the message from our prancestors. My fingers sprang back and forth between the characters and the dictionary. I started to recognize certain meanings without looking them up. The rhythm of their language became familiar, making it easier to fill in the gaps.

As I read, I heard a man and a woman speaking in unison in my head.

We arrived at the merge of mind and machine, bringing the distant future into accurate prediction.

I reread: *the merge of mind and machine.* Our prancestors were describing an evolutionary milestone they had achieved, a milestone that our own kind was now on the brink of. But we called it something different. We called it *the singularity.*

The singularity was the inevitable destination of our relentless yet blind march toward handing over control of our lives to computers. While we hailed every technological advancement as a breakthrough, like virtual assistants and self-driving vehicles, we were also taking fast steps toward the point at which digital intelligence would exceed the functionality of our own brains.

Scientists and enthusiasts referred to this development—estimated to occur for us by the year 2045—as "the singularity" because it was expected that computer processing and human thinking would soon merge to become one, or *singular.*

As I read, the prancestor man/woman voice eagerly explained:

We reached the merge and no longer asked
our computers for information; they began

to deliver the knowledge they determined we needed, including scientific predictions. Where before we could only anticipate such upcoming occurrences as the phases of the moon or the likely path of a hurricane, now we could see how the planet's geology would change and how its life-forms would come and go.

A flare of warmth inflamed my cheeks. They had seen the upcoming death of their kind but also, on the distant horizon, the dawn of our race.

I glanced around the plane. Who were these passengers, wallowing in self-made conundrums, diseases, and concerns, missing the meaning of life for the distractions of the day? I was decoding the most important script in the history of the planet, while the guy next to me penciled numbers into a sudoku grid and the woman across the aisle read from a magazine page headlined "*Celebrity Makeup Tips.*"

I dipped my fingers into the cool water in my cup and dabbed the back of my neck. Our prancestors had acquired the knowledge of how the Earth would metamorphosize over time—that it would freeze and thaw, that the Cambrian explosion of life would occur and lead to a second iteration of humankind.

Yet they were divided, fighting, unable—despite their advancements—to work together to ward off extinction.

Were we headed for the same fate?

CHAPTER 38

We were greeted by the dry air of Southern Arizona as we piled into two SUVs. We drove in silence, trying to make sense of the nearly unbelievable information that each of us had translated on the trip.

After arriving at an assortment of stores connected by a sprawling parking lot, Casey and Elaine ventured into a gun retailer. When they returned, Miguel headed toward a department store.

"Miguel," I said out my window. "Something white."

Ann went to a restaurant with leafy potted plants in the front. Miguel returned with a bicycle, summer clothing for Ann, and a tiny, slender gift box, which he handed to me.

After opening the box, I asked Paul, "Where do you get so much dough?"

Paul tugged one phone off the car charger and put another one on it. "Underground work earns good money from governments, especially yours."

I examined the heart-shaped pendant: mother-of-pearl, on a gold chain. Would Carrie find it a suitable replacement for the zircon? Would it keep her imagination in the clouds?

In less than an hour we were parked in a residential area, overlooking rocky mountains that grew more pink with every glance. We used boulders for seats and devoured chicken salads, packaged in biodegradable containers that Ann had collected at the restaurant. As we read each other's translations, the sun faded away but left the heat of the day behind.

Sunny passed his notes to me, his eyes windless sails.

I lost myself in his carefully printed block letters, hearing the echo of the male/female voice in my ears.

Humans advance. We disconnect from the land. We want to communicate and acquire goods faster. We want to fly. But advanced materials and activities introduce toxins that harm us and our planet. The demand for sophisticated living soon causes scarcity and unequal distribution of resources.

I watched the others as they read, trying to detect a reaction. Damn operatives, they took everything in stride, even a billion-year-old message from an extinct human race. And Mom had become one of them, sipping her iced tea with a straight face as she turned over the piece of paper in her lap.

Casey pulled his nose away from the page Christopher had handed him. "How are we going to—"

"Not now," Paul interrupted. "We'll discuss later how to follow what our prancestors are saying. Let's focus on recovering the white crystal."

"When do we do that?" Ann asked.

"The detective I put on this says Lynette picks up Carrie from gymnastics in forty-five minutes," Paul said. "And if they go directly home, they would arrive there twelve minutes after that."

"Okay," Elle said. "Sunny, call the others."

Jeremy popped onto the screen, unnerved. "Small planes keep flying over us. Musa was hounded with questions from the locals today in Antigua when he got supplies."

"What are those things behind you, Jeremy?" I asked.

Jeremy twisted around. "The tanks?"

"Jesus," Miguel mumbled.

Paul said to Jeremy, "At some point, no matter what my agency sends you, it won't be enough. It may be time to get you out of there."

"Aren't you guys coming?" Jeremy asked. "Aren't we supposed to make sure this thing gets launched?"

"It will take days for us to get there," Ann said. "That may be too long."

Musa and Meredith set an ice chest down and stepped up to the screen.

"Days?" Musa said.

"Let's move you out of there, please," I said.

Musa spoke, but whistles and yells from nearby people in fatigues drowned him out.

"What did you say, Moose?" Sunny asked.

"We're gonna stay. You guys will make it."

Meredith shielded her ears from the *chup-chup-chup* of a landing helicopter. "But y'all better go get that other crystal."

CHAPTER 39

Our SUVs glided past a golf course surrounded by stucco houses topped with pinkish-brown asphalt shingles.

Ann's voice came from the phone in the center console: "A car with two men, parked in front of the house." She had ridden away from us, on the cobalt-blue cruiser, three minutes ago, in shorts and a tank top.

I leaned between the front seats, toward Paul and Elaine. "Does she mean Lynette's house? Could it be Veeder?"

"*Ssshhhh!*" Elaine said. "Ann, what do they look like?"

"White, middle-aged. Brown hair. One has a mustache and a ball cap. I'm passing the house now. The garage door is opening."

Casey, in the other vehicle, was on the three-way call. "If they park in the garage, they're kidnapping them."

"Damn it!" I said.

"David, be quiet," Elle demanded.

I confined my whispering to the back seat, asking Christopher, "What have I done to that little girl and her mom?" I remembered Carrie's delicate fingers holding the crystal, and her sweet voice: *It looks like the clouds.*

"I pulled over," Ann said, "pretending to check my tire."

We braked at a stop sign, not far from the fourth tee box.

Streetlamps flickered on and I realized there wasn't anyone outside, despite the relatively bearable temperature of ninety degrees.

"The car is backing into the garage," Ann said.

Paul gunned our SUV as he commanded, "Miguel, get them out of here. Casey, on foot, to the front of the house with Ann."

"Yep," Casey said.

I grabbed Elle's shoulder. She explained, "He's telling Miguel to drive Mom and Sunny away."

Paul parked us in front of the house that backed up to Carrie's house. He directed me and Christopher: "You guys stay here, hold your guns. If you see Veeder, don't shoot him."

I objected.

"David!" Elle said. "In this suburb, some grandma will witness you shooting him, and you'll go to prison."

"Or more likely"—Paul scanned the tract homes, each with a square window in front and fewer than twenty feet separating one house from another—"your bullet will miss him and go into one of these houses and *kill* a grandma."

He and Elle stepped out and concealed their pistols in the backs of their pants. "I'm getting too old for this part," he muttered.

They hurried up the driveway and to the side of the house, inched around a cactus, and tugged at the wooden gate, which opened. After scampering through the backyard, they swiftly climbed over the rear fence and into the yard of Carrie's house.

"What is Paul, like sixty-seven?" Christopher asked.

"Nimble guy," I said.

A red Corvette pulled into a garage three doors down from us, and my mind followed it, missing normalcy—was it just another day for its owner, getting home from work, preparing dinner, planning a golf game this weekend?

I picked up my Glock and imagined shoving it into Veeder's mouth. I set it down and socked the back of the driver's seat. It was the kind of hit I had delivered to the chair in the hospital after the transplant team wheeled away my dad, to harvest everything but his fatally flawed heart.

"It's okay," Christopher said, unconvincingly.

Tires squealed.

"Get down!" Christopher shoved his head between his knees.

A four-door luxury car turned the corner behind us. As it passed, a figure with a mustache and a baseball cap, sitting in the back seat, held me in his gaze.

And then the car was gone.

I jumped when Paul opened the door. "I saw Veeder," I said.

"Did he see you?"

"Yes, but not Christopher."

"Huh," Paul said, as if it would take a minute for him to decide what this information would mean.

He drove us around the block, and we took hurried steps toward Lynette's front door. Carrie's sunflower sandals and yellow scooter rested on the porch.

"Just us," Paul called out as he led us inside.

Lynette wore lightweight bell-bottom pants and a sleeveless shirt, and sat on the arm of her couch. A picture of her and Carrie—each with a white-flowered lei around their neck—hung on the wall. Her eyes were glued to the muted television, which displayed a banner at the bottom of the screen: *Denlon's fingerprints on gun found in trash at JFK.*

Paul left to inspect the garage; Casey shut the drapes in front of the sliding glass door and peeked out of them.

Ann, watching out the kitchen window, updated me and Christopher. "We scared them off before they took Lynette."

"Carrie wasn't here," Elle added, emerging from the hallway. "Last-minute change. Her dad picked her up from gymnastics."

Lynette sniffled, smearing away her eyeliner with her tears.

"Thank God," I said. "Why would Veeder take them?"

Lynette checked me out, no doubt comparing me—now with glasses, minus most of my hair, and wearing hip jeans—to the photos she'd seen on TV of a shaggy-headed man in loose-fitting trousers. "He said they worked for you, Dr. Denlon."

"No, trust me . . ." I ran out of words.

Elaine took over. "Veeder's plan was probably to take you and then let you escape, and then you'd tell police that David hired people to kidnap you. That leaves everyone to think David's the bad guy, not him."

"That would have worked," Casey said.

Ann nodded. "And then the next news bit would have been 'Denlon kidnaps woman.'"

I carefully approached Lynette. "I'm David. I never introduced myself on the subway."

She stood, still unsure, but offered her hand. "Lynette."

"I'm so sorry." I held her hand in both of mine. "I had no idea that giving Carrie my zircon would put you guys in danger."

She looked over to the television screen, which now asked, *Is Denlon holding his mom and ex-wife against their will?*

I wanted to explain but didn't know where to start.

Christopher broke the silence. "What happened to the crystal?"

"Veeder got away with it," Elle said.

Lynette looked me over again. "No, he didn't."

"But you told us he took it," Casey said.

"That was before I trusted you." She aimed the remote at the TV, now showing a picture of me—with a beard and looking dazed—taken from the security-camera footage at Shakespeare's birthplace. The screen went black.

She walked to her bedroom and returned with the white zircon on a leather strap.

"Oh my God," Christopher said.

"It seemed valuable to me," she explained. "I would only let Carrie wear it on special occasions. I kept it in my jewelry box. When that guy—you call him Veeder?—asked me for it, I gave him one of Carrie's Geo Sparkles, since it looked similar."

Geo Sparkles. It sounded familiar. What were they?

Then I recalled the commercial, featuring six-year-old girls at a kitchen table with magnifying glasses and jewelry-making tools, giggling at fake geological formations. It ended with the jingle "Because smart girls . . . *very smart girls* . . . know that science is preeeeeetty!"

Geo Sparkles were pretend geological formations, used to craft earrings, bracelets, necklaces, and rings, that came in a pink box with the promise of fostering an interest in science by incorporating lessons, like the difference between stalagmites and stalactites, into jewelry making.

First, I laughed only through my nose, but then I couldn't contain myself.

Casey joined me, laughing so hard he had to sit down on a stool. Christopher covered his mouth but could not stop himself either, punching his fist into his leg. Ann smiled wider than I'd ever seen, and Elle declared, "That's fucking awesome."

And then Lynette chuckled along with us, dabbing a tissue to her cheeks.

Paul stepped in from the garage. "I missed something?"

"Veeder thinks he recovered the zircon," Casey said, "but Lynette slipped him a toy." Saying that out loud sent Casey, along with me and Christopher, into another laughing fit.

Paul's eyes found the zircon in Lynette's hand. "How'd you pull that off?"

Lynette shrugged. "He seemed like the type of jerk who would think some single mom in suburbia couldn't fool him. So when he asked for it, I said, 'You can have it. It's nothing special, I think it's fake. Why else would that guy give it to a kid he didn't know?' And then I gave him Carrie's white Geo Sparkle."

Paul contemplated. "Smooth move."

"Police have probably been dispatched," Ann warned.

Elaine said to Lynette, "It would be great if you could forget about seeing us."

"For how long?" she asked.

"Give us a few days," Paul said.

"I'm sorry I have to take the crystal back." I handed her the box. "It turns out that it's an artifact." As she peeked inside at the mother-of-pearl necklace, I said, "Please tell Carrie I will never forget how brave she was that day."

Paul extended a business card to Lynette. It was blank, except for a phone number. "If you ever want to outsmart bad guys for a living, give this number a call."

CHAPTER 40

After stopping at a home-improvement store so Miguel could purchase wire cutters, we parked outside the Tucson airport, away from the main terminal, in view of the light aircraft resting on their miniature rubber wheels. We gathered in between our two SUVs.

"Here's the plan," Paul said. "Since Veeder knows we're in Tucson, his connections do, too, and he's connected all the way up to the president. That means law enforcement is monitoring every road and commercial flight out. So we're going to sneak into a small plane and take off in a hurry. It'll aggravate air traffic control, but I don't know what else to do."

"Will they send the military after us?" Christopher asked.

"I'm hoping they'll just think I'm inexperienced."

"You're right, Elle," I said. "You operatives do a lot of hoping."

Elle buried her face into the part of her sweatshirt with the patch of polka dots from her mother's blouse.

A Tesla pulled to the side of the road behind us. A man with East African features climbed out of it, and Paul left to meet him.

Across the tarmac, three vehicles parked in the field and shut off their headlights.

"They're getting into position," Ann said. "Please just be cops."

"What's the difference?" I asked. "Whether it's law enforcement or Veeder's people, they're both out to get us."

Casey wrapped the Velcro straps of an ankle holster around his leg. "Regular law enforcement probably won't open fire on a plane."

Mom sighed. I put my arm around her.

When Paul returned, I asked, "Who was that?"

"Magan. He supplied intel some years back that helped us stop a lot of the Somali piracy. Your president rewarded him and his family with citizenship. He's done well. An engineer. Nice car. Plane."

Magan quietly departed in his Tesla.

"Leave most everything behind," Casey said as we abandoned the SUVs. "Being too heavy on this flight could kill us."

The chain-link fence was no match for Miguel's cutters. But before he could finish the job, bright white lights barreled down the road at us; we bent behind the prickly brush while a Hummer with a law-enforcement emblem sped by.

Miguel then finished snipping, and Casey pulled the fence open as a bolt of lightning streaked across the sky. Paul ignored it, ducked through the hole, and ran. The night swallowed him.

Mom stepped through and then Miguel; my stomach sank as they trotted into the black.

More headlights appeared across the tarmac, near the others. When they switched off, Sunny and I sprinted blindly until the white tail of a plane came into view. Paul whistled and we followed the sound, beyond that plane to another.

Elaine boarded after me and I hugged her.

"It's okay," she said, but I kept hugging.

Christopher climbed in, and then Ann and Casey.

"Call Musa and the others now, if you can," Paul said to Sunny. "I don't know what kind of internet we'll have in the air."

Sunny's right leg tapped. He glared with apprehension at the open mousehole part of his window.

Ann lightly stroked Sunny's knotted hair. "Sunny?"

He jolted out of thought, prepared his laptop, and handed it to Paul, who balanced it at the front for everyone to see.

The weary faces of our three comrades appeared from inside a tent.

"Where are you?" Jeremy asked.

Paul lit up a map with a keychain flashlight. "About to take off in a small plane and hop down to you. Maybe twenty-four hours. But maybe longer."

Meredith's face needed good news. "You got the other keystone? Sunny, what have you translated?"

When Sunny didn't answer, Mom asked him, "Have you flown on a small plane before?"

He shook his head no, holding himself as if it were chilly and not, as our moist faces attested, like a sauna.

Christopher answered Meredith. "We recovered the crystal. But their message is overwhelming; I don't think we know where to start."

"About four minutes," Paul said. "Start somewhere and talk fast."

Casey took the lead. "Okay, well, I hope you guys are sitting down. This transporter has to take a group of people to a planet in another star system of our galaxy, to colonize, to continue the existence of our kind."

Musa and the others kept their eyes on us. Had the screen frozen?

Casey further explained, "Our prancestors warn that we must get this first ship launched, to ensure that at least some of us go colonize and continue humanity."

Jeremy eventually asked, "Why can't we continue living here?"

"Because Earth is only the birthing ground for humankind," Ann said. "Our species comes into existence here, but this isn't where humans are supposed to live, once we've evolved and developed. There are other planets, with conditions more suitable to us. The transporter takes us to the closest one."

Paul stuffed his map into the thin, elastic pocket near the floor. "Seatbelts!"

"Birthing ground?" Meredith asked.

"Yes," I said, clipping my belt. "Our prancestors explain there are two kinds of planets in our galaxy for human beings—birthing and habitation. Earth is a birthing planet, with the conditions for evolution that can create a humanoid species."

Jeremy pushed his hair out of his face as if seeing us with both eyes would help him comprehend. "Conditions for evolution?"

"Birthing planets have extremes, like ice ages and greenhouse periods," I said. "Forces that allow Mother Nature to naturally select the fittest, leading to new life-forms that are more and more complex, until eventually, humankind is born."

They stared and said nothing. Elaine clarified, "Think of it like an unborn baby. It can't develop without the conditions of the womb, but once it matures, it has to leave to survive. Earth is the womb of our race."

The propellers whirled into a haze; Sunny looked for something to hold on to.

"I get it," Meredith said. "Mother Earth brought humankind into being, but we're too advanced now, and too numerous. We're just hurting her, and ourselves, if we stay."

"Exactly," Christopher said. "Our prancestors say that if we don't leave, we either fight each other to death over resources, or the planet kills us off, so it can go into its recovery period."

"To recover from what?" Jeremy asked.

"That was Casey's part," Christopher said as Casey pulled a crinkled paper from his only remaining belonging—a toiletry bag—save the gun on his ankle.

"Intoxication." Casey struggled to read his notes in the dark. "And there's one problem in particular; we're not sure how to translate this. They call it the material that lives beyond its purpose . . . it's used in daily functions . . . food storage . . . buildings . . ."

"Plastic?" Musa suggested.

We collectively paused.

"Plastic," Sunny said, keeping his nose to the window, clearly doubting our tiny plane's ability to fly. "That's it."

"They said it poisons the oceans and kills the plants and animals," Casey reported. "The Earth heats up and then goes through an ice age. Elaine has been translating the numbers. Elle, how long does it take for Earth to recover?"

"I'm not sure," she said as she nervously eyed Paul, seemingly anxious for us to get in the air and away from whoever was in those vehicles, shining their headlights toward us. "At least a million years. But I think the number is bigger, like a hundred million."

After passing the computer back to us, Paul put large headphones over his ears. "Here goes." He mumbled quickly to air traffic control; all I caught was "requesting to taxi."

"But won't we just screw up the next planet, the habitation planet, like we've done here?" Meredith asked.

"No," Sunny said, keeping his fearful eyes on the propellers. "The destination planet is the right kind of host for advanced humans."

"How so?" Meredith asked. "Like, how can a planet that's good for humans not produce them?"

The one time it was appropriate for Sunny to scream—over the piercing buzz of the engines—he wanted only to hold himself and stare out the window. Nevertheless, he sucked in a determined breath, turned toward the laptop screen, and delivered a quick synopsis.

"The same challenges that prompt evolution—extreme temperatures, scarcity of resources—also make it too difficult for us to survive here without using chemicals and toxic materials to build our houses, drive our cars, mine for resources, and so on. In other words, the very circumstances that bring us to life in the first place become obstacles to us maintaining our species. But the habitation planets have more accommodating conditions—fair weather, natural shelters, more abundant sources of food—making it much easier for us to sustain ourselves there."

Sunny's animation was gone; he spoke rapidly, from memory. "These stable conditions mean we can live in a sophisticated way, absent conflict with each other or the environment, which means humans can thrive. However, these stable, accommodating conditions are unable to spur the kind of radical evolution that would lead to the *creation* of humankind. Habitation planets, therefore, could never give birth to a complex species like humans. To populate these planets, humans must migrate to them after developing on a birthing planet."

"That's incredible," Jeremy said.

I was sure that Sunny agreed, but he had done his part and now returned to the window, as if keeping an eye on the wing would ensure that it didn't fall off.

When our plane rolled toward the taxiway, more cars—some in the field beyond the runways, others near the buildings—switched on their headlights.

"C'mon, Paul," Ann muttered. "Get us out of here."

"Keep going guys," Musa said.

"The habitation planets are dying without humans." Casey aimed his phone's light at his page of notes. "They need a species that can do things like use fire and combine elements, because those functions sustain their atmosphere and their plant life."

As we approached the runway, two black SUVs raced toward us from the terminal.

"Are cars allowed to come out this far?" Christopher asked.

"Cut to the chase," Paul said, twisting his headphones to expose one ear.

"What do you mean, Paul?" Ann asked. "What should we tell them?"

Paul's hands jumped from knobs to switches in the cockpit. "Tell them what they need to know to launch the ship without us." He covered his ear again.

"What?" Jeremy asked. "But you guys have the crystals."

"If anything happens to us," Elaine said. "Come for our things. The crystals have survived a billion years on Earth; they'll survive a plane wreck."

Sunny pulled at his hair; Mom nibbled on her fingernail.

"What if people are already on the habitation planet when we get there?" Meredith asked. "Like maybe they've already arrived, from another birthing planet?"

"That could be," Christopher said. "But we either go there for the chance to keep our species alive, or we stay here and go extinct."

"So let's go," Jeremy said. "Let's colonize!"

Paul mumbled into his microphone again, and this time I could make out a series of phonetic letters along with numbers, one of them "niner," and the phrase "holding short." He leaned toward the small windshield, searching the night sky for planes.

Sunny slapped his hands onto his face, covering his eyes, but I didn't know if he was expressing his fear of flying or anticipating the news we were about to deliver to Jeremy, Meredith, and Musa.

"There's an issue with launching," Casey said, having to raise his voice over the screech of the engines. "We can't do it without doctors and farmers and teachers, physicists, engineers . . . people to serve in all areas."

Paul accelerated. Part of his garble was "cleared for takeoff," as if he were insisting on it instead of asking permission.

"Why do we need all those people?" Meredith asked.

Casey looked to Elle, who said, "If I'm translating the number correctly, it takes about a century to get to the new world. The ship is a flying city; we establish a society, for the hundred-year journey."

Our speed increased. Paul flipped up his microphone, talking to himself. "Bugger off, ATC. Waiting doesn't work for us."

We could hardly hear Meredith over the noise of the plane. "But we won't live for a hundred years."

"We have kids," Ann yelled. "And they have kids. And that's who colonizes our new home."

"How many people do we need?" Musa asked.

Sunny braced himself, seeming to expect the rattling plane, now in full throttle, to fall apart.

"Elaine." Musa spoke louder. "How many people do we need to launch this thing?"

The end of the runway quickly approached. Were we too heavy?

"The way I translate it," Elaine shouted, "the number is at least three hundred. But it could be three thousand."

The bumping beneath us stopped; the nose of the plane finally sought the sky.

"What?" Jeremy said. "We gotta find three hundred people—or three thousand—with all those skills"—his voice began to fade away—"and convince them to leave the planet . . . ?"

CHAPTER 41

"Guess it wasn't just cops," Casey said.

I moved into the copilot's seat, a feat that required backing into it and lifting one leg over Paul's head. "If the shots hit the gas tank, how long do we have?"

Paul took off one of his earmuff headphones. "Come again?"

"How long until we run out of gas?"

"No way to know."

"Why don't you seem concerned?"

Paul squinted into the round indicator which still pointed to F. "For Magan to have a plane, he would've run it by my agency. And we insist on self-sealing tanks."

I sighed away tension. The engines blared a one-note song and I released myself into it.

I blinked and lugged my head up, wondering how much time had passed. It came to me slowly that the wooly white line in the distance was the horizon.

"You were out," Paul said. "Glad you could get some shut-eye."

"Where are we?"

He scooted a headphone away. "What's that?"

"Where are we?"

"Near Laredo."

The flat expanse of Texas came into view as the sun rose. Paul gently set our plane down on the only airstrip of an airport with no control tower. Miguel hot-wired a van parked near the hangar.

Elle told the wrinkly woman who smelled like cigarettes at the motel desk that we were a church group on a road trip and needed four rooms.

We parked the van behind the building and replaced its license plates with ones we had stolen on the drive from the airport. Their frames read *Mike's Auto Sales . . . Buy the Best!*

Paul slept while the rest of us ate gas-station food, in the room where Elaine and I were staying. Were the walls gray or dirty?

Ann clicked her laptop shut. "People have flown over the site and posted pictures online. I don't know how long that army is going to be able to protect it. And they're saying we stole a plane. And the—"

"Please," I said. "Just stop."

"And the reports are that we're a band of terrorists."

Sunny, smiling uncontrollably since he had climbed out of the plane, sat up on his haunches on the bed. "Our prancestors gave the habitation planet, the ship's destination, a unique symbol, like a name. So what name should we assign to that symbol, to name the planet?" He gave up on his soggy sandwich, putting it back in its bag and dropping the bag into the metal wastebasket.

I welcomed the diversion of naming the planet we were supposed to colonize. "Sunny, you said it's the space cruiser's *destination*." I began pacing the room. "It's where the transporter is programmed to take us. Where we're meant to go, to avoid extinction."

Mom smiled. "It's our destiny."

"Destiny," Casey said. He retrieved Sunny's bag out of the trash and rescued the half-eaten sandwich. "*Destiny.* Yeah."

Miguel put his thumb in the air.

"Oh, whoops." Elle looked at her phone. "We were supposed to wake up Paul fifteen minutes ago."

We relocated our meeting to his room.

Paul heaved himself out of slumber and called one of his operatives. We watched as he nodded. "Right. Yes."

"Okay then," he sighed. "Well, that's it."

He drank coffee from a flimsy cardboard cup, wincing between each sip. "Listen. My operatives tell me not to enter Mexico by air. They're impounding private planes upon arrival and demanding ransoms. We've got to go by vehicle, but we can't use a stolen van. And they've found our plane, where we left it this morning. Border crossings now have heightened security."

Mom shook her head, walking to the window. Ann cussed under her breath. The wind had kicked up, whistling through the gap between the door and the wall.

Paul dumped his coffee down the sink. "I don't know what fate lies ahead."

Ice cubes crashed down in the machine outside the door, startling us.

Paul bent forward, setting both hands on the fake-marble countertop. "What I'm saying is: get off this train now if you don't plan to be on the launch. Earth has a lot of nooks and crannies. If you want to hide out in one of them, tell me now, while there's still a chance I can make that happen."

"How are we going to get to the site?" Christopher asked.

"That is an answer we don't have yet," Paul said, before unwrapping the circular soap and washing his face.

"How are we going to find enough people to launch the transporter?" I asked.

"There's another one." He grabbed for a towel with his eyes closed.

"Staying here isn't a bad choice," I said. "Staying on Earth means working toward more launches. The singularity is coming. We'll soon invent the materials to build fleets of these ships. Our prancestors couldn't figure out how to work together to send transporters to Destiny, but that doesn't mean we can't."

Ann disagreed by nearly spitting. "Tuh!"

The wind sped up; twiggy branches scratched the window.

Miguel's voice surprised us. "Decision time."

We stared at each other.

"Oh Jesus." Ann stood up. "We don't have time for this. You all know. Everyone has made their decision. Out with it."

"You're going, Ann?" Paul asked. "On a transporter toward another solar system that you won't live to see?"

"Of course," she said. "Life isn't about finding something to live for. It's about finding something worth dying for." She tossed her microwaved noodle cup in the trash.

Paul countered, "But Ann, what if this is a hoax? Someone buried this stuff, the ship and the rocks with messages, so we would—"

"Impossible," Sunny said. "Musa used radiometric dating, and not only is the vehicle too substantial to be a prank, it's made of materials we haven't invented."

Ann stood about five feet, eight inches tall, but she suddenly seemed taller. "I feel like all my life something deep inside me has been asking a question, and this discovery is finally the answer." She pointed to Sunny's notebook. "All that stuff we've translated, about humans living more easily somewhere else, it just makes sense. You know, we tried once, my friends and I, in college. It's not that we were lazy and didn't want to get a nine-to-five job.

It's that it seemed silly to secure a loan to buy a house and maintain a car and go shopping all the time and save for retirement and on and on. We thought, couldn't we live safely, happily, and responsibly, just off the Earth?"

A gale of wind mimicked an infant's cry. Ann waited for Miguel to check the window before she continued.

She quieted her voice. "So we lived in yurts, off the grid, for a month. And you know, you *could* live off the land, if whole communities would embrace that way of life. But how do you convince people to give up the comforts they have known all their lives? Have you ever tried to make your own water safe to drink? To grind your own flour? To feed your own chickens without going to a store? To make your own medicine? It's a lot of work that seems ridiculous when the majority of the population is spewing out chemicals anyway."

Her next word got stuck in her throat and she turned around. She stared up at a cobweb in the corner of the ceiling and then faced us again. "I haven't had children because I don't want to bring another human being into this struggle. But I *would* have kids on that ship. I would give them the opportunity to be the parents of the first generation to live on Destiny."

She plugged a burner phone into a charger and looked at me. "I'm going on the launch, even if you don't."

"I'm going with you," Mom said.

"Mom?" I went to her. "Wait, let's talk."

"Oh, Davey, there's nothing to talk about." Mom pulled her baggie of pills out of her pocket and went to the sink for a plastic cup; I wondered how she would get blood pressure medication on a spaceship. "My husband is gone, and my only child has made a discovery that can save humanity. This is my path. And, dear, it's okay if you don't go."

"What?"

"Maybe you want to be here, to build more ships and ensure fair launches. Whatever you decide, sweetie, is what's meant to be. But your mom is going to be on that transporter."

Miguel gave a peace sign and resumed peering through a gap in the curtains, with binoculars he'd found in the van.

Casey sighed. "Somehow, doing anything else but getting on that transporter is what makes me afraid. I'm in."

Sunny unplugged the cord to his laptop and wound it around its power pack. "There's nowhere else for me to be." He looked at Paul. "But I need to say good-bye to my parents and my sister."

"Get me their contact information," Paul said. "I'll see what I can do."

"And you, Paul?" Casey asked.

The wind continued its assault, vibrating the window and door.

"It's about time that I retire." Paul smirked. "And that transporter beats any retirement community I've ever seen."

Christopher laughed. "And if I'm in outer space, Veeder can't hurt me. Sign me up."

I sat near Elle, touching the dotted material sewn into her sweatshirt. "What would your mom say?"

"I can answer that," Paul said. "I knew Elaine's mother well."

Elaine smiled, delighted for a glimpse of her mother's spirit.

"Sheri was practical, and unafraid. Without a doubt, Elaine's mother would have quickly determined that staying here to deal with partisan politics and red tape, to secure funding and invent new materials, would be much more of a headache than being on the first blast into space."

"Yeah." Elaine laughed. "She'd go, and she'd want me with her."

Sunny smacked the nightstand. "But if we're going to launch a city, we need three hundred people!"

"It's three thousand," Elaine said. "I'm sure of it now."

Miguel took his binoculars away from his face to stare at Elaine.

"Three thousand?" Sunny lowered his voice when Casey's hand pushed an invisible brake in the air. "With all the skills to run a society? And supplies, like plants and animals? How are we going to do this?"

"Our prancestors put a lot of faith in us." Casey lay across the foot of the bed. "I don't think we turned out as good as they were hoping."

Sunny's computer whooped. We each found a view of his laptop as Musa's eyes blinked onto the screen.

"Can you see me? Can you hear me?"

"We got you, Moose," Sunny said.

Behind him, Meredith and Jeremy frantically packed up their camping gear.

Five male hikers came onto the scene. Soldiers screamed in Spanish, *"Go Back! Now!"* The group defied them and kept walking.

Musa's nervous words ran together. "We're moving to higher ground. The Guatemalan government is being pressured by the UN to let a multinational task force into the site. And tourists are flooding the place. When will you be here?"

"We've been delayed," Paul said. "Forty-eight hours, if we're lucky."

Musa scanned the area around him. "I don't know what this place will be by then."

"Please make the decision about whether you want to be on the transporter," Paul said. "Ask Jeremy and Meredith. Because if any of you aren't going, we've got to get you out of there."

"We already talked about it. We're on the launch. But we need you and the crystals." Musa gazed at us and finally said, "Godspeed."

Chapter 42

Paul checked his watch. "I think we're here for the night. But that van gives us away. Miguel, you and Casey can ditch it? Use a taxi service to return?"

Back with Elle in our room, I peeked out the corner of the window at Miguel and Casey walking across the nearly empty parking lot. The weeds growing up through the potholes shimmied in each gust of wind. On the other side of the highway there was no sign of human life, only undeveloped land as far as I could see, with brittle, stickery plants that would someday be uprooted and blown into their tumble.

Elle brushed her teeth, giving the air a minty smell.

I looked away from the window and examined the poster in a warped plastic frame, hanging on the wall. It provided the only real color in the room, since the carpet was worn-out brown and the bedspread was grayish silver—and dull, like ten thousand cycles in the washing machine had drained the dye from its threads. The hot air balloon on this poster, however, offered a shiny checkerboard of red, green, yellow, and blue, and the sight of it, carrying its basket above some kind of crop—rows of strawberries? Lettuce?—would have been soothing except for the ridiculous one-word message beneath it: *Dream.*

It was an unpleasant reminder of that painted rock in my marriage counselor's office. *Faith.*

Where did this habit come from, this human tendency to tell others the obvious? *Hey, you're a person, not a rat, or an oak tree, so you should have faith, you should dream.* Why did these directives always come at the lowest of times, as if to point out that all one has left is an intangible concept? *Faith* was suggested to couples on the verge of divorce; people stuck in dingy motel rooms were told to *Dream.*

I retreated into a steamy shower, scrubbing myself in sevens. Right arm, seven soapy washcloth swishes; left arm, seven more.

Then Elle stepped in.

The water flowed into her cleavage, splashed up onto her mouth, and slowly straightened her hair. Her green eyes shined through the misty cascade. She struggled to say, "David," before tears spilled down her face and blended into the wetness. "I don't know what's going to happen."

I kissed her. "It's not here. None of it is here, in this space."

That confident zeal that was uniquely Elaine's, that had empowered her through life-risking combat and clever scheming, now compelled her to indulge in carnal fulfillment as if it were her last chance to do so.

She knelt down and didn't hesitate. I braced myself against the wall as my leg muscles found it more difficult to work. I fell into a fantasy of us in a dirty movie—skin, steam, saliva—and yet, the moment was sacred, as though we'd been summoned to it, to a union written in the stars.

She stood up with adventure on her face—no, more than that. Invincibility.

A hint of fear bled into my excitement, as if I were on a roller coaster at its apex, about to plummet into the thrill of my life.

Her strong hands left me, in search of the top edges of the shower walls. She secured the toes of her right foot on the handle of the glass door and came off the ground as if she could fly, raising her left leg and tightly wrapping it around me.

I grabbed on to her, guiding her body into the perfect position to receive me. She invited more by tilting her knees outward, dipping into a floating plié.

"Elaine the Magnificent," I whispered, feeling myself deplete, giving everything I had to make love to her, to perform for her so long and so perfectly that it would dissolve the concepts of space and time, of life and death, unlocking the door and allowing us, forever, into a world of only each other.

Elle folded toward me, her arms now around my neck, panting into tiny convulsions. My pressure released and I pulsated inside her, each wave a new level of pleasure, almost unbearable.

And then the water hitting the shower door seemed loud. We hushed our breathing as I helped her find her footing. I glided my hands down her back and held her waist. "I love you."

She ran her fingers through what was left of my hair. "I love you, too."

We left our declarations undisturbed, adding no more words as we slipped into bed naked and fit our bodies together, two parts of a whole.

The bedside lamp—affixed to the nightstand—was just beyond my reach and I didn't want to stretch, lest Elaine, now sleeping on my chest, would be awakened. I shuffled through the pages of my mind, searching for a happy memory or a playful musing, anything to escape the thought that I would soon die, and would go down in history as a wrongdoer.

I could distract myself with nothing but the shadowy hue on the walls, which was, I concluded, not the color of the paint, but years of filth.

CHAPTER 43

"Liam trusts me," Christopher said. "I was always nice to him. I bet I could convince him to let us cross."

I had entered our morning meeting late, after finally dozing off around three a.m.

"Okay," Casey said. "Then there's the plan."

"What's going on?" I asked, rubbing my eyes.

Paul handed me a packaged muffin. "My guys tell me they put Liam Ericson at the border checkpoint here in Laredo, to watch out for us."

"They're using Liam?" I asked. "Because he can recognize me and Christopher?"

"Yep. Put your fake glasses on," Elle said. "Our taxi is here."

Elle and I entered the lot of Billy McGee's RVs to see Paul and Mom, who had arrived ahead of us, pretending to be a couple. Our target was the rig with the *Hot Deal* sign—black letters on a three-by-four-foot cutout of a red chili pepper—displayed on its humongous windshield.

An eager salesman invited Paul and Mom to join him in the motorhome. We browsed our way over and stared at its massive front wheel. I tapped the tire with my toe.

Elaine chuckled. "Conducting analysis, Doctor?"

We approached the door and tuned in to the conversation happening inside. "Congratulations on your retirement," the salesman said. "If you buy today, we throw in all kinds of things."

"Like what?" Paul asked, escaping into his character.

"For one thing, we fill 'er up with gas—that's hundreds of dollars these days."

"Holy moly!" Paul said. "Maybe we should rethink this, honey. America is much bigger than my homeland. All that driving will be too much money on gas."

"Dear, look at this storage space," Mom said.

We peered up the stairs to see Mom admiring small compartments that clipped shut.

"Hey, honey, did you hear me?" Paul asked. "I don't know if we can afford to go anywhere in one of these."

Elaine and I read each other's minds. *We don't have time for this!*

"Tell you what," the salesman said. "We can give you a great deal on an extended warranty."

"We don't need that," Paul retorted.

When Elaine and I boarded the RV, the salesman tugged on his Wile E. Coyote tie and said, "Welcome! Did the 'super sale' bring you in today?"

"Yeah," Elaine said. "And I like peppers."

"Good one!" he said. "Don't forget to check out the bathroom. Bigger than you'd expect, three whole feet wide. Plenty of room to do your business."

I caught sight of the small grocery store across the parking lot with a simple sign. *Food and Supplies.* After pretending to inspect the driver's seat, I joined Mom in the bedroom and whispered my idea.

"Excuse me, Mr. Salesman," Mom yelled out the window.

"Call me Hank," he said as he extended the outdoor kitchen.

"Hank, is that food-and-supplies place part of this business, too?"

"Yes, ma'am. Both establishments belong to Billy McGee's. Whatcha thinkin'?"

In under an hour, Paul and Mom drove away in a motorhome with no warranty but with a free tank of gas and, complimentary, five hundred dollars' worth of products—everything from sliced bread to nail clippers.

When they picked the rest of us up down the street, a boyish grin spread across Casey's face. "Can I drive?" he asked. "My grandparents had one of these."

"Have at it." Paul shifted to the passenger's seat and studied a map. "Let's see, we'll stay along the coast . . ." His phone vibrated and after reading it, he said, "Liam's headed to lunch, let's go. I've got a guy tailing him."

Over the next several minutes, Casey used the blinking dot on the map on Paul's phone to navigate our rig.

"There he is," Paul said, pointing to a car I couldn't see amid the traffic. "He's turning in, there. Can you fit in that driveway?"

The RV's rear tire rolled over the curb; our bodies lifted and dropped. "Oh crap," Casey said. "How did my grandpa do this?"

Paul shut off his map application and handed me his phone. "I have a contact at the Department of Human Services. Sent me pictures of Liam's file."

"Why does he have a file there?" Elle asked.

"He was in foster care," Paul said. "Thought there might be something we could use as leverage."

I scanned the pages on the phone. Familiar phrases stood out. *Doesn't pick up social cues. Difficulty regulating emotion.*

"He was never permanently adopted," Paul continued. "Spent some time in special ed. Seems like the Church was his only constant."

Mom looked at me and then back to the tuna salad sandwiches she was constructing.

I handed the phone to Paul. "I don't think there's anything we can use."

Miguel rapped the window and pointed. Liam walked alone toward the entrance of the Burger Hut with his arms crossed and held awkwardly high on his chest.

A group of teenaged boys near their parked truck stopped shoving each other to stare at Liam. One of them taunted, "Hey, weird dude, what's up?"

Liam redirected himself to the dumpsters on the side of the building. A black cat with begging eyes leapt out from behind one of the steel bins and took a long look at the pear-shaped man staring back at him. Liam slowly squatted and remained still. When the cat ventured closer, Liam gently rubbed its cheek.

The five leggy juveniles, each drinking from a large cup with a fat straw, lost interest in Liam and climbed into their truck, loudly talking in detached conversation—one sang a song lyric, another said, "These shakes are the bomb," and a third lamented, "I fuckin' hate school."

Their truck seemed malformed instead of cool—too tall for its short length and too much space between its frame and those big, deeply treaded tires. As it thumped with noise—music?—and wheeled away, Liam hurried into the restaurant. Miguel and I moved into position, one of us on each side of the door.

When Liam came out and saw me, his lonely eyes sparked a happy greeting before they shrank and darkened.

"You'll be shot if you don't comply," I said. "Walk with us."

Liam stretched his neck around Miguel to view the cat, who sat with his tail wrapped around his body, eagerly staring at us.

"Let's go," Miguel said, pushing Liam.

In the RV, Liam's eyes didn't leave the window, watching the cat scamper behind the dumpster. Miguel tied each of Liam's hands to his body, threading the thin rope through the belt loops in his trousers.

I asked, "You want to feed him?"

Liam squinted at me in repulsion.

Ann dipped her nose into his bag. "The burger's for you, the chicken strips for the kitty?"

Liam stared at his feet—in black sneakers with worn-out rubber soles—as Miguel tied them.

Ann put her hand on Liam's throat. "Answer."

"Yes," Liam quickly said.

I took some of the chicken and reopened the door.

"They love chicken," Mom said. "Remember how Arthur ate it?"

"Hurry, mate," Paul warned.

At the trash bins, I crouched down and called, "Here, kitty." I set one of the chicken pieces on the ground. The cat stayed hidden. I saw Arthur in my memory, telling me with his citrine eyes that everything was okay as long as he was there.

This cat was our leverage.

When he cautiously approached the chicken, I scooped him up and dashed back to the rig. He wiggled out of my hands and hid in a corner of the bedroom.

I tore more chicken into tiny pieces and spread it on a plate near Liam's feet.

"Don't worry," I said to Liam. "We aren't going to harm you."

"Do not credit yourself for showing mercy," Liam responded. "You are being held back from hurting me by the divine force. My hands are tied, but yours are restrained even tighter."

Ann swung to smack Liam in the face, but I caught her hand before it hit him.

"Don't talk like that," Ann said. "It's creepy. Do you hear me?"

Liam returned to gazing at his feet.

The cat slinked out of the bedroom and stopped, eyeing the plate of chicken. When Liam made a soft clicking noise, the cat cautiously stepped closer, but paused again.

"Should we name him?" I asked.

Liam said nothing.

I untied one of Liam's hands and put his bag of food on the table in front of him. After warming a mug of water in the microwave, I plunked a tea bag in it and handed it to him. I set a package of wet wipes on the table.

The scrawny cat moved to Liam's feet and nearly inhaled the chicken. Mom set a bowl of water on the floor.

As Liam bit into his hamburger, Sunny emerged from the bedroom and sat on the vinyl seat across the table.

What was Sunny doing? His interaction with Liam had not been part of our plan. The rest of us looked around at each other.

"Since we're asking you to help us," Sunny said, "I thought we could share some information with you."

Casey looked up at the ceiling vent, his thought clearly written on his face. *Oh boy, here's where this goes wrong.*

Ann raised her eyebrows toward Paul, silently asking, *Should we stop this?*

Liam took another bite of his hamburger.

"It's amazing," Sunny said. "It's a vehicle that transports us across the galaxy." He reached down and lightly touched the spine of the cat, who raised up his back end to make sure Sunny would pet him all the way to his tail.

Liam relaxed as if he were the one getting a back rub.

Sunny continued, "The launch starts out with three thousand people, and the population expands over the century it takes to get to Destiny. That's what the planet's called—where the transporter goes, to another star system."

Liam sipped his tea. I replenished the cat's empty dish.

"But the ship, it's enormous." Sunny's enthusiasm was nearly electric. "It creates a sustainable living environment. It grows a forest! And a three-story garden. It will have animals to feed and clothe us. We'll be a functioning society that is supported by the ship's ecosystem across generations."

Mom stopped loading the small pantry, chicken noodle soup in one hand, peanut butter in the other. Miguel and Ann looked at each other and then back at Sunny, who had apparently translated a lot more of the message from our prancestors.

"It even creates an internal weather system!" There was no harm in Sunny's loud voice, as no one was near the RV. "It self-navigates. And it can tell how many people are on board, their age and body mass, and it determines their nutrient and atmospheric needs. We'll have to bring doctors for health care, and legal people for law and order, and political people for government, and farmers, and botanists, and teachers. We'll have to devise a schedule and—"

"Good Lord," Liam interrupted. "Jesus Christ our Savior!" He peered upward as if he could see through the plastic ceiling. "Oh Lord, you are so great! They don't get it. They don't even get it. But you have put me here so I can show them!"

"Show us what?" Casey asked.

"You speak of an ark."

"That's a *fable*," Ann nearly screamed. "This is a transporter that sustains us on a journey. To another region of our galaxy. A galaxy that exists even though it isn't mentioned in the Bible. Science is fucking real!"

Paul attempted to balance Ann's scissor tongue. "Everyone is entitled to their beliefs."

"Ark or not," I said, "why couldn't this be part of God's plan? But Liam, I have a question for you. If you have such an allegiance to God, how could you kill someone?"

Liam used his free hand to pull a wipe from the package. He carefully—almost angrily—cleaned the area of the table on which he'd eaten. "I've killed no one, Denlon."

Our plan had been to threaten him with murder charges and then agree not to turn him in if he let us through the checkpoint. "There's a grave in the backyard of a Bolivian house that says otherwise."

Liam punched his cup off the table. It smacked into the small oven with a *clang-crunch!* and broke into pieces. "You don't know what you're talking about!"

The cat dove under the driver's seat.

Mom pulled an ice pop out of the freezer, unwrapped it, and handed it to Liam. He stared at it like he'd never seen one before. She touched it to his lips. "Take it. Eat it."

Liam pinched the stick between his fingers and began to lick the raspberry ice, seemingly surprised at how much he enjoyed it.

Casey picked up the cup parts and wiped the floor, releasing a defeated sigh.

"I told him to run away," Liam said. "I shot into the dirt. I pushed all the dirt in the hole."

After sneaking his way back, the cat rubbed his head on Liam's foot.

"Why did you make the rest of us believe you killed someone?" I asked.

He tipped his frozen treat sideways and caught its drips with his mouth. "All I had, to keep Vladmir and Gustav from hurting me, was their belief that I was capable of murder."

"Sorry to interrupt, David," Paul said. "But Liam, how long did you tell the others at the checkpoint you'd be gone for lunch?"

Liam said nothing.

Ann approached him, but before she could choke him, he said, "Half an hour."

"We're at thirty-four minutes," Paul said.

Elle lifted Liam's shirt and taped a gadget to his bare stomach, our Plan B.

Ann came to Liam again. "If you try to remove this or if you alert people to us, we press a button and you explode. Guts everywhere."

Miguel waved something small, rectangular, and black in the air, hopefully too quickly for Liam to perceive that it was our TV's remote control.

Casey added, "And also, your cat will die."

Liam's frightened eyes questioned mine.

"Listen," I said, "all you need to do is get us through the checkpoint and not tell anyone about us. An hour after we drive away, the device will deactivate and you can remove it."

Liam gave the ice-pop stick to Mom and dried his hand on the paper towel she held out, before he brushed his fingers on the purring cat.

"And one more thing," I said, as Elaine executed the final part of our plan. She put her laptop on the table. The screen displayed a headline about the mysterious death of a community leader in central Africa.

"Patrick Veeder uses you, Liam," I said. "He has you giving old clothes and tools to poor people, while he's making millions from their relics. Haven't you noticed that village leaders die after you leave?"

"Lots of people die in those villages," Liam mumbled.

On cue, Christopher appeared at the bedroom doorway. "Veeder murders them, Liam. After he picks up the artifacts that you encourage them to give away. He was using both of us to do very, very bad things."

"Christopher," Liam said, as if he wanted to hug him.

"How are you?" Christopher asked.

Liam's eyebrows nearly banged into each other. "What are you doing with Denlon?"

"Being on the right side." Christopher carefully stepped toward Liam, trying not to scare the cat. "Look, we're telling you the truth about Veeder. Those people didn't die from infections."

"Forty-two minutes," Paul reminded.

We untied Liam and opened the door. I collected the cat in my arms, holding him back when he reached in Liam's direction and meowed as if he were in pain.

Liam paused on the steps. Without looking back, he said, "Let's call him Noah."

He hobbled out, head down, and walked to his car.

I asked Elle, "What'd you make the gadget out of?"

"A bottle cap, toothpicks, a package of sugar, and foil."

We watched Liam drive away, as Casey wondered out loud, "Think he'll cover for us?"

Chapter 44

Ann picked up the only part of a disguise we had left—a wig—and plonked it onto my head. She dusted rouge on my face while Elle shaved my forearms and painted my fingernails. I wore Ann's oversized pajama top and tucked myself into bed, blowing on my wet nails.

Elle splattered sunscreen on her face but didn't blend it in. Sunny scrunched his knotted hair into a hat. Mom put a scarf around her head and my fake glasses on her nose. Christopher slicked back his hair with cooking oil, as Mom and Paul hadn't thought to get hair gel on their shopping spree. We practiced our vacation story.

Paul took over driving, steering us into the sea of vehicles at the border checkpoint. The patrol officers overflowed with self-righteousness, chins up and peering down their noses; they clutched the straps of their machine guns with one hand and used the other to stop cars or wave them through.

Elle laid out our passports on the table. "I hope these work."

The door opened and a German shepherd bounded on board, scaring Mom two steps backward. The guard holding the leash was not sorry. The dog's fidgety black nose skimmed the edges of the drawers and along the creases of the couch cushions.

In Spanish, Miguel called toward the bedroom, *"Sweetie, we're at the checkpoint, it's time to wake up."*

I responded in the highest pitch voice I could force my vocal cords to produce. *"We're at the checkpoint? Why didn't you wake me up sooner?"*

Miguel grumbled to himself, *"Because you're a monster."*

"I heard that!" I said.

The guard's rock-hard cheeks softened when he chuckled.

I kept the sheet up to my nose, exposing my fingernails. *"I'm so embarrassed, sir . . ."*

"It's okay, ma'am." He wasn't interested in a lady, only drugs, weapons, and David Denlon. He respectfully averted his eyes from me as the dog sniffed around the bed.

When he led the dog into the bathroom, I peeked out the small bedroom window and into the booth at the checkpoint. Large red letters appeared on a TV monitor—*Breaking News: Stolen van recovered; RV purchased in cash.*

The German shepherd arrived at the front seats and pawed at the floor. He whined and glanced back to his boss. Noah had compressed himself into a fuzzy black ball on the dashboard. His yellow eyes screamed for help.

The guard commanded, "Déjalo," and took the dog outside. He ordered his colleague in the same tone he had used with the dog. *"Get Liam. And have him tell these people their cat has to go to Inspection."*

Within minutes, Liam clomped on board. He ignored us and searched for Noah.

"The dash," Ann said.

Liam cradled Noah in his arms and contemplated Christopher, who stood as he always had, with his shoulders slightly rolled forward in an unthreatening pose.

Christopher pet Noah's head. "Please, Liam."

Liam kept hold of Noah and walked out.

A different guard used a metal rod with a mirror at the end of it to inspect beneath our vehicle. He was younger than the guard with the dog and seemed more invested in finding me. He spoke English to Liam. "Could it be them? Maybe in disguise?"

Elle held her breath; Ann grabbed Casey's arm.

"No," Liam finally responded, "but they don't have papers for the cat. I'm taking it to the boarding house; they'll be back in four days to pick it up."

The guard aimed his eyes up toward our kitchen window, unconvinced. He turned to the canine handler and switched to Spanish. *"You checked the basement compartment and under the mattress?"*

The handler had moved on to the extended cab of the truck in the next lane, and either didn't hear the question or was choosing not to answer. The younger guard reluctantly folded in our outdoor steps. He waved us on, asking Liam, "What's a boarding house?"

"Nice work," Paul said, maneuvering our rolling home onto Avenida 15 de Junio.

Sunny fumbled with a burner phone. "I can't get through to Musa."

"Can you text them?" Paul asked. "Let them know we made it across?"

"You guys need to see this," Elle interrupted, having opened her laptop. "Miguel, can you hook this up?"

Miguel plugged an adapter into her computer, and the TV monitor came alive.

A blonde-haired woman with a British accent reported, "We have breaking news that a location in Guatemala has been identified as the discovery site associated with Dr. Denlon's search for people from the distant past."

"Turn it up," Casey said, a state of alarm overtaking his normal air of confidence.

"Denlon seems to regard these people as a sister race to our own, claiming they existed approximately one billion years ago, before falling into extinction. The United States military has captured pictures of the area, and archaeologists who have been allowed to view those photographs say unequivocally that what has been discovered could only have been created by humans or other intelligent life. They describe the primary find as a large urban structure with a futuristic appearance."

"The whole world is about to know," Christopher said. "Now what?"

"Drive faster," Ann said, consulting the map.

"Some scientists have called this a hoax," the reporter continued, "while others have supported the idea that a race of humanlike beings could have come before us, and could have evolved further than we have, which would explain leaving behind something that seems to be advanced. The US is seeking access to the site, access that has so far been denied by the Guatemalan government and its considerable army of soldiers who keep guard around the clock. Here's what the US president said minutes ago."

The broad-shouldered president had entered office with a full head of hair, but now thin strands waved around in the wind, barely holding on to his scalp. He stood outside the White House, answering reporters with a don't-be-silly smirk. "Guatemala can't keep us out. We're submitting an emergency motion to the UN Security Council today. It was a US citizen who did the research that led to this discovery. Our military is moving into position. By UN resolution or by force, we will soon have control of that site."

Chapter 45

" I got a connection!" Sunny yelled, directing our attention to the TV screen. It was the middle of the night—we had traveled continuously, stopping only for fuel.

"My God!" I said to the sight on the monitor.

Miguel was driving; Ann woke up and shuffled out of the bedroom. "Oh no . . . oh no . . ." Her raspy voice was still asleep.

Paul pulled his toothbrush out of his mouth and yelled from the bathroom, "What is it?"

Sweat trickled over the wrinkles near Musa's eyes. Behind him, pickup trucks delivered metal fence panels. Some of the guards—along with Jeremy and Meredith— hurried to erect them; others scrambled to set up more lights.

Mom answered Paul, "There's a mob at the site. People trying to force their way in."

"Have you figured out how to recruit three hundred people?" Musa asked.

"Three thousand," Elle said.

"We're working on it," I responded.

The screen returned to black, displaying one word in the upper-left corner: *Input.*

"We're working on it?" Casey asked. "Really?"

"What happened?" Sunny slapped the table and grabbed his hair. "Where'd they go?"

Ann looked at me, dejected. "Dave, three thousand people? Skilled? Good-hearted? Willing to drop everything and take off into space? By, like, tomorrow? I don't think we can do this. We need a new plan."

"There have to be some groups of people we can tap into," Christopher said. "Some networks online. Can we send requests on social media?"

Paul came out of the bathroom, smelling like mouthwash. "Then Veeder and his people sneak in, answering your call."

Agitation festered inside me. I had pawned my belongings and used up my savings to find that site, to dig and to test, when no one wanted to help me. The system of the elite, the powerful, and those who fancied themselves so had deemed me crazy. One of my colleagues, Barry Gilroy—a petulant, stubby man whose monotone lectures often put an entire class to sleep, requiring him to drop his book on the floor to signal the end of the hour— had flippantly said he could not recommend to the grant committee "funding David's postdivorce therapy, where he runs into the wilderness looking for people who can't reject him." But now, now that I was right, now that two different human races were being connected across an eon based on my theory and my work, now I was a criminal?

Words flew out of my mouth before I could stop them. "We can't let this discovery fall under the control of the system. We cannot fail our prancestors!"

"No, Professor, we can't!" Sunny agreed.

I stood up, holding on to the cabinet handles. "Our prancestors couldn't avoid the extinction of their race, but they dedicated themselves to helping us avoid ours. They sent us a ship to give us a head start, before the merge. The scientists and peacekeepers of yesterday are speaking to those of us today. If we wait until the merge, until the singularity, like they did, to try to launch the first transporter, the divisions, the fighting, the system—it will be too much to overcome."

"Okay," Elle said, inspired. "So who do we call, to collect three thousand people, the Red Cross?"

I threw my hands in the air. "I don't know how we can call anyone! You've seen the news. The system of power has chewed me up and spit me out. How will we convince any of those groups to listen? How do we get three thousand people to trust us when the news is calling us dangerous?"

"Then we hide out and build the next ship," Paul said. "Our own kind is on the verge of inventing the materials we need. If we quietly assemble people over a few years, we can get three thousand, no problem. Our prancestors did the right thing by creating a spacecraft in secret. They just didn't do it before the whole world was engaged in war. But we can."

Miguel checked the large side mirror before he led our diesel pusher into the next lane, saying, "And we have the crystals. No one else can launch."

"What do you mean by 'the system of power,' David?" Casey asked, before stuffing half a piece of licorice into his mouth, leaving the other half sticking out.

"The system!" I batted a box of cookies off the counter and into the sink. "It's all around us, all the time, and it's gotten so big that it has its own momentum. It constantly seeks to expand itself, at our expense. When we reach the singularity, do you think there's going to be more compassion? That suddenly we're going to feed the hungry and help the poor? No. The evil and greed will be solidified, baked into the programming that will run everything."

"Slow down," Sunny said. "Are you talking about governments?"

"Bigger than that! The network of all the governments, and all the established rules, and all the ways we've been taught to do things."

"Taught to do things?" Christopher asked.

"Yes! Like . . . the system tells us to put our garbage cans out every week and to believe that our trash is whisked away to some place that won't hurt the planet. The system tells us that racism and sexism are supposed to take hundreds of years to overcome. The system lies to us about our own wealth, convincing us that our accumulation of goods and money doesn't have anything to do with why people across the globe are starving."

I swallowed and almost choked. Mom handed me a bottle of water; I guzzled it.

"I got 'em back!" Sunny announced.

"David?" Musa asked, his eyes glazed from a blend of exhaustion and anxiety. "We can't keep control of this site much longer. This is your project. What should we do, my friend?"

"I don't know where to find three thousand trustworthy, skilled people," I said. "Or all the supplies we need. But we cannot give up. We have to find them. Otherwise, those in power in this wretched system will fill that ship with greed and corruption to send to Destiny. They'll find someone we love, and torture them until we turn over the zircon pieces. Or they'll fight over who should be on the launch until the transporter is destroyed."

I opened a second bottle of water. "If we don't get this ship launched, evil will have prevailed again."

Casey had forgotten about his licorice piece; the uneaten half fell from his face when he spoke. "You don't think America has a group, or a commission, that could be assembled, to properly choose a crew?"

I laughed. "Properly choose a crew? Casey, America can't even *properly* choose food. Haven't you seen our stats?

We lead the world in things like adolescent heart disease—we've blocked the arteries of *teenagers*, for Christ's sake."

Paul widened his eyes.

Miguel mumbled from the helm, "I love Ranting David."

Jeremy asked Meredith, "Did he go off like this in *your* class?"

"No. But that would've been cool."

I opened the refrigerator and scanned the contents that had been loaded at Billy McGee's. "Here we go, right here." I grabbed a cheese package, pointing at the long phrase on the label. "They can't even simply call it 'cheese' anymore because most of it isn't! Yet people are getting rich selling it, other countries are now buying it, and many people have never actually eaten real cheese. The more progress we make, the more we kill ourselves."

Musa cut in. "David, put the cheese down. Listen, I think each of us must call who we know. We all know at least one person who knows us so well they will trust us over this media. And that person knows someone, and that person knows someone else."

"My parents will believe me," Christopher said. "And they were missionaries—they know a lot of people who would want to be on that ship."

"Okay, that's it then," Paul said. "Let's get to calling. And may I take a look?" He slipped the package out of my hand and examined it.

I slid my back down the thin wall and sat on the floor. "I nominate Sunny to be the captain of the voyage to Destiny."

Sunny's chin lowered, and his eyes asked, *Really?*

"I second that," Musa said.

"Yes!" Casey high-fived Sunny.

Miguel honked our horn.

"Your ETA?" Jeremy asked.

Paul consulted his map. "Maybe nineteen hours?"

Meredith smiled. "See you soon."

After the monitor shut off, Miguel asked, "Can someone pass me up a piece of that delicious cheese?"

I rolled over onto the floor, laughing. "It's not . . ." I struggled to pull my mouth out of its smile. "It's not food, Miguel!"

Casey and Christopher lost themselves in laughter.

"They didn't exactly have organic food at Bobby McDees." Mom chuckled.

Sunny held up the clipped paperwork from the RV lot, unable to curtail his laughing. "It's *Billy McGee's*!"

Paul had now peeled the plastic from a glossy slice. He stuck the slice to a window and peered closely at it. "Have a look at this! It attaches like a decal, now, doesn't it?" He laughed and inspected it again. "My goodness, does it have glue in it?"

The orange square clung to the window, and the sight of it tickled us to no end. The orchestra of laughter was one of the most soothing noises I'd ever heard.

And then there were gunshots.

Chapter 46

Miguel's blood-splattered arms and head dangled from his limp body, belted into the driver's seat.

Was he dead?

Why did I feel weightless?

The motor home banged onto the ground; we cried out as our bodies smashed down and jerked back up again. The rig landed and gained speed, racing over uneven terrain. As we bounced from wall to cabinet, I grabbed for handholds—the counter, the couch, the microwave door, now open—but my fingers could never find a grip.

We lurched toward the front seats, but with less force than if we had crashed into a static object. Water splashed onto the windshield.

"A lake!" Ann yelled. "We've crashed into a lake! We're sinking!"

Elaine, on the wet floor among bags of chips and packages of instant rice, examined her contorted limbs, figuring out that she needed to lift up her leg to untrap her arm. She looked up at me. "I can get Mom, you get Miguel."

From where I had landed, on top of the table, I scanned the littered seats and floor until I saw the fanny pack that Mom had gotten at the supply store. Unzipping it, I confirmed that it held the zircon crystals.

I stepped into the flood and reached Miguel. Where was he bleeding from?

"Guns." He coughed. "From the side of the road."

"C'mon, buddy," I said, unclasping his seatbelt as water rushed over it.

Elaine led Mom toward the dining area window. She asked her, "You can swim?"

Blood trickled into Mom's mouth from her nose. "Gonna have to remember!"

"Mom," I said. "Just paddle and then turn over and float."

Paul yelled over to Mom, "Swim away from the vehicle as fast as you can!"

The cool lake water cascaded in when Elle slid open the emergency exit window. Mom waded to the edge, but the streaming water dragged her back inside, submerging her face. Elle gave her a shove, getting her out of the current's pull. She disappeared into the obscurity of water and night, and my pounding heart dropped into my stomach.

The chest-high water made it easy to assist Miguel; he floated along with me until I pushed him out the window after Mom. Then I worried that Miguel might grab onto Mom in desperation, and they both would drown.

Only four feet of air remained between the rising water and the ceiling.

"Should I go under and swim through the window?" Christopher asked.

"Go for it. I'm behind you," Casey said. "The rest of you follow Paul."

Christopher and Casey took in deep breaths and disappeared into the dark water.

Paul stood on top of the kitchen counter with a bag of supplies clutched in one hand as he punched the ceiling vent out with the other. "This way!" He tossed the bag up and then hoisted himself onto the roof.

"Can you see Mom?" I yelled. "Is she okay?"

Paul reached back down and took a backpack from Ann, then helped her up through the narrow hole. "I can't see anything, just c'mon!"

Sunny balanced his computer and notebook on his head as he treaded water. I helped him onto the counter, and he handed his things to Paul, who handed them to Ann. Then Paul helped Sunny up and out.

"Let's go!" Paul demanded.

I gave Elle my fanny pack and pushed her up as the water reached the ceiling and engulfed me. I opened my eyes but couldn't see. I felt for the opening and Paul's hand clasped mine. He pulled me up; I gasped when my face finally hit the air.

The RV landed on the lake bed, and as we stood on its roof, the water reached our hips. Elaine and Paul plunged in, following Sunny and Ann, each using one arm to hold supplies above their head as they swam.

Crackling rang out; I looked toward the noise and saw bursts of orange and white light coming from the road up above, the road we'd flown off of.

I sat down until only my head was above water, shivering as I watched the reflection of the moon dance on the black surface around me.

Where was Mom? Miguel?

I inhaled and submerged myself, paddling and kicking underwater in the direction I thought was the shore. My wet clothes weighed me down as I crawled onto land and spotted Mom with the others, behind trees and a boulder.

"Mom, you're okay?"

"I'm fine," she whispered, "but he's losing a lot of blood."

Miguel had slumped onto his side. "You'll be okay," I told him. "We'll get you to a doctor."

Elaine kept her voice low as she asked me, "'Help' in Spanish?"

I whispered the phonetic pronunciation: "I-*you*-thuh."

She and Ann snuck away from the edge of the lake, up the hillside, toward what we could now see, as our eyes adjusted to the moonlight, was a pickup truck.

Elle tucked her gun in her pants and waved. "Ayuda! Hey! Ayuda! Help! Don't shoot! I'm trying to escape these people! Ayuda!"

Ann chimed in, "Me, too! Help us! Por favor!"

Headlights switched on. Ann and Elle kept their hands up as they arrived, screaming in distress. Two men stepped into the glow of the lights and pointed their guns, but Ann and Elle violently clapped the men's gun-holding hands, sending their weapons flying. A blur of elbows and kicking legs accompanied huffs and squeals. Paul and Casey made it up to them just as we heard the *blam!* of a body being slammed into the truck.

I asked Mom, "Are you sure you're okay?"

"Yes, let's go." Mom took custody of the fanny pack and a small duffel bag, hiking up the embankment like a much younger woman. Sunny and I helped Miguel through the weeds and up to the roadside; Christopher hauled up everything else we had salvaged—most importantly, Sunny's laptop and notebooks.

When we arrived, the men were facedown, pinned by Paul and Casey and being stripped of their shoes by Ann and Elle. After Elle harvested the shoestrings, Ann used them to tie the men's hands and feet. Elle then prodded the smaller man in the head with her gun. "Who sent you?"

The man pushed his nose into the dirt in defiance.

Elle clanked her gun onto the hood of the truck and flipped open a knife. Putting the tip near the man's eye, she said, "I'm going to carve out your eyeballs. Then shove this knife up your ass."

She stepped on top of him and cut into his cheek, prompting his screams: "Veeder! Patrick Veeder!"

Dust particles, fluttering in the headlight beams, surrounded Elle and Ann as the women stood and set their hands on their hips.

Fast-blinking red lights soared at us from down the highway.

"Maybe thirty seconds," Casey said.

Ann felt the men's pockets. "Got the keys."

Casey pulled the larger man to a standing position and placed him on the shoulder of the road, leaving his hands and feet tied.

"Hopefully they'll stop for him," Elle said, "or we won't get away."

The emergency lights were nearly upon us as we tore off, Elle at the wheel, and Christopher, Casey, Paul, and Ann hunkered down in the truck bed. Sunny rode with our belongings in the passenger's seat, and Mom and I sat in the back seat with Miguel, her hand on his forehead, mine pressed to his side, trying unsuccessfully to stop the bleeding.

By sunrise we spotted a man unloading a box from an old, unmarked cargo van. We offered him almost all our remaining cash—$7,000—and he happily unloaded the rest of his boxes and relinquished his key.

We parked at the first hospital we could find; Ann accompanied Miguel inside. When she returned, several hours later, we were crowded together on the floor of the van, using burner phones to call our most trusted friends and family.

I stared at my phone; no one came to mind.

Mom asked Ann, "How's Miguel?"

Ann closed her eyes and shook her head. "Too sick to leave."

Chapter 47

"This is what I'm telling you," Paul said into his phone. "It's now or never."

Elle took a break from calling. "Well, either I just convinced four people to go, or they were too afraid to admit they think I'm nuts."

"What'd your parents say, Chris?" Casey asked.

"They were more suspicious than I thought they'd be, but they're gonna meet me at the site. They said they'd pass the information on to their network. So, I'd say, count maybe ten?"

Sunny calculated on a notepad. "Okay, and with the calls Musa and the others made, that brings us to about two hundred and seventy-eight."

"And assuming half the people are lying?" Elle asked.

"Then a hundred and forty or so."

"Still, Sunny, that's a lot," I said. "Can we launch with that?"

"I don't think so, Professor. That's not even close to what we need."

I slouched and secretly gave up hope for our mission. Whatever special place inside myself that I had accessed back in the RV, before Miguel was shot, that had invigorated me to believe I would never give up, seemed nonexistent.

What had I thought, that Weird David, Indigo David, Staring David was going to take on the system and prevail? Was going to save the human race?

A pleasant memory distracted me: my rush of excitement when I first saw those dry-erase boards in the La Paz bunker, displaying graphs and notations about the evolutionary milestones of our prancestors.

I recalled sneaking into the laboratory that night, shining my light on the last photograph on the board. The scratches. The river of red.

I pushed my head close to Sunny, so as not to disturb the others on their calls. "Did you translate that last milestone of our prancestors' evolution? The claw marks and the red color? What did that mean?"

A grim energy overtook Sunny. He dug through his notebook and handed me a loose page. I tucked it into my pocket.

"I don't have phone numbers memorized anymore," Mom said. "Elle, can you help me look people up?"

Elaine opened her laptop. "Yes, Mom. Who first?"

I put on a baseball cap—from one of the few bags we'd managed to take out of the RV—and said, "I'm going to check on Miguel."

438

"Be careful," Mom and Elle called out together.

I stopped at the statue of the Virgin Mary, just outside the main hospital doors, and unfolded Sunny's page of notes. As I read his block letters, the voices of the man and woman returned.

> *The ultimate demise of the human race is delivered by the microscopic material that exists in the twilight between dead and alive. The virus. Mother Earth has peppered her sea and land with viruses; they are her most abundant organism. She need not provide any specific orders to these tiny monsters because humans, in their insistence on advancing at the cost of the environment, will eventually turn the lethal ones on themselves, by terrorism or by accident.*

Mary gazed at me with open arms, standing on a square stone base that read *Trust in God.*

I gazed back at her. *Well, which is it? Should I have faith, dream, or trust?* Today, standing in front of this famous woman—with open, vacant eyes, as if she had fallen asleep without closing her eyelids—I felt something I'd never seen painted on a rock, displayed on a poster, or etched into stone: regret.

I should have insisted that Mom go with Melly to the safe haven of Tuscany. I should have killed Patrick Veeder, if not in the bunker, in Mont-Saint-Michel. I should not have believed that a Hollywood producer would fund my project, and instead of sharing with him my greatest secret, I should have told him that my search had revealed nothing.

Someone in this hospital would soon put Miguel together with the trending news stories. We were out of time. My reputation was gone. We would fail our prancestors.

I entered the building and traversed the wide corridor, quick-stepping out of the way of busy nurses and dodging sick people tethered by tubes to wheeled IV poles. But I couldn't dodge the memory of the last time I had been in a hospital.

> The nurse disconnected the monitors from my dad, the signal that he was gone. I said to his warm, wilted head, "I wasn't mad at you, Dad. It wasn't your fault. I'm sorry I yelled at you. I'm so sorry."

> The organ transplant team stood against the wall, their eyes fixed on the clock.

I sank down into the chair next to Miguel's bed until the hard edge of the backrest uncomfortably dug into my head.

"David." Miguel's voice was weak. "What's on your mind?"

I sighed. "I'm not sure how to explain it."

"Try," he said, wincing as he adjusted himself to face me.

"My dad . . ." I rolled the bedside table out of the way so I could see Miguel's gray face. "He taught me so much, but he didn't just teach me. He helped me see things I couldn't understand until he explained them in a special way."

Monitors beeped overhead. Those goddamned monitors.

"When I grew up and learned about the business he was in, I saw how harmful it was, especially to uneducated people. But he couldn't see it. So I thought I would return the favor. You know, explain something to him, help him see it clearly, like he had done for me so many times."

Miguel moaned.

"Miguel, you look like you're in pain."

"Yeah, but they say more pain meds will put me to sleep. What was your dad's business?"

"He had this company that brought in mortgage loans for banks. He wanted me to take it over." I inhaled the disinfectant smell of the hospital. "He kept saying, 'Just do it for me.'"

The half of Miguel's face that wasn't smashed into his pillow curved into a smile. "Give me the David rant on why taking over your dad's business was such a bad idea."

I had never shared that explanation with anyone other than my parents.

"Well, the American housing industry convinces people to see life success as having a mortgage on a house that's bigger than they need, with lofty ceilings that skyrocket heating bills, and yards that require constant maintenance. It pushes people way in over their heads, into houses they can't afford. Research studies of the elderly show that if people could go back and do things differently, they'd put less money and time into big houses—and for that matter, fancy cars and designer clothing—and more into enjoying each day with their loved ones."

Miguel strained to ask, "Did you tell your dad this?"

"Yeah. So many times. Different ways. I even used charts."

"Charts? He must have laughed."

"What makes you say that?"

"The whole system was telling him that he was helping people. And you were showing him graphs that said old folks are unhappy."

Miguel gave me another half smile.

"Yeah, you're right." I chuckled. "He laughed at my charts."

"Dave, your dad couldn't hear you because he was still trying to save you." He shuddered but forced himself to continue. "He was worried about how you would make a living as an anthro, a cultural, a . . . ah, whatever the hell you do."

We laughed, and I forgot about the beeping.

A nurse in thick clogs walked in and spoke in Spanish. *"I'm glad to see you happy."* She felt the bag on the IV, made a note in her little book, and deposited the book back into her baggy pocket. She looked at Miguel, then over to me, then at Miguel again.

We stared back at her.

Finally, she said, *"Press the call button if you need anything."* She drew the curtain completely around us and disappeared.

"She recognizes us," I whispered.

"Oh yeah," Miguel said. "She's known since I got here. But she seems to be keeping it to herself. It's weird."

I pointed to his abdomen. "What did the doctor say?"

"The bullet caused too much damage. I need a new liver."

I sat up in my chair. "What?"

"Yeah, I'm gonna die. 'Cuz I'd rather die of liver failure on that space cruiser than get a transplant and stay on the planet. C'mon, help me."

Miguel groaned as he hauled himself into a seated position.

"Uh, Miguel, wait, I don't know if you should be doing this."

He pulled the needle out of the top of his hand. "C'mon, David. Just do it for me."

CHAPTER 48

"The doctor said you could leave?" Paul asked, helping Miguel into the van.

Miguel was in too much pain to make up a story.

I stuttered, "Um, as long as we get him a checkup in a day or so. We should get going. Who's driving?"

Elaine scooted into the driver's seat and started the engine.

"What's the plan?" Ann asked. "The guy who sold us the van has put in a report that we took it at gunpoint, and pictures of us are all over." She glanced at Paul's muted laptop, which showed some kind of press conference. The announcement took up half the screen: *Denlon now believed to be in Mexico*.

Elle added, "The orders are to shoot us if we don't comply."

Miguel held out his hand; Paul set a phone on it.

"We need to get out of this van and split up," Mom said.

"Please, let's stay together," Sunny begged.

Elaine drove us to a line of taxis in front of a nearby museum. "Someone find a meeting spot, a hotel maybe, where Miguel can rest and we can come up with a plan. I'm sorry, Sunny. They're looking for a group in this vehicle; we can't travel like this."

"Here." Miguel coughed. "This place."

Ann considered the location on his phone. "This'll work. Tell your driver to take you here." She passed the phone around and Paul distributed the last of our cash.

Ten minutes later we had made it to the shabby part of this southern Mexican town—our four taxis in an eye-catching caravan as we drove alongside a concrete wall with green shards of glass lodged into the top of it. We were successively dumped at a doorway in between a café and a shoe store. With Miguel bent over and taking baby steps, and the rest of us toting disheveled belongings, we were the spectacle we had hoped not to be.

The people on either side of the gravel road, sitting outside their establishments on makeshift benches and old chairs, were hot, tired, and shooing away flies. We entered the small lobby and closed the door behind us, shutting out their wary stares.

"The cops are corrupt here," Elaine said. "When they arrest us, we'll offer them money to let us escape."

"We're out of cash," Ann said.

"Too much media anyway." Paul was looking around the room for ideas. "They're only corrupt when it's not public."

The lobby TV was tuned into an American news station. The bald man being interviewed was familiar to me. Who was he?

Miguel lost his balance and landed on the floor with a moan. Paul squatted to help and Ann put her backpack down as his pillow. Elle locked the front door and closed the dusty drapes on the two windows.

Police sirens sounded from several directions.

Elaine approached the front desk, but the three workers fled to the back office, closed the door, and scowled at us through the office window. One of the men lifted the receiver of a phone, staring at us, as if he were trying to communicate: *This call is about you.*

On the TV, the reporter said to the bald man, "You were tied up in a basement in Bolivia, and Dr. Denlon was there. Tell us about that. Was he the one holding you hostage?"

That was it! He was the hostage that Liam had indeed let go.

The man's eyes were still angry. "He was working with the person who had kidnapped me, that's for sure."

"Would you say that Denlon is a dangerous man?"

"Yes. And manipulative."

Elle shut off the TV. "This isn't helping."

The screaming sirens multiplied, almost drowning out the grunts coming from Miguel, grunts that sounded like he was taking a slug to the stomach every ten seconds.

"You'll be okay," Christopher said. "They'll take you back to the hospital."

"I don't care about me," Miguel snapped. "This mission is everything, and Patrick Veeder is a piece of shit, and it can't end this way, it can't!"

Mom came to me and I embraced her, practicing my Spanish in my head: *Officer, she's seventy-five years old. Please don't hurt her.*

Sunny clutched his computer and notebook, looking even more afraid than he did on the plane.

"I'm sorry." Paul stood and rested his hand on Elaine's shoulder.

"There's nothing to be sorry about," she said, moving the curtains to peek outside. She jumped back when a man banged on the window and screamed, *"You're the people from the news!"*

"What did he say?" she asked.

"Don't worry about it," I said. "Sunny, can you dial up Musa?"

He sat down on the coffee table and flipped open his laptop.

"I'm so sorry," Paul continued, his head low. "I turned us into outlaws trying to go after Veeder."

"No, this is on me," I said. "For making a foolish deal for money. When they arrest us, tell them I hired all of you, but didn't tell you what was really going on."

Paul shook his head. "No, David—"

A rock broke through the glass and somersaulted across the floor.

"Listen to me!" I begged. "They think it's all me. Let it fall on me, because I need you to be on the outside, to take care of Mom, and to watch over the evidence."

Mom put a protective hand over the fanny pack—secured around her hips—and fought back tears.

A fist pounded the door. This time a woman's voice: *"Don't use our town to hide in! Get out of here!"*

Elaine reached for the gun in her pants.

"No," Casey said. "They'll kill us if they spot a weapon. Just put your hands up when they come in."

Too choked up to speak, Sunny turned his screen to me.

Behind Musa, guards were losing a fight with people pushing their way toward the transporter. "We can't control things here anymore, David."

"Musa," I said. "I have to call it, my friend. I'm sorry."

"Where are you?"

"In a hotel lobby. Surrounded. And I have no idea how to find enough people and supplies for the launch."

Sunny wiped his nose on his sleeve.

Musa took a deep, slow breath. "The greatness of this discovery prevails, even if today we don't."

Outside, the sirens abruptly stopped and car doors slammed.

The fear in Sunny's wet eyes melted into surrender. He turned his computer back around and peered into the screen. "Okay, Moose," he said. "See you soon . . . hopefully." He buried his laptop in his bag.

"Listen," I said. "I want you all to work with Musa, to protect the message and the zircon crystals."

"If they take you, we'll never see you again," Elle said. "There has to be another way."

"David, look," Ann said, gesturing.

I ignored Ann and yelled, "There *isn't* another way!"

"David!" Ann said. "He's talking to you."

I looked beyond her pointed finger into the office behind the counter and saw the man on the phone. His compassionate eyes stared at me as he stood right up to the glass. I recalled the name of the hotel, Hotel of the Sacrament, and noticed the crosses on the walls. The frightened worker was dressed entirely in black, with white on the front of his collar, indicating he was a member of the priesthood.

He seemed to be trying to tell me something, in a way that his colleagues, huddled behind him, would not notice. His eyes signaled to his right, repeatedly. To his right was an unmarked door. Did it lead to another office? To the hotel rooms?

A hard knock on the front door was followed by a deep voice. "Police! Open! Right now!"

Elaine whispered, "They wouldn't be speaking in English if they didn't know who we were."

The man in the back office continued to signal. I forced myself to think. We were in Mexico, which meant that this man was likely a priest in the Catholic Church.

The Catholic Church. One of the largest, most wealthy organizations on Earth. A major player in the system of power and, as such, a perpetrator of sins. There had been the atrocity of priests raping children, along with their superiors keeping those assaults a secret, and the continuing iniquity of disallowing women to be priests for no biblical reason, a policy that perpetuated gender discrimination. And none of this was to mention the institution's brutal history of conquering Indigenous peoples.

Why would this person be helping us?

Something heavy struck the front door, cracking it.

The eyes of the man in the collar pleaded. I considered the small statue on the check-in counter. It was the Virgin Mary again, this time holding a cross to her bosom.

"Let's go," I said.

Elle's face questioned me: *You're sure?*

"Let's go, this way!"

Paul and Christopher carried Miguel, one at his legs, the other gripping his armpits. We shuffled through the interior door. As Ann closed it and clacked the deadbolt, we heard the front door crash open and a man yell in Spanish, *"Where are they?"*

We had entered a long hallway with a door at the end of it.

"Was that guy telling us to go out the back and run?" Casey asked.

"Leave me," Miguel said. "Leave me and go!"

"We're not leaving you," Ann said.

The door at the end of the hall swung open; we cowered. Casey put his hands in the air, then looked over his shoulder at us, confused by who had come in.

Chapter 49

"They're gonna break through," Paul said, his calm and collected demeanor long gone.

Again, a heavy tool blasted into the other side of the interior door we'd just locked, causing Mom to scream.

I became paralyzed.

"Shake it off," Elle said, "David, breathe, c'mon!"

Two nuns in gray habits and, behind them, two priests, had charged in through the back door and now stood, facing us, in the narrow hallway.

"We're here to help you," one of the nuns said.

The door behind us was struck again—this time a metal pipe lanced through, sending dagger-sized pieces of wood flying into us. The quaking knocked the cross with the bleeding Jesus from the wall to the floor.

One of the priests said in Spanish, *"Follow us. Fast, right now!"*

We fled out the back door, Paul and Christopher dragging Miguel.

The clergy members directed us into three different cars, parked on the dirt road behind the hotel.

"You okay, Mom?" I whispered, as we huddled under a serape. I heard the other two cars motoring away, ahead of us.

Mom answered by holding my hand.

After several minutes of swerving, the car headed in one direction at a steady speed.

"Stay down and stay covered. We're okay," the nun in the passenger's seat reassured us.

I passed the time by pressing my fingers into the bristles of the floormat, focusing on each prickly needle. A persistent question lingered in my mind. I spoke softly under our blanket. "Mom, I know this is a strange time to ask this."

"Anything, sweetie."

"Did you only have one kid because I was so hard to raise?"

"Oh, Davey, why would you think that?" She fanned some air from outside her blanket up into her face. "Your father and I wanted more kids after having you because you were so much fun. But you know your father had his heart issue. He was afraid of leaving me with too much to take care of."

Her sweaty hand grabbed for mine again.

"I'm sorry I didn't take over Dad's business."

"It's okay, it wasn't your thing."

"But he was trying to leave me a gift. To pass on something. And I didn't accept it."

"Sweetie, your father knew you loved him. That's all that mattered. He never thought he'd live long enough to see what you'd become. He was so proud of you."

I dug my fingertips into the bristles again.

"We're making a quick stop," the nun in the passenger's seat said.

The car ran over bumps and slowed to a halt. The door next to me opened and something was set down in the middle of the back seat. In a matter of seconds, we were again cruising along, as if we were on a highway.

Once the dark of night had completely set in, our saviors finally let us come out of hiding. The woman in the passenger's seat wore silver rings on every other finger, and a turquoise bracelet—more adornment than usual for a Catholic nun. She directed Mom to put on a veil and handed me a black shirt with a white collar.

The driving nun, in her fifties, said in Spanish, *"Tell them it's going to be a long ride, through the night, all the way to Guatemala."*

I let the passenger nun translate, while Mom and I nodded. She continued. "I'm Maria." She pointed to the basket that had been set between Mom and me. "Empanadas and some water. Please eat."

"I'm David and this is my mom," I said.

Maria smiled. "Hi, Mom."

Mom laughed. "My name is Alice."

"Mucho gusto, Alice. This is Magdalena." Maria put her hand on the driver's shoulder. "She goes by Maggie." Unlike Maria, Maggie wore a full headpiece that covered her ears and hair.

Maggie instructed Maria, in Spanish, to ask why I was a murderer. I reacted with a quick breath and then feigned choking on an empanada to hide that I could understand.

"Drink some water," Mom said.

Maria rephrased Maggie's question. "We understand you're trying to kill Patrick Veeder?"

"Why would you think that?" I asked.

Maria translated my response and they quizzically looked at each other.

Mom put her hand on mine. "They don't have a way of knowing what happened. Tell them."

"Where are you taking us?" I asked. "Where are the others?"

After hearing my questions through Maria, Maggie tightly gripped the steering wheel. *"Don't give up any information."*

"They're scared," Maria responded. *"We should tell them who we are."*

"No. This was a crazy plan Roberto had," Maggie argued. *"I'm driving a murderer and his mother to our home. This is a mistake."*

Maria disclosed, "We are from Antigua, Guatemala."

"Maria, stop!"

Maria ignored her. "We live in a monastery and run an organization that serves the poor. For a long time, we've tried to get people higher up in the Catholic Church to understand what a criminal Patrick Veeder is."

"Shut up," Maggie insisted. *"You're putting us in danger!"*

Maria continued. "But Patrick gives large donations to the Church, so we can't get anyone to listen. The archbishop has deemed you a threat, ordering our parish leaders to call him if they find you. Our art historian, Father Roberto Jimenez, said that Patrick Veeder probably lied to the archbishop about you. So Roberto said we had to come help you."

Maggie fumed. *"What are you telling him? I don't agree with how you're handling this!"*

Maria spoke more like a businesswoman than a nun. "One of our connections told us you were at the hospital where she works, so we flew to that city."

I recalled the nurse there, closing the curtain.

"But after we landed, another person we trust called and said he was directing you out the back of the Hotel del Sacramento."

"Wow," I said. "Thank you. But I never set out to hurt anyone. I was just doing research. Patrick Veeder came after *me*."

Maria translated for Maggie and added, *"See, I told you."*

Maggie changed lanes and slowed down. *"Patrick's enemy is not necessarily our friend. I'm leaving them in a gas station. Roberto can get them if he wants them."*

"Please don't do that," I said in Spanish. *"I'm not a murderer and I would never hurt you."*

The nuns looked at each other, and then Maggie squinted at me in the rearview mirror.

"Thank you, Maria, for giving us that information," I said. *"I'm happy to tell you both the whole story."*

Maria gloated.

Maggie rolled her eyes. *"He could still be lying. Right, Dr. Denlon?"*

"So could you," I said.

Maggie smiled. The tension in the car flew out the open windows.

The soft, salty empanadas released more flavor with each bite, as if my taste buds were deciding, one at a time, that it was safe to come out. I chewed, gathering my thoughts, and then I did what I had done throughout my entire career. I presented a true story about people.

We had conferenced in with the other two cars—Father Juan Sandoval driving one and Father Roberto Jimenez driving the other. After twenty minutes, I concluded: *"So when I saw the other hostage on TV in the hotel lobby, I knew Liam had told me the truth, that he had not killed him. And that's where you came in and, literally, saved our lives."*

Father Jimenez spoke and Christopher translated: "I don't know that we've saved you yet. And we are very curious about what your team has found. We've heard some reports, but we don't know what to believe."

"Well," I said into my phone, to my cohorts in the other vehicles, "what do you all think? Should we explain the discovery?"

"I think we're among friends," Paul said.

"Sunny?" I said. "Would you like to tell them about our prancestors?"

"I'd love to," he responded. "But it will take a while."

"We have many hours to go," Maria said, "before we get to Antigua."

As Sunny shared the details of the discovery and explained the message carved into stones by our prancestors, Christopher and I took turns translating his words to Spanish. We delivered the information and answered their many questions, as the miles and the hours passed by, until the sun ushered in another day.

Across the Guatemalan border, we followed a route that passed intermittently through towns and countryside, sometimes providing only a single lane, but always enduring two-way traffic. Double-decker tourist buses and wide-load construction trucks drove within inches of bicyclists balancing baskets, duffel bags, or other people on their handlebars.

When we pulled into the tourist town of Antigua, the narrow streets, packed with cars, slowed us to a crawl. We rolled by storefronts painted in solid colors—yellow, blue, orange—and passed under the iconic arch on Fifth Avenue North. We saw a group of people in their twenties—Americans? Europeans?—engrossed in conversation, walking out of a bright-pink door labeled *Spanish School.*

Just outside the main part of town, Maggie drove us onto a concrete driveway, delineated by black metal fencing and leading to a building that was crumbling under the burden of time. The Renaissance structure stood behind wispy trees and was reminiscent of a haunted mansion in an amusement park.

A ledge along the front of the roof was held up by slender pillars, themselves stacked on top of columns. Light-blue niches in the walls sheltered intricate religious statues; they stared at us with raised hands as if they had been cursed into stone right before sharing valuable information. An arched doorway in the center of the façade appeared as the monument's dark, open mouth.

After we staggered out of our vehicles on cramping legs, Roberto Jimenez came to me with an outstretched hand. *"Welcome to Vida."*

"So you see," Sunny finished answering the latest question, "the supply list isn't like when you're going camping and you pack enough for the stay. It's like we're bringing what we need to sustain a whole city. To start a farm. To open a hospital. To produce clothing and tools."

I translated Sunny's words, and then added, *"And honestly, Father Jimenez—"*

"Roberto, please."

"Roberto." I sighed, rotating my ankle, trying to wake up my foot. *"I have lost hope that this transporter will make it into good hands."*

A hummingbird darted to us, stopping abruptly in midair. It pointed its skinny beak first at me, then Roberto, before shooting away.

Roberto set his hand on my shoulder. *"Here at Vida, we have a saying: Hope doesn't get lost. We do."*

Chapter 50

L ush leaves and twisted vines reached out to us as we dined at an outdoor table, lapping up soup that Sister Maggie pronounced "Peppy-Anne."

"Muchas gracias," I said, an understatement, as Maggie set down more bread.

Vida's arches, fountains, and peeling walls had succumbed to a vast garden that refused to be tamed. The unrelenting plants had taken over the eaves, dangling their radiant petals in front of windows and looping their sticky tendrils around columns. A pathway led from our courtyard table into the grounds, where succulent flowers in every Easter-egg color bloomed from bushes and draped down from branches.

Paul dabbed his mouth with his napkin. "I could stay here for years, couldn't you? I've always run my operations remotely, and these folks will appreciate the rent my agency will pay them, for all of us."

"We'll hang out here, fall off the radar?" I asked.

"We'll do more than that," Ann said. "The US government, Veeder, and the FBC may get the spaceship, but we'll have the crystals, and the message. We'll be in a position to negotiate."

Sunny dunked bread into his bowl. "You don't think they'll be able to translate the symbols?"

Ann took a moment. "We can see if Musa can destroy the rocks."

"Absolutely not." I dropped my spoon and it clanked on the table. "We can't destroy them."

"David, we have photographs," Casey said. "They're saved digitally in several places."

"But they're artifacts," Christopher countered.

"Call Musa," I demanded.

Our third attempt at a video call went through. Musa walked his computer away from the screams of protesters. "I stand with David. These are too precious."

"What about hiding them?" Elle asked.

Jeremy threw tent poles into a truck and stepped toward the screen. "Hide them? They're enormous and really heavy."

"Wait, she's right," I said. "You have that equipment and those big trucks. Hoist some of the tablets into a truck bed. Drive them to a lake. They'll sink and be hidden, but won't be hurt. Knock the rest over so they can't create the translation grid."

Meredith looked around before saying, "That wouldn't be impossible."

Behind her, a soldier fired his gun into the air. She instinctively ducked. The soldier pointed at hikers holding cameras. "Go on! Get back!"

The calm in Musa's voice had run out. "Whatever we're going to do, it's gotta be now."

"Sunny," Paul said, "can you figure out which rocks are the most vital to the message, so they know which ones to drown?"

"The fewer the better, and in order of priority," Jeremy said. "The way things are going, we may not get to moving all the ones you want."

Elaine shifted toward the screen. "We're working on getting you flights here. You guys are gonna love Vida. Best hideout yet."

"How long?" Meredith asked.

"How long for what?" Ann said.

Meredith sent a *help me* look to Jeremy, who finished her question. "How long do we need to stay hidden?"

CHAPTER 51

I checked on Miguel, sleeping in the cool air of a basement bedroom.

Mom stacked his bowl on his bread plate. "He didn't eat much."

Miguel opened one eye. "Sorry, Mom."

She rested her hand on his forehead. "It's all right."

Miguel's eye caught sight of me, then fell shut.

"David," he whispered.

"I'm right here."

"You're gettin' me on that ship?"

I pulled the blanket up to his neck. "You need to sleep, buddy."

Mom pushed me outside and closed the door behind us. "What's going on?"

"We're gonna live here for a bit."

Her head sagged.

"I'm sorry we can't go home. But we'll be safe here."

"At least we're alive," she said.

"That's the name of this place. *Vida.* That means 'life.'"

We poured cups of coffee and joined the others in the courtyard, next to a two-tiered, red-stone fountain.

Down the breezeway from us, Roberto, Maria, and several other members of the clergy trotted into and out of what looked like a classroom, holding phones to their ears.

"I don't like the looks of this," Ann said.

"Me either," Casey agreed. "They seem like they've been planning something all afternoon."

Paul's worried eyes surveyed our whereabouts—backed into a corner of stone walls. "We're worth a lot of money."

"What do you mean?" I asked.

"Governments pay handsome rewards for their most wanted. Especially yours."

More people arrived and peeked over at us before scurrying into that room.

Elaine held my tense hand. "David, act relaxed." She turned to the others. "Let's talk escape."

Roberto stepped out, pausing under ferns in planters that hung from the eaves. He seemed uneasy as he waved at us.

"What about Miguel?" Mom asked.

"That's it," Ann said. "We say we're taking him to a doctor. That probably gets Sunny and Mom out with him."

A group of people—some in hiking shorts, others in multipocketed safari pants, and most wearing long-sleeve, sun-protective shirts—appeared at the rear of the grounds and walked with purpose, directly toward us.

"Well, scratch *that* plan," Ann said.

Paul whispered, "Loaded?"

Casey, Elaine, and Ann nodded.

The oncoming men and women picked up their pace.

Casey looked back at us. "When this goes down, Dave, you and Mom run down the breezeway, into the building, and out the front door. Chris, you and Sunny go the other way, into the yard and around the side. It'll confuse 'em."

Mom grabbed my arm. Sunny squeezed his computer to his chest.

I breathed in and out as deeply as I could, warding off a stare. Roberto moved back inside, but he watched with anticipation from the doorway.

The advancing group fanned out in front of us, amid the foliage. One of the men said, "Which one of you is Dr. Denlon?"

None of us spoke.

He smiled. "Oh, excuse me, maybe I'm wrong." He turned and yelled to Roberto, "Dr. Denlon is over here?"

The people around him introduced themselves.

"I'm Pete."

"My name is Josh."

"Carina."

Roberto hollered back, "Yes, there."

Heavy drips of water fell from the wavy edge of the fountain's upper bowl into its main pool.

"Call me David," I said to the man who had asked.

"David, it's a pleasure, an honor, really. I'm Jason." He firmly shook my hand.

"What's going on?" Ann asked.

"Yes, well, much to explain," Jason said. "But I'll let Sister Maria do that. She should be over here in a minute."

Jason's eyes drank in Casey's good looks. "I thought you were getting ready to shoot me."

"I was," Casey said. "And I'm still not entirely sure that I shouldn't."

Nervous chuckles made the rounds as Casey cautiously offered his hand to Jason.

Night closed in as we made small talk; ropes of tiny lights that had been strung throughout Vida's floral yard began to twinkle.

Maria finished her enthusiastic conversation with two people near the classroom and came to us. Her bronze eyes held heartache. We gave them our attention.

"I work for Interfaith Missionaries," she said. "We have spent decades building a large network of people to serve the poor and politically alienated. We have formed relationships in this country and abroad to obtain resources and expertise that assist us in our missions."

Mom found a seat on the bench, anticipating a long speech.

Maria said, "We help people grow food, raise animals, get access to health care and to justice, among many other things."

Ann hid a yawn. "Sounds like you do amazing work."

Jason and his colleagues seemed to be waiting for us to figure something out.

Maria continued. "We work with every major humanitarian organization around the world. Our expertise is mobilization to worthy causes."

Sunny abandoned his deflated pose and stood up straight. Elle's hand covered her mouth.

I smiled. "Are there three thousand of you?"

Maria smiled back. "Around the world, including who we serve, there are millions."

Ann peered around at the busy people. "That's what this is? You're calling members of your network and saying, 'Do you want to immediately leave on a spaceship, and maybe die?'"

"Well," Jason said, "when she called *us*, she left out the 'die' part."

Maria gestured toward Jason and his colleagues. "These wonderful men and women are from Lawyers Without Borders. They happened to be nearby and we often work together. Most of them may not personally leave on the transporter, but they are here to help us identify who will."

"Oh my God," Christopher said. "We're gonna launch the ship!"

Paul asked Sunny, "Can you get Musa and the others?"

Casey scanned the grounds with fresh eyes. From the gazebo to the pathway to the courtyard, the place was quickly filling up with chatty people ready for action. "Holy fucking shit," he said. "Oh, oops. Sorry, Sister."

"Holy fucking shit is right," Maria said. "We can barely believe this is happening. Listen, in Guatemala, more than half the population lives without enough food, shelter, or medicine. It's a problem that will not be fixed in our lifetimes, and may even get worse. There's suffering similar to this in many places on the planet. But God is giving us this opportunity."

"How much time do you need?" Elaine asked.

"Twenty-four hours is all we can take," Maria said. "As soon as we start directing people to the site, no matter how hard we try to keep things quiet, someone will leak what we're doing."

"And when it gets out," Ann said, "Veeder will organize a way to stop us."

"He's probably already on that," Paul said.

More people excitedly arrived at the classroom and were greeted with hugs.

"I've got them." Sunny held the computer screen toward us. Jeremy wore work gloves and panted, leaning on a loaded truck bed. Behind them, soldiers waved batons at crowds as tanks crawled along in front of the space cruiser.

"Musa," I asked, "can you hold for a day?"

"The rocks?"

"No, still send those to the lake. But we think we can launch this thing in twenty-four hours. Can you keep the site secure and stay that long?"

Jeremy's voice jumped up an octave. "Launch? How?"

"If we don't leave now," Meridith said, "we won't have enough time to escape."

"Musa," Paul said, "the Guatemalan government is keeping their army in place. Seems they are leery of your president. And we have someone here you should meet."

Maria stepped closer to the computer. "My name is Maria Flores. I serve on the board of the Interfaith Missionaries."

"Yes," Musa said. "I'm familiar with your organization."

"There isn't time, so I'll be direct. We're mobilizing now. We'll be there, with enough people and supplies to launch, by sunset tomorrow."

Musa seemed to be replaying her words in his head. When he said nothing, Maria added, "We've already sent you additional security."

"Musa?" Paul asked.

Jeremy erupted with a "Yes!" He embraced Meredith, who stood motionless.

Finally, Musa smiled. "Let's do this."

Chapter 52

The crowd filled up the rooms inside Vida and was flowing into the back garden. Nearly every person handled a phone or an electronic notebook, reaching out to their comrades around the world.

Beyond the courtyard, five women stood beneath a large trellis, the glow of their gadgets lighting up the vines woven through the lattice above them. The shortest one held her phone in front of her face and screamed at whoever was on it, "That's not what I'm doing. This isn't a cult!"

"Hi!"

I took a quick sidestep. A woman wearing fruity-smelling lip gloss had come up beside me.

"Hello, I'm David, nice to meet you."

"I'm Shelly, from Interfaith. I just wanted to introduce myself. My partner and I are going."

"You're brave," I said, my mind still on the petite woman's comment about a cult. "Do you think you'll be able to convince three thousand people to join us? Teachers, architects, farmers?"

"Are you kidding? We're worried about having too many. We've already got people from those professions, as well as psychologists and business professionals." She skimmed her palmtop computer with two fingers, red-speckled polish on her nails. "Let's see. Social workers, international trade specialists, law enforcement officials, mechanics, plumbers, carpenters, ironworkers, medical and legal professionals . . . Yeah, we're making great progress."

A man across the yard waved at her.

"I have to go," she said. "See you on board." Her ponytail bounced behind her as she disappeared into what was now an even larger mass of people.

Sunny saw Maria trotting through the courtyard and called out to her. "Sister, I've translated most of the supplies we need."

"Come with me," she answered, leading him toward the classroom.

"Wait, excuse me," Christopher said.

Maria stopped. "Yes?"

"Do you know people in remote parts of Africa? Like villages in Malawi and the Congo?"

Maria looked to Carina.

After Carina nodded, Maria charged off so fast that Sunny had to run to catch up.

Carina's veiny arms showed her advanced age. Her eyes exuded peace, as if she had done exactly what she had wanted with her life. Her silver hair fell straight down behind her, almost to the small of her back; two pink barrettes, one above each ear, clipped it out of her face.

She asked Christopher, "There are people there, that you want to invite on the ship?"

"Yes. I've sent word about this. But I don't know how they would get here."

Paul pulled his phone away from his head and offered to Carina, "I can get a charter from Lusaka."

"Lusaka." She pinched her chin in contemplation. "Okay. I can probably arrange for at least some of them to be flown there, but we'll have to hurry. C'mon."

Christopher and Carina headed inside the main building.

The people from Lawyers Without Borders had dispersed to phones and computers, except Jason, who stood with the rest of us.

"So, Jason," Casey asked, "are *you* Catholic?"

Jason shrugged. "I am. I don't agree with some things in this religion. But the Catholic Church has an established set of connections throughout the world. I could spend my life trying to create a different system or I could use this platform, already in place, to help people."

Casey smiled. "That's an honest answer."

"How about a drink for everyone?" Jason asked. "They've got great wine here. You look like you need to relax."

"That's up to our friend Davey," Casey said.

It was the perfect time for a glass of wine.

"You guys enjoy a nice red," I said. "I'm going for a walk."

I roamed to the gazebo, which had nearly been consumed by the plants, and studied the buds of the morning glories wrapped around one of its columns. They were purple and shut tight. Casey's words repeated in my head. *Our friend, Davey . . .* That was the first time anyone other than Musa and, oddly, Liam, had called me a friend.

I took the stairs down to the basement and found Miguel hobbling back from the bathroom. I helped him into bed, whispering, "Tomorrow we're getting you on that ship."

The skin on his face had become waxy—like my dad's, at the end.

He pushed his mouth into a smile.

I reclined on the other bed in the room, but my feet danced and my eyes refused to shut. At four a.m., I gave up and found Paul, alone, sipping coffee in the courtyard.

"Can't sleep either, eh?" he asked.

Only a dozen people remained, scattered among the shrubs and trees, speaking into their phones. Some gestured passionately; others read from their notes. Inside the windows, candelabra-style lighting flickered, revealing a small gathering in each room.

"Where'd everyone go?" I asked.

Paul set his cup on the bench. "To the site. There are only so many roads. Roads that are congested and may soon be closed. I've got helicopters coming, but they hold very few people."

I thought about drinking more coffee, but I was already wired. "Hey, that guy watching over Melly in Tuscany, can we reach him? Can I talk to her?"

Paul texted a code. "There's a development I need to share with you."

He opened Elaine's laptop and played the breaking news. A male reporter said, "The US president has made a decision regarding the Guatemalan discovery site, leaving many world leaders stunned. In a statement on social media, the president has deemed the site a 'potential threat to America and to all mankind.'"

"Good Lord," I mumbled.

The reporter spoke as aerial footage of the transporter played on the screen. "The discovery site contains an impressive structure, allegedly built by a race of humanlike beings who went extinct a billion years ago, and who had reached a further point in evolution than our own race has yet to achieve. Although there is no evidence to date of weapons or chemicals among the finds, the US president has stated that he is considering a military strike against Guatemala to take over the site."

"Unbelievable," I said.

The reporter continued, "Guatemala's president called this 'an ignorant and unnecessary move' and added that there has so far been 'no reason to fear' anything that has been found. He has denied US military personnel access to the site, and has called any potential effort to take control of the site 'an act of war.'"

Images of hordes of hikers and long lines of traffic appeared as the reporter said, "Thousands of people are trekking to the site, located on the Cayateña volcano, from all over Guatemala and the world, to get a chance to see or even touch the massive structure, which archaeologists describe as 'an enclosed city of some sort.'"

I shut the laptop, muttering, "At least they don't know it flies."

"They'll figure that out when they see us loading it," Paul said, as his phone played an alert. He read the text and seemed satisfied. After dialing, he handed the phone to me. "Be quick."

"David," Melly said. "Thank you for calling, I was worried."

"How's the painting?" I asked.

"It was tough at first. I just stared at the canvas. But the piece I've got going now, it's one of my best."

"What is it?"

"It's my view from the balcony on the roof, overlooking vineyards, farmhouses, and a row of cypress trees."

"You're not scared, to be up that high?"

"Doesn't seem to bother me anymore, after leaping out of a castle."

I smiled. "Into the ocean."

"In the dark!"

It was refreshing to laugh, and the more she did, the more I joined her.

"How are you, David? I had to shut off all TV and radio. It was overwhelming."

"I'm good. So, keep this to yourself . . . We're going to launch the transporter. It goes to another part of the galaxy, and, well, we're not coming back. I didn't think you'd want to do something like this, but I wanted to, you know, let you decide for yourself."

"I'm not leaving on a spaceship, David."

"Yeah, I figured. Which is why I wanted to talk to you one last time. And thank you for the eleven years we shared."

"You're definitely getting on that thing?"

Her voice was loud enough to reach Paul, who had poured another cup of coffee. His eyebrows raised up, as if he were asking me the same question.

I exhaled a long breath. "I guess it's destiny."

Paul smiled.

"Oh, wow, David, I don't know what to say. I'll miss you. And wherever you're going, I hope you're happy."

"Take good care, Melissa."

As Paul and I worked through the details of getting to the site, particularly how Elaine and I would go by helicopter, Sunny frantically summoned me.

I looked around, searching the darkness, unsure of where he was.

"Professor!" he said again, opening a door and racing up to me.

I grabbed his shoulders in an attempt to quiet him.

"Four pieces of jade!"

"What?" Paul asked.

"We can't lift off without four pieces of fingernail-sized jade."

"Talk slower," I said.

"I finished translating the list of supplies! Jade! Four pieces! The size of a fingernail!"

"Elaine and I aren't leaving on the first helicopter run," I said. "I can get it in town. As soon as the stores open."

Sunny's body released its tension. I hugged him and Paul patted his head, saying, "You've done great work, Captain."

He plodded away, talking to himself, "Jade, fowl, sunflower seeds . . ."

Paul and I sat in silence until morning pushed into the black sky. A streak of purple materialized before our eyes.

"I hope I'm a worthy companion for your last sunrise on Earth," Paul said.

Beams of yellow light appeared as if they'd been switched on.

"This is you and me, isn't it?" I returned. "My find and your intervention?"

Paul raised his cup toward me before drinking.

The purple strip took on a blue tint.

"What would you call that color?" I asked. "That band, above the rays."

"Hm. You don't see that very often." Paul concentrated. "Indigo?"

A delicate, high-pitched whistling noise started up from a bird we couldn't see, and then other birds chimed in with peeps and clucks.

"You know," I said, "it was Sir Isaac Newton who added indigo to the rainbow. He insisted on seven colors in the spectrum, not six, because he regarded seven as a spiritual number."

"Well, that's an interesting bit."

"Yeah, but most people can't distinguish indigo from the other colors. So it doesn't matter as much."

"Nonsense." Paul's eyes still hadn't left the sky. "I think it's intriguing." I had gotten used to his British accent, almost not noticing it, but now it sharply struck my ears. "That color makes you think, question. Reminds you that not everyone can perceive things in the same way. Helps you realize that you don't need to fully understand something to find it beautiful."

Paul glanced at me and did a double take, probably surprised by the gratitude I held in my teary eyes. But instead of becoming uneasy, he smiled warmly. And then we both returned our gaze to that purple-ocean tint—that quirky, yet worthy, shade on the spectrum.

CHAPTER 53

Elaine's laptop chirped; Paul opened it to find Musa. In the background, Jeremy directed people with mesh-screened boxes—Did they contain bugs?—while Meredith took inventory on an electronic notebook.

"People are showing up," Musa said, as if he hadn't believed they would. He appeared ten years younger. "Skilled people and trucks of goods. This is happening."

"Don't get too excited, Musa," I warned. "Launching is still a long shot."

"David," Musa replied, unwilling to let his good mood be dampened, "every amazing feat starts as a long shot. Get here soon."

Mom rushed to me and held both of my hands, her grip tight and prolonged, as if she would never see me again. "I am so proud of my Davey." Paul and I escorted her out the front door and to the helicopter that would take her and Miguel to the site.

She asked Paul, "This helicopter is coming back for Davey and Elaine?"

"Yes, dear." He touched her arm. "Both helicopters are returning. One for them, the other for supplies."

I kissed her cheek and we helped her climb inside. Miguel, on a stretcher, had already been loaded; his eyes were closed and I worried that he had died.

We backed away, watching the chopper rise into the sky.

Roberto honked; he drove over to us in a jeep and stopped. Sunny was inside, and he lifted up the leather straps around his neck to show me the blue and white zircon crystals. Paul got in and stuck his head out the window. "The jade, Dave."

"Four pieces," I said. "Fingernail-sized."

Paul pointed to an empty white jeep on the side of the driveway. "Keys are in it. Though it might be easier to go to the store on foot, given traffic."

The brigade of vehicles—three jeeps, two pickup trucks, a van, and the second helicopter—rumbled away, stuffed with people and backpacks.

As if a loud radio had shut off, Vida became noiseless. And then I noticed one more car—compact, with no trunk or rear compartment—sitting at the end of the property.

The engine started with a wheeze, and as the vehicle approached, I could see the window was down and Casey was at the wheel. He parked next to me.

I fixed my eyes on the car's skimpy tires. "You're not headed up the mountain."

"No." Casey's tone was apologetic. "And I'm not much for good-byes."

He stepped out. "I called my niece, my sister's kid." His voice became somber. "Her dad's a shithead. Doesn't come around much. But Uncle Casey's always been there, on holidays, and, when I'm not working, at her soccer games."

He pushed his toe into the ground as if he were snuffing out an imaginary cigarette.

"She was so sad . . ." He took in a labored breath. "She's too young to understand. It would be different, you know, if my sister and her were going."

"You've made the right decision," I said. "You can't abandon her."

We hugged, squeezing hard, hoping that would keep in the tears.

"What are you going to do after this?" I asked.

"Elaine gave me her savings." A look of *yahoo!* flashed on his face. "So, I think I'm going to buy a small house somewhere and do a whole lot of nothing."

"Good for you." Envy sank into my heart. He was on his way to peace and solitude. Would I ever have those things again?

"But right now, I'm headed to coffee," he said, his eyes brighter. "When Jason found out I wasn't going, he asked me out. And I want you to know, Davey, if it weren't for you, I would have said no."

"Well, don't be late."

I waved until I couldn't see him anymore.

CHAPTER 54

Sitting alone in Vida's courtyard, I sensed faces staring at me. It was unmistakable, that feeling of energy streaming in my direction. I searched the foliage, finding nothing. I turned toward the building, looking into the windows, but saw no people. Then I realized it wasn't people. It was the flowers—along the eves, on the columns, on the vines climbing up the walls. They were all around me, and they had become judgmental.

I grounded myself with analysis. The colorful blooms staring at me were made of molecules. Matter. The same matter that had existed before Earth had formed. The molecules in these flowers had once been cosmic dust, and now, most recently, had manifested as vibrant plants.

Plants that were checking me out. But not as a novelty, as a nuisance. Their essence had observed humanoids across the ages, and I gave them no reason to temper their disdain. They had witnessed, in our prancestors and now in us, that we rarely stopped to acknowledge ourselves as matter, let alone to understand that we were them and they were us, and there was no saving ourselves at the expense of others; there was only saving everything, or nothing.

The orchids were more upset with me than the rest. Mr. Yellow hung on a sturdy vine, stretching open his mouth, as if he were in the middle of screaming, *Another one is here to disappoint!* I looked away, only to be caught in the glare of two white eyes, circled in red. This girl sneered in disgust from beneath her puffy petal hat. *You can't even imagine how you're going to fail.*

I sought comfort in the sky, but was denied. My coveted blue-and-white vista was concealed behind dark clouds swelling into a squall.

Elle called out, "David?"

I found her inside the classroom, packing a satchel and a duffel bag.

"Why don't you go ahead," she said. "I'll stop at the pharmacy and then meet you at the park."

I found solace in the rhythm of walking, studying cobblestones polished by the shoes of a hundred thousand tourists. Closer to the heart of town, I rounded a corner to the view of a green, corpulent landmass. Volcán de Agua. This street ran right into its foothills.

Cayateña was in the other direction, not visible from here.

I finished my jade shopping and wandered through the park until I came upon female statues spouting water from their breasts. The gentle splashing sounds of this fountain centerpiece enticed me to sit on a nearby bench.

A woman balanced a basket of fruit on her head while carrying a baby. Ten-year-old kids, wearing Catholic school uniforms, passed by, the girls holding each other's hands. A green-and-orange iguana sat still on a sturdy branch, aiming its dinosaur face toward the souvenir shops. A man with a bag of flutes played a tune for three young tourists and asked, "You want? Good price!"

The avenues leading away from the square were clogged with cars and tuk-tuks—small three-wheeled vehicles used as taxis. People yelled and cheered in Spanish. Some said, *"We go to space! To a new land!"* Others screamed, *"Government lies! Don't be fooled!"*

Thunder cracked between the mountains, and within seconds, pellets of rain began to fall. People cleared the park, but I stayed seated.

The last two boys to jog toward the cover of the surrounding shops bowed their heads at me, reminding me of my priest disguise.

Elaine approached through the blurry weather. She looked as stunning in her habit as she had the moment I had first seen her, on the flight to Shanghai.

When the drops fell faster, she tucked her pharmacy bag into her oversized purse. "Hello," she said, flirting. "I'm Elle. What's your name?"

"Roger. I'm from Ohio."

She smiled. "What brings you to Antigua?"

"A spaceship. How 'bout you, Sister?"

We laughed and resisted the urge to kiss.

A man stepped out of the historic cathedral, looked up, and read the sinister clouds. He closed and locked the tall church doors before hurrying away.

Elaine leaned her head back. "Sunny said the ship has an ecosystem that produces rain, but it can't be the same as this."

I ignored my ringing phone at first, in favor of watching Elaine embrace the moment, her eyes closed, her palms facing the sky.

But then I saw it was Roberto, so I answered. His nervousness shook me. "Got it," I said, and hung up.

"Elle, this isn't just a shower. A dangerous storm is about to pass over. We have to get to the helicopters."

I stood and held out my hand.

She came out of her meditation. "I don't think a priest and nun would hold hands." She laughed.

"I keep forgetting!"

On our stroll back to Vida, the rain took a break, but the northern sky darkened and started to swirl.

Elaine paused to watch a yellow-and-black butterfly flap its triangular wings. "Sunny also said there will be butterflies."

"C'mon, we need to hurry."

"Wait," she said.

I glanced at the charcoal clouds tumbling toward us. "What is it?"

"I thought we'd have more time to talk about this." She put her hand to her belly. "I'm pregnant."

CHAPTER 55

I paced back and forth in front of Elaine, in Vida's deserted courtyard. She repacked her backpack for the third time, trying to fit in jars of prenatal vitamins.

Thunder vibrated the ground, more like an earthquake than a storm.

"Is Paul sure they can't send both helicopters back?" Elle asked.

"No time in this weather. The first one will barely make it."

"I don't like leaving without you."

It was soothing to pace—I took seven steps, spun into an about-face, and took seven more. "We can't part with any of the supplies you're bringing," I said. "What they weigh, plus you, and the pilot, it's already unsafe."

She zipped her backpack shut. "How will you get there in time?"

"I'll take the jeep. Musa says there's a back road, not on maps."

"If you're not worried," she said, "then why are you pacing?"

I stopped. "Is it fair, dooming our child to a secluded life on a spaceship?"

Elaine pushed the backpack away, as if she were mad at it. "Is it fair, dooming our child to a life where they'll eat chemicals instead of food? Where more money goes to prisons than to the schools they attend?"

"That's America," I said. "We can live somewhere else."

"In peace? After all of this?"

"Elle, what makes life great? What makes it worth living?"

She moved on to packing first aid kits. "Freedom. Purpose."

"Our child will be imprisoned on a transporter for their entire life."

She stood up, digging her hands into her hips. "Most of the people going on this mission are free to wander much farther here on Earth than they will be on that transporter. But they're clamoring to live in that confined space, because their minds and hearts won't be restricted. There is the realistic hope of equality, of working less, so they can spend time with their loved ones, so they can learn, enjoy, relax. And their descendants will live on, in a place where people aren't fighting over resources. What can they offer their grandchildren now? They can't save them from poverty or promise them even an education."

She stomped her foot. "Where is the David Denlon who is the king of ranting against the evils of life on Earth?"

The haughty faces of the flowers just beyond Elaine glared at me. *Yes, where is he?*

She shook her head. "You suddenly want to raise your kid in the system you've been running from your whole life."

"Elaine, we get to live in this world and then endure that ship. And our grandchildren deal with the ship and then get life across our galaxy, on Destiny. But our child, Elle, their life will be entirely lost in the journey."

Elaine's hands came off her hips. "Our kid will be free from most diseases and struggles, and will be guaranteed a healthy lifestyle in a peaceful community. That's not lost!"

Drapes of rain sailed toward us from the north, threatening to arrive before the helicopter.

"Elle, when I first got to college, I thought the campus was immense. Two years in, it seemed tiny. Cabin fever is real. It makes people go crazy."

"Cabin fever is as real as the system makes it," she argued. "People are brainwashed into thinking they have to go far to have fun, to move away from their families to grow up. But true happiness is having your needs met and getting to interact with your loved ones. This transporter makes that *more* possible, not less."

We heard the low-pitched drone of the helicopter flying in from the south.

Elle tried to pick up her backpack, but I snatched it. I put the strap of the satchel over my shoulder and lifted up the duffel bag. She took her large purse and hurried down the breezeway into the classroom, and I tried to keep up, yelling, "I wasn't brainwashed, and I don't know how I would have coped all these years without my traveling."

"Oh, please!" She turned around. "You may have traveled thousands of miles, but you didn't explore those miles. You sat in a little airplane seat, and then you visited museums and ruins, and gave speeches in lecture halls, and ate in restaurants. If you add up all the space you've been in without the meaningless miles that flew by while you slept, it's probably less than on that ship!"

She opened a small door that looked like it would lead to a closet, but it revealed a narrow stairwell. To the roof? She headed up and I toted the bags behind her.

"Still . . . We're making a decision for our child that they should have the right to make."

She didn't look back as she asked, "Don't all parents make decisions for their kids before birth? Poor parents decide to bring their children into hardship, because they want to give them life."

She reached the top and pushed her shoulder into the door, grunting as she fought the wind.

Despite the stairs leading to it, Vida's uneven rooftop was not designed to be walked on. It took several minutes to go a short distance without slipping or losing a bag.

The roar of the chopper grew louder as it hovered over us. Lightning flashed in the approaching sky.

"David"—Elle stumbled, but caught herself—"what are you really afraid of?"

The raindrops sharpened and shot into our eyes. The wind produced a throaty cry, as if death itself were screaming as it shoved us toward the roof's edge. The helicopter swayed, lowering a netted basket.

Elaine tried to take a bag from me, but I pulled it back and yelled, "I'm afraid if things go wrong, I can't protect you! Elaine, we have the resources to have an amazing life here. We have a cause—getting the next ship built—and a baby . . . a child that could grow up and make their own decision about going on the next launch. And the transporter may explode on takeoff, or get shot down, or malfunction!"

My lips involuntarily frowned; tears warmed my cheeks. I threw the bags into the basket and held Elle's arms. "I love you. I know what I can offer you and our child here. I can't predict what will happen on a spaceship."

Elle pressed her wet lips to mine, then released me. "I love you, too. And I'm getting on that ship, no matter what." She climbed into the netting and signaled upward.

The basket violently twisted.

"Elaine!"

She folded into herself.

"Elle!"

The chopper rose as pink lightning flashed, much closer than the last time.

My sneakers had become waterlogged; I struggled to find my footing. When I was finally back at the door, thunder boomed like a cannon, startling me; I tripped down the stairway, ending up in a heap on the floor of the classroom. My burner phone rang in my soaked pocket. I reached in to grab it and felt the four pieces of jade.

I answered, "Musa, the jade! I forgot to give it to Elaine!"

"David, listen to me," Musa said. "Now is not the time to get lost in your head. Do you hear me?"

The sky crackled as I collected myself off the stone floor and ran out of the classroom, into the courtyard.

"You'll be fine." Musa raised his voice. "Bring yourself and the jade. I'm going to give you those directions. I want you to repeat them back to me, okay?"

I searched for my backpack and the hiking boots Roberto had left me.

"David, you'll be alone for several hours. But stay focused. Take the gun Paul gave you. Can you hear me?"

I peeked at the petal faces, now mocking me: *We knew you'd screw this up.*

CHAPTER 56

The road was packed with cars; I passed them on the right, my wheels splashing up the water in the ditch. The broken metal gate from Musa's directions finally came into view. The jeep bounced over rocks and plants as I accelerated around the gate and onto the flooded service road that led up the side of Cayateña.

The rain lessened the farther up I went. In fifteen minutes, I was lowering my window to clear the fog on my windshield, and in twenty more, birdsong replaced the pattering of rain.

The gravel road turned to dirt and then vegetation I could not drive through. I vacated the jeep and journeyed upward, tromping through fields of cornstalks. The mountain seemed to expand as I scaled it, disorienting me.

My clothes dried but soon became saturated in sweat. I stopped to rest, looking back. The dark tempest had consumed the valley below.

Seemingly out of nowhere, two cinder-block structures appeared, small and square. Empty clotheslines spanned the distance between them, and beneath those ropes, five children, barely school-aged, played next to a skinny cow.

I gathered all the quetzales out of my pockets, careful to keep hold of the pieces of jade, and handed the money to the children. I trudged on, but they ran after me, asking with their faces if I'd made a mistake.

"Yes, for you," I said in Spanish. *"For you."*

The children sprinted to their minuscule homes, chickens hop-flying out of the way of their feet. They showed the money to a man putting on a shirt as he walked outside.

"No," he scolded. *"Return that!"*

"It's okay," I said. *"I don't need it. Please take it."*

The man eyed me with concern. *"Where are you going, sir? There is nothing that way. No town. No tour."*

"I know," I said. *"I'm meeting some people. Listen, get to a television or a radio. Remember I told you this—be on the next ship, okay? The next ship—remember."*

The man pulled the children to his side. *"Okay, sir, thank you for the money. Come, children, get inside. Right now."*

I forged on, wondering if this were all a dream. Perhaps I was as insane as that man's eyebrows had suggested. Had any of this adventure really happened? Was I walking toward the barren crest of a volcano, expecting to find people loading a space vehicle that would carry us to another place in the galaxy?

As I shed my outer shirt, a thought bit into me: *I should have asked that man for water.* I considered going back, but when I looked down the hill, there were only bushes.

I couldn't remember when the noises had begun, but now lava pebbles crunched beneath my steps, like cereal being eaten without milk. One scraggly shrub seemed out of place in the stretch of dead earth. When had the plants disappeared?

My lungs solicited me to sit down, but I resisted, anxious that the sun had already dipped into the western sky.

Long off the trail that had either dissipated or never existed, I scampered up steeper terrain, sliding on loose lava rocks. Steam drifted out of dark holes in the ground, like tentacles reaching from the underworld. This was not the way I had originally found the site. Was this even the same mountain?

My trembling calves finally pushed me to the top of the ridge I had been relentlessly pursuing. It had looked to be a twenty-minute hike but had proven to be miles from where I had started. Now I was there, expecting to be nearing the summit. But Cayateña's peak—actually two pinnacles above a small canyon of black rock—seemed as far away as when I had exited the jeep.

Was this where Musa wanted me to head left, or was I supposed to go higher? My idea to reach the mountaintop and search downward for the transporter could not be realized before sunset.

Misty blobs in the shape of ghosts floated alongside me as I continued upward.

When I felt that ten minutes had gone by, I checked my watch. It was nine and a half minutes later. I lumbered on, making my time checks a game.

Another ten minutes seemed to have passed. I looked. Eleven minutes.

I climbed.

And then the world shifted. My vision blurred—was there a vent I wasn't feeling, blowing steam into my eyes? I pulled my heavy wrist up to my face, expecting to see that about ten minutes had passed.

An hour had.

Air chilled my back, and I realized my backpack was gone. My gun was in my right hand.

How had I lost track of so much time? Had I passed out? Walked in a circle? Set my backpack down? Had I needed to use my gun? Why couldn't I remember?

The smoldering land was no longer one volcano, but a range of ridges, as far in every direction as I could perceive. Was I in a crater on the side of the mountain? Is that why I no longer knew which way led up to the top?

CHAPTER 57

I turned in circles, trying to find a reference point. No direction felt more compelling than another as to where I'd been or where I needed to go.

Depleted, I landed on my knees, dropping my gun. I gripped handfuls of seared earth, squeezing the sharp lava bits into my palms.

In satisfying surrender, I released the thinking that I could ever control anything. Arriving, or not, at an interstellar transporter that allegedly rested beyond one of these ridges was up to a much higher force than me.

I collapsed backward. My legs came out from under me, and my head crashed onto the rocky soil. The mountain's energy filled my chest, melding me into the ground; I couldn't tell where my back ended and the dirt began. I observed the burnt gravel lodged into the bloody flesh of my hands, but felt no pain. The life-moderating voice in my head dwindled to a whisper, and then disappeared.

The now was comforting and safe, unencumbered by the past and not bound to any particular future.

Someone was hiking over to me. Who was it? Through the mist I saw those green eyes. I tried to say *Elle*, but my mouth didn't move.

She smiled, unalarmed at the sight of me on the ground. She had always accepted me exactly how I was.

Shade swept over me. Time passed. How much? As the fuzzy cloud drifted away from the sun, the light intensified again, brighter than before.

Elaine had gone, but in her place stood my father. His eyes shrunk into slits when he smiled. Like mine.

"David," he said, and then laughed, shaking his head. "Oh, David."

I reached out my hand and he pulled me up; I was light as a feather.

"Dad, I'm sorry."

"For what?"

"I should have taken over your business."

"Obviously not," he said. "If you'd done that, you wouldn't have made this discovery."

A warm sensation came over me, despite the cool temperature.

"What were you trying to tell me in the hospital?" I asked. "What did I teach you?"

He grinned. "Son, you taught me how to keep moving forward, into the unknown."

I stared at him with the confused look I so often had as a child.

"You showed me," he explained, "how to keep going, even when it was into the arms of an angel at the foot of my bed."

I recalled those last moments of his life, and for the first time, I felt more peace than pain.

"But, Dad . . . how did I teach you?"

He peered into the sky, at the white clouds slow dancing across the blue, and gathered his thoughts.

"Son, you kept going all the way to your PhD. When your colleagues called your hypothesis crazy, you went forward with more research anyway. When I offered you a lucrative business, you kept moving in your own direction, without fear."

"The reason I can't do anything else but move forward," I said, "is because you never taught me how to quit."

His hand found its place on my left shoulder blade. "Then don't quit now."

The cold strangled me. I heaved in air, sensing that I'd been without it for too long. I realized I was again flat on my back, and I contemplated the deep soreness in my arms and legs. *Could they be broken?*

I stood up, holding my gun, bewildered at how it had gotten so heavy.

"Forward," I mumbled, tearing open my parched lips, enduring the metallic taste of blood.

When the ground stopped spinning, each of my blistered feet lifted my boots, step by slow step, landing just inches beyond the other.

Soon, my strides became lighter and longer.

I surprised myself when I started hopping along, steadily and without stopping, unconcerned about time. I skipped around a boulder and headed left, following Musa's directions.

And then I gasped in shock, swallowed a scream, and halted so abruptly that I tipped forward.

It was Musa. My friend. My mentor.

But he was standing with his hands in the air. Behind him, Patrick Veeder pointed a pistol at his head.

What was happening?

I aimed my gun, but with Veeder behind him, any shot would likely kill Musa.

Defeated, Musa struggled to talk. "I came looking for you . . . I didn't see him following me."

Chapter 58

"David, shoot!" Musa implored. "Unload your gun. Don't worry about me. Please!"

Veeder stood up straight, no longer hunched over from his wound. His thick locks of black hair were feathered back, fully exposing his satisfied, smiling face. "David, the world thinks you're a terrorist. But I can help you with that."

I could feel the sting of another blister, breaking open and bleeding into my sock.

"It's simple, David," Veeder said. "We're having a meeting. You're making me the director of the project. My team and I go on the launch."

My scratchy throat asked, "In exchange for what?"

"Well, for one thing, your friend here doesn't get his brains blown out."

Musa's voice turned deep and rough, like I'd never heard from him. "Pull the trigger, Veeder, I dare you!"

"No!" I begged.

"And for another thing, David, I will explain that you have been the victim and not the perpetrator of this whole mess, and save you from prosecution."

"Impossible," Musa said. "Don't listen to him!"

Veeder smiled again. "It's been Liam all along, has it not? He opposed your research because it doesn't fit into his warped sense of religion. He's the crazy bad guy. You and I are a team. The media's gonna love it."

My tongue poked into every corner of my mouth, searching for saliva.

"I've lived a meaningful life," Musa said. "Taking a bullet so this creep is finally exterminated, now that's a noble farewell. For the sake of humanity, David, fire your goddamn gun!"

Veeder's grip tightened on his Beretta.

Musa taunted, "C'mon, Patrick, you vile, self-absorbed waste of a human life, shoot me! David is going to gun you down."

I countered, "No!"

"David, think of what's at stake!" Musa pleaded. "We're so close. Stop worrying about me and shoot!"

I swayed but stayed standing. "Look, Patrick, if you want to be part of this, we can talk."

Musa nearly growled. "You know David's lying! You will rot in a cage if you're even allowed to board that thing."

Veeder gritted his teeth.

I whimpered, "Musa!"

"For Christ's sake, David, shoot!" Musa screamed.

"You're making me do this, David!" Veeder yelled. "You're making me put a bullet in your chest!"

I felt the oncoming rigor mortis of a stare. But this time, the paralysis fell short of taking hold, and the demonic energy fled. A weight lifted from my gut, rose up through my head, and floated away.

What I could see of Veeder, as he hid behind Musa, became clear. He was thinner, and his confidence had been replaced with a mouth twitch.

I tossed my gun down.

Musa shouted, "What are you doing?"

"You need me alive," I said to Veeder. "I'm the only one who can give you the authority to board that transporter."

Veeder huffed. "If you don't give me what I want, I'll settle for revenge."

"Fine. That will give the world more reason to convict you, and the righteous more motivation to launch another ship."

I felt a breeze, but the air was still. I heeded my instinct to throw myself to the ground.

Veeder blasted a shot. My left side exploded with burning and pressure.

Musa grabbed for Veeder's gun; it discharged again. The bullet ricocheted off a boulder and I flinched.

When I opened my eyes, Veeder stood over me, pointing his Beretta at my forehead.

Musa yelled, "No!"

The next shot didn't hurt, and for a moment, I thought death was painless.

CHAPTER 59

Veeder's holler grew longer and louder as he staggered in a circle. Liam was behind him, his stance wide for balance, holding a pistol with both hands. His bullet had penetrated the back of Veeder's leg.

"You imbecile!" Veeder shouted at Liam.

Musa wrenched the gun from Veeder, leaving him yelping in frustration, gripping his bloody thigh.

"I'm not an imbecile." Liam kept his gun trained on Veeder. "I'm a follower of God. You're a criminal."

I clawed at the rocks around me, trying to stand. Musa yanked me up. "Let me see." He lifted my shirt and failed to conceal his reaction: "Dear God."

How bad is it? Am I going to die? I couldn't turn my thoughts into words.

Veeder called out, "Darin!"

We turned to see Darin, Veeder's assistant—unsure of his footing and with a look of dread—hiking down toward us, having come from beyond the next ridge.

Veeder tried to move but his injured leg had gone floppy.

Musa aimed the Beretta at Darin.

"Don't shoot me!" Darin said, parking his feet on the loose gravel and raising his hands. Liam went to him and patted him down, recovering a gun.

"Mr. Veeder!" Now Christopher jogged from the same ridge Darin had come from, calling out with concern. "What happened, sir?"

"Christopher," Veeder said, a note of hope in his pained voice. "You're alive, thank goodness."

Liam, Musa, and I looked on, with confused faces, as Christopher positioned himself under the arm of his former boss.

Christopher glanced at me to make sure he had my attention, before mumbling in French, *"Trust me."* Then he summoned Darin. "C'mon, help Mr. Veeder."

Darin's eyes asked Musa for permission.

"Please," Christopher begged Musa, as if he'd never met him. "We're all going to the same place. These men need medical attention."

Musa lowered his gun and we watched Veeder limp away, leaning on Darin and Christopher.

Liam came to me and pressed his hand on my left side, like he was trying to keep my organs from falling out. "What did Christopher say?"

I held on to Musa's shoulder, convinced that my ribs were on fire. "He said to trust him."

Musa observed the three of them hobbling back up the hill. "Trust him? What's he doing?" His questions were carried away by a gust of wind.

When we reached the top of the ridge, Liam yelled down the other side, "It's Denlon! Please help him!"

Musa and Liam pulled at me to keep walking, but I stayed put, taking in the view from this elevated position.

I opened my mouth to speak, but nothing—not air, not sound—could find its way out.

In the mountain valley beyond me, the spaceship stood like a shiny megahotel, covering the distance of several city blocks. It twinkled in the sun, or did it have star-shaped, blinking lights? Much taller than it was thick, it tapered into a point at the end closest to me. One long side leaned into the volcano, but the other side—a sweeping concaved curve—was completely exposed. Large black squares made up most of its outer surface, but it didn't appear dark; it was a soft mix of blue, white, and reddish brown, reflecting the colors of the sky and the surrounding terrain.

I clung to Liam and Musa, to keep from passing out.

People moved quickly in front of its exposed side—some pushing carts of grain or wheelbarrows of blankets, others carrying canvas bags. Two young men clapped their hands and whistled at reluctant sheep, encouraging them toward the wide ramp that led to a massive opening.

There was a trail along the ridge, and I visually followed it, up past the armed soldiers, all the way up to the top of the transporter. Where on the roof of this massive city-cruiser had those blue and white keystones been placed?

"I know, it's unreal," Musa said. "But we've got to get you to a doctor."

"No, wait."

Below, rope lines—accompanied by guards—held back hundreds of onlookers. Several metal detectors, plugged into generators, acted as gateways to the open space in front of the ship. Nuns holding tablets interviewed people and then directed them through the detectors. Pickup trucks drove back and forth, between the loading ramp and the rope line, hauling everything from copper rods to bags of manure.

"What happened?" A young man with an Australian accent passed off a box of medical supplies to a colleague, and climbed up the embankment to us. "I'm Trevor, a doctor."

"He was shot," Musa said, still unable to mask his concern.

"Can you walk with me?" Trevor asked, leading me down the hill before I could answer. He guided me to a medical station and helped me sit down. "Go ahead, John," he said to his assistant.

John put a stethoscope to my lungs and felt my neck pulse.

My surroundings blurred; when they came into focus again, I watched Veeder leaning into Christopher and Darin, at another medical station. Assistants helped him lie down on a blanket, and a doctor dove into the business of the bullet in his hamstring. Christopher then hurried away from Veeder and Darin, toward a muddy blue jeep beyond the rope line, and I hoped he was greeting his parents.

But why had he helped Veeder?

Trevor inspected my wound, talking to himself in his Down Under accent. "What have we here? Oh yes, well, that's lucky."

A pain deep in my head subsided slightly when I shut my eyes. I opened them again—or was I waking up from a nap?—to John washing the lava pebbles out of my hands. He gave me a bottle of water and after I'd poured most of it down my throat, he smeared something greasy on my lips.

The fogginess started to clear from my mind.

I caught sight of Christopher—his short legs pounding the gravel in small, quick steps—returning to Veeder. What was he doing?

Paul jogged up to us, and I coughed out: "Elaine?"

"She's on board with Miguel." He turned to Trevor. "What's the damage?"

Trevor squirted something on me and then tugged. I cringed, turning my attention to the piles of bandages and medicine on a folding chair.

"The bullet skidded off his rib cage," Trevor said. "Probably cracked a bone. Nothin' that won't heal. David, I'm gonna stitch you up and protect the wound, then work on you for real after we launch."

"Praise the Good Lord," Liam said, exhaling.

"What happened?" Paul asked Musa.

"Veeder shot David."

"And who shot Veeder?"

Musa pointed at Liam.

"Amen," Paul said, igniting a smile on Liam's face.

Musa patted my arm, "It's nice to finally be with you in person."

"I've missed you," I managed to say, but then jumped when Trevor did something that pinched.

Outside the ropes, crowds of people waved and screamed. Signs read *Repent!* and *Thieves!* Groups of happier people held signs like *Beam me up!* and *Tell Yoda I said Hi!*

Veeder lay beyond us, ass up and jolting every half minute as the doctor worked on his leg. Christopher sat beside him, rubbing his shoulder. A military commander listened intently as Darin yammered on, but we couldn't make out what was being said.

Liam asked, "Why is Christopher still with Veeder?"

"Good question," Musa said. "And Darin's been talking to that official for a while now."

Paul tilted his head. "Why haven't they arrested Veeder?"

The commander left Darin and walked over to us without making eye contact until he arrived.

"Can we help you?" Trevor asked.

"It's about Mr. Veeder," he said.

The commander was an oversized man in every respect. Tall and muscular, yes, but somehow more intimidating were his individual body parts—like his kneecaps, the size of croquet balls outlined in each pant leg, and his feet, in black boots that must have been specially ordered to be that wide.

I met his unfriendly gaze. "Yeah?"

"He said you shot him, Dr. Denlon."

"*I* did," Liam said. "Because he shot David and was about to shoot him again."

"That's not the story we heard from the witness, Mr. Darin Scott. He confirmed that you shot first, Dr. Denlon. We're placing you under arrest."

Our shocked faces stared over at the other medical station, where Christopher helped Veeder drink the last of his water. He glanced at us but quickly turned away.

Liam seethed. "Liars!"

"No!" I yelled to the official. "You don't understand. Darin wasn't even there."

"Listen," Paul said to him. "You must believe us."

The commander waved over several men, one with handcuffs.

"Please," Trevor said. "Let me treat him first."

"He will be treated in custody," the commander said, losing his patience.

"I'm the one funding you." Paul's tone became stern. "Nothing happens until I speak with your president."

"We have to do our job, sir," the official insisted.

Veeder got to his feet and steadied himself. He yelled in our direction: "You can't get away with your crimes, Professor!"

"You will burn in hell!" Liam screamed.

The official with the cuffs bent my arms behind me. I groaned, and Trevor argued, "He's injured!"

The moment grew heavy. I watched Paul, waiting for him to do something. This situation could certainly be remedied by his connections, his training, his money, or, at least, his charm. But he stood, barely breathing, with the same eyes that had apologized to me in the lobby of the Hotel del Sacramento.

As the army official clamped the metal bracelets around my wrists, Casey's words came to mind, offering me a stark reminder. *We have to go over the meaning of 'covert.'* Tremors attacked my body—first one leg shook and then the next, then my lips—as I realized there was nothing Paul could do. His expertise was in covert operations—behind-the-scenes endeavors—not this.

I'm getting arrested.

What would this mean? Mom and Elaine would leave the planet, but I'd be stuck in prison?

The official grabbed my arm, wanting me to stand.

"Wait!" Christopher yelled. "I need to say something."

Veeder eyed him disapprovingly.

A hand pressed on my shoulder, presumably the official, now telling me to stay seated.

Christopher spoke—loud enough for us to hear—to the medical assistant wrapping Veeder's leg: "You know that bottle of water you gave me, for Mr. Veeder?"

The assistant gave a slow, confused nod.

"I didn't give it to him." Christopher pointed to the blue jeep, the vehicle he had run over to, before returning to Veeder. "I gave him one of his own bottles, from his rental."

Veeder's face melted into fear, followed by hysteria. He scrambled to the empty bottle and squished it in his hand.

Christopher looked at me with satisfaction in his eyes, satisfaction he'd craved for a long time. "Mr. Veeder's water is top shelf. Or as they say in French . . ."

I smiled. "Poison."

Chapter 60

"Pump my stomach!" Veeder shrieked. "Do you hear me? It will kill me!" He shoved his fingers down his throat, causing himself to choke.

"Patrick, you'll have to make an admission," Christopher said. "The clock is ticking."

"It's poison!" he cried out, in between vomits. "What more do you want me to say? The water in my jeep is poison. Please!"

Darin was dumbfounded. "Poison?"

Christopher asked Veeder, "Who shot first?"

"I did! I was trying to kill that bastard! Now get me to a hospital!"

Christopher joined us, addressing the commander. "Darin lied to you." He yelled back to Veeder, "Isn't that right? You told Darin to lie?"

"Yes, fine, arrest me! I need treatment! We're running out of time!"

The commander signaled for the official to uncuff me. He turned to his troops and ordered, "Ready the chopper.

Get statements—find out who Mr. Veeder poisons. And don't let Mr. Scott get away."

Darin had backed off the scene and now sprinted down the hill, past a metal detector. A soldier gave chase, charging into Darin like a linebacker, drilling him into the ground.

The crowd reacted: *Whoa!*

The commander laughed to himself. "There's an entire army here. Where did that bloke think he was going?" He continued his orders. "Seize the jeep. Be careful with that water."

Veeder coughed and spit. "I need a hospital!"

"I saw an opportunity," Christopher said to us. "I didn't have a chance to explain."

"Excellent work, operative." Paul slapped his shoulder.

"Praise God!" Liam hurried to the large group of bins that sat in front of the pushed-over monuments. He searched among pet carriers holding dogs, cats, turtles, and other animals. Then he snatched one up and returned.

"We can't leave without Noah," Christopher said, before noticing that two people were waving to him from the rope line. "Oh, there they are. There they are!" He trotted away.

"His parents made it," Paul said. "That's good."

A wave of weakness struck me again; Trevor offered more water. I sipped my way back to a clear head and noticed a man in his sixties, beyond the medical stations, seeming disoriented. He dropped his hiking sticks and stumbled, gawking at the enormous, black-paneled fortress, and then asked the heavens, "What's going on? What is this?"

The woman with him nearly screamed, "Don't get upset, Dan, it's okay!" But his head drooped and he fell into her. She embraced him as they toppled to the ground.

"Not the first person I've seen faint today." Trevor took over wrapping the bandage around my chest so John could run to the couple. "The sight of that transporter is overwhelming."

My view of it now was from down the slope, looking up. Every inch of the city-ship seemed as if it would feel slick and polished to the touch. There were no protrusions—no wings, no propellers. Each end, now freed from the granite, narrowed into a sharp vertical edge. The long side facing us dipped inward across the middle and flared out at the top and bottom levels. Was the other side still embedded in the mountain? The bottom floor was ringed with twenty-foot-tall panes of something thick, glassy, and silver. A ramp led up to the warehouse-door entrance on the second of the fifty levels.

Six women in Mayan garb carried full baskets on their heads up the ramp and through the forty-foot-wide open door. Behind them, a teenaged boy pulled a wagon of crated chickens. A line of eighteen men and women stretched from a truck to the transporter so they could pass burlap sacks from one pair of hands to the next.

Handcuffed and flanked by military personnel, Veeder limped by us, scowling. "Do you think this is over?" His voice was hoarse, his face pallid. "That you won? You're so fucking stupid." He gestured with his chin toward the top of Cayateña. "Give it about half an hour."

"Let's go," one of the soldiers said. They dumped him like a dead body into the basket that had carried Elle off the rooftop of Vida. The chopper lifted off, hauling Veeder and his arrogant glare away from us.

"Is he bluffing, to scare us?" Trevor asked.

Soldiers sprinted toward their large antiaircraft guns, focusing them on the crest of the mountain.

"Patrick Veeder lies and cheats," Paul said. "But I don't think he bluffs."

CHAPTER 61

"We have to get this show on the road." Paul monitored the mountain's peak, his eyes fearful.

To our left, a woman and man in their twenties started walking away from their family, but the woman stopped and cried. The man, wearing a large backpack, prompted her along, but she didn't go. A younger girl, behind the rope, yelled, "Sissy, you can do it! You had a dream about it!"

The woman carried an old square suitcase that pulled her arm down. She slowly stepped, then stopped and cried again.

"You don't have time for indecision," Paul said under his breath. He looked around at the troops, most of whom seemed befuddled. Were they supposed to be helping people to the transporter, or keeping them away from it? "Someone has to start telling these people to get on or get the hell out of here."

"Just about done, David," Trevor said. "Keep drinking that water, it has electrolytes."

"There's the professor!" a woman shouted. She and about thirty people assembled around me.

"No, Jesus," Paul said. "This isn't a party."

One by one they turned around, holding up their phones to snap selfies.

"Get out of here!" Paul said, annoyed. "This is very dangerous. Go on!"

"Whatever, old man," one of the women said.

I gazed up at the volcano's cone and asked Paul, "If Veeder wasn't bluffing, then what's coming over the mountain?"

Paul's unease continued to grow. "Something made possible by that system you so accurately complain about."

A couple and a weeping teenaged girl took heavy steps toward our medical station.

"Shit," Paul mumbled, out of their earshot, before putting on a happy face. As they arrived, he said, "I'm so glad you were able to say good-bye to Sunny. But you really must get off this mountain."

This was Sunny's family, and the sight of them riddled me with guilt. Had I lured a curious young man not to a place we called Destiny, but to his death?

Sunny's father shook Paul's hand. "We're so grateful. We couldn't have made it here without your arrangements."

"A pleasure to be of service, now please—"

"Dr. Denlon, it's an honor," Sunny's father said, as if I were a celebrity.

"Your son is brilliant, and such a good man," I responded, forcing myself to stay composed.

Although her eyes were drenched and red, Sunny's mother smiled. "I have never seen him more fulfilled."

Sunny's little sister, in a sweatshirt with beaded pink hearts, put a tissue to her nose and turned away.

"All right then, time to go." Paul could no longer feign hospitality. "Quickly now."

"Davey! My baby." Mom trotted up to us and asked Trevor, "Is he okay?"

I was still bowing my head and waving to Sunny's parents as Paul pushed them away.

"David is good," Trevor said to Mom. "Just getting him rehydrated."

"What happened?" Mom asked.

"Alice, we're in a hurry." Paul put his arm around her. "He'll be fine. Just a scrape." Then he jogged over to a Guatemalan officer. "Sir, you speak English?"

I gazed in silence at the sleek transporter. Mom put her hand on my cheek like she used to when I was young. "Isn't it the most amazing thing you've ever seen, Davey? The locals have named it. A year . . . Aye yare . . . What is it, Doctor?"

"Just call me Trevor."

I studied Trevor for the first time. His tan, happy face put him at about thirty-two years old. He had a muscular build, but seemed ungainly, like he didn't know what to do with his strength.

He answered Mom: "They call it the Ayerfuturo. That's Spanish for something like 'yesterday's future.'"

"Good nickname," I said.

"I've got to get on board, to check on Miguel." Mom tried to hide her concern.

I stuffed my fingers into my pocket. "I've got something for you, Mom." I handed her a chain with an olive-green gem. "I didn't have a chance to get you anything in China. But they have beautiful jade here, too."

Mom closed her hand around the pendant and kissed my cheek. "My Davey. So thoughtful. Thank you, sweetheart."

Paul raced back to us. "Dear," he said to Mom, and that word struck me. It was the second time he had called her that, and I hadn't heard him use that word with anyone else. "I don't want to worry you. But we may have a situation here. Let's get on board as fast as we can, okay?" He touched Liam's arm. "Why don't you and Noah go with Alice? Stay together. Please hurry, the transporter is farther away than it looks."

"We're right behind you guys," Trevor said.

Mom and Pastor Liam, clutching a pet carrier, strolled away toward the glistening space vehicle through a muddle of civilians, soldiers, vehicles, and crates of supplies. The oddness of that scene took me completely away from the pain in my side.

Trevor cut my bandage and packed away his scissors.

I asked him, "Why are you going?"

"Huh?"

"On the ship. Why are you going?"

"Oh." Trevor shrugged. "I've got nothin' really stoppin' me. Orphaned when I was four, foster mom was a doctor. Went to med school with her help. This gives me hope. Maybe the loss of my parents was meant to be."

As he helped me to my feet, a woman in khaki pants and a teal camisole shirt arrived. She wore a leather backpack, and her sunglasses reflected me like a mirror.

"David, this is Dembe," Musa said. "She's staying here, working with Interfaith Missionaries, planning to build another ship."

"Hello," she said. "Oh my goodness, does it hurt?"

"Quite a bit, actually," I said.

"Dembe," Paul cut in, stealing a look at the tip of Cayateña. "We're out of time. Jeremy and Meredith briefed you about the hologram and the stones in the lake?"

"Yes, they were very thorough."

"Sunny gave you the dictionary?" Musa asked.

"Printout and flash drive."

I asked, "Do you have pen and paper in that backpack?"

After she handed me a pen and the printout of the dictionary, I wrote down the location of the second site.

"Can you read that? It's the other place I found zircon crystals. That site should be explored, but keep it a secret."

She looked closely at my writing. "Yes. Wow. Okay."

"You don't have an easy job, Dembe," Musa said, zipping the bag he and Paul had loaded with the bandages and medicine from the folding chair.

Behind the rope, a large group of people—most of them under thirty years old—yelled and waved. One of their signs said *Mission Possible 2* and another promised *If You Build It, We Will Go!*

"You already have passengers?" I asked.

"We do," Dembe said.

"Holy Christ," Paul said. "More people are coming than going. This is not good." He put his face near Dembe's. "Listen to me. Take off, right now. Run down this mountain, as fast as you can."

Dembe didn't move; her long face, like a beautiful statue, was still and calm. It occurred to me that the person Musa would select to oversee the building of another transporter—to negotiate with world leaders, to strategize the next launch—would not be easily frightened off.

"Please," Paul said, his voice so desperate that it made the rest of us uncomfortable.

Dembe's eyes shifted, finding Musa. He nodded.

She slipped the dictionary into her backpack. "Someday," she said to me, "our grandchildren shall meet." She turned and took determined steps down the slope.

"These people have to get out of here," Paul said, looking around at the spectators. He stopped a female commander. "Tell them to leave. Please!"

She responded with open hands. *What more do you want me to do?*

"Paul," Musa said, anxiously glancing at the empty sky above the volcano. "The US military wouldn't really be deployed for something like this, would it?"

"That's not how the system works," Paul said, shaking his head as people flatly ignored the officials' orders to leave—sticking around to snap photos and wave signs. "Veeder would get money to an up-and-coming insurgent group. One that your president could later denounce and declare war on."

The sun had disappeared and now sent farewell streaks of orange across the still-empty sky.

"Are you expecting a plane?" I asked. "Like from the Taliban?"

"If something is coming," Paul said, "it's going to be more than one plane."

As we took our first step toward the ship, a boy timidly approached us and asked in Spanish, *"I go?"*

"Bloody hell," Paul muttered. "What now?"

The boy's sandals were broken, and he used a T-shirt as a satchel to hold underwear, shorts, and something wrapped in foil. Behind the rope, an older couple waved to us.

"Your grandparents?" I asked him.

He nodded.

His grandmother called out to us, "Por favor!"

I asked him, *"What's your name?"*

"Mateo."

"How old are you?"

His dirt-smudged face displayed concern.

"Twelve?"

He whispered, *"Eleven."*

"He's been here all day, waiting for you," Trevor said. "His parents are gone."

"What do you think?" I asked Trevor.

"He'll be better off on the ship, but I'm rather biased."

"He'll need a guardian."

Trevor gulped. "Right."

"That's it then," Paul demanded. "Take the boy. We're leaving."

Mateo lifted one of Trevor's bags, wobbling under the weight of it.

"Here," Trevor said, "I'll trade you." He took the heavy bag and gave Mateo a lighter one.

The grandparents, crying into handkerchiefs, yelled over the noise of the nearby helicopter, *"Mateo, we love you!"*

"Tell them to leave," Paul said.

I tried to shout, but it was too painful.

Paul offered me his elbow, as if we were walking down the aisle. Musa scooped up the last medical bag. Trevor and Mateo followed behind us.

"And not the Taliban, by the way," Paul said, as we marched toward the center of the ship. "There's more leverage with newer factions, the ones nobody's heard about."

My chest throbbed; I leaned on Paul, laboring through each step. "But a squadron of planes?" I panted. "That would be expensive."

"I know money doesn't grow on trees," Paul said. "But it doesn't have to. Governments print it."

With most of the soldiers and security officials now busy manning weaponry, more people could get away with coming under the rope lines to give the space cruiser a closer look.

"No!" Paul tried unsuccessfully to get their attention. "Go back! You're in danger!"

A pregnant woman rushed to us, her arm straight out in front of her and her finger pointed, as if she were going to jab me with it.

"You better be right!" she screamed.

"I'm sorry?"

"My husband is leaving me behind, because I won't go die on a spaceship!"

"Ignore her," Paul said. But I stopped, and then so did Paul, Trevor, and Mateo. "David," Paul complained. "We've still got about thirty-five yards."

"He's one of the astrophysicists in there," the woman cried. "Gabe. He says I'm the one choosing to break up our family. But I know this thing is going to explode!"

"It might," I said, looking up at the structure, now a mix of pink and purple, mirroring the evening sky.

"'It might'?" she squealed. "That's what you have to say?"

Mateo stepped closer to Trevor, unsure of this woman.

"Maybe we're supposed to die," I said. "So you and others are inspired to build more ships."

"Oh my God!" she yelled in response, and then wept into her hands.

A horn bellowed—one long blast, one short, and then another long. The tall gray doors began to slide shut.

"C'mon!" Paul pulled me along, saying to the woman, "Get to safety, ma'am, please."

A soldier—not more than nineteen years old—crossed our path and halted, staring upward. He stiffened as his mouth fell open.

A couple ahead of us inspected the sky and immediately stopped their happy babbling. Next to them, a man looked up, dropped his camera, and took off running.

I didn't look at the sky. Instead, I searched for Mom, who had almost made it to the ramp with Liam. She had seen what was coming over the volcano, and now searched for me in the escalating pandemonium.

More troops hurried to rocket launchers and into tanks.

"Run, Mom!" I said, unable to yell. "Paul, tell her to run up that ramp and get inside!"

"They're trying to kill us!" a woman shouted, pointing upward.

Commanders, some with bullhorns, demanded, "Get on or get away! Move!"

Paul shouted toward Mom, but she didn't hear him. She continued to call for me until Liam guided her to the ground. He tucked Noah's carrier beneath him.

Trevor pushed Mateo to the gravel and toppled onto him. "Get down!" he yelled to the pregnant woman. She froze in shock, staring toward the mountaintop.

Surface-to-air missiles screeched into the sky, leaving trails of white smoke. Explosions sounded off above us, rattling our bones.

Musa's bloodshot eyes came at me. "We're not gonna make it."

I finally looked up. There were too many planes to count. And too many bombs.

Chapter 62

The Ayerfuturo's door closed behind us and sealed, becoming a seamless wall. Had Mom made it on?

A crowd of people cheered: "Denlon! Yeah!"

I was still reeling from how Paul and Musa had dragged me on board, amid detonating bombs that were pulverizing lava rocks within feet of us.

Liam was sitting on the floor, which looked like a softer version of marble, catching his breath and clutching Noah's carrier. Trevor inspected Mateo for injuries.

Panic constricted my lungs and amplified the deep soreness in my side; I stood on my toes, searching the room.

"I'm right here," Mom said, coming out of a cluster of people. "I'm okay. I'm going to check on Miguel."

I exhaled, but my heart sank again at the sight of Christopher looking around like a lost child, calling out every name his parents might hear over the celebratory shouts and loud talking. "Mom? Dad? Mr. and Mrs. Kiser? Tammy? Dustin?"

"We'll help you," Paul said to him, grabbing Musa. "We'll split up."

"Do it this way," I offered, and explained myself in Musa's ear, since the sensation of hot pokers stabbing into my chest wouldn't permit me to speak up.

Musa, Paul, and Christopher followed my directions, asking people to please pass on that Christopher was looking for his parents, Mr. and Mrs. Kiser. Each person they spoke to immediately found another, relaying the message, and then another, until there were a hundred people dispatching the information.

Gabe's wife had apparently followed us on board and now held her protruding belly as she studied the transporter's interior, an even more surreal spectacle than the sight of this shiny spacecraft from the outside.

We had entered a main gathering area, with smooth, white walls extending all the way up to a ceiling that was too far away to clearly see. In the center of the floor, a railing encircled an opening, exposing the level below. How had everything stayed so clean, so new-looking, over all these years?

Along the far wall, liquid doors levitated in place and didn't drip, each one a sheet of light-blue translucent gel in a rectangular frame.

"What's that made out of?" Musa wondered out loud. "How's it doing that?"

"I can't even imagine," I responded.

A man approached one of the doors, and the frame quickly siphoned the gel into itself. After he passed through, the goopy liquid cascaded back out and again hung in the air, maintaining its flat shape despite being soft and attached to nothing.

Above us, three sizable clear tubes—each wide enough to fit a truck—led up and away, presumably to other places in the city-ship. Like humongous French horns, the tubes were the widest at their open ends, and they curved in a circle around one another before heading off in different directions.

About fifteen men and women had already mastered the flying Segways—blinking hover boards with T-shaped handlebars for steering and wheels for use on the ground—and were now venturing up into the air and inside the tubes.

"Do you think they're alive?" Christopher came up beside me, having given up believing that his parents were on board. "Do you think they made it away from the bombs, Dave?"

I searched for words that didn't come. Leaving his parents behind would have been hard enough. But wondering for the rest of his life if they had been bleeding to death outside the door, at the beginning of a journey he had talked them into . . . that was too much.

A muffled explosion went off outside. It trembled the ship, but hushed the crowd only momentarily.

"Don't these people know we're under attack?" I asked Paul.

"Most were on the ship before it happened," he said. "You can't see out these panels and this thing is pretty soundproof."

"I'm going to look for Jeremy and Meredith," Musa said, worried. He walked away toward a square tower that had one of those gel doors at the base of it.

"Chris, honey!" A woman ran up to us, her gait uneven due to a missing shoe, and with a sling cradling her arm.

"Mom!" Christopher stopped himself before embracing her, minding her injuries. "Are you okay? Where's Dad?"

"Yes, my love. We were in medical when someone said you were looking for us. Dad's got some cuts, but he'll be fine." She smiled and cried at the same time. "We're here, Chris, we're really doing this. We're going with you."

I scanned the inside of this flying biosphere, checking out the grand lobby, and admitted to myself that it gave off a sterile, empty look—mostly since every feature was some version of white, clear, or light blue. But it also instilled in me a sense of safety. It felt clean, high-functioning, and ready.

Another rumble, this time just outside the door—were they trying to bomb their way in?

"I have to alert Sunny," I said.

Paul nodded. "I'll go with you."

Paul and I approached the railing to discover the operation center below—with six-foot-tall hologram maps of the galaxy, touchscreens as big as picture windows, and lightbulb-shaped drones floating about, seeming to be making their own decisions. The command station formed an oval in the middle of the first floor, and surrounding the station was more of what this transporter seemed eager to provide—open space. The sides of the ship on that level were glass-like walls, as opposed to the paneling that covered the rest of this star cruiser, but the walls were dark, allowing no view outside.

Sunny and seven other people were in the command station, some swiping their hands across the giant screens, others seeming to consult with the drones. Sunny had tied his hair, now in dreadlocks, into a short ponytail. When he saw us, he mounted a hover board and shot up and over the railing.

"You learned that quickly," I said.

"It's easy, Professor! Oh my God, what happened to you?"

"We'll explain later," Paul said. "Sunny, surely one of those gadgets down there has let you know we're under assault." He did his best to keep his voice low. "We have to take off."

"We're trying to figure out how to get the protection shield up," Sunny said. "We're not set to launch for an hour."

"The army can't defend us any longer," I insisted, handing him the jade.

Sunny's forehead wrinkled. "But the launch is in three phases. I don't know how to do the third one yet."

"What are the other two?" I asked.

"The first one activates elements on the ship that react to elements in the volcano, like two magnets pushing apart. This repels us from the mountain. The second one creates a field that denies Earth the ability to recognize the ship's mass. That relieves us from the pull of gravity, and our thrusters get us to about seventy thousand feet."

"Seventy thousand feet." I paused to think. "Higher than planes can go."

Another explosion seemed to send rocks crashing into the ship. Those who heard the noises crouched and then looked around with big eyes.

Sunny glided back down to the operation room. His voice came through the speaker system: "Your attention, please. We are lifting off immediately. Make sure to tie down!"

It wasn't until his directive that I noticed harnesses attached to the walls and the railing. When Paul tried to assist me, I said, "No, please, find my mom and help her. I'll be fine."

People ran in front of me, to the nearest bank of harnesses, before I could limp over to them. I turned and located other belts, but they were across the lobby.

More bombs detonated outside. I looked everywhere for Elaine.

"Davey!" Mom yelled, strapped in next to Paul. "Get buckled in!"

I peeked down into the operation room. Sunny and several crew members, as if in disagreement, darted between the touchscreens and the hologram maps, making their cases to each other.

A fiery blast propelled a boulder through one of the panels, sixty feet up the wall of our space city. It crashed down inside, nearly hitting a man and his daughter. The impact caused fissures to snake throughout the polished flooring, scaring people into jumps and shuffles.

I peered up at the spikey-edged hole, then returned my focus to the operation room. Was there something they could do?

Sunny gaped in horror at the breach and slumped into a chair. Some of his companions shook their heads; others covered their faces. The crowd's fear turned into confusion. Now what?

Almost without a sound, a new panel slid from the bottom of the inward-curved wall, raced up, and replaced the broken one. We collectively stared. The transporter had healed itself. Cheers rang out, growing so loud that I wondered if ten thousand people had boarded.

Sunny and his team sprang back into action, securing themselves with straps connected to poles that had emerged out of the floor.

Jet engines buzzed our cruiser—muted roars, but far too close. Were they diving into us?

Everything vibrated. I arrived at a strap, but the ship lurched sideways, knocking me down before I could cinch it. The transporter tipped and I slid across the floor. Sirens blared as the interior became dark. I used my left arm to protect my wound while I extended my right, blindly grasping from side to side, finding nothing.

The walls glowed green, and the floor became an expanse of white light—except where the cracks had formed. A force pushed my body down.

We're airborne.

In an instant, everything seemed normal. The regular lighting returned, the grind of the engine disappeared, and I felt as if the ship were sitting on the ground.

Elaine ran to me and helped me up.

"Elaine the Magnificent," I whispered.

"C'mon, let's get you secured," she said.

We clicked our belts and I became dizzy. People around me held their heads and groaned.

"Where are we?" someone asked.

"Above the clouds!" a woman answered, yelling from her restraint on the railing, where she could see down to the first floor. "You can see out the windows now!"

Everyone in a railing harness stretched their necks to peer down to the level below, exclaiming, almost in perfect harmony: "Ooohh!"

But then our sky city sank, dropping like lead. Our screams trailed off above us.

We picked up speed. Our legs came out from under us; our bodies surrendered to the harnesses. Elaine linked her arm around mine; I put my hand on her abdomen, praying that death would be fast.

But the ship slowed, and our feet met the floor again. Bloodless faces glanced around. *Are we okay?*

"Phases one and two complete," Sunny announced. "Sixty-eight thousand feet and holding."

Liam hugged Noah's carrier.

Frightened, Mateo looked up to Trevor, seeking reassurance. Trevor nodded and patted his head.

Hums and sighs of relief spread around the room and were the only sounds for nearly a minute.

On the opposite wall, Ann was buckled in next to a burly man with a shaved head. I mouthed, *Mark?* Their smiles and nods confirmed it was Ann's husband. I brought my hands together and so did Ann; we exchanged bows.

"Dr. D!" Jeremy yelled from three harnesses over, reaching his fist toward me. I bumped mine into his.

Next to him, Meredith called out, "We're in a dream!"

"You found them, I see," I said to Musa, who kept a tight grip on his harness straps, suspicious of the space cruiser's next move.

"Professor?" Sunny's voice came from the speakers. "As we prepare for phase three, I think our community would like to hear from you."

Shouts of "Woo hoo!" and "Yeah!" filled the room.

Elle guided me to an intercom and I spoke into it: "Thank you, Sunny. I do have something to say, but first, I have a question." I wasn't sure how to ask this, but time was limited, so I simply spit it out. "Elaine, will you marry me?" I lowered myself to one knee.

Her surprised eyes stared into mine. The passengers became silent with anticipation.

"Yes!" she said. "I love you."

As applause and whistles echoed throughout the room, Mom unlatched herself and walked over, wriggling the diamond ring from her wedding finger. "Now this is a gift your father would want you to accept."

"Oh, Mom . . ."

I pushed the sparkly jewel onto Elaine's finger. She knelt beside me and we kissed, eliciting more clapping. I kept my lips on hers, until she pulled her head back. "You're on, Doctor," she said.

Elle and Mom helped me stand. My wound burned, and as I breathed through the pain, I spotted a diagonal row of characters—thick and silver—etched into the lobby wall. Pieces of paper had been taped beneath it, one big letter per page, in Sunny's block-style writing.

Our prancestors had displayed a message they felt was important enough to be the only adornment in the atrium of the transporter. And Sunny had translated it: *BELIEVE.*

My mindful breathing became a long sigh. Mom's hand came to my back as she quietly asked, "Does it hurt to talk?"

I closed my eyes and shook my head. Not even an interstellar space vehicle could rescue me from these nonsensical sentiments. *Faith. Dream. Trust. Believe.* Why were these cheesy concepts inherent in the human condition?

And then I saw a young family, the mom with a baby in a carrier strapped to her chest, the dad holding the hand of a four-year-old girl, each of her pigtails in a red bow. The parents smiled at me, their faith in this transporter, and in a future for our kind on another planet. I glanced back at Meredith, her happy face revealing dimples on each cheek, and recalled her comment, *We're in a dream!* My eyes landed next on Mateo—a Guatemalan boy whose grandparents trusted this journey to provide him with much more than life on Earth could offer. And holding me were Mom and Elaine, who both believed in being part of this mission even when I had doubted.

People shifted, adjusting their harnesses and clearing their throats.

I swallowed. "I see on the wall," I began, addressing the passengers through the intercom, "the word 'believe.'" People started to clap but I interrupted them. "Well, I'll tell you what I believe. I believe that we humans can be evil."

The vigor was zapped from the room. Some of the faces around me became confused.

"It's true," I said. "Humans can be awful—greedy, selfish. You want me to believe? Oh, I do. In the absolute horrific effects of the human race."

A few people booed. One asked, "What are you talking about?" Mark looked at Ann, questioning his decision to leave an entire life behind.

Elaine whispered, "Dave?"

Mom eyed me, worried.

"And that's okay," I said. "In fact, that's great. Because up is only up in relation to down."

The room fell silent. Several people gave me that familiar look: *What the hell is wrong with you?*

"Fast is only fast because we can compare it to slow. Now, that doesn't mean we have to go slow. But the possibility of going slow *must exist* for the possibility of going fast to *also exist*. And therefore, my fellow humans, it's the same for good and bad; choosing good is only possible if bad is one of the options."

Faint smiles, one for about every fifty people, sparked throughout the crowd.

"Yes, I'll tell you what I believe. I believe in humanity's propensity to be bad because without that, none of us would have the opportunity to be great."

Their full attention was back; a few people clapped.

"I believe in our ability to be terribly hateful, hateful to the core. But having that ability doesn't mean we ever have to exercise it. In fact, we *never* have to hate, but we do need to be capable of going that way, so the door is open to go the other—to love each other, to love ourselves, to love unconditionally."

Cheers rang out; the spirit in the room lifted again, stronger than before.

Fluid dripped down my left side, probably blood, but I didn't check. The pain was excruciating, and yet, I ignored it.

"I *believe* that this is just one of many examples of the complexity, the uniqueness, and the beauty of humankind, and I *believe* that our human race should live on."

People whistled and shouts rang out: "Yeah!" "Right on!"

"A billion years ago, a separate race of human beings believed in us. They spent their energy and their time building this transporter for us, knowing that we would have, like them, a strong ability to use it in bad faith. But they believed. They believed that despite our capacity to do bad, we ultimately would choose goodness and, well, look who is sixty-eight thousand feet above the surface of the planet, making the choice to risk our lives for the future of our race!"

Happy screams engulfed me, the loudest I'd ever known. A mother wept, embracing her three children. Christopher and his parents clasped hands with several people in orange-and-red headdresses.

The scene of my father—smiling, sipping wine, telling me how smart I was when I was actually behind on my homework—flashed before my eyes. "We're going forward," I said, "forward in a way none of us could go alone."

I lost my balance; Mom and Elaine held me up.

"We're believing in something outside of us," I said, "something farther into the future than our own life spans. And that is uniquely, beautifully, human."

Joyful hysteria had taken over; people hooted and waved.

"Sunny," I said, "we commit to you as our captain, as we leave our beloved Earth, and start our journey home. To Destiny!"

Trevor kissed Mateo's forehead.

Chanting began and quickly picked up steam: "Des-tah-nee! Des-tah-nee! Des-tah-nee!"

Elaine and I returned to our harnesses, about twenty feet from where Miguel lay on the floor with two belts securing him. When I called out his name, he rolled his head over and slowly produced a thumbs-up. I held up the peace sign, prompting him to smile.

His eyes closed, his face relaxed, and his thumb faded down to his side.

I unclicked my belt to go to him, but the speakers crackled on. There was no mistaking Sunny's serious tone. "Please make sure you're tied in. This is—"

It was unclear if the intercom had given out, or if Sunny had ceased talking.

His voice returned. "This is it. This is the final phase, the one that has to get us into space."

The lively chatter abruptly stopped. I clicked back into my restraint.

"No matter what happens," Sunny said, "we all came together. We pulled off the launch of a star cruiser." A measured tone, wise and decided, had supplanted his youthful excitement. "In this moment, we have nothing to fear; we've already succeeded."

Strangers stretched from their restraints to hold one another as if they were lifelong friends. I winked at Mom and exchanged smiles with Musa and Paul. Elaine put her hand to her heart, on her treasured sweatshirt. I set my hand on hers.

Buckled to the vessel in which I would die, I was finally free.

ABOUT THE AUTHOR

Christine Morse is an attorney and a professor of criminal justice. She is an avid explorer of the world, and a believer in Mark Twain's sentiment: "Travel is fatal to prejudice, bigotry, and narrowmindedness..."

Connect with Christine on LinkedIn: www.linkedin.com/in/christinemorse18

Regardless of where you purchased this book, your review is appreciated.

Made in the USA
Las Vegas, NV
12 May 2022

48818051R00319